COLUMBIA COLLEGE
782.42162H772S C1
C0-AQW-716

"Honey in the Rock"

The
Ruby Pickens Tartt
Collection
of Religious Folk Songs
from Sumter County,
Alabama

Honey in the rock

Mother, mother come and see
   What the Lord have done for me
I am so humble
   Never get tired
I am walkin' by my Savior's side.

-Chorus-
Honey in the rock, honey in the rock
   Oh it taste like honey in the rock
Go taste and see dear Lord 'tis good
   Oh hit taste like honey in the rock.

Brother, brother come and see
   What the Lord have done for me
I am so humble
   Never get tired
I am walkin' by my Savior's side.

Sister, sister come and see /etc./

—See page 109, below.

The
Ruby Pickens Tartt
Collection
of Religious Folk Songs
from Sumter County,
Alabama

"Honey in the Rock"

edited
and with preface, introduction,
and bibliographic essays
by

Olivia and Jack Solomon

Mercer University Press
Macon, Georgia 31207

ISBN 0-86554-336-4

"Honey in the Rock"
The Ruby Pickens Tartt Collection
of Religious Folk Songs from Sumter County, Alabama

Mercer University, Macon, Georgia 31207

Printed in the United States of America

The paper used in this publication meets
the minimum requirements of American National Standard
for Information Sciences—Permanence of Paper
for Printed Library Materials, ANSI Z39.48-1984.

Library of Congress Cataloging-in-Publication Data

"Honey in the rock" : the Ruby Pickens Tartt
collection of religious folk songs
from Sumter County, Alabama
edited and with preface, introduction, and bibliographical essay
by Olivia Solomon and Jack Solomon.
xxxvi + 176pp. 9 × 9" (23 × 23cm.)
Includes index.
ISBN 0-86554-336-4 (alk. paper)
1. Afro-Americans—Alabama—Sumter County—Songs and music—texts.
2. Christian poetry, American—Alabama—Sumter County.
3. Christian poetry, American—Afro-American authors.
4. Folksongs, English—Alabama—Sumter County—Texts.
5. Spirituals (Music)—Alabama—Sumter County—Texts.
6. Sumter County (Ala.)—Popular culture.
I. Tartt, Ruby Pickens, 1880–1974.
II. Solomon, Olivia, 1937– .
III. Solomon, Jack, 1927– .
PS591.N4H57 1991
782.42162'96073076141—dc20 90-42394
CIP

Contents

Preface

Ruby Pickens Tartt of Livingston, Sumter County, Alabama, was a short story writer, painter, librarian, wife, mother, and, perhaps more than anything else, a lover and collector of Afro-American folklore, life, and song. Her achievement as a folklorist ranks with the very best in the history of American folklore collection.

A courageous, compassionate, and generous woman, Mrs. Tartt fought off personal despair during eight years spent in tuberculosis sanitariums; unstintingly gave her help to America's most-prominent folklorists (among them John Lomax, Benjamin Botkin, Alan Lomax, Elie Seigmeister, Carl Carmer, John Jacob Niles, Julia Peterkins, and Harold Courlander); and as a WPA[1] project worker during the time of our great national despair, travelled the dirt roads of Sumter County and gathered tales, reminiscences and life histories, games and riddles, superstitions, and songs. As a single collector of folklore confined to a limited geographical area, Mrs. Tartt has few peers. The body of her collection is a microcosm of Southern and American Negro folk culture as it existed for a hundred years, from about 1850 (the decade or so prior to the War between the States, times within the living memory of former Alabama slaves whom she interviewed) until 1950 (the year during which she aided Harold Courlander with his Sumter County folk music recordings, although her own active life in folklore collection was, for the most part, nearly over).

We never met Ruby Pickens Tartt, an unfortunate happenstance we would readily alter had we the power. In 1931, when she already was about her collection of folk songs, she had lived more than a half century, while one of us was only three years old and the other not to be born for another seven years. Yet we do, indeed, know her. In the songs she saved for all of us we have heard her voice, touched her hand, felt the force of her will and intelligence. We have read the record of a disciplined mind and a heart receptive to wisdom and poetry and music. We have marvelled at her strength, her energy, her passion to capture what she knew, for a certainty, to be a thing of value.

Our research has been somewhat hindered by as-yet-restricted or limited access to certain manuscripts, correspondence, and other personal papers. However, we intend with this book:

- first, to present Mrs. Tartt's collection of Sumter County, Alabama, spirituals as im-

[1]The Work Projects Administration (WPA) was established in April 1935—originally as the Works Progress Administration—and replaced the Federal Emergency Relief Administration. Headed by Harry L. Hopkins, the WPA was a federal agency charged with instituting and administering public works to relieve national unemployment during the Great Depression. In addition to providing construction work for millions of jobless persons (building bridges, roads, airports, schools, and so forth), WPA employed a wide range of talents in such programs as the Federal Theater Project, the Federal Art Project, and the Federal Writers' Project. The Folklore Division was a prominent part of the Federal Writers' Project. The WPA was discontinued in 1943 and its many programs gradually phased out, but the lasting impact of the WPA was far-reaching.

portant texts in Afro-American folksong study and as a source of pleasure to the general reader;

- second, to rectify the neglect of Mrs. Tartt as folksong collector and as nourisher of the Afro-American folksong tradition, both for its own folk performers in Alabama and for other collectors and scholars who drew freely from her abundant knowledge and who might have reaped a far-less-bountiful harvest had she not directed their paths and cleared the way, literally and figuratively, to those fields of memorable song;
- third, to call attention to the efforts of the Work Projects Administration's Federal Writers' Project, Folklore Division, and thereby to stimulate further investigation in this singular attempt to collect American folklore on a national scale; and
- finally, to show something of the spirituals as folk poems that reflect the evolving Afro-American experience as immigrant, slave, folk, and Christian.

As yet, neither a full-scale biography nor a critical assessment of Mrs. Tartt as a folklorist has been attempted. Surely, when all the archives are opened, some assay will be made, but until then certain questions must either be guessed at or remain unanswered. The contours of her infancy, childhood, adolescence, maturity, and old age have been suggested by Virginia Pounds Brown and Laurella Owens in *Toting the Lead Row: Ruby Pickens Tartt, Alabama Folklorist*[2]; but those specific events and circumstances of personal life that impinged upon Mrs. Tartt as a complex and brilliant twentieth-century figure are still uncertain.

Born at the end of Reconstruction, Mrs. Tartt grew up not in the shadow but the reality of the Old South, its great war and aftermath. The Old South did not cease to be on the instant with Appomattox but persisted long after as a cultural entity of which Ruby Pickens Tartt, like thousands of other Southerners, was a part. It was an incredibly complicated moral, intellectual, and physical identity that she and the others assumed and experienced naturally, coherently, and organically, even to her perception of the landscape, of time and seasons, of the earth and sky of Livingston, Alabama.

This milieu she inhabited daily all her life, save for a year in New Orleans at Sophie Newcomb College and another in New York City where she studied art under the portraitist William Merritt Chase and attended the city's operas, theatres, and museums. How these two years away from Livingston and her earlier studies at the Livingston Female Academy under the feminist, reformer, and educator Julia Tutwiler affected her development may only be surmised. Without doubt, however, such influences came to rest on one who was, by her own family's testimony, gifted, mercurial, and "different" from the start. All the photographs of Mrs. Tartt that we have seen, even those in old age, show her to be a beautiful woman by any standard—dramatic in pose, fashionable in dress, her hands strong, her face strikingly lovely, her frame tall and with a purity of bone structure, her eyes deep-set and luminous, with nowhere a hint of the physical suffering she had endured during the illness she conquered at long last.

That Mrs. Tartt was witty and a born mimic, zealous for the comfort of her guests, and that she understood by instinct, observation, and musical and literary training and aptitude the very core of Afro-American folk song, we know from Carl Carmer, the Lomaxes, and her own writings. That she risked censure and scandal from her fellow townsmen for the sake of her conscience, we know from public record. That her desires to read, to write, and to record Alabama Negro folk culture were insatiable, we know from her WPA manuscripts and her fiction. That she forged bonds with Negro men and women at a time when such liaison was extremely difficult, that in some large part they trusted her with their folk-musical and religious inheritance, and that she was fair and honorable with them, we know from a few letters, the great number of col-

[2](University AL: University of Alabama Press, 1981).

lected songs, and from her exemplary WPA Life Histories and Slave Narratives.

How she reconciled the depth and intensity of her intellect and her hunger for expression with her role as wife and mother we shall perhaps never know. However this reconciliation, she came to maturity in a bleak time of survival economy, followed hard by wartime prosperity and the peace won by D-Day and Hiroshima; she grew old in the wake of the civil rights and woman's rights movements, and in the midst of the hard rock and hard drugs, Viet Nam and Watergate era of the 1960s and 1970s. Yet while her contemporaries withered and died of old age and disease, she continued to read and write and paint, to serve in a chair of anguish on the Sumter County Board of Registrars during the time of Negro-voter registration, to flourish like the psalmist's tree planted by the waters. And though she came to death just short of a century span—as Boswell reported of Dr. Johnson, rendering up to God a mind unclouded, and with a soul as bright as any ever shone in the epitaphs she herself copied down—her tombstone reads simply "Ruby Pickens Tartt 1880–1974."

The efforts of Ruby Pickens Tartt in Alabama folksong study and collection antedate all others except those of Professor Newman I. White, the general editor of the famous Frank C. Brown Collection of Folklore in North Carolina. Professor White, while he was teaching at the Alabama Polytechnic Institute (now Auburn University) during 1915–1917 and at Duke University during 1919–1920, gathered and edited more than 800 Alabama folksong texts and fifteen specimen tunes. When John Lomax's monumental folksong recording project for the Library of Congress brought him to Sumter County in 1937, 1938, and 1940, Mrs. Tartt was his hostess and guide. She arranged recording sessions and interviews for Lomax at homes, schools, and churches in various nearby communities—York, Sumterville, Coatopa, Boyd Station, Epes, Belmont—and in her own backyard in Livingston, rounding up preachers, house servants, field hands, railroad trackliners, and honky-tonk musicians, people she had known personally, many as good friends, all her life. At that time Lomax was already a well-known editor and collector of American folklore and would shortly become head of the Folklore Division of the WPA Federal Writers' Project, and Mrs. Tartt was deeply involved in documenting Sumter County oral folk history and lore for the WPA.

The Tartt folksong manuscripts deposited in the Alabama Archives indicate that by 1937 her field studies were complete, that in 1937–1938 she was occupied in the final assembling, editing, and typing of the manuscripts, and that by November 1938 she had submitted the collection to the state WPA office in Montgomery with the understanding that it would be forwarded to the Washington office. While Byron Arnold was conducting field research for his *Folksongs of Alabama*[3] he met Mrs. Tartt at the Alabama Archives. "She had come to the capitol," Arnold said, "to see if by chance copies of any of the hundreds of Negro folk songs that she had been collecting all her life were filed in the Archives. She had sent them in both words and music, during the WPA Federal Writers' Project."[4] The collection was still intact in 1976 when we located it at the Archives. Although several pages bear the notation "Washington Copy/11-8-38/L.H." we can only speculate that the collection remained in Montgomery because the Federal Writers' Project ceased operations before the state office could process and forward it, a circumstance which occurred in other state, district, and regional offices.

Arnold's report of "both words and music" is a bit troubling. Among the Tartt WPA folksong manuscripts at the Alabama Archives are musical notations, in her hand and with her signature or initials, for some *secular* songs, several evidently first drafts, others clear and readable, with, in many instances, multiple versions which exhibit progressive improvement in copying. Unfortunately, we have located no transcriptions for the Sumter County

[3](University AL: University of Alabama Press, 1950).
[4]Ibid., 152.

spirituals. Some explanations for this absence of such transcriptions may be suggested.

Since Mrs. Tartt was trained in transcription and, moreover, by reason of her long familiarity with and love for this folk song, would have been capable of catching some of the subtleties of performance, her musical manuscripts of the spirituals may reside in some as-yet-unexplored repository of her personal effects. On the other hand, given both the intricacies and confusion that existed throughout the administration of the massive federal writer's program (especially toward the end), such manuscripts may have been lost, misplaced, or even borrowed by some state, district, or national editor, and may be languishing in some forgotten archive file. In 1950 Mrs. Tartt, though seventy years old, assisted Harold Courlander in his recordings of Afro-American folk song throughout the Livingston area, and she was still perfectly able to finish or begin the transcriptions of the spirituals, but for some good reason of her own she may have chosen not to do so.

Byron Arnold mentions a hurricane "the previous spring" that destroyed Mrs. Tartt's house and "all her records, pinning her beneath the debris."[5] Perhaps musical transcriptions were among the losses. Another unanswered question if the fate of Mrs. Tartt's WPA drawings. In a letter to Lomax (probably in 1943) she said, "I'm wondering, though, what became of all the stories I sent in? And the drawings."[6] At her request Benjamin Botkin returned some manuscripts from the Washington office; these she sent to Lomax, but their final disposition is still not clear.[7]

If indeed the absence of notation can be attributed to her conscious choice, her decision may be an act of wisdom, for there has not been a single collector of Afro-American folk music during the past 125 years who has not commented on the almost-insurmountable difficulties of its transcription. The spiritual does not exist until it is seen and heard; it is born anew with every performance. Mrs. Tartt, of all collectors, would have been the first to acknowledge that fact.

Though recently a few musicologists have devised improved systems for noting the complexities of rhythm, metrics, scale, and melody, fundamentally there are two ways of presenting Afro-American folk song: the simple delineation of melody and metrical arrangement, or the re-creation of performance in orchestral and choral manner. Both ways are largely dependent on the musical ear and mind of the Western world. Both leave out, for the most part, the modal, tonic, and rhythmical qualities of Central and West African folk music. Both ignore, in particular, the phenomenon of spoken liturgy, poetry, and narrative, that is, the oral-musical formulas and inventions that shape and reshape every performance. Finally, both, at best, barely suggest the musical identity while, at worst, they either neglect all the psychosocial and religious nuances contained by the human voice or mislead entirely in the reconstruction of those nuances and identity.

To be fair, one must assess the aim of any attempt to transcribe or re-create Afro-American folk song. If the purpose is to provide a minimal Western guide, for the Western ear, in "how the song goes," or to rework this folk song for the Western concert stage, then these two methods of presentation may be pragmatically acceptable. But they are not satisfactory to some. The scholar, the purist, or even the amateur lover of Afro-American folk music may assert that some violation, some betrayal, has occurred in either distilled notation or concert expansion; and the folk performer very well may not even recognize a song so transformed or reduced.

Alternatives, however, are at hand: audio and audiovisual recordings, despite the constraint and awkwardness inherent in the recording situation itself are by far the most reliable source of study and enjoyment of the Afro-American musical tradition. Short of active participation and firsthand experience, such recordings, together with written comment based on field investigation, offer the best solution to the problem of musical transcription. For

---

[5]Ibid.

[6]Quoted in *Toting the Lead Row,* 41.

[7]Ibid., 42.

that reason we have appended a "Discography of Alabama Afro-American Folk Songs" (below, page 151) with annotations regarding significant recordings of Afro-American folk music made in Alabama by, for example, John Lomax, Harold Courlander, and Frederick Ramsey. We hope this discography will supplement and complement the textual notes to the Tartt folk songs.

Admittedly the printed texts in this book are far, very far, from the emotional, religious, musical, and poetic substance of the spiritual as it exists in actuality. Only direct experience of performance, within the context of a worship service or associated religious restival, can begin to reveal the sources, dimensions, and power of this folksong tradition. Only in such a real-life situation are music, text, voice, and other physical attributes all of one aesthetic and religious whole. Further, only therein is the single song coherent with the entire liturgical phenomenon, that is, sermon, prayer, testimony, or other discourse, and sacrament, rite, custom, and ritual. Yet, because of their high verbal art, there is much to be gained by consideration of the Tartt transcriptions as specimens of American folk poetry.

Regrettably, even some who praise the spirituals, for one reason or another, have been indifferent to this poetry. Others dismiss it as negligible. Many regard it as shallow, childlike, crude, stereotyped, imitative, debased, deficient in intellectual content, vacant of symbol and trite in metaphor, garbled in syntax, prosaic in diction, deprived of lyric, narrative, and dramatic devices—in short, an enfeebled, bastardized form which lacks all the qualities of noble and beautiful expression. Such charges are made generally and regularly against much Anglo-American folk poetry save the sacrosanct English ballad. A poem made by the folk, it is said, is doggerel chanted by lesser beings, and if such creations are now and then successful, that is no more than a stroke of good luck or the gesture of some inexplicably gifted primitive. Yet something vastly valuable and attractive must lie in this large body of American folk verse: it endures so long, so many people obstinately refuse to abandon it, learn it early in life and never forget it.

To be genuinely "folk" a poem must arise from folk consciousness and folk experience. Though somewhere, somehow it probably emerged from a single intelligence, it is primarily collective. That is, other intelligencies bear upon its form and content, adding, subtracting, and multiplying, and thus it passes into a collective life, shared by thousands who sing and recite it and for whom it has meaning and aesthetic value. The same ideas, emotions, and poetic devices—metaphor, image, symbol, rhyme, meter, diction, syntax—that animate written poetry are present, to lesser and greater degree, in folk poetry; but a particular folk imparts its own special qualities to subject, structure, and conventions, even as the single creator of written poetry speaks in his or her own voice.

The first distinguishing characteristic of folk poetry is language—bold, fresh, drawn from living folk speech, retaining its color, verve, timbre, rhythms, and intonations. By contrast, the shabbiness of imitative folk speech in composed sentimental, minstrel, and other pseudofolk types sticks out like the proverbial sore thumb. A second characteristic is imagery, which, like the language, springs immediately and forcefully from folk life, from the very stuff of daily existence. Whenever these vivid sensory details appear in clusters or as aggregates and are repeated, varied, or counterpointed by other images, they may take on the functions of metaphor and symbol. In the Tartt spirituals, for example, the overpowering images of the deathbed scene congregate so often and so subtly that they acquire immense symbolic meaning. It is true that in some species, notably autograph verse, folk similes are contrived and trite; yet these are, in actuality, a kind of oral shorthand, verbal and intellectual conventions which, like folk sayings and proverbs, have been in common parlance for hundreds of years, and which, once reexamined, recover much of their original spontaneity. Finally, the folk have no schoolmasters to insist on learning a poem by rote. What is memorable is so by its own power; the cheap, pale, and stagnant do not endure; and if a line does not catch the ear and heart, stick to the tongue and brain, it is promptly and forever forgotten.

Careful and fair examination of Afro-American folksong poetry will, by and large, refute charges of primitivism, mediocrity, imitation, and stereotype. This volume of Sumter County spirituals, to the contrary, presents many folk poems of great merit. Hitherto, Afro-American folksong study has been dominated by studies in origins, of the historical and cultural phenomena out of which it evolved. Yet while such studies have enlarged our understanding and heightened our response to this music, discordant findings have often obscured the significance and value of American Negro folk poetry within this singular, compelling folksong tradition. For example, one study may claim an African ancestry, while another discovers sources in European hymnody and secular folk song, and still another compromises with theories of syncretism and acculturation and claims it is bound up with the history of American slavery and the civil rights movement.

Mrs. Tartt's collection provides an excellent means of examining Afro-American folk religious poetry. Here is a wide variety of genres from a continuous folk culture which, though geographically restricted, may be taken as representative of hundreds of similar folk continuums throughout the Southeastern United States. The introductory essay and the textual notes of this volume are designed to help readers discover the breadth and depth of this strain among our nation's folk poetry possessions, and we earnestly desire responses of a clearer understanding and fuller enjoyment of a vital and continuing American folk legacy.

The discussion of origins, now complicated by the admission of additional genres— blues, toasts, jokes, personal narratives, and conversations—and even more intense examination of the social, political, and psychological elements always latent in the subject, is laborious but instructive, particularly in connection with the question of whether or not the spiritual still exists as a dynamic folk entity. The first collectors of Afro-American folk song—Allen, Garrison, and Ware—worried about its demise, a fear handed down to their successors, including Mrs. Tartt and her colleagues, who have all regularly prophesied its doom, possibly the one point of real agreement throughout a century-old debate.

The bones of contention might be less plentiful if there were some reasonable compromise in the matter of defining folklore. Inherent in the antiquarian and linguistic bent of the first Anglo-European folklorists—who never thought of themselves as folklorists and became so almost accidentally—were primitive-survivalist definitions which determine the folk-ness of any phenomenon largely on the basis of its antiquity, agrarian character, and evidences of the distortion that inevitably occurs when a higher, quantatively and qualitatively more restricted order filters down to a larger and inferior group. That is, if an item displays, overwhelmingly, the attributes of a generally extinct specimen, passing from its original time and space into a present dimension, preserving the outline of some Ur-classification, and, moreover, if it exhibits those modifications that invariably accompany processes of diffusion, then it is "folk." This theory so dominated Anglo-American folksong study that the search for Child or English ballads within isolated, uneducated, socially backward, and economically deprived Rip Van Winkle cultures continued unabated until around 1950.

Attitudes that folk items are an endangered species, so charmingly quaint or symbolically significant as to be worthy of preservation, certainly have given us important literary folklore to enjoy—notably in the Brothers Grimm, Hans Christian Andersen, and the writers of the Irish Renaissance. And, unquestionably, such attitudes deeply affected English and American writers—Scott, Hardy, Hawthorne, Irving, Keats, Coleridge, Yeats, Eliot, and Joyce, among others—as well as philosophers and psychologists such as Freud, Jung, and Nietzsche. Yet it was not until the mid-twentieth century with the full emergence of comparative mythology, anthropology, and archaeology that the persistence and universality of myth was demonstrated. Notably the lifelong labors of Stith Thompson in the identification and systematic compilation of worldwide folktale motifs and types, an achievement that marks a continental divide in the history of folklore scholarship, showed that all folk phenomena are organic, rising, falling, and reappearing in new disguises. The attacks of Richard Dorson against "fakelore" or concocted, vitiated lore several times removed from the authentic folk base, stringently corrected irresponsible lapses in research and set folklore firmly on the path of analytical induction. And during the last two decades scholars have begun to chart the flow from folk to popular, the circuitous routes by which folk impulses travel through electronic media, though these latest directions in folklore criticism have not been without opposition from conservative theorists.

Surely, a most important aspect of all folklore (as of life itself) is its evolutionary character, the slow, unconscious transformations of the folk-life continuum in which, though turning points and climactic passages are reached, there are no sudden deaths. The argument that the spiritual is an anachronism today limits the definition of folk song to the narrowest of confines. It is not enough, however, to speak of just the *antebellum* prayer chant, work song, or elegy. In point of fact and realistically, these songs belong to every decade. The early evidence from 1750 to 1880, derived from letters, diaries, journals, and newspapers, is practically all in. Now must be assembled written documents from the last decade of the nineteenth century to 1920-1930, a time marked by one of those climactic passages, the entry of American folk song into early radio and recordings. And now must be made careful inquiry into the past fifty years of Afro-American folk song in both its folk and mass-media existence. Otherwise the spiritual shall not be understood.

Popular treatments of Afro-American folk song began with nineteenth-century minstrel and other staged entertainments for white audiences. With the tours of the celebrated Jubilee Singers of Fisk University and later of groups such as the Tuskegee Institute Choir, the spiritual entered the concert stage throughout America and Europe and soon found its way into operatic and symphonic forms. By 1930 piano-accompanied spirituals performed by Negro singers were attracting large local and regional radio audiences and the tonalities, rhythms, melodic phrases, and vocal styles of Afro-American religious folk music were heard in the jazz and blues of string and brass bands in New Orleans, Memphis, and Chicago. The 1950s rock-and-roll explosion clearly owed much to its antecedents in polyphonic worship-music performance, and popular musical expressions in the 1980s, from the rap song to blues and gospel, everywhere carry the seed of Negro sacred song.

None of this means that the spiritual has lost its folk center; it rather means that the center radiates outward to popular media which, in their turn, are reinterpreted by the folk. Hundreds of Afro-American choirs and congregations, thousands of singers, even those with the hymnbooks Mrs. Tartt urged her singers not to buy for fear they would forget the old songs, understand the roots and evolving transformations of their folk-worship music: they are in enviable possession of both change and the continuity of tradition, of a moment in time as well as an encompassing sense of the history of a song—not textbook history, but that of cumulative, transmitted, and lived folk experience. Whatever popular raiment it wears—gospel, jazz, blues, rock—and however decked with whatever instrument— electric organ, orchestral strings, synthesizer—the folk identity of the American spiritual is essentially what it has always been.

Perhaps the temper of our time is unsuited to sympathetic appraisal of any religious folk song. Whatever the reason, our surveys of recent Negro culture studies show that while field studies of Afro-American lore of all kinds are more than adequate, religious folk song suffers a dearth of narrative and analytical documentation, and that, though commercial and scholarly recordings of secular song are abundant, those of worship and sacred folk music are woefully scant. Our own field research during the last decade in Crenshaw, Elmore, and Tallapoosa counties in Alabama[8] dispel any claims that the spiritual as folk expression is dead or declining. To the contrary, it is wonderfully healthy and widespread, and, moreover, in its structure, motifs, figurative concepts, intellectual and theological substance, its emotional and spiritual attributes, musical qualities, performance styles and circumstances, in both regular and special worship services, it bears very close comparison to that body of song recorded by John Lomax in Sumter County fifty years ago. Further, it exhibits a strong degree of kinship with the Afro-American religious folk song described and documented by numerous observers during the nineteenth century. We are, however, only two researchers. The need for extensive field research and recording in this area is immediate and pressing. Perhaps this collection of Mrs. Tartt's Sumter County folk songs will encourage others to undertake similar study in the South and elsewhere.

We have made no attempt to "clean up" this Sumter County collection. Ordinary standards of correctness are useless and self-defeating in folklore investigation where language is a fundamental agent in the identification of a phenomenon as "folk." Ironically, in a grammatical fault will often lie the poetry and truth of some human experience. Historically, some transcriptions of Negro folk speech have descended to a caricature which insults the people it purports to portray. Mrs. Tartt's song manuscripts are notably free of that flaw: she was extremely careful to avoid exaggerated phonetic spelling, and she recorded folk diction and syntax accurately. These songs, as well as her other WPA manuscripts, show that she had "a good ear" for folk discourse in every sphere, circumstance, and mood— the kitchen, the fields and other sites of labor, the country road and the front yard, pulpit and pew, sidewalk and courthouse square. Everywhere she captures the idiom so revelatory of this folk, the shadings and depths of thought and emotion, the individualized tone imparted to each song by its singer, the verbal expressions, metaphors, and grammatical and structural usages of a speech in which lie the wit, passion, humor, fear, anger, despair, and joy of a people, their dreams and knowledge, the turnings of their earth. For this reason we have presented the texts as she submitted them to the Archives more than forty years ago.

We remain, however, somewhat perplexed in the choice of nomenclature. Anglo-Europeans and some Americans use the terms *man, woman,* or *person of color. Colored,* as in National Association for the Advancement of Colored People, appeared in some mid-nineteenth-century folklore collections and sociohistorical commentary. *Black* is favored by some contemporary social and political organizations, by many contemporary folklore scholars, musicologists, anthropologists, and sociologists, and by many universities and colleges as a title for courses and curricula. *Negro,* preferred by other organizations— for example, Negro Universities Press and United Negro Colleges— historically has been widely accepted by scholars in various academic disciplines, including folklore; it is the designation used by Mrs. Tartt. *Afro-American* is the preference of some historians, sociologists, and folklorists who believe it to be a sensible, practical, objective appellation that combines ethnic origins with both the historical stage of immigration, assimilation, and present citizenship, and who extend that usage to other groups, as for example, Polish-American, Eastern European-American, Chinese-American. We have used all but one of the above designations, *Colored,* and found each apt and helpful. *Black* is used generally in reference to contemporary folklore criticism and theory and as a designation for the folk group; similarly, *white* refers to *that* folk culture or song tradition. *Negro* is employed as a formal appelation of the ethnic identity and with reference to historical folksong criticism. *Afro-American* is used whenever the folk culture and song tradition come under analytical discussion.

[8]Audio tape recordings made during the course of our field research are available by arrangement with the editors and Thomas Russell Library, Alexander City State Junior College, Alexander City, Alabama.

So much is beyond the scope of this book: so many different questions cry out for examination, and so many significant findings could but be touched on or pointed to in the bibliographical essay; and so much yet remains to be learned and told about Mrs. Tartt and about Afro-American religious folk song—a future enterprise for other editors and researchers, the prospect of which we view with much excitement.

For the present, we owe our thanks to many generous hearts and willing hands: to Miss Sarah Ann Warren of the Alabama State Department of Archives who assisted us in the location of the manuscripts and prepared duplicates; to our typists Brenda Croley, Janice Riley, Sabrina Evers, Donna Hall, Martha Murry, Anne Barkley, Sharon Atkinson, Mrs. Tyrone Oliver, Sandra Florine, and Phyllis Hornsby; to the library staff at Alexander City State Junior College, Frances Tapley, Peggy Causey, Joyce Robinson, and Carolyn Ingram; to student assistants Larry Hornsby, Freddie Langford, Alan Guy, and David Florine; to Mr. Joseph Hickerson and Mr. Gerald Parsons, Archive of Folk Song, the Library of Congress, for their supervision of the reproduction of the recordings made by John Lomax in Alabama; to Alan Jabbour, director, American Folklife Center, the Smithsonian; to the Rev. Mr. David Bentley, the Rev. Mr. Joseph Edward Hastings, and the Rev. Mr. G. Gene Williams, all of Tallassee, Alabama, who identified certain scriptural references; to Fannie Pickens Inglis, daughter of Ruby Pickens Tartt, who encouraged our efforts; to Mr. John Neel and his family who received us so hospitably on our trip to Livingston University in quest of Mrs. Tartt's papers; to Ethel Scott, catalog librarian, Julia Tutwiler Library, Livingston University, for her kind assistance; to Hank Willett, for his perusal of our manuscript during its early evolution; to Bill Ferris, director of the Center for the Study of Southern Culture, the University of Mississippi, for his examination of these materials and for his graceful telephone conversations and letters which came at a time when we were on the precipice of despair over putting the book together; to the anonymous readers for Mercer University Press who chastened our excesses, set a plain path, and gave us hope; to Mr. Don Haymes, sometime editor in chief of Mercer University Press, who welcomed and believed in this book; to Edd Rowell, one of the pure in heart. Special note is due to the late Dr. Byron Causey, president of Alexander State Junior College, who faithfully supported our research over twelve years and who arranged for the purchase of the duplications of John Lomax's recordings for the Library of Congress of Alabama folk songs. Without John Lomax there would not be preserved the remarkable Sumter County folk singers or their even more remarkable songs. But without Ruby Pickens Tartt there might not have been any Library of Congress Sumter County recordings at all; and, assuredly, this book would never have been. To John Lomax, to the Sumter County singers, and to Miss Ruby, we and the world are much obliged.

On 27 July 1977, President Asa Green of Livingston University nominated Mrs. Tartt for the Alabama Women's Hall of Fame. The nomination was rejected, but upon a second nomination in 1979 was accepted. On 23 October 1980, a century after her birth, formal installation ceremonies were held at Judson College, Marion, Alabama. In the summer of 1978 we visited her burial place in Myrtlewood, the Livingston town cemetery. Her grave, beside that of her husband, is across the way from the hanging ground of the legendary Sumter County outlaw Steve Renfroe of whom she often wrote. Renfroe and most of the Sumter County singers are all silent now, but their lore and music are all amingle with the memory and spirit of Ruby Pickens Tartt.

—*Olivia and Jack Solomon*
Tallassee, Alabama

An Introduction

The Ruby Pickens Tartt collection of Afro-American religious folk song from Sumter Country, Alabama, brings together an unparalleled anthology of texts from a flourishing folk culture, rich in poetry and music, a body of unforgettable spirituals—story and sermon songs, elegies, laments, chants, moans, jubilee and religion songs, salvation and praise songs, lyric hymns—all of marvelous folk artistry. For two hundred years the spirituals transcribed in this volume have been sung in the American South, descending from generation to generation. Today their impulse reaches throughout the world.

To Mrs. Tartt, as to countless others who have lived intimately with this tradition, these spirituals were—and are—as familiar as a dearly loved face, yet never so familiar as to be common. Melodies sweet and strange are heard from the open windows and doors of small churches and houses silvered by blistering August suns, freezing January rains, and the lion winds of March. They echo down muddy lanes and dusty roads; across open fields, marshes, and dark forests; out of alleys behind cafes and drug stores; from kitchens of fruitcakes and ambrosia, turnip greens and sowbelly; and across front porches among luxuriant ferns and highbacked rocking chairs or pine-plank stools and benches. They roll down long, cool halls of portraits or through open, rotting dogtrots, and rise from beside the barn, smokehouse, or wellhouse, from orchard and garden, scuppernong arbor and meadow. They are the sounds of despair and faith, of old sorrow and young hope, at daybreak and nightfall, in war and peace, at birth and death, in all weathers and seasons, arcing, unfolding, streaming to the heavens, lonely smoke from the chimneys of home. Say but a phrase and we, both the whites who heard and the blacks who sang, remember—"My good Lord done been here"; "Steal away"; "Rock my soul"; "Motherless child"; "Lord, I'm going down in your name"; "Honey in the rock."

But—make no mistake—the remembrance and the possession of these songs is not the same for white and black. Only by the hardest discipline, the most unwavering, patient, and rigorous study, may one enter a folk culture not his own. And remembrance is sometimes an impediment, for a beloved voice or figure does not lend itself easily to dispassionate analysis. Ultimately, *Honey in the Rock* lies beyond rational judgment, and to assess the significance of this musical and poetic tradition, as both an integral part of American Negro folk culture and as human expression is exceedingly difficult. The origins of these songs are obscure, their power mysterious, and though we readily recognize their beauty, to say why they move us so deeply and in such strange manner is quite another matter. At their center is bondage, its bloody war and bitter aftermath, and no man would summon this past time of enslavement except to discover truth.

Both folklore and history teach, though in very different ways. The judgments of the historian are based on examination of substantiated facts, while from folklore studies come revelations of the mind and spirit. The use of a body of folklore as document is perilous: its very substance defies any but the most general classification and discussion. Thousands of vagaries, whims, concepts, motifs, and images manifest themselves in a whole cosmos of folk wisdom and philosophy, folk literature and science, folk music and dance, folk play and religion, all dynamically reshaped, if only slightly, as these are transmitted temporally and spatially by individual bearers. It is almost impossible, therefore, to find in a folk song unassailable evidence of any thesis. What we may find is a sense of and feeling for the folk identity that produced the song. Every word, every fragment of melody inescapably reflects that identity, in everything from large systems of thought and geocultural configurations to the smallest detail of everyday affairs.

Mrs. Tartt's collection is referential to American and Southern history from about 1850, the apogee of the plantation system, until about 1950 when the worst hardships of the Depression were over and the stirrings of black protest began. But such reference is not specific to social and political events. *Honey in the Rock* is by no means a document in history, but here may be encountered the experience of the American Negro as slave, as Christian, as folk; and here may be discovered his mortal life, thought, and heart.

Though the indigenous character of his experience may not be precisely delineated, it is everywhere evident that the American Negro brought with him to the New World his own complete folklife continuum. That this continuum was brutally assaulted by slavery, suffering the stunning loss of its native tongues, is undeniable; that the unwilling immigrant held fast to certain aesthetic, intellectual, social, and psychological modes of his traditional folk life is also irrefutable; that, in forging a new identity, Afro-Americanism, he took what he wanted and needed, and what he could get, from his enslavers is clear, and that he made it his own is important for us to grasp if one is to understand Afro-American religious folk song.

Afro-American musical and religious inheritance from Central and West Africa was vast, strong, and persists to great degree until this day:

- percussive, wind, and string instruments as solo and as accompaniment to song and dance;
- melodic, tonic, and rhythmical elements of a distinct and fascinating character;
- the human body, including facial expression and vocal quality, as visible metaphor, imagery, and symbol, as objective correlative, of song content and meaning;
- particular performance styles, especially antiphonal dialogue between choir or ensemble and a strong bardic leader, characterized by emerging variation and complication, vocally, poetically, and musically, and the repetition of key verbal, melodic, and rhythmical phrases;
- the concept of song as history, both collective and personal (hence the leaning towards verbal art) and as myth (hence the pervasive subscription to rites of birth, life, and death and the interconnectedness of the ordinary and the divine);
- and the function of song as an organic, logically coherent, and aesthetically satisfying part of the worship service.

Why, then, are there no large extant bodies of Afro-American religious song in African dialects? The answer lies partly in the psychology of captive and captor, of forcible mastery and helpless submission, and partly in the history of Afro-American Christianity. Scholars have cited hundreds of instances in which white masters undertook the conversion of slaves. Religious instruction was given by mistresses, tutors, and other members of the plantation household. Slaves attended services in the church of their masters and white preachers were hired to conduct worship for slave congregations. Negro preachers often achieved renown among both whites and blacks, and even on plantations where worship was totally proscribed, secret services were held in homes or brush arbors. The early postbellum period saw the rapid spread of independent Negro churches, most of which were founded under the auspices of established denominations, and during the nineteenth-century Second Great Awakening whites and blacks sometimes attended campground revivals together. But the incompatibility of institutionalized slavery with the teachings of the New Testament is obvious, and efforts to Christianize, in the end tragically ironic, bore hard and deep on the development of Afro-American folk speech, song, poetry, and religious thought and expression.

The vast majority of slaveholders were Protestants—Presbyterians, Baptists, Methodists, and Episcopalians—and their Bible was the King James Version. The religious folk song of those colonial countries in which Catholicism prevailed developed in an entirely different direction from that of the American South where, again and again, slaves heard not the Latin Mass but the King James Bible, and though most could not read, they learned the Scriptures by rote through oral transmission. The King James Bible was the only available written source of their accommodation to the New World, a compendium of history, philosophy, ethics, morality, theology, natural science, and literature. This was the language they learned—paradigms of syntax, diction, and vocabulary, models for figurative devices, patterns of rhythm and meter and of sentence and paragraph structure. Here were folktales, allegories, myths, parables, fables, dramas, proverbs, riddles, sermons, declamations—an entire spectrum of the oral and written literature of the Western world. The substance, themes, and motifs of this biblical literature reached all the way back to the beginnings of civilized man, to the Indo-European of the Mediterranean Basin, even to the very limits of folk memory on the African continent, and the newcomer, stirred by his recognition of familiar mythic images and symbols, was not so comfortless in a strange land. Recently come from a culture where literature, music, and history were highly developed folk-traditional arts, he must have delighted in the comparable folk aesthetic offered by this Bible, the only book he—as well as most whites in nineteenth-century America—ever saw or owned and the first he ever learned to read.

For both slave and slaveholder, the King James Version was a great unifying folk center, a common base of communication, its contents known far and wide, its language and style informing everyday folk speech, thought, and behavior. That it became such a center, in view of general illiteracy, is, on the one hand, incredible; but, on the other hand, consider that the surpassing human need for knowledge, expression, and fellowship for centuries was met chiefly through folk memory and oral perpetuation. Discounting its role in the nurture of moral and ethical behavior, as a spiritual guide, and as the theological base of both institutionalized and folk religion, the Bible has held a place of immeasurable significance in American folk thought, life, and lore.

For the slave in particular the Bible was a golden treasury held out by his oppressor who, though he might have used Scripture as proof of the historical and moral legitimacy of slavery and as an aid to suppress rebellion, built far better than he knew. If the slave was forced to hear an evil doctrine— and few swallowed it—he also tasted glory and has never let it go. Students of the spiritual always point to their recurrent themes of loneliness, exile, despair—indeed, they were once called "sorrow songs"—and quite possibly a life in slavery could not have been borne without the poetic objectivations of faith, hope, and immortality offered by the Bible. Its value to an enslaved people cannot be overestimated, and it is not at all certain that without the Bible, there would have been enough good men, white or black, of North or South, to hold back the forces of dehumanization.

Historians have not always taken into full account the power of Christianity over men's minds in that divisive American war. But the folklorist discerns links, indirect and unconscious, between a body of lore and the great events of the world, the energy unleashed by a short melodic phrase, a tale of martyrdom, a song of rescue. Out of a folk anthology written during the flowering of English literature under Elizabeth and James but orally transmitted and memorized, out of his folk memory of indigenous lore which resembled that contained in the English Bible, and out of the Bible's moral and spiritual instruction and its mythic symbolism, the American slave fashioned a way to live.

Much in his African folk culture prepared the slave for the King James Bible. Keenly attuned to the physical universe, sensitive to plants, animals, stars, sun, the turning of seasons and weather, and disposed towards myth making, he could relate immediately to the six-day creation of the world, the expulsion from Eden, and the fratricide of Cain. Himself a warrior for long years, the slave could follow avidly the battles of Saul, Joshua, Gideon, and David. A riddler and fabulist, he quickly learned to recite Proverbs and the wise sayings of Jesus and easily apprehended the wit and folly of Samson. A practitioner of fertility and death rites, he recognized the sacrificial offerings and taboos of the Hebrews and New Testament water baptism as symbols similar to his own. A maker of lyric song, of praise, satirical, battle, and love songs in his own land, he must have found it pleasant to hear the Psalms of David, Ecclesiastes, and the Song of Songs.

In particular the Old Testament heroes attracted the new immigrant: looming figures of prophecy, adventure, romance, and tragedy—Moses, Abraham, Isaac, Saul, David, Jacob, Job, Daniel, the Hebrew Children—whose stories would be sung and recited for generations to come.[1] But for the New Testament Jesus the slave had few, if any, folk heroic or mythic predecessors. Nor is that surprising. Though prototypes of the Messiah and dead-god-reborn are common in many world mythologies, the Christian Jesus is like none other. In Afro-American folk song the portrait of Jesus is both scriptural and folk: again and again he is "My Jesus," a phrase that bespeaks the warm intimacy of close ties, of friendship and kinship, a concept also applied to the Old Testament characters of the spirituals; he is the impeccable warrior and conquering king on a milk-white horse, leading his Christian soldiers against the armies of Satan; he is the emblem of Christian life and practice, his parables of faith, salvation, and forgiveness forming their own songs; above all, he is the center of the New Testament drama of Crucifixion and Resurrection, the blood sacrifice, the risen Lord who overcame death, hell, and the grave. Jesus' Old Testament counterpart is Job and their sufferings bind Jesus and Job together in the spirituals, as both were bound to the slave through his own hard life on this earth, though Job is quintessential man and Christ is both man and God. As God, Christ saves and forgives, but the spirituals lean heavily towards his humanness: he is the grief-stricken friend of Lazarus, the tender bedmaker of the dying, the old friend we meet once again in the Heavenly City, the fellow slave scourged by his oppressors, the wife, husband, or mother who is faithful in every circumstance—poverty, disease, all misfortunes and joys, even unto death.

This anthropomorphism, directly linked with one of the most appealing aspects of the spiritual, the Christian's personal relationship with God, is sometimes comic: a holy angel cleans mud from a chariot wheel; God hollers out to a sinner, "I'm gettin' worried with your wicked ways"; Job sings the blues because his wife "ain't treatin' him right"; the old conjurer Satan "missed a soul he thought he had." Critics often see here an inappropriate burlesque: the humanizing of the divine in the *Iliad* or *The Second Shepherds' Play* is praiseworthy, yet, somehow, folk comedy in the spirituals is morally and poetically objectionable. But that a folk who exhibit fine, diverse comic skills in oral secular lore should exclude humor from their religious folk song, oratory, and rhetoric would be unnatural and unfortunate. In historical Southern folk worship, both black and white, laughter has never been completely banned from the churchhouse. To this day Southern preachers carry a chest of humorous folk

[1]Though conspicuously absent in contemporary media "gospel," both white and black, where they have been replaced by the "Jesus song" and by other genres derivative of antebellum Afro-American lyric folk hymns and white Protestant hymnody, Old Testament characters still thrive, along with healing, sacramental, and charismatic rites and seasonal festivals (Easter sunrise services, Nativity plays, homecomings, and New Year's watch nights), in American folk worship (especially as sermon topics), in the local Sunday-morning radio "gospel" broadcast, in current "media churchés" (which preserve the revival camp meeting atmosphere and other folk religious strains, episodes of ecstatic conversion, apocalyptic prophecy, and pulpit oratory), and of course in film extravaganzas and television miniseries.

anecdotes, tales, fables, and allegories which serve as attention-getters, narrative and expository transitions, enhancement or shifts of mood, and as a means of simplifying and concretizing theology. Churchgoing is a social act, and worship, no matter how rigidly structured, is communal and human. Surely, judgment of humor in the spirituals as impropriety, or any offense taken at this humanness, misses the mark far and wide.

Comic anthropomorphism is less a matter of characterization, however, than of language. Though its specific sources are widely debated, the high position of verbal art in all Afro-American lore is generally conceded. More than any other kind of American folk song, the spiritual has been shaped by performance: deep within the human voice resides the word, the force that empowers and structures musical and poetic form and incarnates substance and meaning. The term "spiritual" is not a misnomer: these songs arise from the indefinable part of man, neither character, body, nor personality, or even the sum of these, but a part designated throughout recorded history as spirit or soul, that which emanates from the divine and is characterized by creativity.

Since the very beginnings of social man, the Creator has been set apart from his fellows, his special qualities early perceived, feared, and honored; and the Maker—of fire, medicine, weapons, pictures, sounds—became also Prophet, Priest, and King. Skills alone cannot account for a maker's power: he must be invested with the word, for, as John the Apostle said, the Word *is* God. The word as poetry is magic rune and spell which controls nature, destiny, man, the cosmos; the word is the center, source, and means of power of all life; the word lifts man above dust and beasts, gives a tongue to the holdings of his mind and the yearnings of his heart. Who then is to say that image, metaphor, diction, and syntax in the spirituals did not determine the rhythmical, tonal, and melodic arrangement of sound, that the word as poetry gave birth to the word as music?[2]

It is no accident that the great narrative and lyric spirituals exhibit many of the qualities of Elizabethan and Jacobean poetry, or that, down to the present day, the Afro-American folk sermon preserves the syntax, balance, and antithesis of Shakespearean blank verse and the cadence of late-seventeenth-century prose. While West and Central African rhythms and expressive verbal and musical modes undergird ante-and postbellum Afro-American religious folk song and other worship phenomena, there is no way to set aside the overwhelming influence of the King James Bible and of traditional English folk speech in the shaping of Afro-American language, a language that rapidly became fit for ordinary discourse, for narrative, descriptive, and exhortatory oral literature, and for the poetry of secular and religious folk song.

The oral and written speech of the educated master, on whom the slave, for the most part, patterned his own, bore various strains. A reader of Greek and Latin, steeped in Restoration and eighteenth-century Neoclassicism, the Southern planter's public style, bearing like that of his English contemporaries the likeness of Seneca, Cicero, and Milton, was employed for documents, newspapers, letters, journals, and oral declarations. A lover of stage comedies and closet tragedy, the planter relied on that style of "manners" for his parlor and drawing-room social life. The Bible and Shakespeare were his constant companions, and he was thoroughly familiar with English novelists and essayists. In brief, his speech was governed by decorum, appropriate styles for specific circumstances, but far and away the circumstances were ordinary, and for these the English folk language of continuous oral transmission was entirely suitable. Flexible, direct, active, concrete, more than sufficient semantically, pungent with proverbs, images, metaphors, and allusions drawn

---

[2]See Phillip M. Peck, "The Power of Words in African Verbal Art," *Journal of American Folklore* 94/371 (1981): 19-43, for a theory of spoken language as an autonomous entity that determines the dimensions and character of the communicative arts.

from Anglo-American folk life and the King James Bible, this speech served him well. And by daily, intimate association, another folk, a black, immigrant slave people, absorbed this folk speech, imparting to it their own folk experiences and identity.

For many years American Negro speech was reproduced, orally and verbally, as "dialect," in reality often a degrading gibberish of semantic and phonetic distortions vulnerable to attack as a species of prejudice. Today, Afro-American language is more fairly regarded as a fundamentally oral speech learned under the duress of mass enslavement, the survival mechanism accelerating and intensifying its development into a structured instrument for pragmatic, intellectual, and aesthetic communication. World history offers several examples of the preservation of indigenous language by a subject people, and why the American black of today does not speak and write his native tongues is a matter of interesting conjecture.

The degree and kind of subjection, the inherent attractiveness and range of the competing languages helps to determine which takes precedence. In confederations of far-flung dependencies, tributary states may retain their own language for conversation, commerce, scholarship, and literature; or, if the conqueror be sufficiently strong, his language may supplant the indigenous. For whatever reasons, the Afro-American slave chose the language of his conqueror but, as with the King James Bible and this nation, he made it his own. There may be, after all, a portion of the brain reserved for language constructs—remarkably, in only a few short years the African immigrant had a new tongue for his poetry.

On a first reading of the texts collected by Mrs. Tartt one is struck by this poetry, at once natural and supranatural, filled with images drawn from this sunup-to-sundown world and from the ancient marvels of the King James Bible. The language of this poetry is also dualistic: ordinary in its Anglo-American folk idiom, diction, and syntax, yet simultaneously reverberating with the literature of the King James Bible and kindled by all the fears, dreams, and hardships of slaves in a new country, it sometimes reaches the very heights of human utterance.

How this ascent is accomplished cannot be fully explained in the routine manner of poetry analysis. Neither instinctive as in the poetry of children, saints, fools, or riddlers, nor conscious as in literary poetry, this utterance issues abundantly from the American Negro experience. As slave, he gave to the spirituals the themes of loneliness, exile, unbearable burdens, and bondage, and their opposites, joyous fellowship, home, sweet release, and exalted freedom; the syntax of despair and hope; and the diction of a branded body and a redeemed soul. As folk, he brought to his religious song the realities of work, food, and clothing, his physical landscape, and his social intercourse with family and fellows. As Christian, he poured into the spirituals all the inexhaustible substance of the Bible, its legends and mythic tales, dramas and fables, its sociology, morality, and theology.

The theology of the spirituals, often unfairly attacked as ignorant or simplistic, is dead-on a Protestant center: belief in the omnipotence and omniscience of the one God in tripartite form, in salvation through the crucified Christ, and in faith-not-works-alone. True, every now and then a scriptural inaccuracy occurs—the wonder is there are so few in the songs of a generally unlettered people—but the spirituals present both a practical and poetic theology.

First, the spirituals set forth the attributes of Christian practice, in particular the disciplines of praying, moaning, weeping, and singing, and define the Christian life through metaphor, symbol, and imagery as one of harmony with God and with other men and as one of faith that will not be shaken by any obstacle, whether hunger, weariness, beatings, sickness, or the death of beloved friends and family.

Second, both the Old Testament mythos and the New Testament ethos share equal dominion in the determination of Christian conduct: as Moses, Abraham, and David trusted wholly in "Jehovah," were obedient to his commands, endured trials, and kept the covenant of faith; as Christ prayed, healed, taught, and everywhere exemplified the Beatitudes, and as he suffered, died, and was reborn—even so, must the Christian. Without these disciplines, there is no strength for life, no courage to die, and no hope of Heaven.

Third, the spirituals are informed by the New Testament dichotomy of Satan and Christ: redemption from original sin is made possible only by the Crucifixion, and this salvation enables the Christian to triumph over the world, the flesh, and the Devil, and to gain the invisible inheritance of Heaven.

These theological concepts are articulated in the spirituals by various folksong types:

- the exhortatory song in which certain Pauline sins—gambling, drunkenness, lying—are paraded and condemned;
- the salvation song which urges repentance or gives an account of conversion;
- the interior monologue or prayer song which reveals intense psychological states;
- the lament, a song of bereavement, of anguished loss;
- the religion song which celebrates the joys of "being saved" or in the "state of grace";
- the morale-builder or pedagogical song which teaches Christian disciplines;
- the Heaven or Zion song about eternal happiness in the Promised Land;
- the Holy Spirit song which narrates or poeticizes mystic revelation;
- the lyric song of death, either of elegiac tone or in a gripping mood of terror with graphic images of violence and decay;
- the apocalyptic song which evokes the Day of Wrath in the Book of Revelation;
- the sermon song, a miniaturization of the folk sermon from which it borrows principles of organization, rhetorical and oratorical devices, and a preaching style; and
- story songs, folk re-creations of biblical literature.

Such types permit the unfolding of an integrated Christian theology which, whether overt as in the exhortatory and didactic specimens or illustrative as in the story songs, converts the unbeliever, chastens the desires of mortal flesh, points the way to absolution of sin, and lifts the soul to eternal union with God.

The full expression of the spirituals as theology, music, and poetry, and the apotheosis of the Afro-American experience as slave, folk, and Christian, is encountered only in the service of worship where they are part of a single, deeply moving aesthetic, religious, and folk entity. While composed hymns, anthems, and gospel songs are of importance in contemporary folk worship, the strength of the continuous oral tradition is such that it is still possible to study the performance of spirituals during both regular and special services—revivals, sacramental occasions, Christian calendar festivals, funerals, and singings—where the general features of regular worship are altered to achieve specific liturgical, personal, and social aims. Though the African influences are undeniably present, the worship service of the American slave has historically taken its contours from Anglo-American Protestantism, acquiring denominational variations, notably Methodist and Baptist, with minor but pronounced aspects of Episcopalian, Primitive and Free Will Baptist, and Pentecostal and Holiness.

Nineteenth-century white observers invariably evidenced their wonder and excitement over Negro folk worship, its sincere piety and ecstatic happenings. The contemporary investigator, no less moved, hears thousands of echoes from historical Protestant worship, and is plagued by thorny questions: How and why, for example, did the time set aside for "personal testimony" arise? How extensive was the influence of Puritan metrical psalmody, of English plainsong, and perhaps the secular madrigal on the early spiritual and on Negro Sacred Harp? What was the role of the *Book of Common Prayer* in the formulation of Afro-American worship order and language, or of John Wesley's "Order of Worship"? How are the Afro-American folk prayer chants related to formal Anglo-American Protestant prayers of invocation, benediction, and offertory, to the recitation of creeds, collects, and confessions? What folk derivations emerged from readings of the psalter, the gospel, the lectionary, and out of sacramental liturgy? What indigenous African elements prevailed over or were syncretized with traditional Protestant worship forms and practices?

Systematic study of American folk worship, of its origins from and relationships to institutionalized Protestant liturgy and forms and its social, political, and psychological applications, is at present lacking. Hence little can be said conclusively, but it can be observed that Afro-American folk worship, like other species, is immemorial and universal. From primitive times until now, man has made particular conditions for worship: a sacred place—forest, mountain, river, cleared ground, or housing; a celebrant, priest, or leader who incarnates the god or is mediator between the god and worshippers; a group or congregation of believers and participants united by common blood, geosocial background, practices, and presiding mythology; the enactment of worship through dramatic re-creation, pantomime, dance, music, gestures, facial expressions, and vocal qualities; the use of symbolic objects and artifacts in prescribed rites, including the dress and ornaments of the participants; and a generally unalterable presentation order.

In the main, American Negro Protestant folk worship is founded on three constructs—song, sermon, and prayer—out of which all other variations accrue. The presentation of the constructs in the order of regular Sunday service may be outlined as follows:

- the gathering of the congregation in churchyard and building, a social act which may go on for two hours;
- the assembling of worship objects and the initiation of worship processes, including the seating of choir, congregation, and ministers, the proper placement of hymnbooks, collection plates, Bibles, pulpit and chairs, and altar decorations (crucifix, flowers, candles), lasting a half-hour to an hour and marked by continued social exchange, handshaking, and other amenities;
- some signal that the service is about to begin—the approach of the minister to the pulpit, an instrumental prelude, a lifting of arms by minister or elder, or, rarely, the processional of choir and minister, a rite usually reserved for the entrance and exit of the body during a funeral service;
- the opening of worship, an invocatory rite in two stages—the "call to worship" or summoning of participants by choir, elder, or minister, which may be oral, musical, or both, followed by a prayer beseeching the presence of the Holy Spirit, spoken or chanted by minister or elder;
- congregational song directed by a lay leader, elder, or minister, and usually supported by the choir;
- introductory remarks as to occasion and circumstances, announcements of general interest, an extended usage of the Protestant parish notices;
- congregational song, intercessory prayer, and personal testimony;
- performance of "special music" by the choir, often with gradual congregational participation or response;
- the introduction of visiting ministers and other guests, though this may occur at other times;
- prayer invoking the inspiration of the Holy Spirit in the sermon which is to follow;
- the sermon, usually preceded by a reading from the Scriptures, largely extempore and sensitive to congregational mood;
- the invitation to salvation and church membership, which may be prolonged and accompanied by exhortation, prayer, and song;
- the extension of "the right hand of fellowship" to converts and new members, a rite of acceptance during which prayer, songs, and exhortation may continue;
- further announcements and prayers of departure and benediction; and, finally,
- the rites of farewell, informal social exchange in the sanctuary and churchyard.

While this order of liturgy may be shifted for emphasis, with any part expanded or condensed, it has application in all regular and special services, with the exception of the Christmas service when the Nativity drama is often substituted for the sermon. This order is generally descriptive of both white and black Southern folk worship services.

Yet the differences between white and black and between folk and institutionalized worship are many and deep. In the country of the common man, the new America, folk variations of English Protestant liturgy were inevitable. The Reformation and the advent of printing had brought theology and worship to the verge of mass consciousness, and the arguments of English Protestants over liturgical forms and doctrines persisted for a century or more.[3] By the end of the seventeenth century the degree and kind of congregational participation had been fairly well standardized in the Church of England, but within three decades John Wesley began the democratizing of English and American Protestantism with his lay societies, open-air preaching, and the conference system of administration. And despite the early twentieth-century liturgical movement to impose a formal order of worship and restrict congregational improvisation, American Protestant worship has been vulnerable to folk innovation. In contemporary as well as in historic Afro-American folk worship the Protestant liturgy takes on the patina and timbre of its folk practitioners, and though that statement may seem oversimplified its truth becomes evident during continued observation of worship services where liturgical expression is simultaneously individual and traditional, human and social, yet mystic and transcendent.

Beneath the spontaneous idiom may be discovered one outstanding feature that links Afro-American folk worship with both historic formal Protestant liturgy and universal religious expression: antiphony. Antiphony may be defined as the interaction of celebrant and congregation, an emotional, spiritual, and intellectual dialogue manifested by *oral, musical,* and *physical* means. By *physical* is meant symbolic and sacramental movements of the body, from dance to brief obeisance; by *musical* is meant melodic and rhythmical song, accompanied or not by instruments; by *oral* is meant recitation of prayers, creeds, collects, and Scriptures, and the extended address or sermon. The spatial arrangement of minister and congregation itself signifies their dialogue: from the raised pulpit he calls, cries, and chants, and they echo, elaborate, and extend. Enchanter, priest, incarnate or vicarious god, the minister instructs, narrates, exposits, and reveals mysteries to the worshippers, and together they affirm mythic truth.

Antiphony lies at the very heart of the quarrel over the origins of the spirituals. If, as many suppose, the spiritual arose from the chant performed repeatedly under the direction of a naturally gifted speaker or singer, a bardic leader, with the melodies, rhythms, and text gradually refined and shaped into separate songs, then its origins are both communal *and* individual.

The evidence of a century of folksong scholarship has demonstrated that secular folk song, Anglo-American hymnody of the eighteenth century, colonial psalm singing, composed hymns of the nineteenth century, and West and Central African melodic, tonic, and rhythmical patterns all influenced the steadily evolving body of Afro-American folk song. The evolutionary processes of creation and re-creation go on and on and some things may be lost along the way. Often the specific reality disappears—the physical landscape, setting, manners, and customs of ordinary folk life. Again, events, historical and legendary, fade or merge with other similar events. Entire songs, in particular the topic and occasional, may vanish. Characters may descend from the tragic or romantic to the comic, or some sociomoral spectrum gradually slide into oblivion. Much, however, remains.

For more than a decade folklore scholars have demonstrated the existence of formulas used by folk

[3]*The Book of Common Prayer,* born in the litany of Thomas Cranmer, became the official liturgical service book of the Church of England in 1549 (under Edward VI) and underwent major revisions in 1552. Controversy has marked the book's history since the beginning. It was even abolished by Queen Mary in 1553 (but restored by Elizabeth I in 1559) and by the Westminster Parliament in 1645. Not until its second reinstatement in 1662 by Charles II were matters regarding the Anglican liturgy generally—but still today not universally— agreed.

narrators, expositors, singers, and instrumentalists. Essentially mnemonic, the formula—whether of imagery, verbal and nonverbal sound, or of rhythmical and melodic elements—is repeated and varied for purposes of emphasis, transition, and unity. Unobtrusive, yet clearly identifiable in individual folk performers, the formula may also consist of or be reinforced by facial expressions, gestures, bodily movements, and vocal qualities. In Afro-American folk worship oral-musical formulas play a large role in the presentation of liturgy, myth, and theology, unifying song, prayer, and sermon. Employed within the order of the divine, their purpose the manifestation of the essence of God and the transcendence of this earth, they closely approach the ritualistic, the magical, and the mystical. In a very real sense the formula is incantatory, invocative of the god's presence; and the word, or forumlaic utterance, may be repeated over and over, as in states of hypnotic trance, until it acquires meaning far beyond the rational. The supreme art of language provides a seamless governance over literally hundreds of distinct parts, its workings so intricate that we cannot know the dancer from the dance.

In Afro-American folk liturgy, formulaic repetition offers pedagogical, mnemonic, and psychological advantages but, more important, it is fundamental to the antiphony of priest with congregation, and thus is far less a matter of teaching than a manner, a mode of ascent to the divine. The song leader may be an elder, the minister, or any church member of moral authority and with aesthetic skills. His role is to elicit response— musical, poetic, emotional, intellectual, and spiritual—from a group thoroughly familiar with traditional styles and structures, and their communion may be regarded as sacramental. In some worship performances, the leader may overpower the congregation with extensive solo—melodic, recitative, chanted, or sermon-like—while the group responds with a brief chorus at periodic intervals with a constant subsidiary moaning or humming or with a sudden shout. At other times the congregation may share roles equally with the leader. In moments of intense feeling, two or more leaders may emerge, and several sets of melodies, harmonies, and rhythms may surge within the same song. A choir of five to twenty or more singers may serve as leader, one or more leaders may be distinguished within the choir, and there may also be a floor or congregational leader. And any leader, temporarily deprived of his powers or responding to spiritual impulse, may surrender to another singer. The selection of any one of varying antiphonal styles is dependent upon the progress of the liturgical order, and on the mood, intent, and psychological needs of the worshippers.[4]

---

[4]While all the various origins of Afro-American worship-song-performance style may never be discovered, one source warrants more attention: the history of Christian worship music.

Early plainsong, monodic chant which intones toward a reciting note that rises and falls freely as does the voice in natural cadence, and the more elaborate respond of five-syllable cadence were intended as beautiful recitation of the Holy Scriptures, especially the Psalms, and gradually there developed the antiphon, a melodic refrain sung after each Psalm verse and prominent in processionals, the offertory, and communion. This body of vocal ecclesiastical music, *Cantilena Romana* or Gregorian chant, was shaped during the fifth and sixth centuries by the papal choir for the entire Roman Catholic rite. Though in use mainly for the Mass and daily choir offices, with only slight incursions of the plainsong hymns of St. Ambrose and St. Aquinas, this style dominated West European worship music until Martin Luther began to use secular tunes for congregational hymnody. Although the Church of England did not *officially* sanction hymn singing until 1820, after the important Geneva metrical psalter of John Calvin in 1539, Anglican psalters proliferated throughout the British Isles. Meanwhile hymnody flourished among the dissenting sects of the eighteenth century, chiefly among the Congregationalists whose Isaac Watts (the "father of English hymnody") published the four-volume *Hymns and Spiritual Songs* in 1707 and the Methodists whose prolific Charles Wesley wrote some 7,270 hymns. The Afro-American slave immigrant, then, could create a folk liturgical music style out of the Roman-Anglican ecclesiastical tradition, the metrical psalmody of Anglo-American Calvinism and Puritanism, English Watts-Wesley hymnody, and his indigenous African folk-music inheritance.

As a species of folk poetry, the spiritual is also principally structured by repetition which may be strict or loose, simple, incremental, or complex. Every word may be repeated throughout a stanza; only one word, phrase, or line may be varied within a stanza or from stanza to stanza, usually by substitution of the substantive or the verb; alteration may equal but, except in some narrative songs, rarely overcome the repeated elements; and in some instances, the effect of staggered repetition is comparable to that of a rhyme scheme in literary poetry. In all the genres—ballad, ode, lyric pieces, rhymed narratives, unrhymed hymns—repetition reinforces theme, imagery, and symbol, sustains and heightens mood, develops logical argument and narrative, and shows forth the human heart confronting despair and loss, joy and triumph. While the printed text suggests primitive uses of repetition, in performance the effect is quite the contrary: the uses of rhythm, melody, vocal qualities, pitch, and dynamics are of such complexity that the experience of the uninitiated listener is like hearing an unfamiliar opera for the first time.

Indeed, the Afro-American folk worship service bears some comparison with grand opera: of extended duration,[5] from two to six hours, it features numerous actor-singers, with the congregation as chorus and audience and the minister and choir as principals, who enact in music and spoken language the central tragedy of Christianity, the Crucifixion, around which cluster hundreds of related dramas and tales from the Old Testament.

A more significant parallel with opera may be found in performance styles. To begin with, all the actor-singers are naturally gifted in song and speech, and the repeated performance of traditional song styles, during a lifetime, is a maturing process comparable to the singing of a written score again and again. Further, the voice of both males and females is powerful and striking beyond the description of analytical language, the style of any one singer distinct and instantly recognizable yet all multitextured. The minister's sermon is an extended recitative in which the voice rises and falls, hastens and slows, approaches the melodic, shifts to chant, intensifies almost unbearably, and withdraws gracefully. The sermon-recitation is marked by homely, vivid accents of field, marketplace, and daily life employed for the retelling of the parables of Christ and Old Testament stories; the long wail of the despairing prophet, and the rapid staccato of apocalyptic vision and salvation arguments; the sustained lyricism of the Psalms and of Job for the articulation of the soul's dark struggle and sweet release in divine love; balance, antithesis, and long phrase for pronouncements of the very god; the mighty shout of victory over Satan and death; the bright cutting edge of wit, the relaxed tones of intimate conversational humor, deft satiric jabs, and mock gravity which may abruptly turn deathly serious; the jagged cries of new grief, the sonority of long mourning, the yearning ache of unmitigated loss; and the emphatic tones of the teacher and moralist. The voices of the singers re-create the sounds of the natural universe—laughter and weeping, the rushing of winds and waters, the cries of animals, the thunder above mountains; and they interpret the kingdom of the supranatural—angelic throngs, hellish demons, death, and the grave. All these proceed effortlessly, with total control, the hard, labored intake of air after a long, breathless passage, the subtle syllabic elongation or amputation, the quavers, tremors, the full scale of melodic passage, or the narrow differential of tone in chant and shout.

The minister equals the opera lead singer in the kind and variety of vocal skills, though the lead singer's mode is, in some ways, more formally fixed. The minister and his fellow singers are also "operatically" structured, their duets and ensembles developed from a single musical and oral statement into

[5]Such length was—indeed, in some places still is—not uncommon in white rural folk worship also. Primitive Baptist churches hold "preaching Sundays" during which several ministers from the local association preach sermons in sequence from mid-morning until dark. "Foot-washing Sundays" and Sacred Harp singings are of similar duration. (All these are usually interrupted by "dinner on the ground.")

a spectacular labyrinth of polyphony. Heard several times, however, their song begins to reveal the ordering principle of its parts.

The archetypal stanza may be defined as a generally unrhymed quatrain of varying syllabic length and accentual emphasis, with the caesural pause at logical, natural, or psychological breaks of melodic, recitative, chanted, or oral-cadence quality, and of antiphonal structure. Performance modes may be suggested by some common appearances. Leader and chorus may alternate the first three lines:

LEADER: Soon one mornin',
 death come creepin' in de room
CHORUS: Soon one mornin',
 death come creepin' in de room
LEADER: Soon one mornin',
 death come creepin' in de room
TOGETHER: Oh my Lord, oh my Lord,
 what shall I do to be saved?

the two halves of each line may be divided between leader and chorus:

LEADER: Soon one mornin'
CHORUS: Death come creepin' in my room

or the leader may join each antiphonal response:

LEADER: Soon one mornin'
LEADER AND CHORUS: Death come creepin'
 in my room.

Choral comment or response may occur at the end of every line:

LEADER: Got on my starry crown
 CHORUS: Dan-u-el
LEADER: Got on my starry crown
 CHORUS: Dan-u-el
LEADER: Move de member
 CHORUS: Move, Dan-u-el
LEADER: Move de member
 CHORUS: Move, Dan-u-el.

Such brief response is often nonverbal ejaculation:

LEADER: I call for the water
 CHORUS: uh-huh
LEADER: For to wash my hand
 CHORUS: uh-huh
LEADER: I won't be guilty
 CHORUS: uh-huh
LEADER: For the innocent man
 CHORUS: uh-huh.

Narrative and exhortatory quatrains are often linked by a strong chorus stanza, for example, as in the Sumter County Job song:

Rock Mount Zionee, rock Mount Zionee
Rock Mount Zionee in the morning
Swing low chariot, swing low chariot
Swing low chariot in the morning.

The chorus displays varying dominance or equality, of choir, leader, or congregation, and its position is flexible. It may be "lined out," as in some Sacred Harp or nineteenth-century singing school styles, usually by the song leader and occasionally by the respondents. Or it may be sung one or more times at the beginning or end, between stanzas, or at any climactic point.

Further, the archetypal stanza is usually a core song which may develop in several ways. It may be expanded by simple and/or incremental repetition in several similar stanzas. It may be attached to rhymed and unrhymed stanzas or narrative, dramatic, exhortatory, or lyric species. Or it may coexist with a subsidiary chorus or one of equal strength. In contrast to the archetypal core, the rhymed stanzas of some sermon, story, and religious song may reflect Afro-American accommodation to white Protestant hymnody or belong to Anglo-American oral folk tradition where they circulate as "sayings" and recitations for special occasion.

But the main thrust of the spiritual, both as poetry and as song, has been toward the word which is articulated against and with the word before and after. Out of the interior reality of the word arise all rational and suprarational associations. The word shapes syntactical arrangements within both the line and the stanza, and to great extent determines melody, cadence, meter, and rhythm.

Whether or not this process in which the word functions as controller and determinant of the folk song construct was instinct or deliberate or some of both will never be known, but the oral-musical utterance of the archetypal stanza may be considered as a deeply held imprint which yet allows for endless folk interpretation. Visualized three-dimensionally, the imprint might be a massive four-square monolith on which are inscribed hieroglyphs or song runes: as the hieroglyph is adapted to the cursive and other scripts, so the song rune is shaped by the singers; and as the hieroglyph, or alphabetic character, is recognizable whatever the alterations, so also is the song rune both formulaic and improvisational. The monolith is one, the rune is many and dependent on the monolith. The monolith is invested with the word, the linguistic center, the verbal impulse, the animator, galvanizer, the first cause of song.

The formulaic aspect, both monolithic and runic, is best and supremely evidenced in the worship service where there is never a moment of hesitation in the liturgical progression. All goes forward as surely as if some detailed book of discipline were held in hand: song, sermon, prayer, or rite proceed in turn, and with each participant is full knowledge of every element in any possible combination or sequence despite intrusions from this mortal frame, a cough, shuffle, laughter, or murmured conversation. Whatever the leader does, even to facial expressions, gestures, and postures, is expected and affirmed by the answering congregation.

When first pronounced, the four monolithic lines of the leader are usually rhythmic chant or shout, with little if any melodic structure except that inherent in the word. On the second or third repetition the inroads of melody may be stronger, and rhythm, meter, and accentual emphasis subtly altered. And on the fourth and subsequent repetitions there may occur progressively convoluted vocal intensification of every musical and oral element. At some point in the evolving runic utterance the leader reaches a time of climax characterized by a virtuoso display of at least one and usually several vocal styles: perhaps a rapid, almost unintelligible, ecstatic chant of little tonal variation save the chromatic, or perhaps a long, slow dirge, also in only half tones, or an irregular moan, convulsive sob, or a fully melodic solo delivered with great vocal purity.

Choir and congregation are attuned to all these leader styles by means of a thousand musical, physical, and emotional hints. What is finally achieved, aesthetically and spiritually, by this perfect understanding and execution of celebrant and worshippers is orchestral and operatic: human voices as strings, woodwinds, brass, and percussion; harmony as expressed not so much in mathematical parts but in vocal qualities, harsh and tender, strident and muted, male and female, childlike and mature, innocent and wise, sword-sharp and pillow-soft.

Liturgical antiphony determines the voice and tense of the spirituals. Overwhelmingly the voice is that of the *I*-speaker, who in performance is the leader. As Everyman, or the representative Christian, he describes and explains spiritual states of being, especially sin, conversion, and the lifelong pilgrimage to Heaven. As preacher, he exhorts sinners to repentance and Christian conduct. As omniscient narrator and expositor, he re-creates tales and dramas from the Bible. As human and suprahuman witness of Old and New Testament myth, he reveals religious and poetic truth. As teacher, historian, and guide, he conveys the past experience of man and formulates the ethical and moral framework for daily life. As poet, he is the bearer of symbols and the figurative universe, of rhythm and melody, diction and syntax. As priest and mediator, he absolves sin and offers intercessory prayer. And as the vibrant energy, the pure consciousness of the divine, his position is absolute.

The constant overpowering presence of the *I*-speaker in the spirituals has a secular counterpart in the talking-singing bluesman. Though in theory the worlds of the spirit and the body are stringently opposed and with logical appropriateness some songs are considered the Devil's and some are God's, so taut an antithesis is laden with the ambiguities of intimacy, as in close-knit families where love and hate intertwine. Hundreds of Afro-American blues, pop, and jazz performers started out in local churches as choristers or instrumentalists, and the singer of Titanic and Stag-o-lee ballads also cut recordings of gospel songs, though none took "Easy Rider" into church. And while the spiritual keeps its religious identity intact at home or the work place, very rarely is it heard in "juke joints," at blues parties, dances, or any distinctly social gathering. The high regard of its practitioners for Afro-American religious song as sacred expression and as adjunct to sacred phenomena guarantees against impious parody or other debasement. Though Mrs. Tartt's singer Rich Amerson embraced Satan's blues and, by his own admission, his personal life was sometimes scandalous for a professing church member, his performances of spirituals and sermons leave no doubt as to the respect he sincerely paid his Christian-folk tradition.

The reciprocity of secular and religious Afro-American folk song is now confirmed in many studies, and only their most-obvious similarities may be briefly noted here. In particular should be mentioned their common stylistic and structural dependence on the archetypal construct of antiphony—the oral, musical, and poetic leader-respondent formula: the pulpit shout appears as the leader solo in field holler, work chant, and chain-gang cry; in gospel ensembles the preacher-work boss role is assumed by the lead singer; the spinning takeoffs of instrumental folk jazz are rough equivalents of the improvisations and variations in worship-song performance; and the "it" of children's games directs song, dance, and action in the manner of the preacher in worship liturgy.

General correspondences between blues and the spiritual are readily identified: the regular employment of an antiphonally structured three-or four-line stanza which may be developed improvisationally to six, eight, ten, or twelve lines, marked by simple, complex, and/or internal rhyme, the soloist "answering" himself or providing instrumental response, usually guitar or harmonica; comparable vocal qualities which serve as the physical cognate of emotional states, particularly the guttural and falsetto, and the formulaic use of nonverbal sounds, like "uh-huh," as a means of organization, emphasis, and the expression of complex psychological states or suprarational meaning; similar syllabic and accentual patterns, notably in the chant, moan, holler, and other free-flowing species, and the elongation, syncopation, or complication of rhythm and meter according to individual performance needs; the penchant for genre shifts, for example, the expansion of a chorus to narrative or the reduction of a ballad to lyric remnant; the mutual fountain of folk diction and figurative devices that migrate from song to song as a semantic and poetic shorthand; and the importance of oral language, which in the spirituals appears as the oratory and rhetoric of pulpit and in blues as auto-conversation, dramatic dialogue, and confessional revelation.

Such likenesses are exterior. More significant is the interior reality that emanates from continuous historical folk Afro-Americanism, an unmistakable and pervasive texture or mood in both blues and spirituals that is essentially a quest for selfhood and freedom, for the satisfaction of basic human needs, for harmony with the natural and incorporeal universe, for immortality. In a harsh landscape the seeker wanders among unyielding obstacles, singing and speaking over and over the litany of his sorrow. In the spirituals, hope of Heaven balances despair. In blues, flesh answers flesh with the temporary solace of love, work, sex, drink, gambling. The sojourner of the spirituals will one day go home to eternal joy. The quester of the blues can only repeat failed solutions. Yet both find a measure of relief in the act of song.[6]

[6]The Alabama Archives holds only three blues manuscripts, all with musical notation, from Mrs. Tartt. This scarcity is troublesome, for unquestionably she is directly responsible for the large body of blues recorded by Lomax and Courlander in Sumter County, and she

Moreover it is primarily by means of the *I*-voice that the experience of the American Negro as slave, as Christian, and as folk is reconciled in the spirituals. He stands in the doorway with the ancient watchman and cries out for delivery even as mother, father, sister, brother are snatched from him by those who hold the powers of death and life. Day after day he tends the crops of his owners, bending his back to a never-ending row. His bread is bitter and his bed is hard. His house is not is own. He lives on borrowed land. He may not and often cannot read or write. He may not visit his friends or marry without leave. His garments and roof let in rain and wind. His teachers are mother wit and necessity. And yet he forges chains of fellowship and brotherhood; he sings and dances and comes together with others for church and celebrations, even if sometimes in secret; and he learns a language for daily communication and for the pouring out of his pain.

If ever any man were literally prepared for New Testament Christianity, the slave was one: no riches could block his way to the Kingdom, he might just as well be clothed as the lilies of the field; everywhere he looked there was the possibility of death; and no matter how well he was treated (and he was often given humane, even benevolent, care), no matter how intimate he might be with his masters (and they were sometimes remarkably close, as close as brothers and children of one mother), not a single dream or hope of his own could be ever fully realized.

So the King James Bible and Christianity took quick root and flowering in the immigrant captive. Again and again he confronts Satan, plunges into the abyss of exile and into the cold, dark waters of death, his brain burning with its imagery—the tolling bell, hearse, winding sheet, coffin, and devouring maggots. His prayers and outpourings are continual, and in his contrition he hears the voice of Jesus and enters into salvation. His tormented nightmares almost cease and now he dreams sweetly of home, of sleeping on his mother's breast. He urges conversion on others, disciplines his spiritual life, and subdues the flesh. And at last he achieves mystical illumination: angels descend to his room, he is caught up in the fiery chariot, and he beholds the glory of Heaven. He coexists with Old Testament figures and keeps company with Christ. He preaches with John the Baptist and sees visions with John the Revelator. He stands beside the blinded Samson in the temple at Gaza, overhears Christ's conversation with Nicodemus, and murmurs over wind and water miracles. He speaks as Martha and Mary who mourn for Lazarus and he answers as the Christ who raises from the dead. He walks toward the Bethlehem stable and through the gates of pearl. He is present at every station of the Cross and feels every pain of the Crucifixion.

The voice of the Christian has answered that of the slave, and the rhythms, vocabulary, syntax, metaphors, and symbols of both voices are from Afro-American folk life. The soul in Paradise announces, "I ain't no stranger here." The preacher urges, "Don't let nobody turn you round," and shouts, "Where you running, sinner?" The soldier proclaims, "I been in the War so long and I ain't got tired yet." An erring Prodigal Son decides, "I believe I'll go back home." The dying exult, "Lord, I'm going down in your name." The exhausted and humiliated pray, "Oh, Lord, my trouble so hard," "I most done travelling," "My knees is acquainted with the hillside clay," "My soul wouldn't rest contented," "At the end of my row, give me Jesus," "Lord, have mercy," and when peace comes after long anguish, "My good Lord done been here."

This folk voice with its sharp apprehension of a new religion is capable of every range, from the quotidian to the sublime. As far from the evening-news broadcast as the earth is from the sun, so alive that it seems to possess physical being, shape, color, and visual impact, it is intrinsically poetic:

---

wrote an affectionate WPA sketch of bluesman Blind Jesse Harris. Since she had immediate access to blues and was dedicated to what she perceived as her mission to preserve a vanishing folk song, one may only surmise that she either chose not to collect blues or that some manuscripts are lost.

> Old John the Baptist, old John Divine
> Leather girdle round his waist,
> And his meat was locust and wild honey,
> Wild honey, wild honey, my Lord, wild honey.

Even within the conspicuous rhyme of the hymn quatrain, the inherent music and poetry are apparent:

> Go down, angel, consume the flood,
> Blow out the sun, turn the moon to blood,
> Come back, angel, bolt the door,
> Times have been shall be no more.

Thus the tongue of the Afro-American folk humanizes the massive myth and theology of the King James Bible.

The *I* of the spirituals is omniscient and omnipresent, not bound by the ordinary limits of time and space, and the tense of the spirituals is always the eternal present, no matter when or where the action occurs, even if the time is given as the immediate or historical past, the yesterday of the speaker or the day Paul and Silas were freed from prison, the speaker's tomorrow or the millennial tomorrow of Heaven. All mythic creations inhabit immortal domains: the exterior action of *Oedipus Rex* is laid in ancient Thebes, the interior drama forever within our minds; and in Shakespeare's sonnets, poetry is imperishable. But the spirituals go far beyond this timelessness into a kind of time warp, a poetry of relativity that shatters rational sensibilities in the way Einstein's $E = mc^2$ shattered previous laws of physics. The violence of this mind-bend, this trembling possession of Alpha and Omega, would be insupportable, emotionally and intellectually, were it not for fidelity to the folk landscape, the verisimilitude of folk speech, and the acute sensitivity to both physical and spiritual slavery and freedom.

The great hymns of the soul, the apocalyptic and death songs, the re-creations of the Crucifixion and the Resurrection, the fiery outbursts of longed-for freedom—in these incomparable expressions all temporal and spatial reality pass into a divine, eternal order, a graceful translation in which folk speech is raised to poetry:

> I'm goin' out uv this valley
> I'm goin' out uv this valley
> I'm goin' out uv this valley
> God-er-mighty knows I can't stay down here.
>
> Fire in the east, fire in the west
> Fire gonna burn up the wilderness
> God-er-mighty knows I can't stay down here.

The terrifying forest fires that surround the wilderness dweller are also the fires of Judgment Day and Hell, and the life-giving valley is also the Valley of the Shadow of Death. The straightforward speech of the hard-pressed victim who swiftly scans the skies for safety, desperation shearing off articles, expletives, and modifiers, bursts into fearful cries of the Apocalypse that will consume earth and all mankind. Denigrators who have alleged that figurative species and symbols are trite, imitative, or wanting in the spirituals might take another, closer look.

For the rest, Afro-American religious folk song receives its figurative kingdom from the vast cosmogony of Anglo-European Christian lore, a multitudinous body of oral and written myth and iconography originating in pre-Classical and Classical Mediterranean culture, shaped during the early spread of Christianity over the Roman Empire, interpreted and expanded throughout the Middle Ages and Renaissance, and shifting dynamically to the vernacular with the Protestant Reformation.

Some emblems and metaphors may be attributed generally to the broad aesthetic of historic folk Christianity—for example, the deathbed drama, the summoning Death Angel, encounters with Satan, and mystic illuminations all have antecedents in medieval visual art and miracle and morality plays, and numerous images have accrued from the Watts-Wesley hymn tradition. Far and away, however, the figurative aspects of the spirituals are directly derived from the Bible, the angels, beasts, and apocalyptic imagery of Revelation, the chariots of Elijah and Ezekiel, the Pauline metaphors of warrior and battle, the Crucifixion symbolism, and innumerable allusions to Old Testament heroic tales.

Reinforced over and over in folk sermon and song, gradually more and more impacted, such biblical figures become something like a microchip imprint and a name or word— Moses, David, blood, cross—is the code that accesses memory. On the simplest level, this recall is of brief emblematic and didactic signification. But, in point of fact, the key word summons up an entire mythic landscape and the revelation occurs all at once in the eternal present. "Samson"—and with the mere utterance comes the honey-lion carcass riddle, the foxtails and ass jawbone, the betrayal by Delilah, blindness and death, the destruction of the temple. Like the oral-musical imprints of song performance, Afro-American folk religious figures are formulaic, the priest-magician's incantation which brings to very life invisible poetic reality and spiritual truth.

Examination of Afro-American worship-song texts will reveal that figurative species are integrated into larger religious concepts. In Afro-American spirituals God is all, and more, that Protestant theology would have him be: creator of man and the universe, giver of all good gifts, infinite, eternal, all-powerful, all-knowing; a natural deity mythically imaged as the voice of thunder, the tongue of lightning, the speech of the whirlwind whose word sets sun, moon, and stars in place, brings down the world-destroying flood and the fires of the Last Days; a king who leads the Israelites to war and the soul to battle with Satan, a giver of law who covenants with his people and executes judgment justly; the only very God to be worshipped with song, prayer, and rites; the author of fate who presides over the destinies of nations and men, some of whom he chooses for his unsearchable divine intent.

Consider the Good Shepherd symbol. Though nowhere anthropomorphic in the way of Zeus, God's humanization is suggested in his Old Testament association with the earthly keeper of flocks, an image, arising naturally to a pastoral people, which to this day deeply informs Hebraic and Christian thought. The transformation from protective benevolence to slain shepherd-god, prefigured by the Abraham-Isaac story and the grain/animal rites of the Hebrews, was a fortuitous leap to the Son of God, Christ the Lamb and the Shepherd, whose death-sacrifice takes away the sin of the world and assures believers of immortality, their belief and his martyrdom symbolized in the communion of blood and wine, body and bread.

Of all New Testament events, the Crucifixion and Resurrection dominate the spirituals and form the centerpiece of Afro-American folk religion. As a moving drama of the suffering and death of a heroic protagonist who dwelled among humble men, it bore too close a relevance to life under American slavery. As universal myth, it offered a poetic and religious symbolism that could be structured into a theological and liturgical system and understood as a paradigm for moral conduct. And as a superb narrative replete with startling contrasts and a wealth of sensory details, with enchanting ancillary legends, fables, parables, and dramas tied to the main action, a compelling hero poised against a background of familiar folk characters—tax collectors, fishermen, harlots, thieves, murderers, political opportunists, vacillating rulers, corrupt statesmen, and a host of the world's afflicted—and as a tale recounted in the great rhetoric and poetry of King James English, it held, and still holds, enormous attraction for the folk imagination. Inherently memorable, heard again and again from the pulpit, musicalized in hymns and chants, sacramentally and dramatically enacted in the Lord's Supper, foot-washings, and Easter sunrise rites, such a story could not but become an aesthetic-religious imprint of immense psychological effect.

The bondage of Israel was the slave's own, and he longed for a Moses to lead him out of barren exile to the land of milk and honey. If the Pentateuch became his folk epic, the Crucifixion was his folk drama and lyric song. By the waters of Babylon, Savannah, Charleston, Montgomery, Atlanta, in the fields of the American South, the slave sat down and wept and made a song out of the suffering of his Lord and his own. Every detail, from the night in Gethsemane to the tears of Mary Magdalene, is evoked in the spirituals with a sympathy that could have come only from real experience. And, once more, it is the humanness of Christ on which this lyricism is focused: "Were you there when they nailed Him to the tree?" "Tell me, Job, where were you?" "And the blood came trickling down. . . . "

Another symbol, and one closely related to the Good Shepherd originating from Christian lore and literature, is Jordan, by crossing which the wandering Israelites entered the Promised Land. As death, the last mystery, the last river the soul crosses on its way to immortality, Jordan may be a welcomed release from the pain of earthly life or the feared descent into the cold, deep waters of oblivion, a journey impossible without faith and salvation. As baptism, Jordan signifies the death of the sinner, the old man, and the birth of a new, regenerated man under Christ. And as Paradise, or Zion, Jordan is both the physical site of immortal Christian joys and the symbol of union with God. In all its associations Jordan is both folk and Christian. The catalog or roll call of relatives who process to Jordan, a principle of logical development that may be indebted to the *ubi sunt* of medieval Christian literature is, on its deepest level, a metaphorical statement of man's tragic perplexity over the purpose of life, the mystery of death, and the destination of the soul.

Moreover, the gold waistbands, crowns, and stars of glory, often cited as evidence of a bankrupt poetic imagination in the spirituals, are traditional Christian symbols, continuing from the Revelation of John of Patmos through medieval and Renaissance visual art to nineteenth-century gravestone and other carvings, which throughout their long existence have held special meaning for Anglo-European Christian folk. Who, of rag-and-bone existence on this mortal plane, would not yearn for golden, jewel-studded crowns? That such pitiable yearning, such poignant hope for redress of the griefs and grievances of this world, should be telegraphed in the emblematic shorthand seems not so much an aesthetic flaw but a perfectly logical and natural image from the mind of the dispossessed.

Finally, Jordan is freedom. The spirituals are freedom songs, and there can be no question of their role in the overthrow of American slavery or in the twentieth-century civil rights movement. Veiled or open, conscious or unconscious, political and social liberty is one of the major currents in Afro-American folk song. Yet studies during the last two decades have only rarely taken note of the mighty Christian river in which this current swirls. "Free at last! Free at last! Thank God Almighty, I'm free at last!" That bold declaration is the chorus of a folk hymn of Christian conversion, Christian discipline and battle against Satan, and the Christian vision of Heaven. In the end, the freedom of the spirituals is the long, triumphant cry from earth to Paradise, the freedom of the soul from mortal flesh, the transformation of dust to pure spirit.

The Death Angel, the medieval folk herald and the icon of thousands of folk gravestone carvings, summons the Christian to Jordan. Christ himself is the deathbed-maker. And the soul goes home. He who was homeless on earth claims an eternal home in Heaven; he who was clothed in rags here is adorned with precious ornaments there; sickness, toil, and danger are no more; the children of Moses cease their wanderings; the blindness of Samson is healed; the chains of earthly slavery are loosed; and God wipes away all tears. The freedom of this world, sing the spirituals, is imperfect but freedom in Christ is perfect: "And ye shall know the truth, and the truth shall make you free."

Arguments that the institution of slavery was never so cruel as to prohibit the development of diverse and appealing folk arts, that white masters consciously nurtured Afro-American folk traditions and Christianity for profit or suppression of rebellion, or out of noblesse oblige and genuine aspirations toward the freeing of their subjects all have some foundation in nineteenth-century historical evidence; but other documents burn with instances of unimaginably inhumane practices, of emotional and physical cruelty, neglect, and murderous abuse. How shall we read these conflicting records in terms of Afro-American folk song as a road to freedom?

First, that, no matter how benevolent the rule, every slave knew he was a slave. Second, that, no matter how barbarous or kind his treatment, his personal and communal folk aesthetic flourished, in oral narrative, in hundreds of folk crafts, skills, and domestic arts, in dance and the playing of musical instruments, in the observance of customs, rites, festivals, games and celebrations, and in song both secular and religious. That whether the longing for freedom was intense or smothered by kindness, the oppressor handed his slave the means of political and spiritual liberation in the Christian religion and the King James Bible.

The duality of life in the antebellum Southeastern United States was the raison d'être of the Afro-American folk continuum, and to the paradox of slavery and Christianity may be attributed much of its texture, content, organizational modes, themes, motifs, and figurative species. The retention of certain indigenous forms, styles, and expressions together with the accommodation of new but analogous folk life and lore was possible only in these particular historic circumstances, and this duality largely determined the dimensions of Afro-American folk religion and its music which both exhibit, to greater or lesser degree, both specific African and Anglo-European influences as well as characteristics of universal myth, practices, and worship constructs.

The political definition of liberty for all men had little meaning prior to the time of the New Testament. The achievements of ancient civilizations were predicated on slavery. Even the democracy of Greece and Rome was limited to the few. But the teachings of Christ slowly eroded the idea of power by might, and by 1790, cataclysmic revolutions in England, France, and America had vindicated the ideal if not the fact of equality. Nevertheless, man has always had access to spiritual liberty, if only as a dream or poem or as myth, and the coalescing of spiritual freedom in the magnetic Christ helped engender the actuality of political freedom. Scapegoats and sacrificial martyrs the world had produced before, but only in Christ did the life-giving death of a god insure, not fertility and physical regeneration of the universe or reincarnated or everlasting mortal flesh, but clearly a spiritual immortality that frees man from death. It is this Christian immortality that permeates the spirituals as songs of freedom, and nowhere in all of history is this concept articulated quite as it is in evolving Afro-American religious folk song.

The ancient Israelites, though wandering slaves, produced one of the greatest bodies of literature and religion the world has ever seen, a collection which, through a most peculiar world transmission, came to be translated for English-speaking peoples at a time of splendor in their literature. The mathematical chances of the birth of this folk song from mass slave migrations to a country in which that Bible reigned supreme were small indeed, but now and then comes a miracle. Ultimately, Jordan symbolizes the historic thrust toward political liberty which can only mirror its archetype, spiritual freedom. The performance of Afro-American religious folk song, especially in the worship service, is a sacrament of communion with the very God through whom that liberation occurs, and on every page of Mrs. Tartt's collection from Sumter County, Alabama, there are remembrances and signs of that encounter, of thousands of epiphanies, high moments of the brightest illumination and the profoundest revelation, experienced by this folk for nearly two hundred years.

The editors have included commentaries and notes only as aids to the understanding of these selections as human utterance, folk expression, and as poetry. Otherwise these wondrous songs speak for themselves and for the folk who made and sing them—the sweetness of honey bursting from the rock of bondage. Until her last days on earth, Mrs. Tartt was occupied with the Sumter County spirituals. All her life she planned to show them to the world. And ever since we first saw the manuscripts, we have been haunted by Mrs. Tartt and by this poetry and music. We believe this book is what she would have wanted, and though we shall always regret that she herself did not put it together, we are glad that others may see her noble work.

If the claims we make for these texts seem unwarranted; if there are those already familiar with this tradition who would experience again its power; if those uninitiated would learn of this enviable and inimitable folk song; if any should wish to feel the joys and sorrows of our lives on this earth, to look into the hearts and mind of ordinary mortals touched by ordinary concerns and extraordinary yearnings . . . why, then, take down this book and read.

"Honey in the Rock"

The
Ruby Pickens Tartt
Collection
of Religious Folk Songs
from Sumter County,
Alabama

Lord, I wonders where he's gone (a,b)

2

Ordinarily, in the didactic preaching spirituals the shortcomings of church members and the errors of unbelievers are vigorously condemned, and all sorts of sinners—drunkards, liars, gossipers, hypocrites, adulterers—are exhorted to repentance. But here the gambler is presented sympathetically. In variant (b) he is a "po' man," a phrase descriptive both of his miserable state as a lost soul and the speaker's compassion for a fellow human. No explanation is given for the gambler's dramatic rejection of his cards, but the salvation stanza of (b), interpolated from white Protestant hymnody, suggests sudden conversion or death.

The "wonder-where" motif, often cited as a veiled allusion to the separation of slave families, serves as a strong bond of identification between the speaker and the "po' man" whose condition mirrors that of all men. In (a), stanzas 1 and 3 are the archetypal core song. The shortened chorus of (b) could undergo expansion in performance. And in both variants the idiom and rhythms of oral folk conversation regarding the destiny of an old friend have become a lyric of bereavement.

Lord, I wonders where he's gone (a)

Lord, I wonders where's dat gamberlin' man,
Lord, I wonders where's he gone.
Lord, I wonders where's dat gamberlin' man,
Lord, I wonders where's he gone.

He's er gamberlin' all night long,
He's er gamberlin' till break of day.
He roll 'em on de gamberlin' floor,
En he throwed dem cards away.
Lord, I wonders where he's gone.

Lord, I wonders where's dat gamberlin' man,
Lord, I wonders where's he gone.
Lord, I wonders where's dat gamberlin' man,
Lord, I wonders where's he gone.

I wonder where the gamblin' man (b)

-Chorus-
Lord, I wonder where is that gamblin' man,
Please Lord, tell me where the po' man gone.

-1-
The po' man, Lord, he gamble,
He gamble all night long,
He rose from er the table
En he throwed his cards erway.

-Chorus-
Lord, I wonder where is that gamblin' man,
Please Lord, tell me where the po' man gone.

-2-
I come ter Jesus as I was,
Weary en worn en sad,
I found in Him er restin' place,
En He have made me glad.

-Chorus-
Lord, I wonder where is that gamblin' man,
Please Lord, tell me where the po' man gone.

Lord, I'm gonna tell the news

3

The "good news" of New Testament salvation is transformed by the folk to "tell the news," that is, the announcement of an important event to the community. The "news" is at once that of the speaker's death (and here the catalog-of-relatives device shows itself to be rooted in historical reality, for the illiterate slave had only the grapevine as newspaper and letter) and of his resurrection and immortality, signified by Jordan, which he broadcasts, quite as if on earth, throughout Heaven.

Though "summons" may allude to the legal document, the image of Death as a summoning angel has been common in Anglo-European folklore since the Middle Ages. The interchange of subject-verb agreement, as in "Death have," is still widely observable in Southern folk grammar. For "en" read "and." Except for the mother-father substitution and the omission of "in" in the last line of both stanzas, repetition is exact. The folk conversation is well adapted to liturgical antiphony.

In a variant Mrs. Tartt filed with her Group IV, not included here, the catalog of relatives is logically extended to sister, brother, and deacon, and one stanza is altered to "Death have set me free." The Sim Tartt group performed this text for Lomax on the Sumter County Library of Congress recordings in the drawn-out, wailing manner of some Sacred Harp.

Lord, I'm gonna tell the news

-1-

Lord, I'm gonna walk eround in Jordan en tell the news
Lord, I'm gonna walk eround in Jordan en tell the news
If my mother ask for me,
Tell her death have summons me,
Lord, I'm gonna walk eround in Jordan en tell the news

-2-

Lord, I'm gonna walk eround in Jordan en tell the news
Lord, I'm gonna walk eround in Jordan en tell the news
If my father ask for me,
Tell him death have summons me,
Lord, I'm gonna walk eround in Jordan en tell the news

Coming up, coming up before God

4

A folk re-creation of Revelation 7:9-16: "a great multitude, which no man could number, of all nations, and kindreds, and peoples, and tongues, stood before the throne, and before the Lamb, clothed with white robes, and palms in their hands. . . . " These are the martyrs whose robes have been washed in the "blood of the Lamb" and who sing everlasting praise to God.

Note the logic of the exhortation: (1) the holy and righteous are "coming up" before God, as John the Revelator saw them in his vision; (2) the speaker's mother is among them; and (3) the sinner is urged to join the congregation of the redeemed. *Number* has reference both to arithmetical counting and to those of the body of Christ and the church who inherit the Kingdom of Heaven. The striking rhythmical and alliterative effect of "number no man could number," percussive and hypnotic, is the musical counterpart of the apocalyptic imagery and the call to salvation. The conclusion of the passage in Revelation, which appears often on nineteenth-century gravestones, was surely deeply meaningful to the slave, who learned it by heart: "They shall hunger no more, neither thirst any more; neither shall the sun light on them, nor any heat. For the Lamb who is in the midst of the throne shall feed them, and shall lead them unto living fountains of waters; and God shall wipe away all tears from their eyes."

Coming up, coming up before God

-1-

Oh, the holy en righteous number no man could number
The holy en righteous number no man could number
Oh, the holy en righteous number no man could number
Coming up, coming up before God.

-2-

My mother was in that number no man could number
My mother was in that number no man could number
Yes, my mother was in that number no man could number
Coming up, coming up before God.

-3-

John saw that number no man could number
Well, John saw that number no man could number
John saw that number no man could number
Coming up, coming up before God.

-4-

You better jine that number no man could number
Well, you better jine that number no man could number
You better jine that number no man could number
Coming up, coming up before God.

Let hit shine

Widely performed by choirs and gospel groups during the 1930s, a favorite on gospel radio shows, "Let hit shine" is now also in white folk tradition. The light is that of Christian example taught by Christ in the Sermon on the Mount: "Let your light so shine before men, that they may see your good works, and glorify your Father, who is in Heaven" (Matthew 5:16). Liza Witt and Betty Moore gave Lomax a spirited performance of "Let hit shine" for the Library of Congress recordings.

Let hit shine

-1-

This little light of mine I'm gonna let hit shine
Oh, this little light of mine I'm gonna let hit shine
This little light of mine I'm gonna let hit shine,
Let hit shine
Let hit shine
Let hit shine.

-2-

All in the church He told me to let hit shine
All in the church He told me to let hit shine
Well, all in the church He told me to let hit shine,
Let hit shine
Let hit shine
Let hit shine.

-3-

Everywhere I go, oh I'm gonna let hit shine
Everywhere I go, oh I'm gonna let hit shine
Everywhere I go, oh I'm gonna let hit shine,
Let hit shine
Let hit shine
Let hit shine.

Carry me safely home

6

Several common motifs and structural elements may be observed here: the idea of heaven as home, which came naturally and with intense yearning to a dispossessed people; the pillow of the deathbed, in other songs arranged by the Death Angel or Jesus, but here a comfort disdained by the dying Christian who gives up his soul on the instant; the train metaphor of the passage to immortality; the New Testament figure of the Christian as a soldier "of the cross"; and the allusion to a biblical character who functions as a paradigm of some theological belief or virtue, here the faith necessary for discipleship. The personal character of the Christian experience is conveyed in the conventional image of the dying clasped in the arms of God. The liturgical "Lord, have mercy" became a vivid phrase in folk speech, a poignant cry in crisis, at conversion, baptism, sickness, and death. Peter is central to the evangelical argument: as he followed Christ, so must the sinner in order to "go home" to heaven.

Carry me safely home

-1-

Lord, have mercy when I come ter die, good Lordy,
Lord, have mercy when I come ter die,
Because the Lord gonna take me in His arms, good Lordy,
En carry me safely home.

-2-

Stop dat train en let er soldier ride, good Lordy,
Stop dat train en let er soldier ride,
Because the Lord gonna take me in His arms, good Lordy,
En carry me safely home.

-3-

Fisherman Peter was on the sea, good Lordy,
Fisherman Peter was on the sea,
Said drop you net en follow me, good Lordy,
En I'll carry you safely home.

-4-

Need no pillow when I come ter die, good Lordy,
Need no pillow when I come ter die,
Because the Lord gonna take me in His arms, good Lordy,
En carry me safely home.

Oh Lord, I'm in your care (a,b)

In variant (a) the Old Testament's Daniel, emblem of faith steadfast under slavery, imprisonment, and the threat of death, and the mother, a folk figure of honor and a symbol of Christian practice, exemplify the theme: total reliance on a loving, protective God through the discipline of prayer. The "arms" image occurs throughout the Psalms and Isaiah—an everlasting refuge, they rescue from "compassed" enemies and strengthen the exhausted soul. In the New Testament the arms of Christ offer forgiveness and rest for the weary.

In (b) the Hebrew children of the fiery furnace also signify faith, the enemies of the Psalmist have become "evil thoughts," and the figure of the orphaned child emphasizes the need for reliance on the Heavenly Father. In both variants the speaker simultaneously occupies earthy and spiritual dimensions; hence he may "hear" the prayers of Daniel and the Hebrew Children.

Oh Lord, I'm in your care (a)

-1-

Oh, Daniel prayed three times er day,
Oh, Daniel prayed three times er day,
Daniel prayed three times er day,
These are the words I heard him say,
Oh Lord, oh Lord, I'm in your care.

-Chorus-

Oh Lord, I'm in your care,
Oh Lord, I'm in your care,
Just thrown your arms around me
So my enemies cannot harm me,
Oh Lord, oh Lord, I'm in your care.

-2-

Mother prayed I'm in your care,
Mother prayed I'm in your care,
Just thrown your arms around me
So my enemies cannot harm me,
Oh Lord, oh Lord, I'm in your care.

Oh Lord, I'm in your care (b)

-Chorus-

Oh Lord, I'm in your care
Oh Lord, I'm in your care,
With you lovin' arms around me
No evil thought can harm me,
Oh Lord, I'm in your care.

-1-

My mother's gone, en father too
My mother's gone, en father too
My mother's gone, en father too,
All my hopes depend on you,
Oh Lord, I'm in your care.

-2-

The Hebrew boys was in the fire
The Hebrew boys was in the fire
The Hebrew boys was in the fire,
One by one I heard them cry,
Oh Lord, I'm in your care.

-Chorus-

Oh Lord, I'm in your care
Oh Lord, I'm in your care,
With you lovin' arms around me
No evil thought can harm me,
Oh Lord, I'm in your care.

Three religion songs (a,b,c)

8

These three texts demonstrate the accumulations, borrowings, substitutions, and omissions that regularly occur in folk song transmission. In (b) the "you can't cross there" tag is logically derived from the Jordan River motif, and in (c) the religion chorus serves as an introductory stanza. In (c), stanza 1 announces the salvation theme; stanza 2 brings the theme into sharp focus with the deathbed scene; in stanzas 3 and 7 the metaphor of the fast-approaching death-train and the image of the doctor intensify the drama of death, and the migratory Jordan stanzas 4, 5, and 6 represent the passage from death to immortality.

Variant (b), structured by the Jordan River symbol, is distinguished from (a) and (c) by the catalog of relatives and antiphonal dialogue. Variant (a) borrows the doctor of (c), is similar to (b) in theme and structure, but distinct in the "gamblin' man" stanza, in the inner and end rhyme of stanza 1, and in the oratory of folk sermon—"Death ain't sparin' no po' sinner man's life." Note the folk discourse of "Where you going now?" in (b), and in (c) the cry of the parents, "Lord have mercy my child is dying." For a version of (b), see James Weldon Johnson and J. Rosamund Johnson, *The Books of American Negro Spirituals,* 2 vols. (New York: The Viking Press, 1925, 1926; 9th repr. in one binding, 1964) 2:100.

You'll need that true religion (a)

-1-
Death is slow but death is sho'
Death is slow but death is sho'
When death comes somebody must go.

-Chorus-
Then you'll need that true religion
Then you'll need that true religion
You better get your soul converted
Then you'll have that true religion.

-2-
Gamblin' man, you gambles too long
Gamblin' man, you gambles too lone
Death ain't sparin' no po' sinner man's life.

-Chorus-
Then you'll need that true religion
Then you'll need that true religion
You better get your soul converted
Then you'll have that true religion.

-3-
The doctor stood en looked-ed sad
The doctor stood en looked-ed sad
This is the hardest case I've ever had.

-Chorus-
Then you'll need that true religion
Then you'll need that true religion
You better get your soul converted
Then you'll have that true religion.

You can't cross there (b)

-Chorus-
Oh your must have that true religion
You must be converted in your soul
Be converted or
You can't cross there.

Where you going mother
Where you going now
Going down to the river of Jordan
But you can't cross there.

-Chorus-
Oh you must have that pure religion
You must be converted in your soul
Be converted or
You can't cross there

Where you going father
Where you going now
Going down to the river of Jordan
But you can't cross there.

Sister, Brother, etc.

-Chorus-
Ev'y body they must have that pure religion
They must be converted in their soul
Be converted or
They can't cross there.

You gonna need that pure religion, halle-luh, halle-luh (c)

-1-
All I want is er pure religion, halle-luh, halle-luh
All I want is er pure religion, halle-luh, halle-luh
All I want is er pure religion,
Pure religion take you home ter heaven,
You gonna need that pure religion, halle-luh, halle-luh.

-2-
Mother en father roun' the bedside crying',
halle-luh, halle-luh
Mother en father roun' the bedside crying',
halle-luh, halle-luh
Mother en father roun' the bedside crying',
Lord have mercy my child is dying,
You gonna need that pure religion, halle-luh, halle-luh.

-3-
Train comin' done turn the curve, halle-luh, halle-luh
Train comin' done turn the curve, halle-luh, halle-luh
Train comin' done turn the curve,
Fixin' ter leave this sinful world
You gonna need that pure religion, halle-luh, halle-luh.

-4-
Crossin' Jorden don't have no fear, halle-luh, halle-luh
Crossin' Jorden don't have no fear, halle-luh, halle-luh
Crossin' Jorden don't have no fear,
Jesus gonna be our engineer,
You gonna need that pure religion, halle-luh, halle-luh.

-5-
Jorden deep ain't got no bound, halle-luh, halle-luh
Jorden deep ain't got no bound, halle-luh, halle-luh
Jorden deep ain't got no bound,
Ef you ain't got religion you'll surely drown,
Then you gonna need that pure religion,
halle-luh, halle-luh.

-6-
Jorden river is chilly en cold, halle-luh, halle-luh
Jorden river is chilly en cold, halle-luh, halle-luh
Jorden river is chilly en cold,
Got to have pure religion in your soul,
You gonna need that pure religion, halle-luh, halle-luh.

-7-
Doctor standing looking sad, halle-luh, halle-luh
Doctor standing looking sad, halle-luh, halle-luh
Doctor standing looking sad,
The hardest case I ever had,
Then you gonna need that pure religion,
halle-luh, halle-luh.

God gonna trouble the water

10

A seriocomic ballad of the adventures of the soul as it confronts Satan, imaged as the trickster who would beguile the Christian from his narrow path. John 5 records Christ's healing of a cripple at the site of the pool where an angel of the Lord periodically "troubles" the water, that is, invests it with divine properties. To "wade in the water" is to undergo the spiritual regeneration symbolized by the New Testament rite of baptism. The migratory Satan stanzas may appear to bear no substantive or logical relationship to the chorus them of rebirth, but rebirth frees the soul from the sin that Satan personifies. "Got happy" is a Southern folk expression for the religious ecstasy of conversion or other transcendent expereience. The comic tone of the stanzas and the characterization of Satan as a folk magician, which gives affront to some critics, should be understood as a reflection of a folk culture in which humor is a weapon of survival and a nourisher of hope. See Alan Lomax, *Folk Songs of North America* (Garden City NY: Doubleday, 1960) 470, for a composite.

God gonna trouble the water

-Chorus-
I'm er wadin', I'm er wadin' in the water, chillun
I'm er wadin', I'm er wadin' in the water, chillun
I'm er wadin', I'm er wadin' in the water, chillun
God gonna trouble the water.

-1-
Oh, Satan is er liar en er conjurer too,
God gonna trouble the water,
Ef you don't watch out he'll conjure you,
God gonna trouble the water.

-2-
I 'members the day, I 'members hit well,
God gonna trouble the water,
When Jesus freed my soul from hell,
God gonna trouble the water.

-Chorus-
I'm er wadin', I'm er wadin' in the water, chillun
I'm er wadin', I'm er wadin' in the water, chillun
I'm er wadin', I'm er wadin' in the water, chillun
God gonna trouble the water.

-3-
One day, one day I went out ter pray,
God gonna trouble the water,
My soul got happy en I stayed all day,
God gonna trouble the water.

-4-
Ole Satan mad en I am glad,
God gonna trouble the water,
He missed er soul he thought he had,
God gonna trouble the water.

Soon as my feet strike Zion won't be trouble no more

Musically and poetically, the chorus strongly contrasts with the stanzas: varied conversational rhythms, the characteristic caesura, the repetition of "trouble," the impacted syntax of introductory adverb clause, the folk double negative, and the first-person speaker of the chorus, against the mnemonic rhymed couplet and onmnscient point of view of the Adam stanza and the bold imperatives, exultant pulpit cadence, and godlike voice of the Angel stanza.

In the curiously satisfying manner of folk poetry, the song telescopes the beginning and ending of the King James Bible, Genesis and Revelation: the premise of the theological argument is Adam who represents the original sin from which man shall be freed in fabled Zion. In stanza 2 God orders an angel of the apocalypse to execute the final destruction of mankind, earth, and Satan. The "flood" may be Noah's, but a more probable source is the flood of Revelation 12 which gives an account of the birth of the Messiah to "a womon clothed with the sun, and the moon under her feet" (Rev. 12:1) and of the war in Heaven in which Michael and his angels fought against and expelled the dragon Satan: "And the serpent cast out of his mouth water like a flood after the woman, that he might cause her to be carried away by the flood. And the earth helped the woman, and the earth opened her mouth and swallowed up the flood which the dragon cast out of his mouth." (Rev. 12:16-17) The sun and moon images derive from the Day of Wrath which John envisions from the Book of Seven Seals opened by the Lamb (Rev. 6:12-17). "Bolt the door" alludes to Revelation 20:1-3 which narrates the millennial imprisonment of Satan in the bottomless pit by an angel who bears a key and a chain.

On the Courlander disc anthology the entire Zion song is performed by Dock Reed and Earthy Anne Coleman and the Angel stanza appears in Rich Amerson's Job sermon and song. See also John W. Work, *American Negro Songs and Spirituals* (New York: Howell Soskin Co., 1940) 117. On the Lomax Library of Congress Alabama recordings, the Angel stanza appears in several different songs.

Soon as my feet strike Zion won't be trouble no more

-Chorus-

Soon as my feet strike Zion won't be trouble no more
Soon as my feet strike Zion won't be trouble no more
Trouble Lord, I'm trouble, won't be trouble no more
Trouble Lord, I'm trouble, won't be trouble no more

-1-

A for Adam, he was er man
Placed in the garden at God's command
Adam the father of the human race
Violated the law en God drove him from his place.

-Chorus-

Soon as my feet strike Jordan won't be trouble no more
Soon as my feet strike Jordan won't be trouble no more
Trouble Lord, I'm trouble, won't be trouble no more
Trouble Lord, I'm trouble, won't be trouble no more

-2-

Go down, angel, consume the flood,
Blow out the sun, turn the moon into blood,
Come back, angel, bolt the door,
Times have been shall be no more.

-Chorus-

Soon as my feet strike Zion won't be trouble no more
Soon as my feet strike Zion won't be trouble no more
Trouble Lord, I'm trouble, won't be trouble no more
Trouble Lord, I'm trouble, won't be trouble no more

Seal up your book, John

12

A Revelator song notable for its classic uses of balance and incremental repetition, for its fusion of New Testament apocalyptic images, its folk diction and syntax fitted out as pulpit rhetoric and prophecy, and its sensitivity to simultaneously occurring dimensions of time and space.

The vision of the speaker, superimposed on the apocalyptic vision of John the Revelator, includes all time and eternity: the remote past during which the Revelator, from exile on Patmos, wrote his letters to the seven churches; the immediate past of the dead mother who now dwells on the island with the prophet; the present of the "leader" or preacher who, as head of the church to which the speaker belongs, has received a "letter"—the Book of Revelation itself—from John; the eternal present in which the speaker and the prophet coexist spiritually; and the rapidly approaching future, the last days which John prophesied.

Similarly, the book is more than one. On the first level it is Revelation, the account John authored. Second, it is the fabulous Book of Seven Seals (chapters 5–11) held in the hand of God, unreadable by any except the Lamb (Christ), its Seventh Seal unveiled to Seven Angels who preside over the *dies irae.* Third, it is the prophetic book of the seventh or rainbow angel (who has one foot on earth and one on the sea) of Revelation 10, which John, obeying the voice of God, eats ("And I took the little book out of the angel's hand, and ate it up; and it was in my mouth sweet as honey, and as soon as I had eaten it my belly was bitter." Rev. 10:10), that is, the mystical source of inspiration for John's prophecies; finally, it is the Book of Life (Rev. 20:11-12) from which the dead are judged on the last day.

The seals are also several. In Revelation 10 the angel of the Seventh Seal speaks, seven thunders respond, and the Voice says, "Seal up those things which the seven thunders uttered, and write them not" (Rev. 10:4). In the final chapter of Revelation, after the vision of Paradise, the angel of the Seventh Seal, who is John's guide and also the voice of Christ, commands, "Seal not the sayings of the prophecy of this book; for the time is at hand" (Rev. 22:10), and warns man against any omissions or additions (Rev. 22:18-19). Hence John's book, as the Book of the Seven Seals, is "sealed" by divine or angelic authority against mortal corruption; and, for the folk speaker in this spiritual, the sealing of John's book stands for the end of man and time, the final realization of the Revelator's prophecies.

See Lomax, *Folk Songs of North America,* 480, for a similar song. Courlander recorded a variant from Rich Amerson and Earthy Anne Coleman in Sumter County (*Negro Folk Songs of Alabama,* FE 4472, Folkways); see Courlander, *Negro Folk Music U.S.A.* (New York: Columbia University Press, 1963; repr. 1969) 234, for musical notation.

Seal up your book, John

-1-

I saw John writing way out on that island
I saw John writing way out on that island
John, John, seal up your book, John
John, don't you write no more.

-2-

He wrote the revelations, he was a writer
He wrote the revelations way out on that island
John, John, seal up your book, John
John, don't you write no more.

-3-

He wrote my leader er letter way out on that island
He wrote my leader er letter en while he wuz writing
John, John, seal up your book, John
John, don't you write no more.

-4-

John wrote the seven churches, he wuz er writer
He wrote the seven churches way out on that island
John, John, seal up your book, John
John, don't you write no more.

-5-

I saw my mother way out on that island
I saw my mother way out on that island
John, John, seal up your book, John
John, don't you write no more.

Clim'in' up de hills

14

The ecstatic ascent of the Christian to the godhead is symbolized in the climbing of the Old Testament Mount Zion. The anguished soul is sustained by intimations of glory which arise from his prayers and tears. Lomax recorded several versions of this hymn for the Library of Congress, those of Dock Reed and Rich Amerson especially moving. See also the Courlander recordings for a duet by Dock and Vera Hall Ward.

Clim'in' up de hills

-Chorus-
Lord, I'm clim'in' up de hills
Of Mount Zionee, my Lord,
Wid de glory in er my soul.

-1-
Praying at de hills of Mount Zionee
Moaning at de hills of Mount Zionee,
Lord, I'm clim'in' up de hills
Of Mount Zionee, my Lord,
Wid de glory in er my soul.

-2-
Groaning at de hills of Mount Zionee
Moaning at de hills of Mount Zionee,
Lord, I'm clim'in' up de hills
Of Mount Zionee, my Lord,
Wid de glory in er my soul.

Good-bye, Sammy

A testament of bereavement and farewell, of pity and brotherhood. The William Francis Allen, Charles Pickard Ware, and Lucy McKim Garrison collection (*Slave Songs of the United States* [New York: A. Simpson and Company, 1867], variously reprinted—see bibliography) early evidenced the use of given names in Afro-American folk song. In "Godd-bye, Sammy" the diction is direct and personal, and the repetitions of "good-bye, farewell, Sammy" and "en de Lord" are sorrowing cries. The dead friend is imaged as a runaway, the ambiguous "en de Lord" suggests both Sammy's mystical union with God and the spiritual state of the speaker whose farewell is given "in" the Lord (cf. such phrases as "in Christ," recurrent in New Testament Christian salutation and prayer). Vera Ward's performance, included in the Sumter County Library of Congress recordings, though without Christian allusions, is a poignant realization of this elegiac spiritual.

Good-bye, Sammy

-1-

Good-bye, Sammy, good-bye en de Lord
Oh good-bye, Sammy, good-bye en de Lord
Oh Sammy, good-bye, Sammy, good-bye,
I'm gwine shake glad hand wid Sammy en de Lord,
Oh Sammy, oh Sammy.

-2-

Sammy, Sammy runned erway en de Lord
Oh Sammy, Sammy runned erway en de Lord
Oh Sammy, Sammy, Sammy runned erway,
I'm gwine shake glad hand wid Sammy en de Lord,
Oh Sammy, oh Sammy.

-3-

Farewell, Sammy, farewell en de Lord
Oh farewell, Sammy, farewell en de Lord
Oh Sammy, farewell, Sammy, farewell,
I'm gwine shake glad hand wid Sammy en de Lord.

You got ter move

16

The spontaneous "holy dance" of Protestant folk worship draws its authority from the Old Testament, for example, King David's dance on the return of the Ark of the Covenant (2 Sam. 6:14). The emphasis on bodily response to spiritual phenomena is appropriate to the theme—the power of God to whom all, high and low, must bow. The key phrase "When the Lord gits ready" suggests the strain of tragic fatalism which turns up now and then in the spirituals. The folk phrase "I declare," an ejaculatory response, emphasizes divine omnipotence. The Alabama Archives holds another Tartt manuscript that omits the chorus and rearranges the order of the stanzas.

You got ter move

-Chorus-
You got ter move
You got ter move I declare
You got ter move
When the Lord gits ready
You got ter move.

-1-
Well you may be blind
En cannot see
But when the Lord gets ready
You got ter move.

-Chorus-
You got ter move
You got ter move I declare
You got ter move
When the Lord gits ready
You got ter move.

-2-
Well you may be high
Well you may be low
But when the Lord gits ready
You got ter move.

-3-
You may be rich
En you may be po'
But when the Lord gits ready
You got ter move.

-Chorus-
You got ter move
You got ter move I declare
You got ter move
When the Lord gits ready
You got ter move.

-4-
The Bible say you must repent,
You got to stand in judgment,
For when the Lord gits ready
You got ter move.

I heard the angels singing

17

A chaste, coherent spiritual of a sweet, reflective mood. The transcendent, mystical experience is conveyed in the metaphor of angelic song brought down to earth—"'bout noon," "just above my head," "all in my room." Lomax recorded the song several times for the Library on Congress as sung by Dock Reed, Vera Ward, and the Sim Tartt group, with Clabe Amerson as soloist-leader.

See also Byron Arnold, ed., *Folk Songs of Alabama* (University AL: University of Alabama Press, 1950) 160.

I heard the angels singing

-1-

One day 'bout noon
One day 'bout noon
One day 'bout noon
I heard the angels singing.

-2-

Heaven's in my view
Heaven's in my view
Heaven's in my view
I heard the angels singing.

-3-

Just above my head
Just above my head
Just above my head
I heard the angels sining.

-4-

All in my room
All in my room
All in my room
I heard the angels singing.

Until I found the Lord

18

"Found the Lord" is a folk expression for redemption, similar to "getting religion," though the latter suggests the emotional camp-meeting conversion while the former is reminiscent of the Psalm attributed to David ("I sought him, but he could not be found," Psalm 37:36), the interior, agonizing struggle of a soul "under conviction." The phrase is inherently ironic: it is not the Lord who is lost but the sinner, and when the Lord is "found" so is the sinner reclaimed. The struggle is aptly conveyed by the folk phrase "wouldn't rest contented" (cf. Augustine's "our heart is restless until it repose in Thee," *Confessions,* book 1), by the ejaculation "Lordy," in the psychological applications of poetic repetition, and by images of the weeping sinner.

Until I found the Lord

-1-

Lord, I prayed en I prayed
I prayed en I prayed
Lordy my soul wouldn't rest contented
Lordy my soul wouldn't rest contented
Until I found the Lord.

-2-

Lord, I moaned en I moaned
I moaned en I moaned
Lordy my soul wouldn't rest contented
Lordy my soul wouldn't rest contented
Until I found the Lord.

-3-

Lord, I cried en I cried
I cried en I cried
Lordy my soul wouldn't rest contented
Lordy my soul wouldn't rest contented
Until I found the Lord.

I stood en rung my hands en cried

A hymn of the homeless and tormented. The stanzas belong to traditional Protestant hymnody—rhymed couplets within quatrains of a seven-syllable pattern, and derivative language—but in the folk phrases "My mother took en lef' me" and "I jus' stood en rung my hands en cried" lie images of desolation, the abandoned child, and the wordless handwringing of utter grief. The strict repetition of the chorus orally re-creates the rhythms of weeping and the gestures of immemorial sorrow.

I stood en rung my hands en cried

-Chorus-
I jus' stood en rung my hands en I cried
Lord, en I cried
I jus' stood en rung my hands en I cried.

-1-
My mother took en lef' me
Here in this world alone
I have no friends en relations
Has er right to seek er home.

-Chorus-
En I jus' stood en rung my hands en I cried
Lord, en I cried
I jus' stood en rung my hands en I cried.

-2-
Sometimes I wants to be in er company
Then ergin I wants to be alone
I looked er round en see
How the worl's been tossin' me.

-Chorus-
En I jus' stood en rung my hands en I cried
Lord, en I cried
I jus' stood en rung my hands en I cried.

God-er-mighty knows I can't stay down here

20

In Hebrew-Christian thought and literature the valley is both the pleasant domain of peace and the psalmist's "shadow of death" (Psalm 23:4). The terrifying forest fires that at times surround the wilderness dweller are also the fires of Judgment Day and Hell. The speaker bitterly prophesies doom in language at once conversational and poetic, and the "God-er-mighty knows" of ordinary discourse is heightened to a profound tragic curse. Repetition, images, language, and rhythmical contrast evoke a mood of unrelieved despair. As the American slavery to which it alludes, this song crushes with its apocalyptic fear.

Mary Amerson recorded an excellent performance of this song for the Lomax Library of Congress project in Sumter County.

God-er-mighty knows I can't stay down here

-1-

I'm goin' out uv this valley
I'm goin' out uv this valley
I'm goin' out uv this valley
God-er-mighty knows I can't stay down here.

-2-

Fire in the east, fire in the west
Fire in the east, fire in the west
Fire gonna burn up the wilderness
God-er-mighty knows I can't stay down here.

Dis is er mean old world to. try to live in (a)
Dis ole world is er mean world (b)

Note in the variant texts the shifts in diction and syntax, the addition of the "cry" stanza in (a), and the omission of one line from each quatrain in (b). The theme is pervasive in the spirituals: earthly tribulations, too well known by a slave people, the "mean world" where even the comfort of blood kin is denied and where hope is scant and difficult, may be endured only through Christian disciplines, praying, and crying, which are emphasized by the urgent folk phrases "you got ter" and "so hard."

Dis is er mean old world to try to live in (a)

-1-

Dis is er mean old world to try to live in,
To try to stay in until you die,
Dis is er mean old world to try to live in,
To try to stay in until you die.

'Thout a sister,
'Thout a brother,
'Thout a father, Lord,
'Thout a mother,
Dis here's er mean old world to try to live in,
To try to stay in until you die.

-2-

You have ter moan sometime to try to live here,
To try ter stay here until you die,
You have to moan sometime to try to live here,
To try to stay here until you die.

Ain't go no sister, Ain't got no brother,
Ain't got no father, Lord, Ain't got no mother,
Dis is er mean old world to try to live in,
To try to stay in until you die.

-3-

You have to pray so hard to try to live here,
To try to stay here until you die,
You hve to pray so hard to try to live here,
to try to stay here until you die.

'Thout a sister,
'Thout a brother,
'Thout a father, Lord,
'Thout a mother,
Dis is er mean old world to try to live in,
To try to stay in until you die.

Dis ole world is er mean world (b)

Dis ole world is er mean world to
Try to live in
To try ter stay in until you die.

Without er mother,
Without er father
Without er sister, Lord,
Ain't got no brother.

Dis ole world is er mean world
to try ter live in
To try ter stay in until you die.

You got ter cry sometime
To try ter live in
To try ter stay in until you die.

You got ter pray so hard
To try ter live in
To try to stay in until you die.

Lord, dis ole world is er mean world
To try ter live in
To try to stay in until you die.

You got ter moan so hard
To try ter live in
To try to stay in until you die.

Oh Lord, when I die

22

No matter the terrors of death--it frees the soul from the bondage of flesh and ends in union with Christ, here conventionally imaged as the embrace of Jesus, the Good Shepherd. "Doubting Thomas" is the New Testament disciple who asked to see the nail prints on the risen Christ. "Weeping Mary," a recurrent figure throughout the body of Afro-American religious folk song, is variously the Mother of Christ, the sister of Lazarus and Martha, and the Magdalene—here the last.

Since the Bible offers no accounts of their deaths, why are Thomas and Mary cited as exemplars of the death of a Christian? Both are emblems of sin and redemption, and it is in their lives, not the manner of their deaths, that we seek the correct attitude towards dying. Let me come to death having lived as Thomas, who doubted yet believed, as Mary Magdalene who sinned yet was forgiven and who, in newly bestowed grace, anointed the feet of Christ as a memorial while he yet lived.

Exquisitely balanced, strong and simple in language, this is a lovely folk hymn of faith.

Oh Lord, when I die

-1-

Let me die in the arms of my Jesus
Let me die in the arms of my Jesus
Let me die in the arms of my Jesus
Oh Lord, when I die.

-Chorus-

Oh Lord, when I die
Oh Lord, when I die
Oh Lord, when I die
Oh Lord, when I die

-2-

Let me die like weeping Mary
Oh let me die like weeping Mary
Let me die like weeping Mary
Oh Lord, when I die.

-3-

Let me die like doubting Thomas
Oh let me die like doubting Thomas
Let me die like doubting Thomas
Oh Lord, when I die.

-Chorus-

Oh Lord, when I die
Oh Lord, when I die
Oh Lord, when I die
Oh Lord, when I die.

Hear what my Jesus say

In Protestant folk worship the "mourner's bench" is reserved for sinners "under conviction" of their sins, to which the sinner comes while minister, elders, choir, and congregation sing, pray, and exhort. This dialogue of the saved and the sinner reflects that custom: the sinner is urged to renounce the world and "bow so low," a phrase connoting self-abasement and humility, but the struggle is inconclusive, the sinner promising only to "pray er little longer." "Hear what Jesus (or the bible) says" commonly precedes reading of Scripture. "My Jesus" signifies both the possessive relationship between God and man and the state of salvation which Christ represents. Note the shift in speakers and point of view, from the omniscient exhorter-preacher to the sinner wavering towards salvation, the corresponding shifts of the caesural pause, and the subtle alterations in the refrain tag as the salvation struggle intensifies during the three stanzas.

Hear what my Jesus say

-1-

Oh moaner, can't you give up dis world
Oh moaner, can't you give up dis world
Oh moaner, can't you give up dis world
And hear what my Jesus say.

-2-

Have to bow so low to give up dis world
Have to bow so low to give up dis world
Have to bow so low to give up dis world
And hear what my Jesus say.

-3-

Well I'll pray er little longer to give up dis world
I'll pray er little longer to give up dis world
Well I'll pray er little longer to give up dis world
And hear what my Jesus say.

For my Jesus ever more

24

A song which celebrates the virtues and practices of the redeemed Christian. To the other disciplines has been added "mourning," that is, the compassionate sharing of sorrow within the Christian fellowship. "Build" suggests the parable of the wise and foolish men. Repetition in the three quatrains is absolute except for the central verbs and the few displacements of "Lord" and "Lordy."

For my Jesus ever more

-1-

I'm gonna build right on de shore
Lord, I'm gonna build right on de shore
I'm gonna build right on de shore
For my Jesus, Lordy, for my Jesus ever more.

-1-

I'm gonna pray right on de shore
Lord, I'm gonna pray right on de shore
I'm gonna pray right on de shore
For my Jesus, Lordy, for my Jesus ever more.

-1-

I'm gonna mourn right on de shore
Lord, I'm gonna mourn right on de shore
I'm gonna mourn right on de shore
For my Jesus, Lordy, for my Jesus ever more.

Borrowed land

Here the economic and social realities of Southern history are woven into a relgious context: the phrase is drawn from sharecropping and/or tenantry, but in the spiritual sense all earthly life is "borrowed" from God. "Going back with Jesus," a common Protestant folk metaphor for the election of the redeemed at the Second Coming, implies full ownership of the land of eternal Zion.

Borrowed land

-1-

We're down here livin' on borrowed land
Borrowed land, borrowed land,
We're down here livin' on borrowed land,
I'm gwine back wid Him when He comes.

-2-

We're down here prayin' on borrowed land
Borrowed land, borrowed land,
We're down here prayin' on borrowed land,
I'm gwine back wid Him when He comes.

-3-

We're down here moanin' on borrowed land
Borrowed land, borrowed land,
We're down here moanin' on borrowed land,
I'm gwine back wid Him when He comes.

The bar of judgment

26

The fear of Judgment Day is a strong motivation for repentance. In contrast to those preaching spirituals that paint ghastly images of Hell and the apocalypse or promise relief of burdens, this one faces squarely the doctrine of individual responsibility. The device of the catalog of relatives logically develops the evangelical argument.

Cf. "The lonesome valley" or "You got to go to that lonesome (or lonely) valley, / You got to go there by yourself," widely present in both white and Afro-American religious folk song. Allen, Ware, and Garrison, quote Thomas Higginson (a colonel in the Union army and commander of the first Negro regiment) to explain that to descend to "de (lonesome) valley" implied going to the "anxious seat" ("mourner's bench") of the camp meeting (*Slave Songs of the United States,* 5n).

The bar of judgment

-1-

Oh, I got to stand at the bar of judgment,
Oh, I got to stand there for myself,
Oh, there's no one else to stand there for me,
I got to stand there for my self.

-2-

My mother's got to stand at the bar of judgment,
My mother's got to stand there for herself,
Oh, there's no one else to stand there for her,
My mother's got to stand there for herself.

-3-

My father's got to stand at the bar of judgment,
My mother's got to stand there for himself,
Oh, there's no one else to stand there for her,
My father's got to stand there for himself.

-4-

Everybody's got to stand at the bar of judgment,
Everybody's got to stand there for themselves,
Oh, there's no one else to stand there for them,
Everybody's got to stand there for themselves.

Lord, won't you come by here

"Come by here" is a Southern idiom for transportation and visiting, some intrusion into the pattern of daily routine, as in "The train doesn't *come by here.*" The speaker's plea arises out of the terrible loneliness of the orphan, and the petitionary stanzas lead climactically to the triumphant conclusion, "Lord, I'm goin' down in your name," one of the most splendid lines in all American religious folk song (see the song by that title below). The amplification of the archetypal unrhymed antiphonal quatrain to six lines occurs in response to performance circumstances where mood determines such aesthetic heightening. Oral-musical qualities of the pulpit cadence dominate this artistically superior and moving prayer of the desolate.

Lord, won't you come by here

-1-

Oh Lord, won't you come by here
Lord, won't you come by here
Oh Lord, won't you come by here
Lord, won't you come by here
Oh Lord, won't you come by here
Lord, won't you come by here

-2-

Now Lord, hit's er needy time
Now Lord, hit's er needy time
Oh Lord, hit's er needy time
Now Lord, hit's er needy time
Now Lord, hit's er needy time
Now Lord, hit's er needy time

-3-

Lord, I'm er motherless child
Lord, I'm er motherless child
Oh Lord, I'm er motherless child
Lord, I'm er motherless child
Lord, I'm er motherless child
Lord, I'm er motherless child

-4-

Lord, won't you hear me cry
Lord, won't you hear me cry
Oh Lord, won't you hear me cry
Lord, won't you hear me cry
Lord, won't you hear me cry
Lord, won't you hear me cry

-5-

Lord, I'm goin' down in your name
Lord, I'm goin' down in your name
Oh Lord, I'm goin' down in your name
Lord, I'm goin' down in your name
Lord, I'm goin' down in your name
Lord, I'm goin' down in your name

Wheel in the middle uv the wheel (a,b)

28

None of the old Testament prophets seized the imagination of the nineteenth-century folk quite in the same way as did Ezekiel whose writings, like those of John the Revelator, are invested with the mystic symbols, fabulous images, and elaborate metaphors that fed a people starved for poetry. The "wheel in the middle of a wheel" is from Ezekiel 1:16.

Variant (a) may be taken as the traditional spiritual as sung in Sumter County, Alabama. The "wheel way up in the middle of the air" of concert versions appears here as a "wheel in the middle of the wheel" and the chariots of both Ezekiel and Elijah (who enters the song by association) are merged. In (b) the chorus of the Ezekiel spiritual has been attached to migratory preaching stanzas, and thus the mystic wheel is allied with daily Christian conduct.

Wheel in the middle uv de wheel (a)

-Chorus-
Move wheel, wheel in the middle uv de wheel
Move wheel, wheel in the middle uv de wheel.

-1-
Ezekiel saw dat wheel uv time
Wheel in de middle uv er wheel
En ev'y spoke was a human kind
Wheel in the middle uv a wheel.

-Chorus-
Move wheel, wheel in de middle uv de wheel.

-2-
Elijah saw dat chariot comin'
Wheel in de middle uv er wheel
He got on board en he never stop runnin'
Wheel in de middle uv er wheel.

-Chorus-
Move wheel, wheel in de middle uv de wheel.

-3-
What kind er wheel are you talkin' 'bout
Wheel in de middle uv er wheel
Oh what er wheel are you talkin' 'bout
Wheel in de middle uv er wheel.

-Chorus-
Move wheel, wheel in de middle uv de wheel.

Wheel in the middle of a wheel (b)

-1-
Wheel, wheel in the middle of a wheel
Wheel, wheel in the middle of a wheel,
You must not lie,
You must not steal,
Wheel in the middle of a wheel
Wheel in the middle of a wheel,
You must not lie,
You must not steal,
Wheel in the middle of a wheel.

-2-
You may talk about me
Just as much as you please,
More you talk, I'll bend my knees.
Wheel in the middle of a wheel
Wheel in the middle of a wheel
Wheel, oh wheel in the middle of a wheel

Lord, I'm goin' down in your name

The song opens with the declaration of a weary soldier who has kept faith to the end. Thereafter variations shine against the quiet textures of simple words—*to weep, to pray, to go to heaven, to be humble, to obey*—but these are burdened with the full meaning of faith, hope, and salvation. In stanzas 2, 3, and 4 the caesural pause is filled with "Lord" as this word occurs in both conversation and pulpit sermon and prayer, and folk speech is raised by its own emotional power to poetry.

Lord, I'm goin' down in your name

-1-

Lord, I'm goin' down in your name,
Lord, I'm goin' down in your name,
If I die on the battle field,
Lord, I'm goin' down in your name.

-2-

I'm goin' to weep, Lord, in your name,
I'm goin' to weep, Lord, in your name,
If I die on the battle field,
I'm goin' to weep, Lord, in your name.

-3-

I'm goin' to pray, Lord, in your name,
I'm goin' to pray, Lord, in your name,
If I die on the battle field,
I'm goin' to pray, Lord, in your name.

-4-

I'm goin' to heaven, Lord, in your name,
I'm goin' to heaven, Lord, in your name,
If I die on the battle field,
I'm goin' to heaven, Lord, in your name.

-5-

I'm er humble en I will obey,
I'm er humble en I will obey,
If I die on the battle field,
I'm er humble en I will obey.

I started to make heaven my home

30

Content, rhyme ("roam/home"), diction ("weak en worldly," "prone to sin," "no hope for tomorrow"), stanzaic form (quatrain conforming roughly to hymn meter), and the metaphor of Heaven as home for the pilgrim are all derivative of white hymnody. But in the coinages "boasted" and "tossted" the folk mind has created fresh poetic images of assault. "Boasted" may be "bossed," as in servitude, occupation, which would agree in rhyme and rhythm—*boss-ted/toss-ted*—and also may be semantically appropriate. "Tossted," as in "tossed about," implies capricious, violent movement, as in a storm; hence, the speaker in his helpless terror and despair hears "the kind word of Jesus." (See Luke 8:24 for Jesus' rebuke of the storm, and Matthew 11:28 for the words of comfort, "Come unto me, all ye that labor and are heavy laden, and I will give you rest.") Hearing the "kind word of Jesus," he is "saved," that is, undergoes a conversion from sin, renounces the hopelessness of "dis world," and begins the Christian "newness of life" (Romans 6:4) which ends with eternal life.

I started to make heaven my home

-1-

Sometime I'm boasted, tossted, en driven,
Sometime I knows not where ter roam,
I heard the kind word uv Jesus,
En I started to make heaven my home.

-2-

I know that I am weak en worldly,
My heart is prone ter sin,
No hope in dis world for tomorrow,
So I started to make heaven my home.

Cotton chopping song

Title and structure suggest the use of the spiritual as work song, the questions shouted by a boss, the responses by the "hands." As in secular "hollers" and shouts, the responsive dialogue is shorn of articles and adjectives. Note the balanced progression of respondent and personified symbols— "you-mountain," "sinner-rock," "mother-lord"—the powerful pulpit question, the urgent brief refrain. The "gettin'-up morning" is the day of the world's destruction by fire. The image of sinners in desperate flight is drawn from the "last-days" prophecies of Christ. See also Johnson and Johnson, *The Books of American Negro Spirituals,* 2:40.

Cotton chopping song

-1-

What you gwinter do in the gettin'-up morning
When hit's raining fire down?
Go to the mountain,
Mountain cried out,
You can't hide.

-2-

Sinner, what you gwinter do in the gettin'-up morning
When hit's raining fire down?
Go to the rock,
Rock cried out,
You can't hide.

-3-

Mother, what you gwinter do in the gettin'-up morning
When hit's raining fire down?
Go to the Lord,
Lord cried out,
You can't hide.

Gimme Jesus

32

A hymn of invitation sung at the end of the sermon when the minister invites church membership or some religious affirmation. Carefully balanced through repetition of text and metrical devices, it presents a natural excellence in language: the "fo'-day prayer" or that devotion just at dawn; "at the end of my row," an expression from field labor, implying both the joy of finishing an arduous task and the despair that comes when one can no longer endure burdens; "O, sinner, you must come down," a reference to both the literal act of coming to the altar or mourner's bench and to repentance; "give" is significant—the soul is beyond all help except for Christ who freely gave his life for mankind. See "Give Me Jesus" in Johnson and Johnson, *The Books of American Negro Spirituals,* 1:160-61. On the Lomax Library of Congress recordings, "Gimme Jesus" is sung by Dock Reed.

Gimme Jesus

-1-

At the 'fo-day prayer give me Jesus
At the 'fo-day prayer give me Jesus
At the 'fo-day prayer give me Jesus,
Oh sinner, you must come down.

-Chorus-

Gimme Jesus, gimme Jesus,
You may have all the world
But give me Jesus.

-2-

Oh that good old Daniel, give me Jesus
Oh that good old Daniel, give me Jesus
Oh that good old Daniel, give me Jesus,
Oh sinner, you must come down.

-Chorus-

Gimme Jesus, gimme Jesus,
You may have all the world
But give me Jesus.

-3-

At the end of my row give me Jesus
At the end of my row give me Jesus
At the end of my row give me Jesus
Oh sinner, you must come down.

When the love comes twinkle-lin' down

Afro-American folk hymns of the Crucifixion re-create events by a variety of means. Some narrate and dramatize in the manner of a ballad; some cluster metaphors and images for a lyric impression; and others, like this specimen, utilize the *ubi sunt* ("where are") dialogue of early and medieval Christian poetry, a figurative device which brings the folk consciousness directly, immediately to the scene. As a witness in the immutable spiritual present tense, the speaker is invested with the power and duty to exhort: Where were *you*—elders, kinsmen, hypocrites, sinners—when the Lord died? Had you seen, you would possess salvation. And the Sermon on the Mount chorus (Matthew 7:7) sums up his exhortation.

Stanzaic structure (unrhymed quatrains of six to eight syllables), the strong, clear caesural pause, antiphonal dialogue, and extensive incremental repetition all point to the traditional core song which has undergone little alteration. In *The Books of American Negro Spirituals* (1:41, cf. 1:175), Johnson notes that *twinklin'* is a variation of *trinkling* (in turn a dialectal variant of *trickling*). If *twinklin'* images Christ on the cross, then here is a metaphor of miracle and sacrament in which the blood of the Saviour descends as the glittering stars of holy love. The strength of language and symbol, the force of drama and feeling, and the poetic development of this hymn show that for the immigrant slave the Crucifixion was the living truth of his new religion. Dock Reed sings Mrs. Tartt's text on Lomax's Library of Congress recordings.

When the love comes twinkle-lin' down

-1-
Oh brother, you oughter been there
Brother, you oughter been there
Brother, you oughter been there
When the love come twinkle-lin' down.

-2-
My mother, you oughter been there
Mother, you oughter been there
Mother, you oughter been there
When the love come twinkle-lin' down.

-3-
My elder, where were you
My elder, where were you
My elder, where were you
When the love come twinkle-lin' down.

-Chorus-
Oh seek, seek, seek en you shall find,
Knock en the door shall be open,
Ask en it shall be given,
When the love come twinkle-lin' down.

-4-
Oh my sister, where were you
My sister, where were you
My sister, where were you
When the love come twinkle-lin' down.

-5-
Oh sinner, you oughter been there
Sinner, you oughter been there
Sinner, you oughter been there
When the love come twinkle-lin' down.

-6-
Oh pretender, you oughter been there
Pretender, you oughter been there
Pretender, you oughter been there
When the love come twinkle-lin' down.

Travelin' on

34

The metaphor of the traveller occurs throughout Anglo-American Protestant literature and hymnody. As another great folk hymn proclaims, the "poor, wayfaring stranger / travelling through this world below" seeks the blessedness of home, a pervasive symbol in nineteenth-century Christian lore, especially songs, poems, and gravestone inscriptions. The fullest expression of the sojourner analogy, John Bunyan's *Pilgrim's Progress* (1678), was known, read, and loved well into the early 1900s, but biblical and folk sources were probably of more direct influence in its dissemination. In the wanderings of the Israelites toward the Promised Land, both slave and master might find a paradigm of the interior journey of the soul: see Numbers 20:14-21 in which Moses requests but is refused peaceful passage through Edom to Canaan "by the king's highway" (implicitly a promist not to despoil vineyards and fields), and Numbers 21:21-24 which narrates a similar incident with the Amorites who offer battle and are defeated by Israel. English and American folktales, songs, legends, and nursery rhymes abound in references to "the King's Highway," a road of, to, and from adventure, romance, comedy, and tragedy.

Travelin' on

-1-

Travelin' on
Travelin' on
I am travelin' up the King's Highway.

-2-

Travelin' on
Travelin' on
I'll reach my home some day.

-3-

The trials may upset me
Along the way,
But I'll reach my home some day.

-4-

Travelin' on
Travelin' on
I'll reach my home some day.

Set down side uv de lamb

The Old and New Testaments are brought into close symbolic and theological relationship in the figures of Christ, the Lamb of God, and Father Abraham, the keeper of flocks whose intended sacrifice of Isaac prefigures the Crucifixion. The sacred and the profane mingle freely. For "Father of Abraham" read "Father Abraham": the *of* is an attempt to render the folk pronunciation of *father* in which the *r* is trilled *err* and followed by a weak guttural—*fath-err-raugh*. This pronunciation permits the traditional division of the line into two roughly equal syllabic parts, with the caesura before *set*. For *super* read *suffer*—God promises Adam he will "suffer in the heel" (Genesis 3:15). The two barrels of pork and meal allotted to the slave are such sufferings in this life; Mary and Martha, the sisters of Lazarus to whom are assigned the traditional blue of the Virgin, are examples of Christian faith and practice; "reeling and rocking" is both religious and secular dance.

Compare variations on the theme: "Father Abraham [sittin' down side ob de Holy Lam']"in Johnson and Johnson, *The Books of American Negro Spirituals* 1:144; and "Sittin' down beside o' the Lamb" in John W. Work, *American Negro Songs and Spirituals,* 58. Rich Amerson sang this song for Lomax on the Library of Congress recordings.

Set down side uv de lamb

-1-

Father of Abraham set down side uv de lamb
Father of Abraham set down side uv de lamb
I kin reel en I kin rock, set down side uv de lamb.

Oh, two barrels of pickled pork,
Two barrels of meal
Make God's chillun super in de heel,
Set down side uv de lamb.

-2-

Father of Abraham set down side uv de lamb
Father of Abraham set down side uv de lamb
Mary en Martha dressed in blue
Make God's chillun super in de heel,
Set down side uv de lamb.

Father of Abraham set down side uv de lamb
Set down side uv de lamb.

Can't hide, sinner, you can't hide

36

An apocalyptic spiritual (cf. "Cotton Choppin' Song" above) based on the Day of Wrath in Revelation 6:12-17. The first and third stanzas are cast as questions, the second and fourth as expository statements; but in the last stanza the speaker shifts dramatically from exhorter to sinner, and it is the rock that cries out "You can't hide." "Turn your bed around" is a magical practice to ward off evil, of no avail to these fleeing sinners.

Can't hide, sinner, you can't hide

-1-

Where you runnin', sinner, you can't hide
Where you runnin', sinner, you can't hide
Where you runnin', sinner, you can't hide
Can't hide, sinner, you can't hide.

-2-

My mother dying, can't hide
My mother dying, can't hide
My mother dying, can't hide
Can't hide, sinner, you can't hide.

-3-

Why'd you run to de mountin, can't hide
Why'd you run to de mountin, can't hide
Why'd you run to de mountin, can't hide
Can't hide, sinner, can't hide.

-4-

Turn your bed around, you can't hide
Turn your bed around, you can't hide
Turn your bed around, you can't hide
Can't hide, sinner, you can't hide.

-5-

I went to de rock, can't hide
Fer to hide my face, can't hide
Well the rock cried out, can't hide
No hiding place, you can't hide.

When the train rolls up

Not a single word in this song refers specifically to Christianity, yet metaphor, images, and diction identify it as religious. No invention excited nineteenth-century America like the train, and there are hundreds of railroad folk song. Here the "glory train" replaces the chariot as the mode of transportation to Heaven, the eternal railway station where friends and loved ones will be reunited after death. The metaphor should be set in its historical and folk context: such an engine, descending out of nowhere to a crossroads, breathing fire like the dragon chariots of the Israelites, brought the larger world to Southern rural folk (goods, news, gold, and strangers), carried them west, east, and north, and brought them back for a joyous homecoming.

See the same theme and essentially the same phrasing in "When the train comes along" (in John W. Work, *American Negro Songs and Spirituals,* 94): "When the train comes along, I'll meet you at the station . . . I may be blind an' cannot see . . . I may be lame an' cannot walk."

When the train rolls up

-1-

I may be blind
En I cannot see,
But I'll meet you at the station
When the train rolls up.

-Chorus-

Oh brother, when the train rolls up
Oh brother, when the train rolls up
I will meet you at the station
When the train rolls up.

-2-

I may be lame
En I cannot walk,
But I'll meet you at the station
When the train rolls up.

-Chorus-

Oh brother, when the train rolls up
Oh brother, when the train rolls up
I will meet you at the station
When the train rolls up.

Some say give me father

38

One of the finest laments in the Tartt collection, its diction and idiom lifted out of a life of hardship, its symbolism refined from a folk culture in which woman is multifaceted: in blues she is the force that drives a man to drink, despair, and madness; in the play-party songs, a delight of gaiety and youth; and in the spirituals a guardian and teacher, wise and generous, beneficent and enduring, the source of all good for her children. The motherless child is the most far-reaching metaphor of slavery in all Afro-American folk song. Dock Reed and Vera Hall sing slightly different texts on the Library of Congress recordings.

Some say give me father

-1-

Some say give me father
I say father will do
So when you git on your bed's affliction
Git your mother who will stand by you.

When your mother is dead
You has er hard time
Oh, when your mother is dead
You has er hard time
Oh, when your mother is dead
You has er hard time
Livin' in dis world alone.

Making for the promised land

As leader of the Israelites out from their Egyptian bondage, Moses was a natural hero for the American slave, and the journey to the Promised Land had both contemporary and spiritual meaning. As in other songs, he is "old" Moses, an affectionate term for a friend, whom the speaker, in the eternal present, envisions as one of a band of pilgrims, including his mother and father, to Canaan. "Shall I be the one?" is reminiscent of the question put to Christ by the disciples, "Lord, is it I?" (Matthew 26:22, 25) but in this context refers to the ultimate destination of the soul. "Making for" is an idiom for "going towards." The "right hand" is the hand of Christian fellowship.

Making for the promised land

-1-

I see old Moses coming, coming, coming,
I see old Moses coming, making for the Promise Land.

-Chorus-

Good Lord, good Lord, shall I be the one,
Good Lord, good Lord, shall I be the one,
Good Lord, shall I be the one,
Making for the Promise Land.

-2-

I see my mother coming, coming, coming,
I see my mother coming, making for the Promise Land.

-Chorus-

Good Lord, good Lord, shall I be the one,
Good Lord, good Lord, shall I be the one,
Good Lord, shall I be the one,
Making for the Promise Land.

-3-

I see my father coming, coming, coming,
I see my father coming, making for the Promise Land.

-Chorus-

Good Lord, good Lord, shall I be the one,
Good Lord, good Lord, shall I be the one,
Good Lord, shall I be the one,
Making for the Promise Land.

-4-

I met my mother this morning,
I gave her my right hand,
I met her again this evening,
She was talkin' 'bout this Promise Land.

Don't you grieve

40

The refreshing image of the Heavenly Train "loaded with bright angels" humanizes immortality and makes a frolic of death. The soul about to enter Paradise is going up and down the cars greeting his mother, his elder in the church, and, presumably, all his old friends. The "don't you grieve" tag is common in Protestant folk songs. *Howdy* is pronounced *how-doo* and *hi-dee* in Alabama folk usage.

Don't you grieve

-1-

I spied that train er coming,
Don't you grieve,
And hit's loaded with bright angels,
Don't you grieve,
And hit's loaded with bright angels,
Don't you grieve.

-2-

I'm gonna tell my mother howdy,
Don't you grieve,
I'm gonna tell my mother howdy,
Don't you grieve,
And hit's loaded with bright angels,
Don't you grieve.

-3-

I'm gonna tell my elder howdy,
Don't you grieve,
I'm gonna tell my elder howdy,
Don't you grieve,
'Cause hit's loaded with bright angels,
Don't you grieve.

All the friend I had dead en gone

This is a nearly perfect elegiac spiritual in which structure, language, metrics, rhythm, and melody all sustain the tone of sorrow. The ordinary folk phrase "dead and gone" is carried to the very limits of bereavement. The mother who dies "shoutin' " has embraced the faith all her life and now dies joyously in her Christian hope. And no other allusion could have been so dramatically and poetically effective as Mary Magdalene at the tomb of Christ—when the angels ask the cause of her tears, she answers "Because they have taken away my Lord, and I know not where they have laid him" (John 20:13). Dock Reed's version appears both on the Library of Congress recordings and the Courlander series; the McDonald family also sang it for John Lomax.

All the friend I had dead en gone

-1-
All the friend I had,
All the friend I had,
All the friend I had,
Dead en gone.

-Chorus-
Gone to the grave yard,
Gone to the grave yard,
All the friend I had,
Dead en gone.

-2-
Weepin' Mary, weep no longer,
All the friend I had,
Dead en gone.

-3-
My poor mother died er shoutin',
All the friend I had,
Dead en gone.

He's coming again so soon

42

The Christian disciplines are here linked with the Second Coming. Note the insistent syntax of "got to live to be ready" and the emphatic noun-verb nonagreement of "he come."

He's coming again so soon

-1-

You got ter pray ter be ready when He come
You got ter pray ter be ready when He come
You got ter pray ter be ready when He come,
He's coming again so soon.

-2-

You got ter moan ter be ready when He come
You got ter moan ter be ready when He come
You got ter moan ter be ready when He come,
He's coming again so soon.

-3-

You got ter live ter be ready when He come
You got ter live ter be ready when He come
You got ter live ter be ready when He come,
Yes, He's coming again so soon.

Play-pary or rock song

The title indicates the natural passage of the spiritual into play-party, dance, and game traditions of children. "Chile uv God" is the answer to the plight of the motherless child. The harp metaphor recurs throughout the spirituals and Protestant hymnody. Captain Strong may have been a real person. The epithet "gypsy Jew" designates any person of rapid, babbling speech, but the reference may be to charismatic "talking in tongues." "Don't be shame" demonstrates a common grammatical peculiarity, the absence of the past tense sound *ed* or *t.* One of the copies of this text is dated "November 28, 1938."

Play-party or rock song

-1-

Shout along, children, don't be shame
Shout along, children, don't be shame,
You jes got er tongue like gypsy Jew
You jes got er tongue like gypsy Jew.

-2-

You touch one string en the whole heavens ring
You touch one string en the whole heavens ring,
You jes got er tongue like gypsy Jew
You jes got er tongue like gypsy Jew.

-3-

Captain Strong, don't be shame
Captain Strong, don't be shame,
You jes got er tongue like gypsy Jew
You jes got er tongue like gypsy Jew.

-4-

You don't b'lieve I'm er chile uv God
You don't b'lieve I'm er chile uv God,
You jes got er tongue like gypsy Jew
You jes got er tongue like gypsy Jew.

Ain't no stranger here

44

A courtesy of folk life functions as a metaphor for the joys of salvation and eternal life—"I got introduce to de Father en Son"—as if the Almighty and Christ were neighbors and friends of the speaker; and another ordinary phrase—"I ain't no stranger here"—proclaims his membership among the redeemed. In stanza 2 the interpolation from the hymn "Come, we that love the Lord" (here become "Come *ye*") is appropriate to the mood of jubilation and to the theme, the congregation of brothers in the faith.

Ain't no stranger here

-1-

Well, I ain't no stranger here,
Well, I ain't no stranger here.
Well, I got introduce to de Father en Son
I ain't no stranger here.

-2-

Come ye dat love de Lord
En let yo joys be known.
Well, I got introduce to de Father en Son,
Ain't no stranger here.

Hallelujah, I ain't no stranger here,
Hallelujah, I ain't no stranger here.
I got introduce to de Father en de Son,
En I ain't no stranger here.

Anyhow

Everyday "backsliding" Christians parade through the spirituals: a sister who dresses too fine, a brother who cheats on his wife, an old gossip, a jealous heart, and these squabbling churches of "Anyhow." "Treat you wrong" is an expression for the multitude of small personal sins committed among intimates. Anecdotes about greedy, lustful, cowardly preachers are plentiful in Afro-American humorous lore. "Bowing at the cross" signifies both the repentance of the sinner and the correction of the backslider. The idea of the Holy Ghost as the guide of Christian conduct is based in New Testament theology. Metrics, rhyme, figures, and diction suggest some influence from Protestant hymnody.

Anyhow

-1-

Ef yo' brother treat you wrong,
Let de Holy Ghost be yo' guide.
Fer at de cross you den bow,
En go to heaven anyhow.

-Chorus-

Anyhow, anyhow, anyhow,
My Lord, at de cross you can bow
En go to heaven anyhow.

-3-

Ef yo' pastor treat you wrong,
Let de Holy Ghost be yo' guide.
Fer at de cross you ken bow,
En go to Heaven anyhow.

-Chorus-

Anyhow, anyhow, anyhow,
My Lord, at de cross you can bow
En go to heaven anyhow.

De las' word I heerd him say

46

A sermon song in which a zealous reformer accosts the liar, the backslider, and the hypocrite, none of whom has "prayin' on his mind." Damnation is uttered fiercely, if a bit comically, echoing the pulpit style of revival and camp meeting: "God don' lac it and I doan neither." Such exhortatory songs emerged as a strong genre with the spread of independent Negro Protestant churches in the last two decades of the nineteenth century.

De las' word I heerd him say

-1-

I met dat liar de udder day,
I spoke ter him 'bout prayin'.
De las' word I heerd him say
He didn't have prayin' on his mind.

-Chorus-

Liar, God doan lac hit en I doan neither,
God doan lac hit en I doan neither,
God doan lac hit en I doan neither,
Hit's er scanderlus en er shame.

-2-

I met dat hypocrit de udder day,
I spoke ter him 'bout prayin'.
De las' word I heerd him say
He didn't have prayin' on his mind.

-Chorus-

Hypocrit, God doan lac hit en I doan neither,
God doan lac hit en I doan neither,
God doan lac hit en I doan neither,
Hit's er scanderlus en er shame.

-3-

I met dat backslider de udder day,
I spoke ter him 'bout prayin'.
De las' word I heerd him say
He didn't have prayin' on his mind.

-Chorus-

Backslider, God doan lac hit en I doan neither,
God doan lac hit en I doan neither,
God doan lac hit en I doan neither,
Hit's er scanderlus en er shame.

Been in de war so long

This is the soliloquy of a seasoned, able soldier who has spent his life in the soul's warfare against evil. The images of nightlong vigils and the folk declarations of pride and courage, challenged afresh in new, endless battles, place the song in the highest ranks of American folk poetry. "I am de one dat God sot free" has obvious reference to emancipation, though the deeper implications are to spiritual freedom. The comic overtones of the migratory Satan stanza may diminish the tragic tone, but as the enemy of all good, Satan belongs in the extended war metaphor.

"I ain't got tired yit" is a recurring theme in the spirituals, whether of bravado or genuine hope. See, for example, "I don't feel weary and noways tired" in the song by that name as it appears in Allen, Ware, and Garrison, *Slave Songs of the United States,* 70.

Been in de war so long

-1-

I been in de war so long, I ain't got tired yit,
I been in de war so long, I ain't got tired yit,
Well, my head been wet wid de midnight dew,
The 'fo'-day star was a witness, too,
I been in de war so long en I ain't got tired yit.

-2-

Do you want to know reason Satan don't lac me?
Been in de war so long, ain't got tired yet,
Been in de war so long, ain't got tired yet,
I am de one dat God sot free
En I ain't tired yit.

-3-

My knees is acquainted wid de hillside clay,
Ain't got tired yit.
Feet placed on de rock of eternitay,
Ain't got tired yit.

-Chorus-

Oh, been in de war so long, ain't got tired yit.
Oh, been in de war so long, ain't got tired yit.

-4-

Ole Satan is mad en I am glad,
Ain't got tired yit.
Missed a soul he thought he had,
En I ain't got tired yit.

-Chorus-

Oh, been in de war so long, ain't got tired yit.
Oh, been in de war so long, ain't got tired yit.

Anywhere, anytime

48

Singing and preaching have been added to the list of Christian practices and the choral tag emphasizes an everyday religion that is expressed "anywhere, anytime." "So God can use you" refers to the fulfillment of divine purpose through Christian discipline. Note the progression and balance of substantive and verb within the otherwise strict repetition: *everybody pray, everybody moan*; *preacher preach*; *you sing, you live.*

Anywhere, anytime

-1-
Everybody oughter pray so God can use them
Anywhere en anytime.
Everybody oughter moan so God can use them
Everywhere en anytime.

-2-
Every preacher oughter preach so God can use him
Anywhere en anytime.
Every preacher oughter preach so God can use him
Anywhere, anytime.

-3-
You oughter sing so God can use you
Anywhere en anytime.
You oughter sing so God can use you
Anywhere, anytime.

-4-
You oughter live so God can use you
Anywhere en anytime.
You oughter live so God can use you
Anywhere, anytime.

Don't let nobody turn you 'round

To "get turned around" is to suffer confusion, stop short of a purpose, or reverse direction, for good or ill. The Christian is exhorted to hold steadfast against temptation, here imaged as the devil who perverts and frustrates Christian purpose and as the earthly gambler who would lure the redeemed back into sin. The syntax forcefully conveys the exhortation, and the oral repetition of "turn you round" poetizes the satanic bewilderment of which the song warns.

"Don't you let nobody turn you roun' " is the title of the more complete version as cited by John W. Work in *American Negro Songs and Spirituals,* 89. The present version repeats the chorus with variations.

Don't let nobody turn you 'round

-1-

Don't you let de devil turn you 'round,
Turn you 'round, turn you 'round.
Don't you let de devil turn you 'round, turn you 'round,
Jes' keep on to Calver-ree.

-2-

Don't you let dat gambler turn you 'round,
Turn you 'round, turn you 'round.
Don't you let de devil turn you 'round, turn you 'round,
Jes' keep on to Calver-ree.

-3-

Don't you let nobody turn you 'round,
Turn you 'round, turn you 'round.
Don't you let de devil turn you 'round, turn you 'round,
Jes' keep on to Calver-ree.

Fightin' fer de city

50

The city is that of Revelation 21:2—"And I, John, saw the holy city, new Jerusalem, . . . —the eternal order as well as the spiritual church, and of Hebrews 11:10—"For he looked for a city . . . whose builder and maker is God." The metaphor of the Christian warrior which appers in the chorus is not directly supported in the stanzas but the argument is logically developed: the mother already occupies the city, the sinner yearns for the building "not made wid hand" (2 Corinthians 5:1, "For we know . . . we have a building of God, an house not made with hands, eternal in the heavens"); and the hypocrite will have no entrance there. The image of the mother hiding behind the altar of God appears comical, but the idea of hiding in God (or in Christ or in the "Rock of Ages") has ample precedent in the Bible and in Protestant hymnody.

The "where sabbaths have no end" theme appears from time to time, for example, in "Sabbath has no end" (Allen, Ware, Garrison, *Slave Songs of the United States,* 69) and in "Ev'ry day'll be Sunday bye and bye" (John W. Work, *American Negro Songs and Spirituals,* 213).

Fightin' fer de city

-1-

My mother is gone on a journey,
She's gone dere to stay,
She's hidin' behind de altar,
Gettin' ready fer Jedgerment Day.

Well, I'm er fightin' fer de city, I believe.
Lord, I'm er fightin' fer de city, I believe.
Where sabbaths have no end.

-2-

I went up on de mountin.
I met dat sinner man.
He's looking for dat buildin'
Of de house not made wid hand.

Oh, I'm er fightin' fer de city, I believe.
Lord, I'm er fightin' fer de city, I believe.
Where sabbaths have no end.

-3-

Some folks says dey's got er religion.
They's nothin' but a hypocrite.
Ef de truth was tole en de heart was searched,
They've never been born of God.

Oh, I'm er fightin' fer de city, I pray.
Lord, I'm er fightin' fer de city, I pray.
Where sabbaths have no end.

God's gettin' worried wid yo' wicked ways

Here is a sermon song rich in folk comedy and dead serious as moral exhortation. The couplets owe something to the tradition of oral folk secular rhymes. The dramatic scene which frames the sermon is a folk version of Old Testmant prototypes in which God, exhausted and confounded by the sins of mankind—as in the stories of Noah, Jonah, and Sodom and Gomorrah—sends an angel to warn of or accomplish destruction. While the chorus pounds at sin, the stanzas suggest remedies in prayer, repentance, church going, and the renunciation of worldly goods. Both the metrically regular couplets and the freer rhythms of the chorus exhibit the authentic folk idiom of pulpit and conversation.

In stanza 4 *tinkle* may be *tingel,* as in discolor or stain, or *tinsel* (pronounced *teen-shul,* similar to *tinkle*), suggesting the tawdry brightness which poorly imitates the shine of real silver; in either case, the associated meaning is that of tarnish, debase. Throughout the Old and New Testaments, gold and silver are ambivalent symbols: when sanctified for and by worship, they represent the divine ("The silver is mine, and the gold is mine, saith the Lord of Hosts," Haggai 2:8; the City of God is variously jewelled and of pure gold, Revelation 21:15-21; Exodus 25–30, which describes the Ark of the Covenant, the altar, and furnishings of the Tabernacle); yet they also stand for spiritual barrenness, false gods, and oppressive sin (Exodus 32, in which Aaron, during the absence of Moses, makes a golden calf for worship, a violation of the first commandment; Acts 3:6, "Forasmuch then as we are the offspring of God, we ought not think that the godhead is like unto gold or silver . . . "; Psalms 19:20, "The judgments of the Lord . . . more to be desired are they than gold . . . "; James 5:3, "Your gold and silver is cankered; and the rust of them shall be a witness against you, and shall eat your flesh as it were fire").

God's gettin' worried wid yo' wicked ways

-1-

God settin' happy on his throne
De angel drooped his wings en moan
I'm tired uv yo' wicked ways
I'm tired uv yo' wicked ways
God's gettin' tired uv yo' wicked ways.

-2-

Go down angel en bolt de do'
Dat time whut's been shan't be no mo'
I'm tired uv yo' wicked ways
I'm tired uv yo' wicked ways
God's gettin' tired uv yo' wicked ways.

-3-

Walk in yo' room en fall on yo' knees
It's Lord have mercy ef you please
God's worryin' wid yo' wicked ways
God's worryin' wid yo' wicked ways
God's gettin' worried wid yo' wicked ways.

-4-

Silver shall tinkle en gold shall ruin
God is getting' worried wid yo' wicked doin'
God's worryin' wid yo' wicked ways
God's worryin' wid yo' wicked ways
God is gettin' worried wid yo' wicked way.

-5-

Go to de church en weep en moan
Jes wells ter plead as to stay at home
God's worryin' wid yo' wicked ways
God's worryin' wid yo' wicked ways
God is gettin' worried wid yo' wicked ways.

How long, Jesus?

52

"How long" is the famous biblical cry for vengeance and justice, a favorite phrase of orators and preachers: "How long, O Lord, holy and true, dost thou not judge and avenge our blood on them that dwell on the earth?" (Revelation 6:10). The speaker puts the question to Jesus: How long will you allow the devil his day? Though the encounter with Satan is humorous, as such anecdotes often are in nineteenth-century American folklore, the devil's cruel and coarse joke elicits only weary grief from the beleagured Christian.

How long, Jesus?

-1-

How long, Jesus, how long Jesus
I met de devil t'other day
How long, Jesus, how long Jesus
En whut you reckon de devil say?
How long, Jesus, how long Jesus.

-2-

Dat Jesus wuz dead, en my Lord gone away,
How long, Jesus, how long Jesus
En he wuz jes' back from de funeral dat day.
How long, Jesus, how long Jesus.

Got Jesus in dat lan' where I am bound

This is a vision of the Promised Land, drawn from the prophecies of the New Jerusalem in Revelation and proclaimed with the simple dignity of folk speech. The first stanza is an invitation to join the speaker on his way to Canaan. Stanzas 2 and 3 describe Paradise as freedom from death and sickness. Stanza 4 is a statement of salvation. Stanza 5 summarizes the vision of joy. And stanza 6 offers a last invitation to sinners.

Got Jesus in dat lan' where I am bound

-1-

Come en go to dat Lan'
Come en go to dat Lan'
Come en go to dat Lan'
Come en go to dat Lan' where I am bound.

-2-

Ain't no sickness in dat Lan',
Ain't no sickness in dat Lan',
Ain't no sickness in dat Lan' where I am bound.
Ain't no sickness in dat Lan',
Ain't no sickness in dat Lan' where I am bound.

-3-

No more dyin' in dat Lan',
No more dyin' in dat Lan',
No more dyin' in dat Lan'
where I am bound, where I am bound.
No more dyin' in dat Lan', no more dyin' in dat Lan',
No more dyin' in dat Lan'
where I am bound, where I am bound.

-4-

I got Jesus in dat Lan',
I got Jesus in dat Lan',
I got Jesus in dat Lan'
where I am bound, where I am bound.
I got Jesus in dat Lan', I got Jesus in dat Lan',
I got Jesus in dat Lan' where I am bound.

-5-

Peace en happiness in dat Lan'
where I am bound, where I am bound,
Peace en happiness in dat Lan',
Peace en happiness in dat Lan'
where I am bound, where I am bound,
Peace en happiness in dat Lan',
Peace en happiness in dat Lan'
where I am bound, where I am bound,

-6-

Don't yer want er go to dat Lan'
where I am bound, where I am bound,
Don't yer want er go to dat Lan',
Don't yer want er go to dat Lan'
where I am abound, where I am bound?

He never sed er mumerlin' word

54

Were we suddenly deprived of the great body of American spirituals and told we might save only one, many would name this unblemished folk hymn. Among those songs that lie at the heart of Afro-American folk and Christian experience "Go down, Moses" is a parable of slavery and freedom, "Sometimes I feel like a motherless child" the lyric of exile, "Steal away" the sweet hymn of homecoming, "Deep river" the tragic song of death, and "He never sed er mumerlin' word" the drama of martyrdom.

The speaker is a witness, moved to deep pity and love for "my blessed Lord," a folk term of endearment used for the especially cherished. Each stanza focuses on a separate pain of the Crucifixion and confirms that pity and love, and the central symbolic event of New Testament Christianity is rendered in language so simple, direct, and natural that it could move the stones. Repetition transcends its use as a device for unity and as metrical and verbal reinforcement of theme—it is a cry of compassion uttered over and over: "Not er word, not er word, not er word."

Dock Reed and Earthy Anne Coleman sing "Look how they done my Lord" on volume 5 of the Courlander anthology; on the Lomax Library of Congress recordings it is performed by Vera Hall and Dock Reed as duet and also by Rich Brown.

Also see the very similar "He never said a mumblin' word" as recorded by Work (*American Negro Songs and Spirituals,* 103) and see Rosamond Johnson's arrangement under the title "Crucifixion" (Johnson and Johnson, *The Books of American Negro Spirituals,* 1:174-76).

He never sed er mumerlin' word

-1-

Dey tuck my blessed Lord,
Well, dey tuck my blessed Lord, blessed Lord,
Dy tuck my blessed Lord,
En he never sed er mumerlin' word,
Not er word, not er word, not er word.

-2-

Dey whooped him up de hill,
Well, dey whooped him up de hill, up de hill,
En he never sed er mumerlin' word,
Not er word, not er word, not er word.

-3-

En dey nailed him to de cross,
Well, dey nailed him to de cross, to de cross,
Dey nailed him to de cross,
En he never sed er mumerlin' word,
Not er word, not er word, not er word.

-4-

En dey speared him in de side,
Well, dey speared him in de side, in de side,
Dey speared him in de side,
En he never sed er mumerlin' word,
Not er word, not er word, not er word.

-5-

En de blood come trickerlin' down,
Well, de blood come trickerlin' down, trickerlin' down,
De blood come trickerlin' down,
En he never sed er mumerlin' word,
Not er word, not er word, not er word.

-6-

En he wore dat thorny crown,
Well, he wore dat thorny crown, thorny crown,
He wore dat thorny crown,
En he never sed a mumerlin' word,
Not er word, not er word, not er word.

Hit jes' suits me

A bright jubilee song, which celebrates the joys of religion. Lively meter, half-comic rhymed stanzas, and the folk diction are all appropriate to the real and metaphorical march "around the wall," an allusion to the armies of Joshua at Jericho, also a reference to the nineteenth-century strut performed both in church and on secular occasions. "Three times hidden" may allude to the parable of the hidden talents, or to the concealment of church services from slavemasters, or the "hidden," that is, symbolic, Old Testament prophecies of the Messiah. "Hit jes' suits me" means perfectly agreeable to one's body, sentiments, character, or situation, as a suit of clothes fits the wearer.

The linking of Old and New Testaments here is scriptural as well as poetic. Elijah (1 Kings 17–22, 2 Kings 1–2) prefigures John the Baptist (Luke 1:17; Matthew 11:14; John 1:19-28) in the withdrawal to the wilderness, challenge to the political and ecclesiastical order (for Elijah, Ahab, Jezebel, the priests of Baal, and for John, Herod, Herodias, Salome, the Scribes and Pharisees), passionate preaching of repentance, messianic and/or apocalyptic prophecies, and even in appearance and dress (both wear girdles of animal skins, John eats locusts and wild honey, Elijah is fed by the ravens). However, Elijah is a worker of miracles (including his raising of the widow's son from the dead, as Christ raised Lazarus) while John's role is almost entirely spiritual and moral, a difference evident in the manner of their deaths: John is martyred through beheading, his work finished as the minsitry of Christ begins; Elijah is caught up to heaven by a whirlwind in a chariot of fire, his mantle falling on his successor Elisha. In this song, the contemporary chariot which Elijah boards is "another train" running forever, that is, Elijah foreshadows both John and Christ, and his prophecies are fulfilled in Christ, who, as divinity, never ceases because he is fixed in spiritual time ("never stopped runnin' "). The association of Elijah's death chariot with Ezekiel's apocalyptic chariot is natural; both represent eternity. Ezekiel's prophecies of the destruction of Jerusalem by Nebuchadnezzar of Babylon, the restoration of the Temple, and the coming of a new priesthood and Davidic king are conveyed in poetry marked by dense, exciting images and symbols, none more striking than the vision of the godhead in chapter 1 of his book: a fiery chariot drawn by four brilliant cherubim, each of four wings and four faces, carries the crystal throne of God, whose appearance is that of a burning man; the four wheels are ringed with human eyes and move but do not turn and appear to contain in the middle another wheel, all moving harmoniously, in any direction, according to the spirit of the cherubim. In this text, Ezekiel's wheel is endlessly flowing time in which all "humankind" moves; and the chariots of both Elijah and Ezekiel represent the unbroken line of "dis here religion" by which profession the speaker, a present-day Christian, enters that spiritual realm.

See Byron Arnold, ed., *Folk Songs of Alabama,* 117, and Newman Ivey White, *American Negro Folk Songs,* 98.

Hit jes' suits me

56

-1-

Oh, dis here religion is three times hidden,
En hit jes' suits me.
Dis here religion is three times hidden,
En hit jes' suits me.
Oh, dis here religion is three times hidden.
God said I had it,
En de devil say I didn't,
En hit jes' suits me.

-2-

Oh, come on elders, let's go round de wall,
En hit jes' suits me.
Don't want ter stumble, doan want ter fall,
En hit jes' suits me.
Well, dis here religion is more'n a notion,
It keeps your body in er workin' motion,
En hit jes' suits me.

-3-

Elijah saw 'twas another train comin',
En hit jes' suits me.
Elijah saw 'twas another train comin',
En hit jes' suits me.
Elijah saw 'twas another train er-comin'
He jumped on board, en hit never stopped runnin',
En hit jes' suits me.

-4-

Ezekiel saw dat wheel uv time,
En hit jes' suits me.
Ezekiel saw dat wheel uv time,
En hit jes' suits me.
Ezekiel saw dat wheel uv time,
En every wheel was humankind,
En hit jes' suits me.

Oh John, preaching in the wilderness

A sermon song. Beyond the regularity of meter and rhyme are the immediacy of oral folk speech and the oratorical and rhetorical pulpit—the shouted question, the proverb, the citation of scriptural texts, the emphatic rhythmical *Hallelujah* accompaniment, illustrative biblical figures, and symbols and imagery drawn from both Old and New Testaments. The *I*-voice is the preacher and the song his discourse which is developed around John the Baptizer, his New Testament model with whom he feels an empathetic bond.

The confusion regarding "John" is not limited to the spirituals. Some Christian historians have argued, on the grounds of stylistic similarities and a strong oral-folk tradition, that John the "beloved disciple," son of Zebedee and brother to James, composed the Fourth Gospel and was also the writer of Revelation as well as author of the three epistles of John; others hold that the gospel attributed to John was the work of a later editor and that the John of Patmos was some other person. John the Baptist and John the Revelator were both exiled prophets, one at the beginning of Christ's ministry, the other supposedly during the time of the Domitian persecutions. "John the Divine," that is, the Apostle John, and John the wilderness preacher were martyred—the latter, according to the New Testament, by Herod at the wish of the dancing Salome, the former, according to some oral accounts, murdered on the same day as his brother James, though another tradition claims that John of the Fourth Gospel died peacefully, after digging his own grave, at Ephesus.

The merging here of the three Johns, however, is poetically satisfying: the John of the chorus is clearly the baptizer-wilderness prophet; the appositive "John the Baptist, John Divine" in stanzas 1 and 2 merges the writer of Revelation ("St. John the Divine" in the King James Version superscription) with the baptizer; in stanza 1 the Johns are associated with the Book of Life in Revelation, with the rite of baptism as practiced by John the Baptist, and with the sacrament and theology of baptism as articulated in John and the other gospels, and through the symbolic act of name inscription—here by a finger dipped in the blood of Christ and "pure devine," that is, the blood of the godhead. In stanza 2 the obscure "ladder's claw" may allude to some apocalpytic beast or to heavy Gothic or other ornamental letters which appear in some editions of the Bible at the beginning of books, letters the slave, ironically, could not read but which might resemble a ladder and claw. The tree-fruit analogy appears variously in the gospels as one of the sayings of Christ and still circulates as a folk proverb. The letter of John the Revelator telescopes the Old and New Testaments—"the mighty shoutin' in Galilee" alludes to the Resurrection and the harp-willow tree to the Babylonian exile of the Israelites whose enslavement was so bitter that when their captors required a song, they hung their harps silent on willow trees (Psalm 137:1-4), an image that would not have been unnoticed by the American slave.

58

Oh John, preachin' in the wilderness

-1-

Oh, John the Baptis', John Devine,
Who gonna write dis name uv mine?
Dey ain't gonna write hit wid pen uv brass
Dey ain't gonna write hit wid pen uv gold,
Dip my finger in my Jesus blood,
Write my name in pure devine.

-Chorus-

Oh John, halleluiah,
Oh John, preachin' in de wil'erness.

-2-

Oh, John de Baptis', John Devine,
Who gonna write dis name uv mine?
Read hit down by de ladder's claw,
Angels gonna lock de lion's jaw.
Read down fudder, you'll find hit dere.
Judge de tree by de fruit hit bear.

-Chorus-

Oh John, halleluiah,
Oh John, preachin' in de wil'erness.

-3-

John wrote er letter t'other day,
Whut yer reckon dat letter say?
Hang my harp on de willer tree,
Heer'd er mighty shoutin' in Galilee.

-Chorus-

Oh John, halleluiah,
Oh John, preachin' in de wil'erness.

I ain't going to lay my religion down

To "lay it down" is, in Southern folk speech, to be done with something, to give up after long struggle. The chorus, a negative statement of affirmation, summarizes the theological and evangelical argument, and in its emphasis on the "bold" religious stance of the speaker, unites the disparate subjects of the stanzas. The "tallest tree" stanza, a theme current also in white religious and secular folk song, functions as the salvation reference point. Stanza 2 gleefully relates the image of a "grumberlin' " Satan chained in hell. Stanzas 3 and 4, a brief sermon on the evils of riches as opposed to the New Testament "pure religion and undefiled" (James 1:27), contains the germ of social protest. And stanza 5 confirms the speaker's state of salvation. The rhymed couplets are expanded to quatrains by the intervention of the antiphonal response. Note the contrast between the stanzaic regularity and the heightened folk speech of the chorus.

I ain't gonna lay my religion down

-Chorus-
No, no, no, no, my Lord,
I ain't gonna lay my 'ligion down.
No, no, no, no, my Lord,
I ain't gonna lay my 'ligion down.

-1-
Well, de tallest tree in er Paradise,
I ain't gonna lay my 'ligion down.
Well, de Christian call it dat tree of life,
I ain't gonna lay my 'ligion down.

-Chorus-
No, no, no, no, my Lord,
I ain't gonna lay my 'ligion down.
No, no, no, no, my Lord,
I ain't gonna lay my 'ligion down.

-2-
I wonder what Satan grumberlin' 'bout,
I ain't gonna lay my 'ligion down.
Well, he's chained in Hell, en he can't come out,
I ain't gonna lay my 'ligion down.

-Chorus-
No, no, no, no, my Lord,
I ain't gonna lay my 'ligion down.
No, no, no, no, my Lord,
I ain't gonna lay my 'ligion down.

-3-
If 'ligion was a thing money could buy,
I ain't gonna lay my 'ligion down.
Well, de rich would live, en do po' would die,
I ain't gonna lay my 'ligion down.

-4-
Ef de rich don't pray, to Hell dey'll go,
I ain't gonna lay my 'ligion down.
En de devil gonna get 'em, I'm pretty sho,
I ain't gonna lay my 'ligion down.

-5-
Want er know de reason I walk so bold?
I ain't gonna lay my 'ligion down.
Well, I got Jesus all in my soul,
I ain't gonna lay my 'ligion down.

They cannot crown my Lord 'til I get there

60

Poetic conventions, metrical and stanzaic structure, content, language, and the mood of reflection all strongly suggest the nineteenth-century sentimental hymn in which the prevailing subject, death, is presented in stock metaphors and diction. The pilgrim journeys to the "other shore," the "beautiful land" which he reaches "when the sun goeth down," where we "never grow old," and there are "stars in my crown." Cloying, tasteless, aesthetically inferior though these may be, in performance their hackneyed figurative language gains new life from thousands of voices singing "sweet on a bright Sabbath morning," and this song is like its kindred—full of tender yearning and touching faith, with even a bit of laughter in its image of the Christian hitching on angel wings for the first time.

They cannot crown my Lord 'til I get there

-1-

I was thinking of this life,
How we must take time en die
En go marchin' thru eternity,
Some have left here yesterday,
Some are on their way today,
But they cannot crown my Lord
'Til I get there.
'Til I get there,
'Til I get there.

-2-

Some have laid their burdens down,
En I still have mine to bear,
But they cannot crown my Lord
'Til I get there.
'Til I get there,
'Til I get there.

-3-

Some are old en some are blind,
Some haven't even got er dime,
But they sing en pray en cry all de time,
But one mornin' bright en fair
Hitch my wings en try de air,
But they cannot crown my Lord
'Til I get there.
'Til I get there,
'Til I get there.

-4-

I was thinking of a friend
Who just left the other day
And has gone to that other shore,
But one thing that makes me smile,
They have left us on this side,
But they cannot crown my Lord
'Til I get there.
'Til I get there,
'Til I get there.

Jerdan is so chilly and cold

Here is a gathering of recurrent metaphors and the language of pulpit and the Bible, yet not so much a mixed bag after all. The gambler and the Christian, the river Jordan and the glory train, the miry clay of sin and the rock of eternal life, the miracles of Christ and a home in heaven—all are united by the theme of salvation and by the "Jerden" (a common folk pronunciation still in use) symbol of the chorus.

Jordan is a scared river associated with miracles of healing and the passage of the Israelites into the Promised Land, and also with New Testament baptism. Elijah smites Jordan's waters with his cloak so he and his successor Elisha may cross on dry ground shortly before Elijah's ascent to heaven (2 Kings 2:8); Naaman, commander of the Syrian armies, is healed of his leprosy by Elisha who sends him to bathe in Jordan seven times (2 Kings 5); in the Book of Joshua, which narrates the conquest of Canaan and the fulfillment of the hope for the Promised Land, the Israelites and their priests, who bear the Ark of the Covenant, pass over Jordan on dry land, as under Moses they crossed the Red Sea, and Joshua sets a memorial of twelve stones in the places where the feet of the priests stood; and John baptizes converts and Jesus in Jordan (Matthew 3:7-17). Such scriptural references led to the symbolism of Jordan as the unfathomable mystery of death, the passage from earthly life to the new, eternal life of the spirit: the coldness of its waters parallel the coldness of physical death which is countered by the faith of the believer ("I got Jesus all in my soul"); the shoe motif may allude to John the Baptist who said "There cometh one mightier than I after me, the latchet of whose shoes I am not worthy to stoop down and unloose" (Mark 1:7), and bears comparison with Exodus 3:5 in which God tells Moses to take off his shoes, "for the place whereon thou standest is holy ground" (that is, the site of the burning bush which burns but is not consumed and which signifies the presence of God).

Note in stanza 3 the lovely imge of an invisible soul singing as it goes home over Jordan.

62

Jerden is so chilly and cold

-1-

Stoop down Jonas en untie my shoe, untie my shoe,
Stoop down Jonas en untie my shoe,
Got ter go to Jerden by myself, by myself,
Jerden is so chilly en cold, chilly en cold.

-Chorus-

Jerden is so chilly en cold, chilly en cold.
Jerden is so chilly en cold, chilly en cold.
Jerden is so chilly en cold.
I got Jesus all in my soul, in my soul.

-2-

Got ter go to Jerden by myself, by myself,
Got ter go to Jerden by myself, by myself,
Well, I doan want no gambler to bury me, bury me.
Well, I doan want no gambler to bury me, bury me.

-3-

I'm goin' home on de mornin' train.
I'm goin' home on de mornin' train.
You won't see me, but you'll hear me sing, hear me sing.
Jerden is so chilly en cold, chilly en cold.
Jerden is so chilly en cold, chilly en cold.

-4-

My Lord ain't no lyin' God, lyin' God,
My Lord ain't no lyin' God.
My Lord did jes' whut he said, whut he said,
My Lord did jes' whut he said—
Heal de sick en raise de dead, raised de dead.

-5-

Took my sin en give me grace, give me grace,
Took my sin en give me grace,
Took my sin en give me grace.
Took my feet out de mirin' clay, mirin' clay,
Took my feet out de mirin' clay,
Took my feet out de mirin' clay,
Placed dem on de rocks of eternitay, eternitay.

-Chorus-

Oh Jerden is so chilly en cold, chilly en cold.
Oh Jerden is so chilly en cold.
Jerden is so chilly en cold, chilly en cold.
I got Jesus all in my soul.

Let dat liar erlone

The villainous liar, usually in company with other assorted sinners, turns up in a song of his very own. The comic stanzas derive from versified folk orations, but the portrait of the liar, a born troublemaker kin to the hypocrite, is right on target. The odd little train of the first stanza harks back to Anglo-American mumming performances which conclude with a request for reward, usually food and drink. Liza Witt sings a gospel "Liar" on the Lomax recordings from Sumter County.

Let dat liar erlone

-1-

I come ter yo' house lac er train on de track,
Give me little meal, I got ter hurry back.
Ef you doan wan' ter git in trouble
Let dat liar erlone.

-2-

Er liar en er hypocrit keeps up er fuss,
Both is bad, but de liar am wuss.
Ef you doan wan' ter git in trouble,
Let dat liar erlone.

-3-

He will tell sich er lie 'twill spize yo' mind.
He will mix er little truth ter make hit shine.
Ef you doan wan' ter git in trouble,
Let dat liar erlone.

-4-

Stop en let me tell yer whut dat liar will do,
He'll always come wid sumpin' new.
Ef you doan wan' ter git in trouble,
Let dat liar erlone.

-5-

He will bring you news 'bout women en men.
Ter make you fall out wid yo' bosom frien'.
Ef you doan wan' ter git in trouble,
Let dat liar erlone.

Little black train is comin'

64

"Little black train" is a famous spiritual which has entered choral concert and jazz repertories as well as Kurt Weil's folk opera *Down in the Valley*. The story of "good King Hezekiah" (here "Keziah") is told in 2 Kings 20: the "message" delivered by Isaiah from God is, "Set thine house in order; for thou shalt die, and not live" (20:1). Hezekiah "turned his face to the wall, and prayed" that God remember "I have walked before thee in truth and with a perfect heart" (20:2-3). God is moved to revoke the decree and Isaiah heals the king with figs (20:4-7). This parable of imminent death, judgment, and healing, related in a terse folk idiom, is oddly though naturally juxtaposed with the contemporary railroad, the symbolic "black train" of death. See Mary Alice Grissom, *The Negro Sings a New Heaven* (Chapel Hill: University of North Carolina Press, 1930) 10, for didactic and preaching stanzas; also see White, *American Negro Folk Songs,* 65, for another Alabama text. Line 2 of stanza 3 is obscure; the allusion may be to the king of Assyria who is besieging the Israelites.

Little black train is comin'

-1-

Oh, de little black train is a-comin'
Hit'll git yo' bizness right.
Better fix yo' house in order,
Kaze hit may be here tonight.

-Chorus-

Oh, de little black train's er comin',
Hit's comin' round de curve,
It's puffin' en hit's blowin',
Hit's strainin' every nerve.

-2-

God sent Keziah a message,
A message from on high,
Better git his bizness fixed all right
Kaze hit may be here tonight.

-3-

Keziah turned t' de wall a-weepin'
He seed king in Caaz,
He got his bizness fixed all right,
He gave him fifteen years.

-Chorus-

Oh, de little black train's er comin',
Hit's comin' round de curve,
It's puffin' en hit's blowin',
En hit's strainin' every nerve.

Rock my soul in de bosom of Abraham

The New Testament story of the rich man (called "Dives" after the Vulgate translation of the adjective *rich*) and the beggar Lazarus (Luke 16:19-31) has had wide appeal for impoverished masses who have seen in it grim justice and hope for the rectification of their suffering. In Afro-American folk religious tradition, the parable is given expression by hundreds of sermons and folk narratives and many spirituals, particularly the Lazarus-Dives ballad and this famous "rocking" chorus to which various migratory stanzas are attached.

Rock has numerous imagistic associations: the rhythms of lullaby which croon the child to sleep, as here the soul, the child of Christ, is clasped to the bosom of the guardian Abraham; the swaying movements of worshippers; the reeling and rocking of Noah's ark, and by extension the stormy tumult of conversion from sin; and the analogical sexual connotation in blues and other secular folk music.

Lomax recorded an extraordinary performance of "Rocky my soul" from Richard Brown in Sumter County which points up the startling differences between folk and concert styles. (Brown-Owens, *Toting the Lead Row,* 30-32, briefly relates the recording session, and includes some of Rich's text along with a photograph of Rich and John Lomax.) See also the version of this chorus offered by Allen, Ware, and Garrison, *Slave Songs of the United States,* 73.

Rock my soul in de bosom of Abraham

Well, rock er my soul in de bosom of Abraham,
Rock er my soul in de bosom of Abraham,
Rock er my soul in de bosom of Abraham,
O, de rock er my soul.

Ole Satan is er liar en er conjurer, too,
Oh, de rock er my soul.
Ef you don't mind he'll conjure you.
Oh, de rock er my soul.

O, rock er my soul in de bosom of Abraham,
Rock er my soul in de bosom of Abraham,
Rock er my soul in de bosom of Abraham,
O, de rock er my soul.

Rough, rocky road, en you 'most done travelin'

66

The Christian pilgrim is bound for heaven, not only in the sense of being on his way, but of necessity, of a surety; that is, his faith and salvation in Christ can lead nowhere but heaven. Consider the strange image of a soul carrying a soul and the subtle contrast between the solid rock of his assurance in Christ, whereon his name appears as on a gravestone, and the troublesome rocks of his journey. The alliterative quality, the syntactical *in medias res,* the idiomatic "most done" (almost finished with some task), and caesural balance, create a mood of quiet victory, and these are the outpourings of a hard-pressed soul finally, blessedly almost home. See Johnson and Johnson, *The Books of American Negro Spirituals,* 2:140, for a related song, "Mos' done toilin' here"; also see White, *American Negro Folk Songs,* 112, for another Alabama text.

Rough, rocky road, en you 'most done travelin'

-1-

Oh, de rough rocky road, en u'm most done travelin',
De rough rocky road, en u'm most done travelin',
Oh, de rough rocky road, en u'm most done travelin',
U'm bound to carry my soul to de Lord,
Bound to carry my soul to my Lord,
Bound to carry my soul to my Jesus.

-2-

Oh, my name is written on de solid rock,
My name is written on de solid rock,
Oh, my name is written on de solid rock,
I'm gwine home to live wid my God forever,
Gwine home to live wid my God forever.

-3-

Oh, I'm bound to live in my Jesus' home,
I'm bound to live in my Jesus' home,
Oh, I'm bound to live in my Jesus' home,
Gwine home to live with my God forever.

Oh, I'm bound to carry my soul to Jesus,
I'm bound to carry my soul to Jesus,
Oh, I'm bound to carry my soul to Jesus,
My name is written in de solid rock.

-4-

Oh, de rough rocky road, en u'm most done travelin',
De rough rocky road, en u'm most done travelin',
Oh, de rough rocky road, en u'm most done travelin',
En u'm bound to carry my soul to de Lord.

Stay in de field 'til de war is ended

Compare "Fightin' for de City" and "Been in the war so long," above. The rhymed couplets of the stanzas exhibit the conventional metaphors, images, and diction of Afro-American salvation and heaven songs while the lovely chorus has the quality of recitative and long pulpit cadence. The intervening choral tag expands the couplet to a quatrain and skillfully relates the war metaphor of the chorus to the migratory stanzas.

See also the song "about dat gospel war," "Die in de fiel'," in Johnson and Johnson, *The Books of American Negro Spirituals,* 1:68-69.

Stay in de field 'til de war is ended

-Chorus-
I'm gwine er stay in de field, ole warrior,
I'm gwine er stay in de field,
I'm gwine er stay in de field,
Until de war is ended.

-1-
When I gets to heaven, set right down,
Until de war is ended,
Ax my Lord fer a starry crown,
Until de war is ended.

-2-
Oh, I will never fergit dat day,
Until de war is ended,
When Jesus washed my sins away,
Until de war is ended.

-3-
Oh, when I gets to heaven, gonna talk en tell,
'Til de war is ended,
How I did shun dem gates uv hell,
'Til de war is ended.

-4-
See dat hypocrit settin' dere,
'Til de war is ended,
You tetch dat hypocrit ef you dare,
Until de war is ended.

-Chorus-
I'm gwine stay in de field,
Stay in de field, ole warrior,
Stay in de field, ole warrior,
Until the war is ended.

Time is windin' up

68

This is a forceful, brilliant song of the Apocalypse. Time on earth is "windin' up," almost finished (in the sense of rewinding thread on a spool) but the last days of destruction will be followed by a new Heaven and new Earth, the inauguration of a new time (as a clock is wound up and set in motion again). Deepening the paradox is the twin image of the hand of God and the hand of the clock. The gambler stands for all sinners who are warned of Judgment, and "Lord, have mercy," the liturgical phrase sprinkled throughout sermons, prayers, and congregational responses, becomes a litany of confession and petition.

Liza Witt and Betty Moore recorded for Lomax a very fine performance which vocally evokes the terror of the Day of Wrath. In 1950 Harold Courlander recorded two songs with very similar apocalyptic themes: "This may be your last time" and "It's getting late in the evening," both duets by Rich Amerson and Earthy Anne Coleman (see *Negro Songs from Alabama,* 34-35, 38-40).

Time is windin' up

-1-

Time, time, time is windin' up,
Time, time, time is windin' up.
Oh, destruction in dis lan',
God's done moved his han',
En time is windin' up.

-2-

Go tell dat gambler time is windin' up,
Go tell dat gambler time is windin' up,
Oh, destruction in dis lan',
God's done moved his han',
En time is a-windin' up.

-3-

Lord have mercy, time is windin' up,
Lord have mercy, time is windin' up,
Oh, destruction in dis lan',
God's done moved his han',
En time is windin' up.

Traverlin' shoes

Comfortable shoes were a rarity for the slave. In a famous spiritual, the redeemed shouts that all God's children will one day "walk all over God's heab'n" in glory shoes. (See verse 4 of "All God's chillun got wings," Johnson and Johnson, *The Books of American Negro Spirituals,* 1:71-73; and verse 3 of "Goin' to shout all over God's heav'n," John Work, *American Negro Songs and Spirituals,* 180.) Here too shoes are transcendent, symbols of salvation and Christian practice, fit for travelling to the other world.

The stanzas present a small Everyman drama. Death summons first the Gambler, emblem of all unconverted sinners, but he has not the sturdy shoes of faith and salvation, and then the Preacher, representative of the redeemed Christian who is "willin' to go," a phrase that connotes an affirmative, realistic attitude: though the Christian fears death, he accepts it with the strength born from his disciplined exercise of virtue and from his salvation experience. The dialogue of the three folk characters is cast in the folk conversational mode, while the walking rhythms of the chorus are evangelical and didactic in style and content.

Vera Hall performed "Travellin' shoes" and Dock Reed and Vera Hall sang a duet version of "You got shoes, I got shoes" or "Going to shout all over God's heaven" for the Harold Courlander anthology (two of the sixty-seven songs Courlander elected to also include in his *Negro Songs from Alabama,* 40, 56). Fanny and Peggy Lou Herod gave Frederick Ramsey a variant of "Travellin' shoes" of more extended development for his *Music from the South.*

Traverlin' shoes

-1-

I got no, I got no,
 I got no traverlin' shoes.
I got no, I got no,
 Lord, I got no traverlin' shoes.

Well, you better get yo' traverlin' shoes,
Well, you better get yo' traverlin' shoes,
Well, you better get yo' traverlin' shoes,
 Lord, you better get yo' traverlin' shoes.

-2-

Well, Death went over to dat Gambler's home,
Gambler come en go wid me,
 Come en go wid me,
 Come en go wid me.
Dat gambler said "I'm not willin' to go,
 Caze I go no traverlin' shoes."

I got no, got no, got no,
 I got no traverlin' shoes.
Got no, got no, got no traverlin' shoes.

-3-

Well, Death went over to de preacher's home,
Preacher come en go wid me,
 Come en go,
 Come en go.
Dat preacher said, "I'm willin' to go,
 Caze I got on my traverlin' shoes."
Got my, got my,
 Got on my traverlin' shoes.

Walk in Jerusalem jes' lac John

70

Jerusalem is the holy, eternal city envisioned in the Book of Revelation: to "walk in Jerusalem jes lac John" (the Revelator) is to experience Christian immortality. The "ready" motif of the chorus is derived from the discourses of Christ on the "last days" and final judgment ("Therefore, be ye also ready; for in such an hour as ye think not the Son of man cometh," Matthew 24:44). As witnesses of the death and resurrection of Lazarus and of Christ, Mary and Martha stand for the salvation and eternal life made possible by the crucifixion. The children of Moses, now at home in the New Jerusalem, are "all dressed in red," a color suggested by their miraculous passage through the Red Sea and, more importantly, by the blood of the lamb sprinkled on the doorposts as a token of their exemption from the last plague brought on the Egyptians, that is, the slaughter of the firstborn; the subsequent institution of the Passover which commemorates the deliverance and freedom of the Israelites in the Feast of the Unleavened Bread and the sacrifice of the Paschal Lamb prefigures the Crucifixion and the rite of the Last Supper ("For even Christ, our passover, is sacrificed for us," 1 Corinthians 5:7; "Behold the Lamb of God, who taketh away the sin of the world," John 1:29; and Matthew 26:17-28; Luke 22:7-20; Mark 14:12-26). Thus, by means of these allusions to the Old and New Testaments, the song is theologically correct and poetically unified; moreover, it resonates with a powerful epic sweep from the time of Moses to Christ to the present and into the eternity of the New Jerusalem.

This is a jubilee hymn of pleasant melody often performed in concert. See Johnson and Johnson's version, "Walk in Jerusalem jus' like John," *The Books of American Negro Spirituals,* 2:58-59.

Walk in Jerusalem jes' lac John

-Chorus-
Lord, I wants to be ready,
I wants to be ready,
I wants to be ready,
To walk in Jerusalem jes' lac John.

-1-
Don't sing en pray yo'self away,
Walk in Jerusalem jes' lac John.
Mary weep, en Martha moan,
Walk in Jerusalem jes' lac John.

-Chorus-
Lord, I wants to be ready,
I wants to be ready,
I wants to be ready,
To walk in Jerusalem jes' lac John.

-2-
Well, who was dem yonder all dressed in red?
Walkin' in Jerusalem jes' lac John.
Well, dey looks lac de chillun dat Moses led.
Walkin' in Jerusalem jes' lac John.

-Chorus-
Well, I wants to be ready,
I wants to be ready,
I wants to be ready,
To walk in Jerusalem jes' lac John.

We gonna have a good time bimeby

For *bimeby* read *bye-and-bye* (by-and-by), an American folk designation for an inexact time beyond the future. *Way* extends the temporal dimensions to eternity. Compare "In the Sweet By and By" ("There's a land that is fairer than day") from white Protestant hymnody.

The joys of reunion in Paradise are figured by the happenings of daily life and an Old Testament allusion, the chorus animated by the secular "gonna have a good time. The "mother" of stanza 1 is preeminent in the roll call of relatives. "Jacob's ladder"—which topic has several songs of its own—is drawn from Jacob's vision of angels descending and ascending a ladder to heaven (Genesis 28:10-15) during which God blesses him with land and descendants. "Border land" suggests the imminence of death, as if the speaker stood at the very edge of his translation to the spiritual sphere. Stanzas 4 and 5 contrast *howdy* and *good-bye,* pointing to the timelessness of heaven where there are no farewells, only greetings, a persistent theme in both Christian hymnody and in the spirituals. Throughout, folk speech has become the language of Christian hope. That the chorus is the archetypal song is indicated here by the obvious dependence of the couplet on the two successive lines in each quatrain. Evidently Mrs. Tartt was aware of the flexible position of the chorus, for she was careful to record the order of occurrence in actual performance. See Byron Arnold, *Folk Songs of Alabama,* 161, for another Alabama version. Also see the "bye-and-bye" theme in two versions with that title in John Work, *American Negro Songs and Spirituals,* 63, 228.

We gonna have a good time bimeby

-Chorus-

Way bimeby, we gonna have a good time,
Way bimeby, way bimeby.
Way bimeby, we gonna have a good time,
Way bimeby, way bimeby.

-1-

Will meet my mother dere,
Meet my mother dere,
And we gonna have a good time,
Way bimeby.

-2-

Well, I'm clim'in' up Jacob's ladder,
Clim'in' Jacob's ladder,
And we gonna have a good time,
Way bimeby.

-3-

Well, I'm livin' on border lan',
I'm livin' on border lan'.
Lord, we gonna have a good time,
Way bimeby.

-4-

Well, hit's always howdy dere,
Hit's always howdy dere.
Lord, we gonna have a good time,
Way bimeby.

-5-

Well, hit's never good-bye in heaven,
Hit's never good-bye in heaven.
Lord, we gonna have a good time,
Way bimeby.

Wouldn't mind dyin' if dyin' wuz all

72

In Afro-American religious folk song death may be the road to eternal life, but the human fears of its terrors are squarely faced. The first stanza focuses on its utter loneliness while in stanza 2 death is imaged as a violent seizure ("got you" is a phrase used in ghost "jump stories" such as "Bloody Bones" or "Big Toe" and in children's chase games, connoting the sudden capture of an unsuspecting of fleeing victim), and the speaker dreads "standing the test," the final "weighing in the balances" (Daniel 5:27). In stanza 3 the folk idiom "got ter see a king" counters the awful solemnity of Judgment Day with the casualness of ordinary life, as if facing the ruler of the universe were the same as "got to see" a fellow about thus and such. Stanza 4, borrowed from the Ezekiel song, appears unrelated to the other stanzas, but the speaker's vision of death and judgment occurs in the very kingdom of Ezekiel's divine chariot, and the ancient prophet and the speaker coexist in spiritual and poetic time. In any spiritual there is at least one line which leaps off the page and lays hold of the heart—"I wouldn't mind dyin' if dyin' was all," a plain folk statement, which in its very ordinariness sharply calls up the image of those who, with a last breath, reach for a steadying, comforting hand.

Wouldn't mind dyin' ef dyin' wuz all

-1-

Wouldn't mind dyin', but I gotter go by myself,
Wouldn't mind dyin', but I gotter go by myself,
Wouldn't mind dyin', but I gotter go by myself,
Well, I wouldn't mind dyin' ef dyin' wuz all.

-2-

After death got you, got to stand a test,
After death got you, got to stand a test,
After death got you, got to stand a test,
Well, I wouldn't mind dyin' ef dyin' wuz all.

-3-

By en by, got ter see a king,
By en by, got ter see a king,
By en by, got ter see a king,
Well, I wouldn't mind dyin' ef dyin' wuz all.

-4-

Ezekiel saw a wheel way in middle of a wheel,
Ezekiel saw a wheel way in middle of a wheel,
Ezekiel saw a wheel way in middle of a wheel,
Well, I wouldn't mind dyin' ef dyin' wuz all.

Rocky, chillun

The extent to which spirituals were used as secret codes by slave brotherhoods, especially insurrectionary ones, may never be known. Mrs. Tartt's note does not say whether the "night meetings" were social, political, or both, but textual evidence points to origins in "reeling and rocking" spiritual or play party which borrowed a tag from religious folk song. *Rock* has both secular and religious associations— "rock, chariot" of the spirituals and "rock me, mama" in blues. *Chillun* is a designation for both young ones and Christians, as in "God's chillun." "Pull de root," "turn yo' right side," "turn yo' lef' side," and "turn yo' face" are dance calls or ring-game instructions.

Compare "Rock of Jubilee" (Allen-Ware-Garrison, *Slave Songs of the United States,* #33, p. 25) of similar theme and similar "calls" and/or "instructions."

Ricky, chillun

This one they danced by at night meetings.

-1-
Rocky, chillun, rocky, Jesus comin'
Rocky, chillun, rocky, Jesus comin'
Comin' in de mornin', Jesus comin'
Comin' in de mornin', Jesus comin'.

-2-
Pull de root, chillun, Jesus comin'
Pull de root, chillun, Jesus comin'
Turn yo' right side ter me, Jesus comin'
Jesus comin', comin' in de mornin'.

-3-
Pull de root, chillun, Jesus comin'
Pull de root, chillun, Jesus comin'
Turn yo' lef' side ter me, Jesus comin'
Jesus comin', comin' in de mornin'.

-4-
Pull de root, chillun, Jesus comin'
Pull de root, chillun, Jesus comin'
Turn yo' face ter me, Jesus comin'
Jesus comin', comin' in de mornin'.

Job, oh Job

74

With the story of Job the slave could all too readily identify. As the emblem of suffering Job appears everywhere in Afro-American folk religious literature, song, and sermon. The Library of Congress recordings show that the Job song was highly developed in Sumter County, and this text, in structure, dramatic development of subject and theme, and musical and poetic qualities, is unmatched by any other song-sermon in the collection.

Each section presents a dialogue between four speakers—the messenger of the disasters, the speaker-interlocutor, Job himself, and the congregational voice which chants response—and each stanza repeats the first save for the varying of the substantive: cattle, daughters, oxen, servants. Again the hero is "old" Job, one well and affectionately known, the folk nickname imparting immediacy and sympathy. The idiomatic "What you reckon?" is answered by the poetry of the King James Bible, "Blessed be the name of the Lord," the phrase which sets the story of Job beyond an ordinary test of faith into the realm of tragedy. The marvelous "Rock Mount Zion" chorus appears to bear little relationship to the stanzas, but the migratory stanza functions both as the cry of Job, exemplar of the Christian tragic paradox, and of the congregation who also suffer and still believe.

See also "New verses to Job, oh Job," below. All the performances of the Job song that Lomax recorded bear out Mrs. Tartt's note on the manuscript—"Beautiful." A variation of the Job song was recorded by Harold Courlander, as sung by Rich Amerson and Earthy Anne Coleman ("Job, Job," *Negro Songs from Alabama,* 24, 28, Folkways disc FE4472; also Dock and Vera's duet of the Job song, Folkways disc FA2038 and FE4473; and see Courlander, *Negro Folk Music U.S.A.,* 52-56, for text and comment).

Job, oh Job

-1-
Oh Job, oh Job, uh-huh,
Your cattle is dead, uh-huh,
Oh what you reckon, uh-huh,
Old Job said, uh-huh,
Oh the Lord giveth, uh-huh,
And he taketh away, uh-huh,
Blessed be, uh-huh,
The name of the Lord, uh-huh.

-Chorus-
Oh rock Mount Zion
Rock Mount Zion
Rock Mount Zion in the morning,
I wanter go to heaven
Wanter go to heaven
I wanter go to heaven in the morning,
Swing low chariot
Swing low chariot
Swing low chariot in the morning.

-2-
Oh Job, oh Job, uh-huh,
Your daughter 's dead, uh-huh,
Oh what you reckon, uh-huh,
Old Job said, uh-huh,
Oh the Lord giveth, uh-huh,
And he taketh away, uh-huh,
Blessed be, uh-huh,
The name of the Lord, uh-huh.

-Chorus-
Oh rock Mount Zion
Rock Mount Zion /etc./

-3-
Oh Job, oh Job, uh-huh,
Your oxen 's dead, uh-huh,
Oh what you reckon, uh-huh,
Old Job said, uh-huh,
Oh the Lord giveth, uh-huh,
And he taketh away, uh-huh,
Blessed be, uh-huh,
The name of the Lord, uh-huh.

-Chorus-
Oh rock Mount Zion
Rock Mount Zion /etc./

-4-
Oh Job, oh Job, uh-huh,
Your servants 's dead, uh-huh,
Oh what you reckon, uh-huh,
Old Job said, uh-huh,
Oh the Lord giveth, uh-huh,
And he taketh away, uh-huh,
Blessed be, uh-huh,
The name of the Lord, uh-huh.

-Chorus-
Oh rock Mount Zion
Rock Mount Zion /etc./

Tell me, Job

76

This is a sermon-song indebted to the narrative and dramatic framework of "Job, oh Job," the "Were you there?" motif of the Crucifixion spirituals, and the catalog of punishments from "He never sed a mumerlin' word." Like "Job, oh Job" this sermon-song is structured by dialogue, here the antiphony of the interlocutor and Job. As in "He never sed a mumerlin' word" Christ is "my blessed Lord" and Job's "I wuz dere" has been substituted for "not er word." Job's presence at the Crucifixion is correct in doctrine and interesting as poetry: spiritual reality does not participate in measurable, historical time, and Job's own sufferings surely make him a compassionate witness.

Tell me, Job

-1-

Tell me, Job, tell me where wuz you
When dey tuck my blessed Lord?
Job says, "I wuz dere," Job says, "I wuz dere."
"I wuz dere, I wuz dere,
When dey tuck my blessed Lord."
Job says, "I wuz dere."

-2-

Tell me, Job, tell me where wuz you
When dey whooped him up de hill?
Job says, "I wuz dere," Job says, "I wuz dere."
"I wuz dere, I wuz dere,
When dey whooped him up de hill."
Job says, "I wuz dere."

-3-

Tell me, Job, tell me where wuz you
When dey nailed him to de cross?
Job says, "I wuz dere," Job says, "I wuz dere."
"I wuz dere, I wuz dere,
When dey nailed him to de cross."
Job says, "I wuz dere."

-4-

Tell me, Job, tell me where wuz you
When dey blopped him in de face?
Job says, "I wuz dere," Job says, "I wuz dere."
"I wuz dere, I wuz dere,
When dey blopped him in de face."
Job says, "I wuz dere."

-5-

Tell me, Job, tell me where wuz you
When dey speared him in de side?
Job says, "I wuz dere," Job says, "I wuz dere."
"I wuz dere, I wuz dere,
When dey speared him in de side."
Job says, "I wuz dere."

Live tergether, little chillen

While it is possible that "gwiner j'ine de ban' " has reference to the insurrectionary slave brotherhoods, the subject of the song places it well within the tradition of the salvation folk hymn in which Christian practices—praying, singing, weeping, moaning—are enumerated: the "band" is also that of Christian brethren on their journey to the Promised Land.

See "Walk together children," Johnson and Johnson, *The Books of American Negro Spirituals,* 2:180-82. Also compare the very similar "Children, do linger" ("O member, will you linger?") in Allen-Ware-Garrison, *Slave Songs of the United States,* 51.

Live tergether, little chillen

Sung at night to children in slavery times.

Pray tergether, little chillen, I'm gwiner j'ine de ban'.
  Little chillen, I'm gwiner j'ine de ban'.

Sing tergether, little chillen, I'm gwiner j'ine de ban'.
  Little chillen, I'm gwiner j'ine de ban'.

Weep tergether, little chillen, I'm gwiner j'ine de ban'.
  Little chillen, I'm gwiner j'ine de ban'.

Moan tergether, little chillen, I'm gwiner j'ine de ban'.
  Little chillen, I'm gwiner j'ine de ban'.

Live tergether, little chillen, I'm gwiner j'ine de ban'.
  Little chillen, I'm gwiner j'ine de ban'.

Don't you be uneasy

78

This is a fragment of the longer "Jesus gonna make up my dying bed" (which see, below). Mrs. Tartt's manuscript notes that it was sung by "A. A. Anderson, Shiloh Zion Church, Boyd, Ala."—the single instance in all Mrs. Tartt's collection of spirituals where an informant is named.

Dock Reed sings a similar song on the Lomax recordings for the Library of Congress. Also Harold Courlander recorded a version sung by Dock Reed, with the title "Jesus going to make up my dying bed" and the first line "Oh don't you worry 'bout me dyin' " (*Negro Songs from Alabama,* 49). John Work collected at least two songs on the "don't be uneasy" theme: "When I'm dead (don't you grieve after me)" and "O mother, don't you weep (when I am gone)" (*American Negro Songs and Spirituals,* both on 119).

(Note: The manuscript title reads *Don't,* despite the *doan* of the text.)

Don't you be uneasy

-Chorus-

Oh, doan you be uneasy,
Oh, doan you be uneasy,
Oh, doan you be uneasy,
Jesus gonna make up my dyin' bed.

-1-

Oh, when I am er dyin',
I don't want nobody to moan.
All I want yer to do fer me
Is jes' give dat bell a tone.

-Chorus-

Den I'll be crossin' over,
I'll be crossin' over,
Den I'll be crossin' over.
Jesus gonna make up my dyin' bed.

-2-

Oh, when I'm dyin'
I doan want nobody to cry.
All I wants yer to do fer me
Is to close my dyin' eye.

-Chorus-

Oh, I will be sleepin' in Jesus,
I will be sleepin' in Jesus,
Oh, I will be sleepin' in Jesus.
Jesus gonna make up my dyin' bed.

Move de member

"Move de member" is a "reelin' and rockin' " spiritual of impeccable balance achieved through subtly varied repetition within the individual stanzas and from one stanza to the next. Each stanza focuses on a conventional symbol of immortal life in heaven—"rockin' shoes," "white robe," and "starry crown." "Move" signifies both joyful religious experience and the close bond of "members" with each other and with Christ. Why Daniel, the Old Testament prophet who interpreted dreams? Perhaps for reasons of rhythm, or because Daniel was a favorite folk figure, or because his visionary qualities are appropriate for ecstatic worship.

Compare "You got ter move" (above). The Rosie Hibler family sings "Move members move" on the Courlander recording series (transcription included in his *Negro Songs from Alabama,* 11-12), and Mary Jane Travis and her family sang it for John Lomax. Allen-Ware-Garrison's "Good news, member" is of very similar theme and arrangement (*Slave Songs of the United States,* 97-98).

Move de member

-1-

Got on my rockin' shoes, Dan-u-el,
Got on my rockin' shoes, Dan-u-el,
Shoes gwineter rock er me home, Dan-u-el,
Shoes gwineter rock er me home, Dan-u-el.

-Chorus-

Move de member, move, Dan-u-el,
Move de member, move, Dan-u-el,
Member move so slow, Dan-u-el,
Member move so slow, Dan-u-el.

-2-

Got on my long white robe, Dan-u-el,
Got on my long white robe, Dan-u-el,
Move de member, move, Dan-u-el,
Move de member, move, Dan-u-el.

-3-

Got on my starry crown, Dan-u-el,
Got on my starry crown, Dan-u-el,
Move de member, move, Dan-u-el,
Move de member, move, Dan-u-el.

Lyin' in de arms uv the Lord

80

This is one of two songs in Mrs. Tartt's collection that contains a direct reference to the War between the States. It is an exhortation to hope, what some scholars of the spirituals have termed a "morale builder." The figurative contrast between the alarums of war and the peace of "Lyin' in de arms uv de Lord" emphasizes the duality of God who is both the wrathful scourge on the "mighty fiel' uv battle" and the loving father, the Good Shepherd. The progressive catalog of Christian believers, the metrically regular quatrains, and leader-respondent structure create a high degree of stanzaic unity. The soldier of the chorus may seem unrelated to the exhortation of the stanzas, but the Yankee is an earthly deliverer even as is God who comforts after long spiritual warfare.

Lyin' in de arms uv de Lord

-1-

Come my lovin' brudder en doan git so weary
Lyin' in de arms uv de Lord,
Come my lovin' brudder en doan git so weary
Lyin' in de arms uv de Lord.

-Chorus-

Oh yes, de Yankee rode er hoss
in de mighty fiel' uv battle,
Oh, de Yankee shot er cannon
in de mighty fiel' uv battle,
Lyin' in de arms uv de Lord.

-2-

Come my lovin' sister en doan git so weary
Lyin' in de arms uv de Lord,
Come my lovin' sister en doan git so weary
Lyin' in de arms uv de Lord.

-Chorus-

Oh yes, de Yankee rode er hoss
in de mighty fiel' uv battle,
Oh, de Yankee shot er cannon
in de mighty fiel' uv battle,
Lyin' in de arms uv de Lord.

-3-

Come my lovin' deacon en doan git so weary
Lyin' in de arms uv de Lord,
Come my lovin' deacon en doan git so weary
Lyin' in de arms uv de Lord.

-Chorus-

Oh yes, de Yankee rode er hoss
in de mighty fiel' uv battle,
Oh, de Yankee shot er cannon
in de mighty fiel' uv battle,
Lyin' in de arms uv de Lord.

My good Lord done been here

A few spirituals are handed down essentially unchanged, some exhibit major structural and poetic shifts, and others—like this one—accumulate migratory or improvised stanzas around a memorable chorus. Stanza 1 often appears in a song of sinners, gamblers, drunkards, and liars. Stanza 2 belongs to the "lonesome valley" song of white and black folk tradition. Stanza 3 utilizes the anchor motif of many Jordan and comic Satan songs. "Oh, my good Lord done been here" exemplifies the way in which the folk idiom, as in "He done been here," after the departure of some visitor, takes on transcendent meaning. "Bless my soul and gone er-way" is the soul's satisfaction after the descent of the Holy Spirit. See John Work, *American Negro Songs and Spirituals,* 132, for this chorus and other migratory stanzas. Vera Hall sings a version on Lomax's Library of Congress recordings.

My good Lord done been here

-1-

I wouldn't be no sinner,
En I tell yer de reason why,
A certain pain might strike me,
En den I'll slowly die.

-2-

En, some says John de Baptis'
Wuz nothin' but a Jew.
But de Holy Bible tell me
Dat John wuz a preacher too.

-Chorus-

Oh, my good Lord done been here,
Bless my soul en gone er-way.
My good Lord done been here, chillun,
En bless my soul en gone er-way.

-3-

I went down on Jerden,
Saw dat island stream,
Soul got ankerled [anchored] in Jesus,
An de devil can't do me no harm.

-Chorus-

Oh, my good Lord done been here,
Bless my soul en gone er-way.
My good Lord done been here, chillun,
En bless my soul en gone er-way.

Lord, trouble so hard

Over and over Afro-American folk hymns pour out weariness and yearning for rest— again and again comes the utterance, "Oh, Lord, my trouble so hard," as it does in the bitter reality of suffering. The omission of the verb *is* in line 1, the conversational, ungrammatical "don't nobody know," the sighing murmur "Yes indeed," all these demonstrate how folk speech of daily life became the music and poetry of the great Afro-American sorrow songs. The migratory rhymed quatrain, common in preaching and other didactic species, though folk conversation, does not measure up to the poetic power of the chorus.

Vera Hall and Dock Reed sang "Trouble so hard" for the Lomax Library of Congress recordings. They later sang "Troubled, Lord, I'm troubled" for Courlander (*Negro Songs from Alabama,* 43). As variations on the "trouble-so-hard" theme one may also compare "Soon as my feet strike Zion won't be trouble no more" (above) and "All time trouble in my heart" (below). Allen, Ware, and Garrison published three versions of "(This is) the trouble of the world" (*Slave Songs of the United States,* 8 and 99). Perhaps the best-known "trouble" spiritual is "Soon-a will be done (with the trouble of this world)," one version of which appears in Work, *American Negro Songs and Spirituals* (109).

Lord, trouble so hard

Oh Lord, my trouble so hard
   Oh Lord, my trouble so hard.
Don't nobody know my trouble but God
   Don't nobody know my trouble but God.

Wait, let me tell you whut yer sister will do
Before yo' face she have a love fer you
'Hind yo' back she scandalize yo' name
Jes' de same yer has ter bear de blame.

Oh Lord, my trouble so hard
   Oh Lord, my trouble so hard.
Don't nobody know my trouble but God
   Don't nobody know my trouble but God.
Yes indeed, my trouble so hard.

Didn't you hear my Lord call?

Common Afro-American folksong conventions are gathered here: antiphonal dramatic dialogue (which serves as a basic structural element), simple and incremental repetition, the two-line refrain, and associative lyric imagery. The idea of God "calling," that is, speaking directly to man, is drawn from the Old Testament—"And the Lord called unto . . . " (for example, 1 Samuel 3:4, 6, 8). The "heaven bells" metaphor is recurrent throughout nineteenth-century Protestant folk and composed hymnody. The "lightnin' flash" is emblematic of the terrible might and the awful glory of God, and the (turtle) dove of both the Holy Spirit and Christ in agony. These images convey a transforming mystical experience which absolves all human impurities—"not a bit of evil in my soul."

John Lomax made several recordings of this lovely spiritual in Sumter County: Rich Amerson sang it for him, as did Dock Reek. Rich Amerson and Earthy Anne Coleman harmonized on the same song (with such variations as are common to unwritten folk song) for the Courlander recordings—"Didn't you hear my Lord when he called" (*Negro Songs from Alabama,* 13; also in Courlander's *Negro Folk Music U.S.A.*, 241-43, with more text and discussion on 68-69).

Didn't you hear my Lord call

-1-

Didn't you hear my Lord call?
Yes, I heered my Lord call.
Didn't you hear my Lord call?
Yes, I heered my Lord call.
My Lord call in my soul,
My Lord call in my soul.
Oh, not a bit of evil in my soul,
Not a bit of evil in my soul.

-2-

Didn't you hear heaven bells ringin'?
Yes, I heered heaven bells ringin'.
Didn't you hear heaven bells ringin'.
Yes, I heered heaven bells ringin'.
Heaven bells ringin' in my soul,
Heaven bells ringin' in my soul.

-3-

Didn't you see dat lightnin' flash?
Yes, I seed dat lightnin' flash.
Didn't you see dat lightnin' flash?
Yes, I seed dat lightnin' flash.
Lightnin' flashin' in my soul,
Lightnin' flashin' in my soul.
Oh, not a bit of evil in my soul,
Not a bit of evil in my soul.

-4-

Oh, didn't you hear dat turkle dove moan?
Yes, I heered dat turkle dove moan.
Didn't you hear dat turkle dove moan.
Yes, I heered dat turkle dove moan.
Turkle dove moanin' in my soul,
Turkle dove moanin' in my soul.
Not a bit of evil in my soul,
Not a bit of evil in my soul.

Work on the buildin' for the Lord
Lord, I feel like I got to go to Jurden
There's sumpin' on my mind whut's worryin' me

84

Mrs. Tartt's manuscripts indicate that these three folk hymns were sung to the same tune. In the source song, "Work on the building for the Lord," the building is the spiritual church, battered by the "rain" of sin, which the Christian must repair. In the second song the central metaphor shifts to "Jurden," the soul's intimation of death and yearning for the Promised Land. "He stopped my feet from travelin' " is obscure, but the "building" song implies that divine intervention effected conversion while the "Jurden" song hints at the imminence of death in the phrase "my time ain't long." The third text demonstrates the use of the catalog of relatives for extended development. Though none of these songs possesses great lyric or dramatic qualities, their folk language is noteworthy: "Lord, I got sumpin' on my mind what's worryin' me, / I declare hit's worrying' me, God knows hit's worryin' me," the repeated words of a heart freeted, bewildered by the loss of a kinsman to death.

See Byron Arnold, *Folk Songs of Alabama,* 162, for "Workin' on the building," popular with radio gospel quartets during the 1940s.

Work on the buildin' for the Lord

-1-

Hit's er rainin', hit's er rainin',
en er leak's in de buildin',
Hit's er rainin', hit's er rainin',
en er leak's in de buildin',
Hit's er rainin', hit's er rainin',
en er leak's in de buildin',
Work on de buildin' fer de Lord.

-2-

Well, he stopped my way of travelin',
hit's a leak's in de buildin',
Well, he stopped my way of travelin',
hit's a leak's in de buildin',
Well, he stopped my way of travelin',
hit's a leak's in de buildin',
To work on de buildin' fer de Lord.

-3-

Hit's er rainin', hit's er rainin',
en er leak's in de buildin',
Hit's er rainin', hit's er rainin',
en er leak's in de buildin',
Hit's er rainin', hit's er rainin',
en er leak's in de buildin',
So work on de buildin' fer de Lord.

Lord, I feel like I got to go to Jurden

-1-

Lord, I feel jes' lac I got ter go to Jurden, Jurden,
I feel jes' lac my time ain't long, so long,
Lord, I feel jes' lac I got ter go to Jurden, Jurden,
I feel lac my time ain't long.
That my time ain't long.

-2-

Well, he stopped my feet from travelin',
travelin', Jurden, Jurden,
I feel jes' lac my time ain't long, so long,
Well, he stopped my feet frum travelin',
travelin', Jurden, Jurden,
Feel jes' lac my time ain't long.
That my time ain't long.

There's sumpin' on my mind whut's worryin' me

Lord, I got sumpin' on my mind whut's worryin' me.
I declare hit's worryin' me, God knows hit's worryin' me.
Lord, I got sumpin' on my mind keeps on worryin' me.
Let us pray a prayer.

Oh, my mother's dead en gone,
  en that's whut's worryin' me.
Oh Lord, hit's worryin' me,
  God knows hit's worryin' me.
Oh, my mother's dead en gone,
  en that's whut's worryin' me.
Let us pray a prayer.

Oh, my father's dead en gone,
  en that's whut's worryin' me.
Oh Lord, hit's worryin' me,
  God knows hit's worryin' me.
Oh, my father's dead en gone,
  en that's whut's worryin' me.
Let us pray a prayer.

Oh, my brother's dead en gone,
  en that's whut's worryin' me.
Oh Lord, hit's worryin' me,
  God knows hit's worryin' me.
Oh, my brother's dead en gone,
  en that's whut's worryin' me.
Let us pray a prayer.

Oh, my sister's dead en gone,
  en that's whut's worryin' me.
Oh Lord, hit's worryin' me,
  God knows hit's worryin' me.
Oh, my sister's dead en gone,
  en that's whut's worryin' me.
Let us pray a prayer.

I feel like my time ain't long

86

The speaker's recognition of his approaching death and the parade of kinsmen whom he will join are framed by images of the hearse and the funeral bell. Though "outrun me and gone on to Glory" may strike the reader as comic, the allusion is to the New Testament metaphor of the Christian life as contest, race (1 Corinthians 9:24), and wrestling match (Ephesians 6:12), and perhaps, if only for the wording, to John 20:4: "So they ran both together; and the other disciple did outrun Peter, and came first to the sepulchre [Jesus' burial place]."

Vera Hall sings it on the Lomax recordings for the Library of Congress. Compare variants with the same title in Johnson and Johnson (*The Books of American Negro Spirituals,* 2:174-75) and Work (*American Negro Songs and Spirituals,* 135); the Work and Johnson variants are virtually the same, but both are very different from this Sumter County text.

I feel like my time ain't long

-1-

Oh, de hearse keep a-rollin' somebody to de graveyard,
Oh, de hearse keep a-rollin' somebody to de graveyard,
Oh, de hearse keep a-rollin' somebody to de graveyard,
Oh Lord, I feel lac my time ain't long.

-2-

Oh, de bell keep a-tonin' somebody is er dyin',
Oh, de bell keep a-tonin' somebody is er dyin',
Oh, de bell keep a-tonin' somebody is er dyin',
Oh Lord, I feel lac my time ain't long.

-3-

Oh, my mother outrun me en she gone on to glory,
Oh, my mother outrun me en she gone on to glory,
Oh, my mother outrun me en she gone on to glory,
Oh Lord, I feel lac my time ain't long.

-4-

Oh, my father outrun me en she gone on to glory,
Oh, my father outrun me en she gone on to glory,
Oh, my father outrun me en she gone on to glory,
Oh Lord, I feel lac my time ain't long.

-5-

Oh, my sister outrun me en she gone on to glory,
Oh, my sister outrun me en she gone on to glory,
Oh, my sister outrun me en she gone on to glory,
Oh Lord, I feel lac my time ain't long.

-6-

Oh, my brother outrun me en she gone on to glory,
Oh, my brother outrun me en she gone on to glory,
Oh, my brother outrun me en she gone on to glory,
Oh Lord, I feel lac my time ain't long.

The old ark's er movin'

"The old ark's er moving" is among the best-known of those spirituals that have entered popular tradition. The terms *reel* and *rock* are applied directly to the symbolic subject, Noah's ark safe on the mountaintop while the waters of the Flood recede, a fit metaphor for the redeemed soul. The migratory rhymed couplets of stanzas 2, 3, and 4 are logically and poetically related to the ark of the chorus: as Noah was rescued from world destruction, so shall the Christian cross Jordan River and enter the kingdom of heaven.

Compare "De ol' ark's a-moverin' an' I'm goin' home" in Johnson and Johnson (*The Books of American Negro Spirituals,* 2:25-27) and "The old ark's a-movering" in Work (*American Negro Songs and Spirituals,* 175).

The ole ark's er movin'

-1-

The ole ark she reel,
The old ark she rock.
The ole ark she reel from mounting top.
Sing the old ark's er movin', movin', movin',
Ole ark's er movin', movin' 'long.

-2-

Way down yonder 'bout Jurden stream
Think I heered de chillun say dey been redeemed.
Sing the ole ark's er movin', movin', movin',
Ole ark's er movin', movin' 'long.

-3-

Jurden river deep en wide
None can cross but de sanctified.
Sing the ole ark's er movin', movin', movin',
Ole ark's er movin', movin' 'long.

-4-

When I gets to heaven, gonna talk en tell
How Jesus freed my soul from hell.
Sing the ole ark's er movin', movin', movin',
Ole ark's er movin', movin' 'long.

God knows I am the one

88

"God knows" is a strong preface to a passionate declaration of some truth or sacred oath, here the statement of redemption. The doctrine of spiritual rebirth is found in the conversation of Jesus with Nicodemus (John 3). The "blood of the lamb," that is, the sacrifice of Christ, washes white the robes of the redeemed (Revelation 7:13-14). Repetition, both simple and incremental, is a musical and poetic proclamation of the saved whose daily life, his very speech and walk, mark him as one born of the Spirit.

Vera Hall sings Mrs. Tartt's text on the Lomax Library of Congress recordings.

God knows I am the one

-1-

God knows I am the one,
God knows I am the one,
God knows I am the one that's born of the spirit.
Too glad I'm the one,
Too glad I'm the one that's born of the spirit.
God knows I am the one,
God knows I am the one,
Been washed in the blood of the lamb.

-2-

Well, I talks lac the one,
Lord, I talks lac the one,
Lord, I talks lac the one born of de spirit.
God knows I am the one,
God knows I am the one,
Been washed in the blood of the lamb.

-3-

Well, I walks lac the one,
Lord, I walks lac the one,
Lord, I walks lac the one born of de spirit.
God knows I am the one,
God knows I am the one,
Been washed in the blood of the lamb.

-2-

Well, I lives lac the one,
Lord, I lives lac the one,
Lord, I lives lac the one born of de spirit.
God knows I am the one,
God knows I am the one,
Been washed in the blood of the lamb.

John saw that number

89

In this wondrous folk sermon on the Apocalypse "that number" is the elect, garbed in white, the mystical 144,000 of Revelation (Revelation 7:4; 14:1, 3). The vision of God and the sacred lamb (Revelation 4ff.) is set, like Ezekiel's wheel, "way in de middle of de air. The cry "holy" is that of the "four beasts" (literally "living [creatures]") who sing praise at the throne of God (Revelation 4:8—a combination of the four "living creatures" or "cherubim" seen by Ezekiel in his vision [Ezekiel 1:5ff.; cf. 10:20] and the "seraphim" observed by Isaiah [Isaiah 6:2ff.]). Stanza 1 introduces the author of Revelation, again fused with John the Baptist (see above on "Oh John, preachin' in the wilderness") whose description is drawn from the gospels. In stanza 2 the Revelator is rescued from hellish perils—frogs and snakes plagues (recalling those called down by Moses on the Egyptians)—by a heavenly messenger who is the sum of all the angels in Revelation, a mighty folk angel flying from hell to heaven gathering wind, stars, and moon, crying out the song of praise "holy" across the vast spaces of the cosmos. In stanza 3 the scriptural text is incorrectly cited: the seven-headed beast rising from the sea is found in Revelation 13:1. *Read* is invested with both real historical irony and poetic symbolism: few slaves could read and John of Patmos could not "read," that is, understand, the mystical book of seven seals ("And I wept much, because no man was found worthy to open and to read the book," Revelation 5:4) which is revealed only by the Lamb of seven horns and seven eyes, the crucified Christ (Revelation 5:5ff.). The Nicodemus stanza is the logical conclusion of the sermon: without the second birth, which Jesus taught to Nicodemus, no man may take his place among the redeemed spirits in John's New Jerusalem.

The "holy" chorus is migratory; on the Lomax Sumter County recordings made for the Library of Congress it is freely interpolated in Rich Amerson's sermon on Job. Compare the different version of "John saw the holy number" in Johnson and Johnson (*The Books of American Negro Spirituals,* 1:158-59) and see the discussion (with various text samples) in Miles Mark Fisher, *Negro Slave Songs in the United States,* 63-65.

John saw that number

90

-Chorus-

John done saw dat number way in de middle of de air
John done saw dat number way in de middle of de air
Cryin' "Holy," cryin' "Holy,"
cryin' "Holy, my Lord," cryin' "Holy."

-1-

Ole John the Baptist, old John Deevine
Leather girdle around his line
And his meat was locus' and wild honey
Wild honey, wild honey,
my Lord, wild honey.

-2-

Ole John de Baptist, ole John Deevine
Frogs an' de snakes gonna eat old John so bad.
God tole de angel "Go down see 'bout John."
Angel flew frum de bottom uv de pit
Gathered de wind all in his fist
Gathered de stars all 'bout his wrist
Gathered de moon all 'round his waist,
Cryin' "Holy," cryin' "Holy,"
cryin' "Holy, my Lord," cryin' "Holy."

-3-

Read, read, read de Revelations
Third chapter en fourth verse
And you'll find him dere
Where he say unto me,
"There is a beast rose out uv de sea
Having ten horns and ten crowns.
On his horns writte 'blaspheme.'
Weep lac a willow, moan lac a dove
You can't go to heaven, 'thout you go by love."
Read it, read it, John couldn't read it,
my Lord John couldn't read it.

-4-

There was a man of the Pharisee
Name' Nicodemus, ruler of the Jews,
Same came to him by night
Says "I know their teacher came from God
'Cause no man can do these mi'cles
'cept God be wid him there.

-Chorus-

John done saw dat number way in de middle of de air
John done saw dat number way in de middle of de air
Cryin' "Holy," cryin' "Holy,"
cryin' "Holy, my Lord," cryin' "Holy."

John couldn't read it, John couldn't read it
John couldn't read it, my Lord,
John couldn't read it.

Thank God a'mighty I'm free at las'

The story that President Lincoln wept when he heard "Motherless child" but bowed his head for "Free at last" may be apocryphal, but surely few of us can fail to be humbled by this great song of freedom, a freedom of both body and spirit which fills all the surrounding space with a long, triumphant shout. Poised against this liberty is Satan, the adversary of God and man's supreme enslaver who would capture souls for all eternity. The migratory seriocomic stanzas are coherently developed within a progressively intensified dialogue of the Christian and Satan; their encounters are underscored at every line by the choral tag that serves far more than the ordinary purposes of didactic emphasis, rhythm, or stanzaic expansion. Rather, the constant antiphonal response is a moral and psychological stengthening for the hard-pressed soul. The refrain is now world famous as the last words of Martin Luther King, Jr.'s "I have a dream" speech (28 August 1963) and as the words inscribed on his tombstone: "Free at last! Free at last! Thank God Almighty, we *are* free at last!"

Dock Reed and Vera Hall sang "Free at last" for both John Lomax and Harold Courlander (see Courlander, *Negro Songs from Alabama,* 46); their duet, harsh and tender, mingles chant, conversation, melody, and ecstatic shout. Also compare Johnson and Johnson's "I thank God I'm free at las' " (*The Books of American Negro Spirituals,* 2:158) and Work's later but straightforward version of the same, "Free at last" (*American Negro Songs and Spirituals,* 197).

92

Thank God a'mighty I'm free at las'

-Chorus-
Free at las', free at las',
Thank God a-mighty I'm free at las'
Free at las', free at las',
Thank God a-mighty I'm free at las'

-1-
One day, one day I was goin' to pray
Thank God a'mighty I'm free at las'.
I met ole Satan on my way
Thank God a'mighty I'm free at las'.
Whut you reckon, whut you reckon ole Satan had to say?
Thank God a'mighty I'm free at las'.
Young man, young man, you's too young to pray
Thank God a'mighty I'm free at las'.
Ef I'm too young to pray, I ain't too young ter die
Thank God a'mighty I'm free at las'.

-Chorus-
Free at las', free at las',
Thank God a-mighty I'm free at las'
Free at las', free at las',
Thank God a-mighty I'm free at las'

-2-
Oh Satan mad, en I am glad
Thank God a'mighty I'm free at las'.
He missed a soul he thought he had
Thank God a'mighty I'm free at las'.
I ain't been to heaven, but I been told
Thank God a'mighty I'm free at las'.
The streets is pearly en de gates is gold
Thank God a'mighty I'm free at las'.
Whut you reckon, whut you reckon ole Satan had to say?
Thank God a'mighty I'm free at las'.
That Jesus was dead and God gone away
Thank God a'mighty I'm free at las'.

-Chorus-
Free at las', free at las',
Thank God a-mighty I'm free at las'
Free at las', free at las',
Thank God a-mighty I'm free at las'

-3-
But Satan is a liar and a conjurer too
Thank God a'mighty I'm free at las'.
An ef you doan min', he'll conjure you
Thank God a'mighty I'm free at las'.
Better min', better min' how you walk on de cross
Thank God a'mighty I'm free at las'.
Yer feets might slip en yo' soul be lost
Thank God a'mighty I'm free at las'.

-Chorus-
Free at las', free at las',
Thank God a-mighty I'm free at las'
Free at las', free at las',
Thank God a-mighty I'm free at las'

I got a home in the rock

93

This is a well-known concert spiritual, appearing usually with stanzas from the story of Lazarus and "Dives" (Luke 16:19-31). In this text "between heaven and earth" suggests the great gulf fixed between the beggar and the rich man. The Psalmist calls God "the rock of my salvation" (Psalm 89:26), Christ is the New Testament counterpart, and the Christian finds "home" in that "rock." The curious image of the Savior "moaning" in the rock refers at once to his death, to the Christian discipline and worship mode of moaning, and generally to religious ecstasy. "King Jesus" is a familiar folk designation, possibly drawn from the mocking "King of the Jews" written above the cross (Matthew 27:37 and parallels). The folk "don't you see" emphasizes an argumentative or expository point.

John Lomax recorded several versions of "I got a home" by various Sumter County singers for the Library of Congress. Compare the variant offered by both Johnson and Johnson ("I got a home in-a dat rock," *The Books of American Negro Spirituals,* 1:96-98) and Work ("Got a home in that rock," *American Negro Songs and Spirituals,* 169), which includes the Lazarus-Dives verses.

I got a home in the rock

You got a home in the rock en don't you see
You got a home in the rock en don't you see
Don't you see way between the heaven en earth
   Think I heard my Savior say,
"I got a home in the rock," en don't you see.

Somebody moanin' in dat rock en don't you see
Somebody moanin' in dat rock en don't you see
Don't you see way between the heaven en earth
   Think I heard my Savior say,
"I got a home in the rock," en don't you see.

King Jesus is dat rock en don't you see
King Jesus is dat rock en don't you see
Don't you see way between the heaven en earth
   Think I heard my Savior say,
"I got a home in the rock," en don't you see.

Nora built the ark

94

The preaching tone of this rare Alabama spiritual is evident from the first line. It is the preacher's voice that unifies the disparate elements of the sermon, his long pulpit phrases punctuated by *says* and *er* (the sound for *a* and *and,* also transitional nonverbal ejaculation), his questions answered by congregational chant "Nora, Nora, Nora." There are no preliminaries: we plunge *in medias res,* Noah's hammer crying out repentance in the teeth of public ridicule, and there we leave him, for Noah is the "jumping-off place," a well-known exemplum, a proof in point: Noah is God's man, his Ark—like the Ark of the Covenant— is a sacred trust, a vessel bearing life out of world-death, and not for a moment does the antiphonal "Nora" chorus allow us to forget him as a symbol of faith and obedience. Subsequent stanzas show Noah's opposites. Stanza 3 presents "Mister Hypocrite" and offers pulpit commentary in pithy folk contrasts and a proverb. Stanza 4 warns the disobedient "sinner man" of the futility of flight and of the coming Judgment when souls will be weighed "in the balances" of Daniel's prophecies (Daniel 5:27). Stanza 5 presents a parable of disobedience in Jonah who resisted God's call to preach to Nineveh and obedience in the "inchworm" that, in accordance with God's command, withers the gourd(vine) of Jonah's refuge (Jonah 4:6-7). In the final stanza morbid images of death and burial, while not obviously related to theme and subject, provide a brilliant conclusion to the sermon: all—Noah, the hypocrite—come finally to death. Note the uses of *link* and *wind* as both adjective and verb. *Lotion* suggests "commotion" or "locomotion." *Ways* is transitional ejeculation in the sense of *well.*

Dock Reed and Vera Hall sing a version of "Noah, Noah" on the Courlander anthology (see Courlander, *Negro Folk Music U.S.A.,* 246-47 for sample text and music and 44-45 for more text and discussion; the recording is on Folkways FE 4473). John Lomax recorded a Noah song by Rich Amerson for the Library of Congress. Compare White, *American Negro Folk Songs,* 99-100, for another (untitled) Alabama Noah song. See also Dorothy Scarborough's discussion (with texts and music) of this spiritual as adapted for a "hammer song" in *On the Trail of Negro Folk-Songs,* 222-23.

Nora built the ark

-1-

You 'members de time Nora buildin' de ark
On dis dry lan'
Er Nora kept buildin', says, on de ark
The hammer cry "You better repent," my Lord.
Who built this ark? Nora, Nora, Lord.
Who built this ark? Nora, Lord.

-2-

Dey call old Nora a foolis' man
For buildin' de ark on dis dry lan'.
Says, Nora kept buildin' er, says.
Who built this ark? Nora, Nora, Lord.
Who built this ark? Nora, Lord.

-3-

Says, I met a Mister Hypocrite the other day
Er, says, he's always up er never down
Always right er never wrong
Says, jes' so the sinner live er jes' so he die
Jes' so the tree fall er jes' so it lie.
My Lord, who built the ark? Nora, Nora.
Lord who built the ark? Nora, Lord.

-4-

Sinner man er you may run away er
But you gotta come back er at Judgment Day.
You gotta go fore dem bars of God.
The balance is dere er you must be weighed er
Says after you balance dem balance too low
Says down in hell you er sho to go.
My Lord, who built the ark? Nora, Nora.
Lord who built the ark? Nora, Lord.

-5-

Says de gourdvine grows er over Jonah's head
Er inchworm come along en cut it down
Er he cut it down at God's command.
My Lord, who built the ark? Nora, Nora.
Lord who built the ark? Nora, Lord.

-6-

Ways, dig my grave er wid the silver spade
En the link er of chain fer to link er me down
Er en a windin' sheet for to wind me up
In de lotion of friends all standin' 'round
Er de dirt come tumblin', end de coffin sound
Er en de creepin' things wuz on de ground.
My Lord, who built the ark? Nora, Nora.
Lord who built the ark? Nora, Lord.

I doan know when ole death gwine call me home

96

The death song is one of the oldest and earliest collected of Afro-American folk songs. In this Alabama lament, death is "old Death," a familiar, one known long and well, perhaps even a mother calling the child home from play at evening. In stanza 2 the first two lines derive from "Motherless child," the third line is indebted to Protestant hymns of faith; and in the last two lines the ascent to heaven is figured by the metaphor of the soul riding the splendid horse of fame in the sky, an allusion to the pale horse of death in Revelation 6:8.

Vera Hall and Dock Reed sang this text in duet for Lomax.

I doan know when ole death gwine call me home

I doan know when old death gwine call me home,
call me home
I doan know when old death gwine call me home,
call me home
He's callin' ev'ry day, en he won't let nobody stay
I doan know when old death gwine call me home,
call me home

Sometimes I feel discouraged
Feel like all uv my work's in vain
I'm built on solid rock, en I lay my Bible down
I mount de horse uv fame
En ride him in de sky.

I doan know when old death gwine call me home,
call me home
I doan know when old death gwine call me home,
call me home
He's callin' ev'ry day, en he won't let nobody stay
I doan know when old death gwine call me home,
call me home

I'm so glad I got my religion on time

"I'm so glad . . . " is exquisitely molded from two other spirituals into a new unity, with an astonishing purity of text, diction, rhythm, and stanzaic structure. Stanzas 1, 2, and 3 have their origins in "Death come to my house," especially the personification of death as a thief and murderer who invades the sanctity of home and family and carries away the mother, the source of earthly joy and comfort. Stanzas 4 and 5 descend from the famous "Somebody knocking at your door"; the shift in imagery from the thief to the voice of Jesus is dramatic and coherent. In stanzas 6, 7, and 8 the traditional metaphor of death as sleep "on Jesus' breast" has become a beautiful folk Pietà. Stanzas 9 and 10 have migrated from certain "religion" songs, and though they do not possess the musical and poetic qualities of the other stanzas, they conclude the interior drama with joy. In the choral tag the allusion to the story of the rich young ruler (Matthew 19, Mark 10, Luke 18) locates physical death within the theological context of salvation: the eternal life the rich ruler seeks is lost when he refuses Christ's injunction to sell all his possessions and give the money to the poor.

Dock Reed and Vera Hall sing Mrs. Tartt's text on Lomax's Library of Congress recordings. See "Death come to my house" (Johnson and Johnson, *The Books of American Negro Spirituals,* 2:108-109) and "Somebody's knocking at your door" (Johnson and Johnson, 1:85, and Work, *American Negro Songs and Spirituals,* 192). Compare variations on the death's-visit, death-as-robber themes: "Death's gwineter lay his cold icy hands on me" (Johnson and Johnson, two versions, 2:93-95, 2:96-99) and "Death ain't nothin' but a robber" (Work, 113).

98

I'm so glad I got my religion on time

-1-
Soon one mornin' death come creepin' in de room
Soon one mornin' death come creepin' in de room
Soon one mornin' death come creepin' in de room
Oh my Lord, oh my Lord, whut shall I do to be saved.

-2-
Death done been here, took my mother en gone
Death done been here, took my mother en gone
Death done been here, took my mother en gone
Oh my Lord, oh my Lord, whut shall I do to be saved.

-3-
Death done been here, lef' me er motherless chile
Death done been here, lef' me er motherless chile
Death done been here, lef' me er motherless chile
Oh my Lord, oh my Lord, whut shall I do to be saved.

-4-
I heard a voice I never heard before
I heard a voice I never heard before
I heard a voice I never heard before
Oh my Lord, oh my Lord, whut shall I do to be saved.

-5-
Called lac Jesus, never heard de voice before
Called lac Jesus, never heard de voice before
Called lac Jesus, never heard de voice before
Oh my Lord, oh my Lord, whut shall I do to be saved.

-6-
Gwine lay my head, my head on Jesus' breast
Gwine lay my head, my head on Jesus' breast
Gwine lay my head, my head on Jesus' breast
Oh my Lord, oh my Lord, whut shall I do to be saved.

-7-
Gwine breathe my life, my life out sweetly dere
Gwine breathe my life, my life out sweetly dere
Gwine breathe my life, my life out sweetly dere
Oh my Lord, oh my Lord, whut shall I do to be saved.

-8-
Ain't gonna die, jes' gonna sleep away
Ain't gonna die, jes' gonna sleep away
Ain't gonna die, jes' gonna sleep away
Oh my Lord, oh my Lord, whut shall I do to be saved.

-9-
Angel, angel, cleanin' up de chariot wheel
Angel, angel, cleanin' up de chariot wheel
Angel, angel, cleanin' up de chariot wheel
Oh my Lord, oh my Lord, whut shall I do to be saved.

-10-
I'm so glad I got my religion on time
I'm so glad I got my religion on time
I'm so glad I got my religion on time
Oh my Lord, oh my Lord, whut shall I do to be saved.

All time trouble in my heart

"All time in trouble" is a variant of "Lord, I want to be a Christian," often a concert selection and now common in both white and Afro-American hymnody, in which some critics have seen an implied condemnation of hypocrisy in white churches and/or a veiled protest against slavery. In stanza 1 *disturber* is one who breaks the harmony of a community, especially that of Christians within the church congregation, but the disturbance is "in my heart," suggesting the tumult of personal struggle. *Troubled,* as verb, implies deep concern while the phrase *in trouble* connotes those obstacles that arise from the workings of fate or the exercise of individual choice, though both meanings apply to the agonizing struggle to find the serene faith required of the Christian. This Sumter County text offers a new and more realistic dimension to a song known primarily as a straightforward prayer.

Dock Reed recorded Mrs. Tartt's text for Lomax's Library of Congress recordings in Alabama. See Johnson and Johnson, *The Books of American Negro Spirituals,* 2:72, and Work, *American Negro Songs and Spirituals,* 76, for the traditional text of "Lord, I want to be a Christian."

All time trouble in my heart

Lord, I doan want er be no disturber in my heart,
in my heart.
Lord, I doan want er be no disturber in my heart,
in my heart.
In er my heart,
In er my heart,
In er my heart,
In er my heart,
Lord, I'm all time in trouble in my heart.

Yes, I want er live lac Jesus in my heart, in my heart,
Yes, I want er live lac Jesus in my heart, in my heart,
In er my heart,
In er my heart,
In er my heart,
In er my heart,
Lord, I'm all time in trouble in my heart.

Low down chariot and let me ride

100

The Old Testament chariot, recurrent symbol of death, transfiguration, mystic apprehension, and apocalypse, gives passage to the New Testament Christian who seeks entrance to Paradise. "Ticket to ride" points to the contemporary train that would slow down for passengers while the chariot must descend or "low down." The theme is progressively developed over ten stanzas: the speaker has a right, by virtue of his salvation, to reide; he begs and prays for passage, as the Christian prays for the mercies of God and the promise of immortality; his mother, father, brother, and sister, under the bond of Christ, already enjoy immortality, and he waits his turn humbly; the proof of his membership among the redeemed and his imminent death, the train ticket, is in hand. This text is distinguished by its quiet use of several Afro-American folk-song traditions: the antiphonal dialogue of leader and respondent, perfectly balanced statement and choral response, in every line; folk conversation as unique expression of spiritual states and of Christian theology; a traditional Christian symbol, with contemporary overtones, which unifies the stanzas and inherently accommodates the catalog of relatives; and incremental repetition which permits logical and poetic progression.

Dock Reed's performance of this text for the Lomax Library of Congress recordings is illustrative of its mood of humility, sorrow, and petitionary hope. Dock Reed and Vera Hall sang the same song (with natural variations) for Harold Courlander's recordings in 1950 (Courlander, *Negro Folk Music U.S.A.,* 250, with the text as here, plus more on p. 72; Folkways discs FA2038 and FE4473).

Low down chariot and let me ride

-1-

Let me ride, let me ride,
Let me ride, let me ride,
Oh, let er me ride, let er me ride,
Oh, low down chariot en let er me ride.

-2-

Got a right to ride, let er me ride,
Got a right to ride, let er me ride,
Got a right to ride, let er me ride,
Oh, low down chariot en let er me ride.

-3-

I'm beggin' to ride, let er me ride,
I'm beggin' to ride, let er me ride,
I'm beggin' to ride, let er me ride,
Oh, low down de chariot en let er me ride.

-4-

I'm prayin' to ride, let er me ride,
I'm prayin' to ride, let er me ride,
I'm prayin' to ride, let er me ride,
Low down de chariot, en let er me ride.

-5-

My mother done rid, let er me ride,
My mother done rid, let er me ride,
My mother done rid, let er me ride,
Low down de chariot, en et er me ride.

-6-

My father done rid, let er me ride,
My father done rid, let er me ride,
My father done rid, let er me ride,
Lown down de chariot, en et er me ride.

-7-

My brother done rid, let er me ride,
My brother done rid, let er me ride,
My brother done rid, let er me ride,
Lown down de chariot, en et er me ride.

-8-

My sister done rid, let er me ride,
My sister done rid, let er me ride,
My sister done rid, let er me ride,
Oh, low down de chariot, en et er me ride.

-9-

I'm 'umble to ride, let er me ride,
I'm 'umble to ride, let er me ride,
I'm 'umble to ride, let er me ride,
Lown down chariot, en let er me ride.

-10-

Got my ticket to ride, let er me ride,
Got my ticket to ride, let er me ride,
Got my ticket to ride, let er me ride,
Oh, lown down chariot, en let er me ride.

Servant choose yo' seat and set down

102

Detractors would point to the stock metaphors of paradise as evidence of a limited poetic imagination, but understood as ritual symbols of glory, and within the historical context of slavery, these regain their significance as expressions of the Afro-American folk mind. Who of marginal survival would not dream of soft white garments in heaven? And what slave would not rejoice to hear his master invite him to sit in a chosen chair? The long days of hardship are ended, the earthly servant is now the beloved of God and takes his deserved seat.

The better-known version on this theme is "Sit down servant, sit down! (an' rest a little while)" as, for example, in Work, *American Negro Songs and Spirituals,* 65. And the overwhelming joy of the servant is of course expressed in "My soul's so happy an' I can't sit down" or "Sit down . . . I can't sit down" (see Arnold, *Folksongs of Alabama,* 176).

Servant choose yo' seat en set down

-1-

Oh Jesus, jes' give me a starry crown
Oh Jesus, jes' give me a starry crown in de heaven
Choose yo' seat, en set down in de heaven
Choose yo' seat, en set down, trouble over,
Choose yo' seat, en set down, trouble over,
Choose yo' seat, en set down.

-2-

Oh Lord, jes' give me a long white robe
Oh Lord, jes' give me a long white robe in de heaven
Choose yo' seat, en set down in de heaven
Choose yo' seat, en set down, trouble over,
Choose yo' seat, en set down, trouble over,
Choose yo' seat, en set down.

-3-

Oh Lord, jes' give me a gold waist band
Oh Lord, jes' give me a gold waist band in de heaven
Choose yo' seat, en set down in de heaven
Choose yo' seat, en set down, trouble over,
Choose yo' seat, en set down, trouble over,
Choose yo' seat, en set down.

Low down death right easy

In all the Tartt collection there is no more tender portrait of the death of one of God's faithful servants. The death scene is directly imaged from folk life—the offices performed by friends and kinsmen for the dying, arranging pillow and linens, keeping watch at the bedside, waiting for the lowering chariot of the death angel. Perfect metrical and verbal balance in each quatrain, repetition and contrast in language and rhythm, and folk speech empowered by Christian hope, all convey the mood of leave taking: one of the folk has gone home.

The "death" of the title does not occur in the stanzas; rather it has become "chariot" in stanza 1, the core or archetypal stanza. This substitution may be explained by similarities in phrasing to "Low down chariot and let me ride" (above in this volume), which is an entirely different song. Lomax recorded performances of "Low down death" from Dock Reed and Vera Hall and others in Sumter County.

Low down death right easy

-1-

Jes' low down de chariot right easy,
Right easy, right easy,
Jes' lown down de chariot right easy
An' bring God's servant home.

-2-

Jes' tiper 'round my room right easy,
Right easy, right easy,
Jes' tiper 'round my room right easy,
And bring God's servant home.

-3-

Jes' move my pillow 'round right easy,
Right easy, right easy,
Jes' move my pillow 'round right easy,
And bring God's servant home.

-4-

Jes' turn de cover back right easy,
Right easy, right easy,
Jes' turn de cover back right easy,
And bring God's servant home.

Everybody ought to love their soul

104

Several Christian doctrines are presented here: the immortal existence of the soul, hence the necessity of honoring and caring for it; the yearning for heaven where angels forever perform those worship rites that exist only in imperfect form on earth (singing, moaning, and praying); and the exhortation to the gambler. Though this text may not lay claim to greatness, it exemplifies well the subjects, language, and structural components of Afro-American hymnody.

Everybody ought to love their soul

-1-
God knows I love my soul
God knows I love my soul
My soul dat live en never die
God knows I love my soul.

-2-
Oh, gambler don't yer want ter go
Oh, gambler don't yer want ter go
In de heaben whur de angel don't never git tired
Er singin' en moanin' en prayin'.

-3-
God knows I want ter go
God knows I want ter go
In de heaben whur de angels don't never git tired
Er singin' en moanin' en praying'.

-4-
Ev'ybody oughter love dey soul
Ev'ybody oughter love dey soul
Dey soul dat live en never die
Ev'ybody oughter love dey soul.

Thanky fer de risin' sun

This is the Sumter County version of one of the oldest collected American spirituals, which some commentators have identified as a code for secret slave meetings and in which others have detected a pagan or Islamic spirit. Language, imagery, and development, both logical and psychological, suggest a morning devotion: the petitioner give thanks for the day and for his right to pray (a right not easily won in historic Christianity and not always possessed by the American slave), exhorts the gambler to repentance, and forthrightly ponders over his own troubled soul. The tone is deeply introspective. The question of the last stanza hints of arduous moral conflict, of St. Augustine's "dark night of the soul" illumined by a symbolic and real rising sun which, although a blessed relief, has not chased away all the terrors of nightmare. The implied analogy and contrast between the speaker and the gambler is of subtle importance to the prayer monologue: both kneel, one to pray, the other to shoot dice; both have passed a wakeful, tormented night and must face the sun of truth; thus the speaker's exhortation to the gambler is also to his own soul, his doubt mirrored in the gambler's sin. In the refrain *Holy* the praise song of the angels and the redeemed in the Book of Revelation (4:8), is the voice of God, and the morning is not only the present one but the morning of the soul's resurrection in the Heavenly City. See John Lowell, Jr., *Black Song: The Forge and the Flames. The Story of How the Afro-American Spiritual Was Hammered Out* (New York: The Macmillan Co., 1972) 263, 264, for comment on the sun imagery in the spirituals.

Thanky fer de risin' sun

-1-

Oh Lord, thanky fer de risin' sun
Oh Lord, thanky fer de risin' sun
Oh Lord, thanky fer de risin' sun
In dis mornin', in dis mornin' when de Lord say "Holy."

-2-

Oh Lord, thanky fer de prayer I pray
Oh Lord, thanky fer de prayer I pray
Oh Lord, thanky fer de prayer I pray
In dis mornin', in dis mornin' when de Lord say "Holy."

-2-

Oh, gambler git up offa yo' knees
Oh, gambler git up offa yo' knees
Oh, gambler git up offa yo' knees
In dis mornin', in dis mornin' when de Lord say "Holy."

-2-

Oh Lord, am I right or wrong
Oh Lord, am I right or wrong
Oh Lord, am I right or wrong
In dis mornin', in dis mornin' when de Lord say "Holy."

De world can't do me no harm

106

Here is a religion song which asserts the mystical powers of salvation to protect the Christian from the harmful influences of the world. Stanzas 1, 3, and 5 exhibit the leader-respondent structure of the core song, or unrhymed choral quatrain subsequently varied by simple and/or incremental repetition, here *sing, know,* and *prays,* which may be understood both as Christian disciplines and as magical rites. The metrically regular stanzas 2 and 4 juxtapose the comical folk encounter of the Christian and the conjuring devil with the "letter" figure derived by the folk from the letters of Paul and John the Revelator, but in this text a letter from "King James," joyously received ("surged me through and through") by the redeemed soul, a personal message of salvation through Christ whose sacred name the believer must confess. The import of any letter to the slave must have been enormous, as is this from the ruler of the universe to his Christian servant, read not by the eye and mind but by the spirit.

De world can't do me no harm

I can sing my religion, yes, yes,
I can sing my religion, yes, yes,
I can sing my religion, yes, yes,
De world can't do me no harm.

Oh, I went down on Jordan
I struck dat island stream
Landed me over on de other side
Devil say "Now you gone."

Lord, I know I got religion, yes, yes,
Lord, I know I got religion, yes, yes,
Lord, I know I got religion, yes, yes,
De world can't do me no harm.

King James wrote me a letter
It surged me through and through
And every line I read
'Twas in my Jesus' name.

Lord, I know I got religion, yes, yes,
Lord, I know I got religion, yes, yes,
I prays my religion, yes, yes,
De world can't do me no harm.

Good news

In this Christmas spiritual the "news" is the birth of Christ and also the salvation message of the New Testament. Similarly, "hunting for the Lord" has dual meaning: the search of the magi for the Christ child and the soul's desire for redemption. Stanza 1 declares the speaker's membership in the brotherhood of Christians, imaged as a name on a legal document witnessed by the Holy Ghost and written by the Recording Angel of Revelation, also the Nativity Angel of the chorus. The slave surely would have known of mnemonic religious alphabets, and he, as well as his master, was familiar with the fine-tooth comb, a practical invention for the removal of head lice and other parasitic infestations, hence the metaphor of hunting Christians. The organization of the stanzas around the Christmas chorus is associative, as in a folk sermon, the birth of Christ the first premise of the salvation the speaker professes, without which he would perish in hell. See Lovell, *Black Song,* 337, for comment on stanza 3; also Miles Mark Fisher, *Negro Slave Songs in the United States* (Ithaca NY: Cornell University Press for the American Historical Association; repr. New York: Russell and Russell, 1968) 29.

Dock Reed and Vera Hall sang "Good news" for John Lomax solo and in a vigorous duet.

Good news

-Chorus-
Good news, good news,
Angel brought tidin's down
Good news, good news,
I'm huntin' fer de Lord.

-1-
God knows I am a Christian
Knows I ain't ashame
De Holy Ghost is my witness
An' de angel done sign my name.

Wa'n't dat good news, good news,
Angel brought tidin's down
Good news, good news,
I'm huntin' fer de Lord.

-2-
Oh, one dark night in December
Christ our Savior was born.
De bright light shine from heaven
Down by Bethlehem's stable door.

Wa'n't dat good news, good news,
Angel brought tidin's down
Good news, good news,
I'm huntin' fer de Lord.

-3-
Oh, you may be a white man
White as de dribberlin' snow
Ef yo' soul ain't ankeld {anchored} in Jesus
To hell you showly go.

Now ain't dat good news, good news,
Angel brought tidin's down
Good news, good news,
I'm huntin' fer de Lord.

-4-
Oh, 'H' stands fer old hell
You may go dere ef you please
Search old hell wid a fine-tooth comb
You won' find na'y Christian dere.

Now ain't dat good news, good news,
Angel brought tidin's down
Good news, good news,
I'm huntin' fer de Lord.

I believe I'll go back home

108

Mary Grisson collected a ballad of the Prodigal Son story (Luke 15:11-32) to which this song belongs (*The Negro Sings a New Heaven,* 36, eleven stanzas which closely parallel the New Testament account). The Alabama fragment opens with the confession of the penitent, a voice from another time and place which speaks in a present folk idiom, simple, forceful, and natural, evoking the New Testament parable, the division of inheritance, the "riotous living" of a foolish son, the homecoming feast, and a brother's jealousy. Thousands of miles and years later is a homelier, more familiar landscape where a happy father shouts "I 'magine this my chile." The structural and poetic center is the chorus, the core song, its last line the climatic moment of spiritual awareness. Again, repetition transcends folk-song function: "I believe I'll go back home" is the decision of every lonely, despairing soul who has tried the world and found it wanting.

Vera Hall sings this text on the Library of Congress recordings.

I believe I'll go back home

I believe I'll go back home,
I believe I'll go back home,
I believe I'll go back home,
En acknowledge that I done wrong.

-1-

When I was at home I was well supplied.
I done wrong for leaving; now I'm dissatisfied.
I believe I'll go back home,
I believe I'll go back home,
I believe I'll go back home,
En acknowledge that I done wrong.

-2-

My father saw me comin'; he met me with a smile,
He throwed his arms around me—"I 'magine this my chile."
I believe I'll go back home,
I believe I'll go back home,
I believe I'll go back home,
En acknowledge that I done wrong.

You jes' as well get ready

This is an exhortatory spiritual that warns against sin and reminds of death and judgment. The basis of argument is derived from the teachings of Christ on the unpredictability of death for which "no man knoweth the hour." From that premise the speaker proceeds logically to the practices of Christian life—praying, weeping, talking. The colloquial phrase "you better mind" means, variously, to obey as in injunctions to children, to give attention, to be strict in observance, or to consider carefully, all of which are applicable here. Compare "You'd better min' " in Work, *American Negro Songs and Spirituals,* 212.

You jes' as well get ready

-1-

Oh, you jes' wells ter get ready, you got ter die,
Oh, you jes' wells ter get ready, you got ter die,
Oh, it may be today or tomorrow
Can't tell the minute or the hour
Jes' wells ter get ready, you got to die.

-2-

You better mind how you talkin'
You better know whut you talkin' about,
You better get in touch wid Jesus,
You better mind, you better mind, you better mind,
You better get in touch wid Jesus,
You better mind.

-3-

You better mind how you pray,
You better know what you prayin' 'bout.
You better get in touch wid Jesus
You better mind.
You better mind, better mind, better mind,
You better mind, better mind, better mind,
You better get in touch with Jesus,
You better mind.

-4-

You better mind how you weep
You better know what you weepin' 'bout.
You got ter give er incount [account] in Jedgement,
You better mind.

Ankle in Jesus

110

A plumb (line) is a carpenter's device to determine the verticality; a plumb-weighted line is also used for sounding. Both meanings are suggested here: the navigational aspect is apparent in the choral tag where the soul is securely "anchored" in Christ, while the architectural context is appropriate to the idea of keeping the straight and narrow path of the Christian life, a state denied to pretenders (hypocrites), tattlers (gossips), and liars. The identification of God as a personified abstraction is rare in the spirituals, but in this song the speaker invokes the aid of Justice in the practice of Christian virtue. The antiphonal structure of this text is outstanding in performance—a version by Dock Reed and Vera Hall appears on Courlander's anthology (see "Plumb the line" in Courlander's *Negro Songs from Alabama,* 55). On the Library of Congress recordings it is sung by Dock and Vera and by the Reverend B. D. Hall family. See also Lydia Parrish, *Slave Songs of the Sea Islands,* 67-70.

Ankle in Jesus

-Chorus-

Help me Lord, plum. the line
Help me Lord, plum. the line
Help me Lord, plum. the line

-1-

Can't no pretender plum' de line
Can't no pretender plum' de line
Can't no pretender plum' de line
Can't no pretender plum' de line
Ankle in Jesus, plum' de line.

-2-

Can't no liar plum' de line
Can't no liar plum' de line
Can't no liar plum' de line
Can't no liar plum' de line
Ankle in Jesus, plum' de line.

-3-

Can't no tattler plum' de line
Can't no tattler plum' de line
Can't no tattler plum' de line
Can't no tattler plum' de line
Ankle in Jesus, plum' de line.

-4-

Help me Jestice plum' de line
Help me Jestice plum' de line
Help me Jestice plum' de line
Help me Jestice plum' de line

Oh Lord, plum' de line
Oh Lord, plum' de line
Oh Lord, plum' de line
Ankle in Jesus, plum' de line.

Honey in the rock

This spiritual is traditional in language, structure, theme, and the catalog of relatives and sinners, all of whom are exhorted to salvation. The biblical allusion is to Deuteronomy 32:13, in the "Song of Moses," his last speech to the Israelites: "and he made him [Jacob] to suck honey out of the rock." But the Old Testament symbol of God's providence for a hard-pressed people is newly associated with the grace of salvation offered by the New Testament Christ, an experience at once comforting, as imaged in "walkin' by my Savior's side," and ecstatic, as symbolized by "honey." This transforming sacrament is conveyed with the spontaneity of folk syntax and diction—"Go taste and see dear Lord 'tis good." On one of the manuscript pages Mrs. Tartt has written "Lovely." The same page is entitled, in her hand, "Unpublished Folk Songs."

Vera Hall gave John Lomax a version of this song for the Library of Congress recording project in Sumter County.

Honey in the rock

Mother, mother come and see
  What the Lord have done for me
I am so humble
  Never get tired
I am walkin' by my Savior's side.

-Chorus-

Honey in the rock, honey in the rock
  Oh it taste like honey in the rock
Go taste and see dear Lord 'tis good
  Oh hit taste like honey in the rock.

Brother, brother come and see
  What the Lord have done for me
I am so humble
  Never get tired
I am walkin' by my Savior's side.

Sister, sister come and see /etc./

Gambler, gambler can't you see /etc./

Sinners, sinners can't you see /etc./

Down on me

112

The migratory rhymed "heaven" stanzas, affirmations of Christian faith, starkly contrast with the brilliant chorus—"Look lac ev'ybody in dis whole 'roun worl' is down on me"—a cry from the very dregs of self-humiliation, of the rejection all men feel at some time or other, so despairing that the assurance of the stanzas seems like a mocking whistle in the dark.

John Lomax recorded several variants of this text by Dock Reed and Vera Hall as well as one by a female vocal backed by a blues band. Compare "Down on me" in Work, *American Negro Songs and Spirituals,* 115.

Down on me

-Chorus-
Down on me, down on me,
Look lac ev'ybody in dis whole roun' worl'
Is down on me.

-1-
Never seed de like since I been born
People keeps er runnin'
En de train done gone.

-Chorus-
Down on me, down on me,
Look lac ev'ybody in dis whole roun' worl'
Is down on me.

-2-
When I go to heaven
Don't you know I'm gonna shout
It's no one there to turn me out.

-3-
Ef I could I showly would
Stand on de rock
Where Moses stood.

-4-
When I get to heaven gonna talk en tell
How I shourned
Dem gates in hell.

-5-
Mary and Martha
Luke and John
All God's prophets is dead en gone.

-6-
When I get to heaven
Gonner set right down
Ax my Lord fer a starry crown.

-Chorus-
Down on me, down on me,
Look lac ev'ybody in dis whole roun' worl'
Is down on me.

Jesus gonna make up my dying bed

Another of those stunning metaphors from folk life is the lyric impulse of this elegiac spiritual—Jesus the maker of the dying bed. The reference is to the cleansing, dressing, and "laying out" of the body before burial, rites enacted thousands of times in nineteenth-century rural America by kinsmen and friends, here performed by the Savior of mankind. In stanzas 1 and 2 the story of Saul (Paul) serves as the exemplum of conversion and divine power. Stanzas 3, 4, and 5 shift to the speaker's vision of his own death. In stanza 6 the unbuckling of the sword is the Christian warrior's consciously willed decision to die in Christ and gain immortal life. And throughout the song, the variety and complexity of tenses, the past of Saul and the eternal present in which Saul and the speaker coexist, the earthly present and future, and the future immortal of the speaker, create a multidimensional setting.

Each stanza carries a separate chorus which reinforces and extends the interior drama. In his blindness Saul cries, "Oh, Lord have mercy," and upon his salvation, "Oh, I'm anchored in Jesus." On his deathbed the speaker exults, "Then I'll be sleeping in Jesus," and "Then I'll be dying easy." At Jordan he shouts, "Then I'll be crossing over," and as he pierces the gold sand, "Then I'll be gone to glory."

Mrs. Tartt attributed the text to A. A. Anderson ("Sung by A. A. Anderson / Shiloh Zion Church / Boyd, Alabama" appears at the foot of the page), but she must also have heard the song many times from her friend Dock Reed who made several beautiful recordings for the Library of Congress. Dock also recorded a version for Harold Courlander (see *Negro Songs from Alabama,* 49). In the Ramsey recordings series it is sung by Horace Sprott. Compare the versions in Work, *American Negro Songs and Spirituals,* 112, and Arnold, *Folksongs of Alabama,* 170. See also "Don't you be uneasy," above, and the comments there.

Jesus gonna make up my dying bed

114

-1-
Saul was on his way to Damascus
He was a wicked man
Just before he reached the city
They were leading him by the hand.

-Chorus-
Oh Lord have mercy
Oh Lord have mercy
Oh Lord have mercy
Jesus gonna make up my dying bed.

-2-
The power of God fell upon old Saul
Just lac on you and I
Just before he reached the city
I heard him begin to cry.

-Chorus-
Oh I'm anchored in Jesus
Oh I'm anchored in Jesus
Oh I'm anchored in Jesus
Jesus gonna make up my dying bed.

-3-
In my hour of dying
I don't want no body to cry
All I want you to do for me
Is to close my dying eye.

-Chorus-
Then I'll be sleeping in Jesus
Then I'll be sleeping in Jesus
Then I'll be sleeping in Jesus
Jesus gonna make up my dying bed.

-4-
In the hour of dying
I don't want no body to moan
All I want you to do for me
Is give that bell a tone.

-Chorus-
Then I'll be dying easy
Then I'll be dying easy
Oh don't you be uneasy
Jesus gonna make up my dying bed.

-5-
In the hour of dying
Somebody will say I'm lost
Just come on down to the river
And Jesus will tell you I crossed.

-Chorus-
Then I'll be crossing over
Then I'll be crossing over
Then I'll be crossing over
Jesus gonna make up my dying bed.

-6-
I'm goin' down to the river
I'm goin' jes' lac er man
An buckle my sword from roun' my side
And stick it in the golden sand.

-Chorus-
Then I'll be gone to glory
Then I'll be gone to glory
Oh don't you be uneasy
Jesus gonna make up my dying bed.

See thy lovin' Lord

The chorus is the song of the women who visit Jesus' tomb and announce the Resurrection to the disciples (in Matthew, Mary Magdalene and "the other Mary"; in Mark, Mary Magdalene, Mary the mother of James and Joses, and Salome; in Luke, women of Galilee, including Mary Magdalene, Joanna, and Mary the mother of James; in John, only Mary Magdalene; in this text, Mary the mother of Jesus). Their amazement over the miracle is conveyed by the imperatives *rise, come, see. See* is critical to both the gospel accounts and this song: in Matthew 28:6-7 the angel urges the women to *see* the empty tomb and promises that the disciples will later *see* the risen Lord; and in John 20:29, in the episode of Thomas the Doubter, the risen Lord says, "blessed are they that have not *seen,* and yet have believed." Thus the historic past of the Crucifixion is brought into the present of the Christian believer.

In the chorus the repetition of "loverin' brotherin," apart from its musical values, creates an emotional dimension not easily described but readily apparent in performance. Stanza 1 telescopes the Crucifixion (Mount Calvary) and the Resurrection (Galilee where Christ appears) through the image of an angelic band. In stanza 2 note the substitution of Mary the mother of Jesus for Mary Magdalene which, though scripturally inaccurate, reflects the importance attached to the mother emblem in Afro-American folk thought. In stanza 3 belief in the Resurrection is directly and causally related to salvation and to the immortal disposition of the soul by the allusion to the Book of Seven Seals (in Revelation) whereon the Recording Angel writes the names of the saved and the *excushuns* (excuses, sins) of the damned. The allusion to Adam and Eve in stanza 4 is a first premise of New Testament theology, that is, without original sin, the Crucifixion would have been unnecessary. In stanza 5 the comic image of King Jesus "heisting" the window to hear the prayers of Daniel is a folk signification for the martyrdom of Christ as the fulfillment of the Old Testament. To *see* the risen Christ, then, is to understand New Testament theology—original sin, Old Testament messianic prophecy, and the sacrificial death and resurrection of Christ which make possible salvation and immortal life.

Jim Carter gave Lomax a vigorous performance of this text for the Library of Congress project.

See thy lovin' Lord

116

-Chorus-

Rise en come erlong my loverin' brotherin
Come erlong my loverin' brotherin
Come erlong my loverin' brotherin
See thy loverin' Lord.

-1-

Angels come marchin' down from Mount Colverree
And the news come down from heaven
He's gone on to Galilee.

-2-

Sister Mary went to the garden
Her son fer to see
En de voice rung out in de garden
He's gone on ter Galilee.

-3-

The books of seven seals
Is lying full of excushuns
Dey is nary man sufficient
Till Christ he rose again.

-Chorus-

Rise en come erlong my loverin' brotherin
Come erlong my loverin' brotherin
Come erlong my loverin' brotherin
See thy loverin' Lord.

-4-

The devil tempted the woman
The woman tempted the man
De foolish notions in dat man
Dat brought sin in our land.

-5-

Moses en King Danuel
Prayed three prayers a day
King Jesus heisted dat window
Fer ter hear whut Danuel say.

Shepherd, shepherd

The pervasive symbol of Christ the Shepherd is given touching expression in this folk pastoral where the unforced flow of childlike dialogue, a bit like Blake's "The Lamb," is burdened with a remarkable poetic and psychological progression: the innocent confidence of "They will never go astray no more" ends with the ineffable sadness of "They will never run together any more." No matter that they are sheep and goats, sinners and saved, both were once God's creatures on a green earth, but now on the Day of Judgment their fellowship is forever lost. Compare "Shepherd, shepherd" in Work, *American Negro Songs and Spirituals,* 68. The last stanza of Mrs. Tartt's text is uncommon.

Shepherd, shepherd

Shepherd, shepherd, tell me where'd you lose yo' lamb
Shepherd, shepherd, tell me where'd you lose yo' lamb
Your sheep's all gone astray
Your sheep's all gone astray.

Pray to the Lord fer ter call 'em back again
Pray to the Lord fer ter call 'em back again
They will never go astray no more
They will never go astray no more.

Sheep's on the right hand en de goats on the left
Sheep's on the right hand en de goats on the left
They will never run together any more
They will never run together any more.

Tall angel at de bar (a, b)

118

In (a) the speaker envisions heaven: the "bar" is the judgment bar of God; the "tall angel" is presumably the Recording Angel of the Apocalypse in Revelation; and the juxtaposition of the Paul-Silas imprisonment with the poignantly comic image of "skippin' over Jerdon" brings the time of the New Testament and the future eternity of the mother into the present time of the speaker who experiences all these simultaneously.

Version (b) is a Lazarus song, notable for its dramatic development and the folk re-creation of scriptural text, to which the (a) chorus has been attached, not without associative logic: the death and raising of Lazarus prefigures that of Christ, and the "tall angel" is transformed into the angel of the Resurrection. The assignment of Mary's line "If you had been here, my brother would not have died" to Christ, though unscriptural, imparts a fresh folk insight into the New Testament tragedy—Christ is both the friend who sorrows over Lazarus and, from his superior vantage of tragic prescience, mourner of his own imminent death. The harsh rebuke in stanza 2 is also unscriptural but in the spirit of the account given by John (11:1-46) where Christ, on two separate occasions (John 11:21-27, 39-40), speaks of his divine powers to a troubled Martha. And the omission of the raising of Lazarus, well known to any congregation, does not constitute a flaw but rather serves to heighten the promise of personal resurrection in stanza 4 and the apocalyptic prophecy of stanza 5.

See Arnold, *Folksongs of Alabama,* 165, for a version of (a) as a ring shout at a church cakewalk (also titled "Tall Angel at the Bar").

Tall angel at de bar (a)

-Chorus-
Tall angel, tall angel
Tall angel at de bar.

-1-
Lord, I wonders whut's de matter,
Tall angel at de bar,
I wonders whut's de matter,
Tall angel at de bar.

-2-
Heaven struck Silas,
Tall angel at de bar,
Den heaven struck Silas,
Tall angel at de bar.

-Chorus-
Tall angel, tall angel
Tall angel at de bar.

-3-
Yonder come my mother,
Tall angel at de bar,
She is skippin' over Jerdon
Tall angel at de bar.

-Chorus-
Tall angel, tall angel
Tall angel at de bar.

Tall angels at the bar (b)

-1-
Tall angels, tall angels at the bar
Tall angels, tall angels at the bar
Ef I had er been here, tall angels at the bar
Ef I had er been here, tall angels at the bar
My brother wouldn't have died, tall angels at the bar
My brother wouldn't have died, tall angels at the bar.

-2-
Will you hush your cryin' Mary, tall angel at the bar
Will you hush your cryin' Mary, tall angel at the bar
Ef you had er been here, tall angel at the bar
Ef you had er been here, tall angel at the bar.

-3-
Your brother Lazarus is dead, tall angel at the bar
Your brother Lazarus is dead, tall angel at the bar
Tall angel, tall angel at the bar
Tall angel at the bar.

-4-
You'll see your brother ergin, tall angel at the bar
You'll see your brother ergin, tall angel at the bar
Tall angel, tall angel at the bar
Tall angel at the bar.

-5-
There's trouble in the land, tall angel at the bar
There's trouble in the land, tall angel at the bar
Tall angel, tall angel at the bar
Tall angel at the bar.

New verses to Job, oh Job

120

The seven rhymed stanzas circulate throughout Afro-American folk hymnody, attaching themselves to various choruses, here the powerful "Rock Mount Zion." This particular sequence derives from sermons preached by Rich Amerson and Dock Reed whose performances for Courlander and Lomax, though individualized in vocal and personal qualities and preaching style, demonstrate the role, sequence of appearance, and structural and stylistic affinities of sermon and song in worship services. Both performers would have known that the slayer of Goliath was David, but the error in stanza 7, either deliberate or made under the stress of preaching, is interesting as poetic compression. Both David and Christ were shepherds, the one a literal keeper of flocks, the other of the spirit, and the one is heir to the other, that is, Christ descends from the "stem/root of Jesse" (Isaiah 11:1, 10; Romans 15:12), David's father, and so also the "son of David" (Matthew 1:1 and often elsewhere). In Amerson's sermon the Pilate stanza is the starting point of a long segment on the Crucifixion that, on a manner similar to that of this text, fuses Job and Christ. Joshua and David, who have their own songs, are cited as exemplars of triumphant Christians who inherit immortal joy. The heaven stanzas, commonplaces of Protestant folk-religious lore, are central to the development of sermon theme. Amerson and Reed are backed by brief congregational response, as in *uh huh,* and in the "Rock Mount Zion" chorus they modify the preaching mode to that of song leader.

New verses to Job, oh Job

-1-

I call for the water uh huh
For to wash my hand uh hun
I won't be guilty uh huh
For the innocent man uh huh.

-Chorus-

Rock Mount Zionee, rock Mount Zionee
Rock Mount Zion in the morning.
Swing low chariot, swing low chariot
Swing low chariot in the morning.

-2-

Oh one these mornings uh huh
Bright and fair uh huh
Oh me en my Lord uh huh
Gonna try the air uh huh.

-3-

Lord I ain't been to heaven uh huh
But I've been told uh huh
That the gates are pearl uh huh
And the streets are gold uh huh.

-4-

Ef you git to heaven uh huh
Before I do uh huh
Just tell them all uh huh
I'm coming too uh huh.

-5-

Oh Joshua wuz uh huh
The son of Nun uh huh
When he got to heaven uh huh
His work was done uh huh.

-6-

One day, one day uh huh
I wuz walkin' 'round uh huh
En the elements open uh huh
En the love come down uh huh.

-7-

King Jesus was
A shepherd boy
Killed Galiath
En shout fer joy.

-Chorus-

Oh want ter go to heaven
Want to go to heaven
Want to go to heaven
Want to go to heaven in the morning.

Swing low chariot, swing low chariot
Swing low chariot in the morning.
Rock Mount Zionee, rock Mount Zionee
Rock Mount Zionee in the morning.

Watch-a-man

In both the Old and New Testaments the watchman is associated with oppression, liberation, and the Apocalypse. The cry "How long," recurrent in the Bible, is emblematic of the yearning for freedom. While internal evidence suggests "Watch-a-man" may have served as a secret signal for slave insurrections, it is foremost a hymn of spiritual bondage: in folk speech undergirded by scriptural echoes, in the balanced quatrains and the repetition of an aching cry, and in its images of a domestic scene—sister, brother, father, mother standing in the doorway—this spiritual blazes with the dream of deliverance for this world *and* the next.

Watch-a-man

-Chorus-
How long, how long, how long, watch-a-man, how long?

-1-
Oh the watch-a-man standin' in the watch-a-man's door.
How long, watch-a-man, how long?
How long, how long?
How long, watch-a-man, how long?

-2-
Oh my sister standin' in de watch-a-man's door.
How long, watch-a-man, how long?
How long, how long?
How long, watch-a-man, how long?

-Chorus-
How long, how long, how long, watch-a-man, how long?

-3-
Oh my father standin' in de watch-a-man's door.
How long, watch-a-man, how long?
How long, how long?
How long, watch-a-man, how long?

-4-
Oh my mother standin' in de watch-a-man's door.
How long, watch-a-man, how long?
How long, how long?
How long, watch-a-man, how long?

-5-
Oh my brother standin' in de watch-a-man's door.
How long, watch-a-man, how long?
How long, how long?
How long, watch-a-man, how long?

He's got his eyes on me

The chorus provides the logical basis of the argument which is developed in the stanzas. An anthropomorphic God "settin' in de kingdom" sees all, hence we must not commit sin. The "I would not be" motif has a counterpart in American secular folk song: "I wouldn't marry" (a preacher, farmer, lawyer, and so forth) in the Cindy and Yellow Gal cycles. Though sermon-songs that focus intently on earthly sins may not move us to tears or laughter, they remind us vividly of our ordinary humanity and, like the others, have their place.

Compare the version of "He's got his eyes on you" in Work, *American Negro Songs and Spirituals,* 216.

He's got his eyes on me

-Chorus-

He's got his eyes on me my Lord
He's got his eyes on me my Lord
My Lord settin' in de kingdom
With his eyes on me.

-1-

I would not be a peacebreaker
I tell you the reason why
My Lord settin' in de kingdom
With his eyes on me.

-2-

I would not be a deceiver
I tell you the reason why
My Lord settin' in de kingdom
With his eyes on me.

-3-

I would not be a pretender
I tell you the reason why
My Lord settin' in de kingdom
With his eyes on me.

-4-

I would not be a gambler
I tell you the reason why
My Lord settin' in de kingdom
With his eyes on me.

-5-

I would not be a liar
I tell you the reason why
My Lord settin' in de kingdom
With his eyes on me.

Israelites shoutin' in the heaven

124

A jubilee song which identifies the redeemed Christian as the inheritor of Old Testament faith. The glory shout as an ecstatic rite of Protestant folk worship has ample biblical authority, including the battle shout of the ancient Israelites, here transformed into a praise song in heaven.

The typed manuscript presents some difficulties in reading and analysis quite uncommon with Mrs. Tartt. *Monor* is probably a typographical error: read *minor prophets*; the Hebrew children are not prophets per se but, rather, the companions of the prophet Daniel who are cast into a fiery furnace but miraculously delivered (Daniel 3). For *wouldn't* read *wasn't there*. The congregational responses *so hard, to see God,* and *goin' home* should be printed on separate lines, as they are once in each of the choruses. *Wouldn't bow* should appear as the concluding line of stanza 1, and in stanzas 2 and 3 the chorus should be printed separately.

These short antiphonal refrains, subtly placed at points of rhythmical, emotional, and logical stress or transition, display overall a structuring quality similar to that of rhyme or of syllabic patterns in written poetry. In stanza 1 the Hebrew children who "wouldn't bow" are now with other Israelites in heaven, the "home" towards which the speaker is tending. In stanza 2 "to see God," derived from John 3:3 ("Except a man be born again, he cannot see the kingdom of God"), associates the Hebrew children of Old Testament faith with the story of Nicodemus, exemplar of New Testament salvation, and both of those with the present speaker who shares their journey. "So hard" refers to the speaker's burdens in life, his "crosses" and "rocky road" and by extension to the ordeals of the Hebrew children and the Israelites. The theme of the embattled Christian, pitted against a seductive or unsympathetic world, who often has nobody even to "tell his troubles to," is expressed throughout the spirituals and Protestant hymnody where god is viewed as a caring father and Jesus as friend and counselor. See, for example, "I Must Tell Jesus" (1893) by Elisha A. Hoffman in *Baptist Hymnal* (Nashville: Convention Press, 1956) 298.

Rich Amerson recorded a version of Mrs. Tartt's text for both Lomax and Courlander (compare "Israelites shouting" in Courlander, *Negro Folk Music U.S.A.*, 248).

Israelites shoutin' in the heaven

There were three monor prophets
Lived in the days of old
Well one Shadrac Meshoc
And the other was Abedingo.

-Chorus-
Wouldn't shoutin' in the heaven
Wouldn't bow
Israelites shoutin' in the heaven
Goin' home Israelites shoutin' in the heaven
Goin' home Israelites shoutin' in the heaven.

Christ spoke to Nicerdemus
As a man would to a friend
Said you cannot enter heaven
Unless you be born ergin
To see God
Israelites shoutin' in the heaven
To see God Israelites shoutin' in the heaven
Goin' home Israelites shoutin' in the heaven
Goin' home Israelites shoutin' in the heaven.

When I get to heaven
I want to see my Lord
Gonna tell him 'bout my crosses
And 'bout dis rocky road
So hard
Israelites shoutin' in the heaven
So hard Israelites shoutin' in the heaven
So hard Israelites shoutin' in the heaven
Goin' home Israelites shoutin' in the heaven
Goin' home Israelites shoutin' in the heaven.

In that land

Here are five migratory, traditional rhymed couplets, all allied to the theme of eternal heavenly joy, to which is attached the famous "in that land" chorus. *Fare* should be understood in the sense of "How are you getting along?" and for Christian landless slaves there was no doubt that the Promised Land could but improve their lot.

See "In this lan' " in Work, *American Negro Songs and Spirituals,* 84, for a related text.

In that land

-Chorus-
In that land, land, land
In that land, land, land
Lord I know I will fare better
In that land.

-1-
Talk erbout me much as you please
More you talk I'm gonna bend my knees
Lord I know I will fare better in that land.

-2-
Jordan river deep en wide
I got er home on the other side
Lord I know I will fare better in that land.

-3-
When I get to heaven gonna sing en shout
'Cause nobody there kin turn me out
Lord I know I will fare better in that land.

-4-
When I git ter heaven gonna sit right down
Ask my Lord for a starry crown
Lord I know I will fare better in that land.

-5-
Jordan River is chilly and cold
Chill my body but not my soul
Lord I know I will fare better in that land.

Ananias, Ananias

126

A pearl of great price, this text belongs in the highest order of all American folk poetry. Like a runic inscription, it appears deceptively simple, yet its utterance unlocks archetypal myth held by a people for so long and so deeply that one sound, one letter imprinted with thousands of associations, reveals symbolic truth. Its taut intellectuality, terse drama, and evocative lyrical intensity present a dimension at once tragic and joyously triumphant, and Mrs. Tartt's collection, or any other, can show few songs which offer a comparable aesthetic and spiritual experience. Largely, this achievement rests on language, rhythms, stanzaic structure, and brilliantly focused New Testament allusions which function as metaphors, as poetic distillations of the great overriding theme of the chorus and refrain line: "whut kind er man Jesus is."

That question, the identity of Christ, is posed throughout the Gospels by his disciples, by the political and religious establishment, by his ordinary fellowmen, all who hear his teachings and witness his miracles. (The Gospel of John provided a philosophical, theological, and mystical context for the early church and later interpreters; see John 1 for the doctrine of the *Logos, Word*: the Word is God, Christ is the Son of God in whom the Word was "made flesh" [v. 14], and believers become "sons of God" [v. 12] "born, not of blood, nor of the will of the flesh, nor of the will of man, but of God" [v. 13]. The revelation of divinity occurs at Caesarea Phillipi, "And Simon Peter answered and said, Thou art the Christ, the Son of the living God" [Matthew 16:16], after the miracle of the loaves and fishes and before the Transfiguration.) Jesus' ministry widens, the paradox deepens, he calms a storm on the Sea of Galilee, and the disciples ask, "What manner of man is this, that even the wind and sea obey him?" (Mark 4:41). In the song, the question is echoed by Saul (unscriptural, though logical; cf. Acts 9:5, "Who art thou, Lord?") whose story, an arresting parable of spiritual blindness and sight, had, and still has, wide appeal in folk Protestant song and sermon: the early Chistian Ananias, in response to a vision, visits Saul (Paul) in Damascus after Saul's conversion, and, as the human instrument of divine purpose, restores Saul's sight and assists with his recovery and baptism (Acts 9:10-19). The stone of stanza 3 is the stone of burial rolled away at the Resurrection (Matthew 28:2; Mark 16:4; Luke 24:2; John 20:1; only Matthew reports that the angel of the Resurrection moved the stone, and in any case the removal is symbolic of Christ's divinity). The risen Christ appears to Saul on the road to Damascus where Saul had intended to persecute Christian believers. Thus the three stanzas are coherently linked with each other and with the chorus by means of allusions to New Testament scriptures which set forth the human-divine paradox.

The language here is fresh and natural, full of Saul's wonderment at the wind and water miracle and his own encounter with the resurrected Christ. Accustoming himself to his new belief, Saul asks again and again what kind of man Jesus is, calling over and over the name of his new Christian benefactor and friend Ananias, and these repeated inquiries carry not a tinge of doubt—they are, rather, affirmations of faith. The use of the ballad-like stanza and dialogue (with Ananias as silent respondent), the removed setting (Damascus, the house of Ananias, some time after the ministry of Jesus and immediately after the conversion of Saul) heighten the idea of Christ's divinity, which is metaphorically conveyed by the allusions. Note that the logical order of question and answer is reversed, the ruminative folk conversational mode following the spare, balanced, authoritative pronouncement of godhead: "He spoke ter de win', en de win' obey."

Vera Hall gave Lomax a lovely performance of this text for his Library of Congress recording project in Sumter County.

Ananias, Ananias

-1-

He spoke ter de win', en de win' obey,
Tell me whut kind uv er man Jesus is;
Ananias, Ananias, tell me whut kind er man Jesus is.

-2-

He spoke ter de water, en de water obey,
Tell me whut kind uv er man Jesus is;
Ananias, Ananias, tell me whut kind er man Jesus is.

-3-

He spoke ter de stone, en de stone obey,
Tell me whut kind uv er man Jesus is;
Ananias, Ananias, tell me whut kind er man Jesus is.

-Chorus-

Ananias, Ananias, Ananias, Ananias, tell me
Whut kind uv er man Jesus is.

Lord, pray wid de heaven

128

"Lord, pray wid de heaven" is a vision of death and heaven. The first stanza, a narrative and expository framework that introduces the themes of prayer and heaven, is heavily infused with folk speech and the rhetoric of the pulpit, and the coming of Judgment Day is imaged as scanning the sky for weather signs. In the second and third stanzas the scanning image is extended to the dying mother and father who yearn for heaven with the wonderful "long-lookin' eye," and the pulpit line "Behol'," an echo from the words of Christ on the cross (John 19:27), is answered by the congregational "Good Lord, let her go." The fourth stanza describes paradise: the twelve pearly gates flung wide, angels bidding welcome, and—one of the most delightful images in all Afro-American folk poetry—"King Jesus hangin' on de golden hinges," the Lord of heaven as a boy swinging on the gate, eagerly awaiting long-expected visitors. The "holy" of the chorus are the redeemed who pray with the hope of heaven and who, as they leave this world for eternity, hear the vibrant folk phrase "Say he ain't acomin' here no more."

Lord, pray wid de heaven

-1-

Yes, I'm er lookin' to de east, er lookin' to de wes',
En hit lookser lac Judgerment Day.
En ev'y po' soul dat never would er pray,
Lord, he wish he had er prayed dat day.

-Chorus-

De holy pray wid de heaven in dey mind,
De holy pray wid de heaven.

-2-

Behol' my mother when she 'bout to die,
Good Lord, let her go.
She's er lookin' to de heaven wid long-lookin' eye,
Say she ain't a-comin' here no more.

-Chorus-

De holy pray wid de heaven in dey mind,
De holy, Lord, pray wid de heaven.

-3-

Behol' my father er 'bout to die,
Good Lord, let him go.
He's er lookin' to de heaven wid long-lookin' eye,
Say he ain't a-comin' here no more.

-Chorus-

De holy pray wid de heaven in dey mind,
De holy, Lord, pray wid de heaven.

-4-

Behol' dem twelve pearly gates,
Dem gates flew open wide.
King Jesus hangin' on de golden hinges,
De angels biddin' me to come inside.

-Chorus-

De holy pray wid de heaven in dey mind,
De holy, Lord, pray wid de heaven.

Oh, show de weary traveler

The call to preach is an important minor theme in Afro-American sermon and religious song. Here, in the first stanza, the speaker, weary and walking a lonesome road, experiences the mystical revelation of holy love; in the second, he struggles with doubts and fears of inadequacy; and in the third, he resolutely faces his destiny—the God-called cannot choose, he is chosen as watchman and symbolic trumpeter who will guide other weary travellers to heaven.

Richard Jolla gives an account of his call, and Sudie Griffith chants the Watts hymn "Go Preach My Gospel" on the Ramsey recordings. Compare "Let us cheer the weary traveller" (with its "Balm in Gilead" third stanza) in Work, *American Negro Songs and Spirituals,* 190.

Oh, show de weary traveler

-1-
One day, one day I wuz weary
Walkin' in de lonesome road.
My Savior spoke unto me,
En filled my heart wid love.

-Chorus-
Oh, show de weary traveler,
Oh, show de weary traveler,
Oh, show de weary traveler,
Erlong de heavely road.

-2-
My cross is great en heavy
Whilst I am in my youth
I'm feered I'll not er be able
To preach de word uv truth.

-Chorus-
Oh, show de weary traveler,
Oh, show de weary traveler,
Oh, show de weary traveler,
Erlong de heavely way.

-3-
En he choose me as de watchman
Ter blow de trumpet dere.
Go show de weary traveler
Erlong de heavenly road.

Lord, I'm on my way

130

The Christian is always "on my way" in the spirituals, Satan gives battle at every step, and prayer is the chief weapon against him. The opening line is straight from life—"I wonder what Satan wanted wid me"—but implicit in the musing is a feeling of uneasiness: the speaker knows only too well what Satan wanted. The metaphor of running is drawn from hunting: compare the proverb "run the devil up a tree" or "around the stump." The determined, courageous faith of the Christian is dramatically conveyed in the Miltonic diction and rhythms of "beat back, beat back the hosts of hell," a metaphor which likens Satan and his fellows to beasts.

Lord, I'm on my way

-1-

I wonder whut Satan wanted wid me,
Lord, I'm on my way.
Wonder whut Satan wanted wid me,
Lord, I'm on my way.

-2-

Oh, pray we'll run de devil,
Pray we'll run de devil,
Oh, pray we'll run de devil,
I am on my way.

-3-

Beat back, beat back de hosts uv hell,
Lord, I'm on my way.
Oh, pray we'll run de devil,
Pray we'll run de devil,
Oh, pray we'll run de devil,
Lord, I'm on my way.

Blow, Gab'le, in de army

131

Gabriel is the "announcing" angel of prophetic vision in both the Old and New Testaments. (See Daniel 8:15-27 where he appears to Daniel, explains the vision of the ram and the goat, and predicts the fall of Antiochus Epiphanes who suppressed Jewish holy rites and desecrated the Temple at Jerusalem; also Daniel 9:20-27 in which he calls for the restoration of the Temple after the Babylonian captivity; Luke 1:5-25 which narrates his visit to the priest Zacharias to announce the birth and role of John the Baptist; and Luke 1:26-38, the Annunciation of the Nativity to the Virgin.) In this song Gabriel is merged with the last of the seven angels of Revelation whose trumpet announces the end of time and the inauguration of the eternal kingdom of God (Revelation 11:15). Metaphors of battle, armies, and the soldier are pervasive in the Old Testament: the ancient Israelites, in their long quest for a home in Canaan, were defeated or victorious according to the will of God whose covenant they kept or broke; and the Psalms and prophetic books image interior struggles of the soul as warfare. In the New Testament the battle is that of the Christian against moral evil, sin, and Satan: Paul writes in Romans 13:12, "The night is far spent, the day is at hand; let us, therefore, cast off the works of darkness, and let us put on the armor of light"; the extended metaphor of the Christian as soldier in Ephesians 6:10-17 has been widely circulated among American folk ("the whole armor of God," "breastplate of righteousness," "feet shod with the preparation of the gospel of peace," "the shield of faith," "the helmet of salvation," and "the sword of the spirit"); and the end of the world and time in Revelation, envisioned as the last battle at Armageddon (16:13-16) in which the kings of the earth and the great beast of seven heads and two horns are defeated by the armies of the Word of God, the King of Kings, and Lord of Lords (19:11-21), was a frequent and well-loved sermon topic in folk Protestantism. The river of stanza 3 suggests both the Jordan (passage through death) of other spirituals and the "pure river of water of life, clear as crystal, proceeding out of the throne of God and of the Lamb" (Revelation 22:1) on the banks of which grows the tree of life (22:2), a symbol prominent in the incident of the woman at the well to whom Jesus proclaims, "Whosoever drinketh of this water shall thirst again; but whosoever drinketh of the water that I shall give him . . . [it] shall be in him a well of water springing up into everlasting life" (John 4:13-14).

The brilliant chorus of this song has entered popular media tradition, especially jazz and dance. The stanzas, bound to scriptural references and the traditional catalog of relatives, articulate with the plain dignity of ordinary speech the idea of Christian life as battle and Christian death as victory, imaged by a great army crossing a river.

Blow Gab'le in de army

132

-1-
Blow Gab'le in de army uv de Lord,
Blow Gab'le in de army,
Blow Gab'le in de army uv de Lord,
Blow Gab'le in de army,

-Chorus-
Blow, Gab'le, blow, blow,
Blow, Gab'le in de army;
Blow Gab'le in de army uv de Lord,
Blow Gab'le in de army,

-2-
Oh, my sister gotter die in de army uv de Lord,
My sister gotter die in de army.
Cross de river wid de army uv de Lord,
Cross de river wid de army.

-Chorus-
Blow, Gab'le, blow, blow,
Blow, Gab'le in de army;
Blow Gab'le in de army uv de Lord,
Blow Gab'le in de army,

-3-
Oh, my brudder gotter die in de army uv de Lord,
Blow Gab'le in de army.
Cross de river wid de army uv de Lord,
Cross de river wid de army.

-Chorus-
Blow, Gab'le, blow, blow,
Blow, Gab'le in de army;
Blow Gab'le in de army uv de Lord,
Blow Gab'le in de army.

Ef I had my way, I'd tear de buildin' down

133

Here is a folk re-creation of the Samson story in Judges 13–16. The rhymed stanzas are narrated by the omniscient *I* who brings the characters and adventures of legend into an immediate folk past and, in stanza 2, into the time of the New Testament. The Old Testament distinguishes between Delilah, temptress of Samson's last adventure, and his wife (his Hebrew parents opposed the match), "a daughter of the Philistines." (His wife's deception and his own jealousy drove Samson to burn the Philistine cornfields and later to slay a thousand of them with the jawbone of an ass. See stanza 4 which alludes to Samson's withdrawl to the "rock of Etam" where he was taken captive by his own people of Judah who feared reprisals from the Philistines for Samson's burning their cornfields.) Here, as in other songs and retellings, the two women are one, Delilah "fine en fair."

Since few of the folk, white or black, brought up on the heroic tales of the Old Testament would confuse the Philistines, ancient foes of the Hebrews, with the Pharisees, the priestly caste that opposed Jesus, there is reason to believe that the Pharisee substitution is a deliberate linking of Old and New Testament events. In any case Delilah is the universal seducer who certainly would have tempted the blameless Timothy had she the opportunity. The seriocomic stanzas are countered by the tragic choral cry of the blind Samson who prays for the return of his strength to bring down the temple of Dagon in Gaza—"Ef I had my way," a folk phrase that suggests Samson is setting his own will against God, when in fact Samson's prayer and the divine will are one.

Lomax recorded a Samson song from Jeff Horton for the Library of Congress, and Courlander presents a Samson story-song on his Folkways anthology, *Negro Folk Music of Alabama* (FE4418); also see Courlander, *Negro Folk Music, U.S.A.*, 49-50, for similar text.

Ef I had my way, I'd tear de buildin' down

-1-
Delilah wuz a woman,
She wuz fine en fair.
Pleasant ter in looks,
En coal black hair.

-Chorus-
Ef I had my way,
Ef I had my way, oh Lord,
I'd tear de buildin' down.

-2-
Whether she went ter Timothy,
Lord, I can't tell.
Er lady uv de Pharisee
Pleased Samson well.

-3-
Samson mother tole him
Hit would grieve her mind
Ter have him marry
A woman er dat kind.

-Chorus-
Ef I had my way,
Ef I had my way, oh Lord,
I'd tear de buildin' down.

-4-
Samson went th'oo the cornfiel'
Dey plotted, but he wuz gone.
Many thousan' formed de plot
En hit 'twa'nt many days 'fo' Samson wuz foun'.

-Chorus-
Ef I had my way,
Ef I had my way, oh Lord,
I'd tear de buildin' down.

-5-
Samson tole his wife
Fer ter shave his head
Shave hit lac de pa'm uv yo' hand
My strength will become er nachel man.

-Chorus-
Ef I had my way,
Ef I had my way, oh Lord,
I'd tear de buildin' down.

Little angels

This perhaps is a Sunday School song. The devices of the secular nursery counting song are here carried into a religious context. The chorus implies both the Sunday morning ride to church and the train-chariot ride to heaven.

Compare another version (also from Alabama) of this counting song in White, *American Negro Folk Songs,* 103.

Little angels

-1-

There's one, there's two, there's three little angels,
There's four, there's five, there's six little angels,
There's seven, there's eight, there's nine little angels,
There is ten little angels in the band.

-Chorus-

I'm gonna ride Sunday morning,
Sunday morning, Sunday morning,
I'm gonna ride Sunday morning,
Sunday morning soon.

(Goes to one hundred.)

Clear the line before you call

136

The writings of the New Testament, especially 1 Corinthians and James, show that early Christian congregations were often beset with quarrels. This sermon-song offers a remedy for personal disputes in prayer, an idea drawn from James whose exhortatory tone, vigorous condemnation of sin, and theme of faith-without-works, all couched in homely accents and realistic folk images, have had great appeal in historic American Protestantism: "Confess your faults one to another, and pray for one another, that ye may be healed." (James 5:16) In view of this scriptural basis, the borrowing (line 2 of both stanzas) from the hymn "What a Friend We Have in Jesus" (Joseph Scriven, 1820–1886) is appropriate.

In the Old Testament, *call* is both a summons from God, often expressed by transcendent means, and a petition to Him (for mercy, forgiveness, guidance); the New Testament adds the dimension of discipleship and the new covenant of blood; in this text *call* may be understood as communication of the believer with God. However, the phrase "clear de line befo' you call" is ambiguous: a version in Arnold's *Folksongs of Alabama* (166) suggests a telephone metaphor, which could have evolved naturally over the course of the song's dissemination; possibly, the origins are in the work song, for example, railroad "tie tamping" (in which roadbed ballast is redistributed beneath the crossties by means of iron tamping picks, bars, or shovels) and "track lining" (realigning track, using heavy crowbars) songs or "calls," rhythmical sounds chanted, shouted, or sung by a section leader and with the work crew's rhythmical response; or the metaphor may derive from a military or social order, as in clearing the "line" or chain of command before one "calls" on a person of authority. In any case, the implication is that personal grievances must be resolved and set aside before one may approach God. *Naught* and *a naught* should be understood both as the indefinite pronoun, as in *anything,* and as a specific noun, as in *zero.*

See Elie Siegmeister's description of Sumter County tie tamping and track lining, which he observed with Mrs. Tartt, in "Letter from Alabama," p. 25 in *The Music Lover's Handbook* (New York: William Morrow and Co., 1943; rev. ed. *The New Music Lover's Handbook,* 1973, p. 11). Dock Reed sings this text on the Sumter County Library of Congress recordings.

Clear the line before you call

You got ter clear de line befo' you call, 'fo' you call,
'Caze God is angry wid us all, wid us all,
En ef you ever 'spects ter git to heaven,
You got to clear de line befo' you call.

-1-

En ef you has a naught agenst yo' sister,
Take her to the Lord, Lord in prayer,
En ef yer ever 'spects ter git to heaven.
You got ter clear de line befo' you call.

You got ter clear de line befo' you call, 'fo' you call,
'Caze God is angry wid us all, wid us all,
En ef you ever 'spects ter git to heaven,
You got to clear de line befo' you call.

-2-

En ef you has a naught agenst yo' antie,
Take her to the Lord, Lord in prayer,
En ef yer ever 'spects ter git to heaven.
You got ter clear de line befo' you call.

You got ter clear de line befo' you call, 'fo' you call,
'Caze God is angry wid us all, wid us all,
En ef you ever 'spects ter git to heaven,
You got to clear de line befo' you call.

"Honey in the Rock"

Bibliographical Essays

General Bibliography (For further reading)

Afro-American folklore, life, and song investigation is a most important segment of American folklore studies. Several general studies should be cited as background and commentary.

Eugene D. Genovese's *Roll, Jordan, Roll: The World the Slaves Made* (New York: Pantheon Books/ Random House, 1974) offers a penetrating analysis of American slavery with discussions of folk religion and worship, the Christian tradition, family structure, daily life and work, folk beliefs and customs, and the interpersonal relationships between masters and slaves.

In *Black Culture and Black Consciousness: Afro-American Thought from Slavery to Freedom* (New York: Oxford University Press, 1977), Lawrence W. Levine surveys and interprets thousands of nineteenth- and twentieth-century Negro folklore items gathered from every conceivable source.

In *The Slave Community: Plantation Life in the Antebellum South* (New York: Oxford University Press, 1972), John W. Blassingame's psychosocial approach to the "peculiar institution" (slavery) is distinguished by the judicious use of numerous primary sources, including nineteenth-century published slave autobiographies, unpublished slave memorabilia from records of the Bureau of Freedmen in North Carolina and Louisiana, contemporary accounts of foreign travellers and American whites, and period illustrations and photographs. Introduced by essays on African survivals, acculturation, and folk culture, Blassingame's study focuses on behavioral patterns and personality types and he concludes that the slave emerged with his self-identity intact.

In *Long Black Song: Essays in Black American Literature and Culture* (Charlottesville: University Press of Virginia, 1972), Houston A. Baker provides a stringent, bracing view of historically evolving Afro-American culture, with emphasis on its treatment by Black writers, especially Frederick Douglass, Booker T. Washington, James Baldwin, David Walker, Richard Wright, and W. E. B. Du Bois.

The writings of William Edward Burghardt Du Bois (1868–1963) spanned sixty years. Of these the most influential has been *The Souls of Black Folk: Essays and Sketches* (1903)[1] which, though regarded by Du Bois himself as social science and accounted by later critics as the herald of Black activism, poeticizes, in many notable passages, the Black experience after Reconstruction.

A seminal folksong collection was that of William Francis Allen, Charles Pickard Ware, and Lucy McKim Garrison, *Slave Songs of the United States* (New York: A. Simpson and Company, 1867). Allen's introductory essay to the 136 secular and religious folk songs (words and music—melody line only) in their

[1]Various reprints, including Chicago: A. C. McClurg and Co., 1938; Greenwich CT: Fawcett Publications, 1961; Hatboro PA; Folklore Associates, Inc., 1963 (facsimile reprint with an added foreword by Roger D. Abrahams); New York: New American Library, 1969.

collection is one of the earliest documents in Afro-American folksong scholarship.[2]

Another early and important collection was William E. Barton's *Old Plantation Hymns: A Collection of Hitherto Unpublshed Melodies of the Slaves and the Freedman, with Historical and Descriptive Notes* (Boston: Lamson, Wolffe and Co., 1899), a collection of seventy songs with Barton's brief descriptive notes.[3]

---

[2]Various reprints, including New York: Peter Smith, 1929, 1951; New York: Oak Publications, 1965. An excerpt from Allen's introduction appears as "Songs of Slavery" in *The Music Lover's Handbook,* ed. Elie Siegmeister, 683-86 (New York: William Morrow and Company, 1943); rev. ed.: *The New Music Lover's Handbook* (Irvington-on-Hudson NY: Harvey House, 1973).

Allen, Ware, and Garrison were Northern "missionaries" who after the war worked among the freedmen of Port Royal, South Carolina. Their compilation of spirituals evoked a flurry of interest, following which the real vogue for spirituals was galvanized after 1871 when nine student-singers from Fisk University in Nashville (the Jubilee Singers) toured the North with a series of concerts to raise money for their university.

With Allen, Ware, and Garrison should be mentioned Colonel Thomas Wentworth Storrow Higginson (1823–1911). Higginson (among other things, a Unitarian clergyman and the editor of the poems of Emily Dickinson) was commander of the first Negro regiment in the Union army and an interested observer of those in his charge, an interest he related at length in his *Army Life in a Black Regiment* (Boston, 1870; repr., New York: W. W. Norton & Co., 1984) chapter 9 of which deals specifically with the spirituals and includes texts. Higginson collected scores of spirituals as sung by the men in his regiment, and is considered by some as among the first serious collectors of Negro spirituals. Allen, Ware, and Garrison refer often to their correspondence with Higginson and several times quote from his writings, especially his articles in the *Atlantic Monthly.* They acknowledge that to Higginson, above all others, they "are indebted for friendly encouragement and for direct and indirect contributions" to their original stock of songs (xxxvii).

[3]Barton's collection appeared earlier as "Old Plantation Hymns" in *New England Magazine* 19 (1898): 443-65, and was reprinted in *The Social Implications of Early Negro Music in the United States,* ed. Bernard Katz (New York: The New York Times/Arno Press, 1969).

Barton's collection influenced Nicholas George Julius Ballanta(-Taylor)'s *Saint Helena Island Spirituals* (New York: G. Schirmer, 1925) which presented 103 songs, most of those we have come to regard as "classic" spirituals, transcribed from the singing of natives of St. Helena Island, South Carolina, and from the college quartet at Penn Normal, Industrial, and Agricultural School. Though brief, Ballanta(-Taylor)'s introductory essay is a cogent explanation of African concepts of harmonics, melody, and rhythm in the spirituals. (See also his discussion in "Gathering Folk Tunes in the African Country," *Musical America* 44 [25 September 1916]: 3.)

An overview of Black culture, religion, music, verbal art, and folktales is provided in *Black America,* a collection of essays edited by John F. Szwed (New York: Basic Books, 1970).

Another useful background source is *More than Dancing: Essays on Afro-American Music and Musicians* (Westport CT: Greenwood Press, 1985), especially Portia K. Maultsky's essay on West African musical influences, Irene W. Jackson's documentation of Black religious music in the urban Episcopal church of the Northeastern United States, and Lorraine M. Faxio's comments on Blacks in the WPA music sector.

The interaction of Afro- and European-folk elements is dealt with in *The Seed of Sally Good'n: A Black Family in Arkansas, 1833–1953* (Lexington: University Press of Kentucky, 1985) by Ruth Polk Patterson whose grandfather was the son and slave of a planter and a Black female slave.

That the assessment of Afro-American folk song historically has been sociocultural is clear from a collection of previously published criticism edited by Bernard Katz: *The Social Implications of Early Negro Music in the United States* (New York: The New York Times/Arno Press, 1969). Among the nineteenth-century documents that first called attention to the spirituals included by Katz are Lucy McKim Garrison's letter about the Port Royal songs (*Dwight's Journal of Music,* 8 November 1862); James Miller McKim's (Lucy Garrison's father) article on "Poor Rosy" and "No More Peck of Corn" (*Dwight's*

Journal of Music, 9 August 1862), extracted from remarks given in Philadelphia about the Port Royal Relief Society; Thomas Higginson's "Negro Spirituals" which appeared in the June 1867 issue of *Atlantic Monthly* (19:685-94); the observations of George Henry Spaulding on shouts at Port Royal, Beaufort, and St. Helena Island, South Carolina, entitled "Under the Palmetto Tree" (*Continental Monthly,* August 1863, 196-200); brief excerpts from Allen, Ware, and Garrison's *Slave Songs,* from James Weldon Johnson's introduction to *The Books of American Negro Spirituals* (see below), and from Du Bois's "Of the Songs" (from *The Souls of Black Folk*); George Cable's writings on Creole songs and dances (with original illustrations); John Lowell's essay "The Social Implications of the Negro Spiritual" (*Journal of Negro Education,* October 1939, 634-43), a watershed in Afro-American folksong social criticism; excerpts from *Journal of a Residence on a Georgia Plantation, 1838, 1839* by the English actress Frances Anne Kemble (London: Longmans, Green, 1863; New York: Harper and Brothers, 1863); and important early texts and melodies, as well as personal accounts, collected by Henry Cleveland Wood in "Negro Camp-Meeting Melodies" (*New England Magazine* n.s.6 [March 1892]: 61-64), and by William E. Barton in *Old Plantation Hymns* (first published in *New England Magazine* 19 [1898]: 443-65—see above, n.3).

The scholarly controversy over origins emerged almost simultaneously with the national discovery of slave folk song. Richard Dorson's essay "The Negro" in *American Folklore* (Chicago: University of Chicago Press, 1959) summarizes positions and findings up to about 1950. Proponents of the African-genesis theory were led by the musicologist Henry Edward Krehbiel (1854–1923) in *A Study in Racial and National Music,* first published in 1914 (repr. New York: Frederick Ungar, 1962), and by the anthropologist Melville Jean Herskovits (1895–1963), author of *The Myth of the Negro Past* (New York: Harper & Row, 1941),[4] and collector of African narratives and president of the American Folklore Society in 1945.

George Pullen Jackson, who conducted pioneer studies in the secular sources of American folk hymns and especially in the history, hymnbooks, and performance styles of Sacred Harp, advanced the white-borrowings argument in *White and Negro Spirituals: Their Life Span and Kinship* (Locust Valley NY: J. J. Augustin, 1943; see also Jackson's *White Spirituals in the Southern Uplands* [Chapel Hill: University of North Carolina Press, 1933] in which he had earlier insisted that the spiritual is heavily influenced by white hymnody).[5]

The collections of Howard W. Odum and Guy B. Johnson, *The Negro and His Songs* (Chapel Hill: University of North Carolina Press, 1925)[6] and *Negro Workaday Songs* (Chapel Hill: University of North Carolina Press, 1926) called attention to cultural and social attitudes reflected in Negro folk song, and in part affirmed George Pullen Jackson's thesis.

The Alabama collector Newman Ivey White proclaimed a genuine sympathy for the slave, but admitted in *American Negro Folk Songs* (Cambridge MA: Harvard University Press, 1928)[7] "I am fully aware that the white man has certain inescapable prejudices and that I am writing as a white man,"

---

[4]Reprinted with new preface and bibliography, New York: Beacon Press, 1958, 1967. See George Eaton Simpson, *Melville J. Herskovits,* Leaders of Modern Anthropology series (New York: Columbia University Press, 1973) which includes representative selections of Herskovits's writings.

[5]Jackson's comparison of the tunes and texts of white and Negro spirituals in two long chapters of *White Spirituals* has been convincing or at least confusing for many. Yet in 1940 John W. Work (see below) termed *White Spriituals* "one of the most commendable treatises on any phase of American folklore yet published" (*American Negro Songs,* 6).

[6]Repr. with a new foreword by Roger D. Abrahams, Hatboro PA: Folklore Associates, 1964.

[7]Repr. with a new foreword by Bruce Jackson, Hatboro PA: Folklore Associates, 1965. Includes about 800 texts or parts of texts plus fifteen "specimens of tunes."

(19) and almost all his texts are filterings from white informants.

John Wesley Work of Fisk University (Nashville)—home of the celebrated Jubilee Singers, the group which introduced concertized versions of the spirituals to the American public in 1871—believed the Negro so completely restructured white hymns as to make them his own fresh folk creation, as he wrote in *American Negro Songs and Spirituals: A Comprehensive Collection of 230 Folk Songs, Religious and Secular, with a Foreword by John W. Work* (New York: Howell Soskin Co., 1940).[8]

The African theory received its strongest support with the publication of Miles Mark Fisher's *Negro Slave Songs in the United States* (Ithaca NY: Cornell University Press for the American Historical Association, 1953; repr. New York: Russell and Russell, 1968). Fisher argues that in his native Africa the Negro used music as history and brought this usage to America; that the spirituals are therefore not folk songs, religious or otherwise, but rather contemporary history. Using the Allen, Ware, and Garrison collection as a canon, Fisher avers that the South Carolina songs are a code which, when unlocked, reveals Negro life and history during slavery and the war—insurrections, secret meetings, colonization efforts in Liberia, and actual events and persons. While admitting the influences of "non-hymnal" European airs, of some Anglo-American hymns of Watts and Wesley, and of certain nineteenth-century white secular songs, Fisher denies the importance of Christianity in the spirituals except as a superficial religious institution.

Among recent general studies of folk song are Eileen Southern's *The Music of Black Americans: A History*, 2nd ed. (New York: W. W. Norton, 1983; [1]1971) and John Lovell, Jr.'s *Black Song: The Forge and the Flames. The Story of How the Afro-American Spiritual Was Hammered Out* (New York: The Macmillan Co., 1972). Southern's book is a history of Negro music in America from its beginnings in West Africa to the middle of the twentieth century. Examining numerous important secondary sources, the author sets her subject against the wider background of American music in general at each major historical period: the slave as musician and performer in the colonies, New England, the South, and the Middle States; Negro music from the Revolution until 1866; the triumph of Negro blues and jazz and the big bands and orchestras of the 1920s and 1930s; and the Black Renaissance from 1940 to 1960.[9]

Lovell's *Black Song* presents his study of the broad implications of freedom and justice in the spirituals. In part 1 Lovell establishes his thesis of an Afro-American entity and reviews the quarrel over origins, with a resounding vote for the African side: the influence of camp-meeting songs and white hymnody was negligible and the Negro took patterns of mythical framework from the Christian tradition. In part 2 he interprets hundreds of texts as poetry: as songs of freedom, Lovell believes, they made extensive use of mask and symbol; as folk songs they provide a realistic portrait of the Negro and a faithful delineation of his culture. Lovell notes that his research turned up more than 6,000 spirituals, approximately 500 of which are referred to in his study; see pages 223-381 for discussion of these as an Afro-American folksong entity. In part 3, "The Spiritual as World Phenomenon," Lovell provides a compendium of performers, choral groups, organizations, and publications, and studies the influ-

[8]Repr. New York: Bonanza Books/Crown Publishers, n.d. (late 1950s?). Also see John W. Work and Frederick J. Work, *Folk Songs of the American Negro* (Nashville: Work Brothers, 1907; reissued by John W. Work and Fisk University in 1915), an excerpt from which—under the title "What the Negro's Music Means to Him"—appears in *The Black Experience in Religion. A Book of Readings*, ed. C. Eric Lincoln, 44-51 (Garden City NY: Anchor Books/Doubleday, 1974).

[9]An excerpt from Southern's history appears as "The Religious Occasion" in Lincoln's anthology *The Black Experience in Religion*, 51-63. Also see Southern's anthology *Readings in Black American Music*, 2nd ed., ed. Eileen Southern (New York: W. W. Norton, 1982; [1]1971), a collection of essays and articles that complements and supplements her history.)

ence of the spirituals on gospel, blues, jazz, and ragtime, the spiritual in motion pictures, plays, recordings, and television, the relationship of the spiritual to the Jewish and Catholic communities, and the international scope of the spiritual.

The frontispiece of *Black Song* is, fittingly, a photograph of the famous spirituals window in the chapel at Tuskegee Institute, Tuskegee, Alabama, which like Fisk and Hampton has been a great center for the dissemination of the concert spiritual. However, Lovell touches only lightly on the music of the spirituals and is apparently unfamiliar with the field recordings made in Alabama by John Lomax, Harold Courlander, and Frederick Ramsey, and the work of Ruby Pickens Tartt, although he does refer to Byron Arnold's *Folk Songs of Alabama* (University AL: University of Alabama Press, 1950) and the short collection (twenty-eight spirituals with music, only some of which are from Alabama) of William A. Logan and Allen M. Garrett, *Road to Heaven* (University AL: University of Alabama Press, 1955).

George Robinson advances the thesis of stylistic continuity in the passage from spirituals to gospel in *Some Aspects of the Religious Music of the United States Negro: An Ethnomusical Study with Special Emphasis on the Gospel Tradition* (New York: Arno Press, 1977), based on his musical evaluation of choir performances in the Chicago area.

Dena J. Epstein's *Sinful Tunes and Spirituals: Black Folk Music to the Civil War* (Urbana: University of Illinois Press, 1977), buttressed by an extensive survey of primary source materials, makes a good argument for a continuously evolving Black folk song which culminated in a synthesized yet distinct Afro-American identity.

Almost all the major anthologies of American folk songs contain representative spirituals. Duncan Emrich's *American Folk Poetry* (Boston: Little, Brown, and Co., 1974) with texts from the Archive of Folk Song, the Library of Congress, but no musical transcriptions. Both Alan Lomax's *The Folk Songs of North America in the English Language* (Garden City NY: Doubleday, 1960) and John and Alan Lomax's *Folk Song U.S.A.* (New York: Duell, Sloan, and Pearce, 1947) include contemporary documents and/or personal observations. Herbert Arthur Chambers has edited thirty favorite spirituals and six modern compositions in his *The Treasury of Negro Spirituals* (New York: Everson Books, Inc. 1963, 1968) with a pleasant foreword by Marian Anderson. Byron Arnold's *Folk Songs of Alabama,* like most anthologies from Southern states, has a good sprinkling of Afro-American religious and secular songs. And Mary Alice Grissom's *The Negro Sings a New Heaven* (Chapel Hill: University of North Carolina Press, 1930)[10] contains a small but interesting collection of spirituals with musical transcriptions.

Perhaps the most-famous collection of spirituals is that edited by the Negro poet James Weldon Johnson (1871–1938) and his brother John Rosamond Johnson (1873–1954) who arranged the scores, with some additional arrangements (in vol. 1 only) by Lawrence Brown. First published separately as *The Book of American Negro Spirituals* (published and twice reprinted in 1925) and *The Second Book of Negro Spirituals* (1926), the collection was later combined as *The Books of American Negro Spirituals,* 2 vols. in one (New York: The Viking Press, 1925, 1926; 9th printing of combined volumes, 1969; paperback repr. of 1969 ed., New York: Da Capo Press/Plenum Publishing Corp., 1977; 3rd ptg. 1985). James Weldon Johnson's introductory essay sets forth his theory that the songs originated with great, talented minds, unknown singers who passed them on to the folk.

A somewhat controversial collection is *Slave Songs of the Georgia Sea Islands* (New York: Creative Age Press, 1942; repr. Hatboro PA: Folklore Associates, Inc., 1965) by Lydia Parrish. At first ignored or regarded as an amateur, Parrish is reevaluated in the foreword to the 1965 reprint edition by Bruce Jackson, who, although he gently

---

[10]Repr. in Dover's Black Rediscovery series, ed. Philip S. Foner (New York: Dover Publications, Inc., 1969).

censures her lack of contemporary scholarship and her personal attitudes, admits her importance as a documenter of Sea Island folksong culture. Parrish was among the first white collectors to support the theory of African antecedents and influences and to recognize the mutual relationship of secular and religious elements, and was deeply moved by the music she collected and transcribed all her life. Parrish's notes are descriptive of worship rites, religious and social customs, and the work and daily lives of the singers. (Included are lovely photographs of the singers, of Lydia Parrish herself, and the landscape.) The musical notations show her sensitivity to the harmonics, melody, and rhythms which have baffled so many transcribers. Geographical proximity, social and other similarities, and the historical migrations from Georgia to Alabama make Lydia Parrish's collection especially relevant to this edition of Mrs. Tartt's WPA collection.

Another folksong effort by Lydia Parrish was the organization, during the 1930s, of the Spiritual Singers of Georgia, a continuation of whose performance traditions, with emphasis on the African aspect, was recorded by Alan Lomax in 1959 and 1961 as *Georgia Sea Island Songs* (New World Records, #NW 278). Bruce Kaplan and Bill Nowlin also recorded Black folk songs at St. Simons and Brunswick in 1973 (*So Glad I'm Here,* Rounder Records, #2015).

Like Parrish's, Dorothy Scarborough's approach to folksong study was intensely personal. In *On the Trail of Negro Folk songs* (Cambridge MA: Harvard University Press, 1925)[11] Scarborough writes in such a friendly way about her travels and research that the reader shares her excitement over every new discovery. The volume contains scores of texts, both religious and secular.

Frederick Ramsey, Jr. gives a similar account of his field investigations in Alabama, Mississippi, and Louisiana in his photographic essay *Been Here and Gone* (New Brunswick NJ: Rutgers University Press, 1960).

J. Owen Garfield examines the spirituals as fusions of African and Hebrew-Christian concepts of God and man in a series of short sermon-essays entitled *All God's Children: Meditations on Negro Spirituals* (Nashville: Abingdon Press, 1971).

Harold Courlander's outstanding *Negro Folk Music U.S.A.* (New York: Columbia University Press, 1963; repr. 1969) deserves particular attention here since it relies heavily on his field investigations and recordings of Negro folk music in Sumter County, Alabama. Observing that Negro folk music is "the largest body of genuine folk music still alive in the United States today," Courlander first considers West African influences and survivals in Gulla dialect and in oral literature, the reflection of African social and religious attitudes in folk music, and European and African influences. His discussion of spirituals, based on sixteen Alabama texts, emphasizes the interdependence of religious and secular elements, the biblical sources of theme, subject, and poetry, and the relationship of folk hymns to oral analogues, especially the sermon. His investigation of folk song in the context of prison and work demonstrates that individual and circumstantial factors determine both the choice of song and its modification for a specific purpose. Additionally, Courlander surveys the play-party and game-song genre as it appears in thirteen Sumter County specimens, the field holler in Sumter County singer Annie Grace Horn Dodson, the ballads of John Henry, Stagolee, Casey Jones, Lazarus, John Booker, and Frankie and Johnny, and selected Louisiana Creole folk songs. In his final chapters, Courlander deals with dances and musical instruments: the joba, calinda, ring shout, square dance, and reel; drums, washtubs, washboards, metal percussion (pots, pans, saw blades, harrow teeth), gourd rattles, the fiddle, banjo, kazoo, and the harmonica. At least two-thirds of the musical transcriptions are of Alabama songs, and the "Sources of Notated Songs" lists thirty-five recordings made in Alabama.

[11]Repr. Hatboro PA: Folklore Associates, 1963, with a foreword by Roger D. Abrahams. An excerpt from *On the Trail* appears under the title "Negro Work Songs and Blues" in the anthology *The Music Lover's Handbook* (see n.2 above), 686-91.

The first strong signal that scholars were willing to admit electronic media as bearers of folk tradition came in 1959 when D. K. Wilgus, record-review editor of the *Journal of American Folklore* (JAF), began the serious consideration of early commercial country recordings (see in particular his "The Blues of Alabama," JAF 82/326 [1969]: 400-407). In 1974 the position of record-and film-review editor for JAF was assumed by Alan Jabbour who also defended long-playing records (LPs) and film as valid sources of traditional folksong study (see JAF 87/343 [1974]: 106-108). From 1975 until 1981 the record-review editorship at JAF was filled by David Evans (see JAF 88/348 [1975]: 224-26 for his comments on the position; also "Black Gospel Recordings," JAF 89/353 [1976]: 380-83, and "Black Folk Music: Recent Recording," JAF 91/362 [1978]: 91-100). In one provocative essay, "Afro-American Music: Early Commercial and Field Recordings" (JAF 91/360 [1978]: 728-47), Evans chastised professional folklorists for abrogating their responsibilities to talented amateurs in the study of recorded Black music and lamented the scanty reproduction and distribution of field recordings held by the Archive of Folk Song, Library of Congress. Evans's successor Jeff Todd Titon, a blues scholar (see his *Early Down-Home Blues: A Musical and Cultural Analysis* [Urbana: University of Illinois Press, 1977]), continued the emphasis on Afro-American and Anglo-American song (see JAF 94/372 [1981]: 277) as has the current discography editor Norm Cohen. For a time, the JAF film and video essays were generally less comprehensive and specific than those regarding recordings, but increasingly, under Editor Toni Rankin, such folklore and folklife studies are being subjected to more careful scrutiny.

The most far-reaching changes effected by the electronic revolution, however, have been in the mechanics of collection and investigation and the selection, arrangement, and presentation of content. Serious controversy over the direction of folklore scholarship seethed throughout the 1960s, and by 1970 protest movements and the media revolution had transformed both folklore methodology and publications. (See *Southern Folklore Quarterly* 32/3 [1968], essays in theory by Ellen J. Stekhert, John Wilson Foster, and Michael Owen Jones; also see "Towards New Perspectives in Folklore," JAF 84/331 [January-March 1971].) Underground urban lore, gathered electronically and related to the folk-cultural context, surfaced everywhere—scatology, erotica, pornography, obscenity—and one cultural revolution after another was directly addressed (see "The Urban Experience and Folk Tradition," JAF 83/329 [April-June 1970]). By 1974, when Barré Toelken assumed the general editorship of JAF, the era of eye-ear-pencil investigation had ended and the triumph of the analytical culture-conscious folklorist was confirmed.

A 1960s full-length study of urban Negro lore was that of Roger D. Abrahams in *Deep Down in the Jungle: Negro Narrative Folklore from the Streets of Philadelphia* (Hatboro PA: Folklore Associates, 1964; rev. ed., Chicago: The Aldine Press, 1970) which presented unexpurgated field texts. In 1974 came Bruce Jackson's study of the Afro-American "toast,"[12] *"Get Your Ass in the Water and Swim Like Me": Narrative Poetry from Black Oral Tradition* (Cambridge MA: Harvard University Press, 1974).[11] Jackson's allied interest in blues carried him to Texas prisons where, like his predecessor John Lomax, he obtained field recordings of the folk songs that made up the core of his *Afro-American Work Songs from Texas Prisons* (Cambridge MA: Harvard University Press, 1972).[14] In his short study for JAF, "Circus and Street: Psychosocial Aspects of the Black Toast" (JAF 85 [1972]: 123-39), Jackson presented Shine and Stackolee texts. A recent anthology of Afro-American toasts and other narrative lore is *Shucking'*

[12]"Toast" refers to rhyming narrative poetry in Black-American oral tradition. (Of fairly recent vintage, the word in this sense does not appear in Webster's before 1983.)

[13]Recording available from Roundup Records, Box 474, Somerville MA 02144.

[14]A film, ed. Daniel Seeger, is available from Film Images, 1034 Lake Street, Oak Park IL 60303.

and Jivin': Folklore from Contemporary Black Americans, tales, toasts, jokes, and legends gathered by Daryl Cumber Dance (Bloomington: Indiana University Press, 1978).

Electronic research gathering has figured prominently in the study of the Afro-American sermon. Bruce A. Rosenberg's *The Art of the American Folk Preacher,* in which Rosenberg presented his thesis of oral formulas as infrastructure in Afro-American folk-religious oratory, appeared in 1970 (New York: Oxford University Press, 1970).[15] Gerald L. Davis continued this approach in *I got the Word in me and I can sing it, you know: A Study of the Performed African-American Sermon* (Philadelphia: University of Pennsylvania Press, 1985; companion film *The Performed Word*) which focuses on the sermon as a narrative structured by rhetorical units or formulas; the full texts of three exemplary sermons are included.

A pioneer study of Negro preaching was that of William H. Pipes (*Say Amen, Brothers! Old Time Negro Preaching*]New York: William Frederick Press, 1951]) who analyzed sermons recorded in Macon and Green counties, Georgia, under the auspices of Fort Valley State College. As Davis observes, research in American folk religion is in its infancy, and though the history and development of the Black church in American has received a fair amount of scholarly attention, experiential evidence gathered directly from the worship service is lacking. The sermon, like the song, must be documented as a coherent part of the entire folk aesthetic and religious phenomenon. Such investigations are only now beginning, as for example by Jeff Todd Titon in *Powerhouse for God: Speech, Chant, and Song in an Appalachian Baptist Church* (Austin: University of Texas Press, 1988).

The religious-secular aspect, which as dichotomy interested Frederick Ramsey in the 1950s and which Harold Courlander perceived as mutual relationship, continued to fascinate Afro-American scholars. Roger D. Abrahams explored the preacher-streetman antithesis in *Positively Black* (Englewood Cliffs NJ: Prentice-Hall, Inc., 1970). John F. Szwed considered secular and religious styles in Black folksong performance in his essay "Musical Adaptation among Afro-Americans," *Journal of American Folklore* 82/324 (1969): 112-21.[16]

The literature and criticism of blues encompasses a broad area: definitions of folk and popular blues; origins and relationships with other genres; the blues as poetry, as music, and as ethnic identity, cultural microcosm, and social phenomena; and individual recordings, performers, instruments, and vocal styles. The Center for the Study of Southern Culture at the University of Mississippi, headed by William Ferris, has recently issued *The Blues: A Bibliographic Guide,* ed. Mary L. Hart, Brenda Eagles, and Lisa Howorth, with introduction by William Ferris (New York: Garland Publishing Co., 1989). In the *Guide* Ronald T. Bailey and Simon J. Bronner present a background chapter on Afro-American history and folklore. There are other contributions by David Evans on the music of the blues, by Jeff Todd Titon on the poetry of the blues, by Robert Springer on blues as societal expression, and by Craig Warner on American literature and blues. In addition, the *Guide* offers author and title indexes and a section on individual performers.[17]

---

[15]See the critical review by William J. Samarin, "An Analytical Review of Bruce A. Rosenberg's *The Art of the American Folk Preacher,*" in *Folklore Forum* 5 (1972): 106-11. See also Rosenberg's essay "The Formulaic Quality of Spontaneous Sermons" in JAF 83/327 [1970]: 3-20.

[16]Reprinted in *Afro-American Anthropology,* ed. Norman E. Whitten, Jr. and John F. Szwed, 219-27 (New York: Free Press, 1970) and in *Man in Adaptation,* ed. Yehudi Cohen, 3:463-69 (Chicago: Aldine, 1971). See also Szwed's "Negro Music: Urban Renewal" in *Our Living Traditions: An Introduction to American Folklore,* ed. Tristram P. Coffin, 305-15 (New York: Basic Books, Inc., 1968), reprinted in the John Edwards Memorial Foundation Reprint Series (Los Angeles: U.C.L.A. Department of Folk Studies and Mythology, 1970).

[17]Since its founding, the Center has acted as stimulus, disseminator, guardian, storehouse, and sponsor of research and publication in Southern folk life, lore, literature, and the arts, and this *Guide* is a much-needed reference work in blues scholarship.

Oak Publications (New York) has led the field in full-length blues studies: Stephen Grossman, *The Country Blues Guitar* (1968) and (with Stephan Colt and Hal Grossman) *Country Blues Songbook* (1973); Paul Oliver, *Aspects of the Blues Tradition* (rev. ed. 1970)[18]; Jerry Silverman, *Folk Blues: 110 American Folk Blues* (rev. ed. 1968; original 1958); and Samuel B. Charters, *The Poetry of the Blues* (1963) and *The Bluesmen: The Story and the Music of the Men Who Made the Blues* (1967). William C. Handy, with Abbe Miles, *Blues: An Anthology* (New York: Albert and Charles Boni, 1926) has been reissued as *A Treasury of the Blues* (New York: Boni, 1949; repr. New York: Macmillan, 1972).

James H. Cone has investigated religious and secular elements in *The Spiritual and the Blues: An Interpretation* (New York: Seabury Press, 1972).[19] Courlander's chapter on the blues in *Negro Folk Music U.S.A.* (1963; repr. 1970—see above) calls attention to blues rhythms and metrical structure, tonal and vocal characteristics, and the blues as personal expression. Duncan Emrich offers specimen lyrics and an extensive bibliography in *American Folk Poetry* (1974—see above).

To the previously cited studies of Jeff Titon and Bruce Jackson may be added *Blues from the Delta* by William R. Ferris, Jr. (London: Studio Vista Ltd., 1970; repr. Garden City NY: Doubleday, 1978) which offers texts, accounts of Ferris's field investigations, letters from informants, a survey of the historical context, and an analysis of themes.[20]

In his article "Techniques of Blues Composition among Black Folksingers" (JAF 88/345 [1974]: 240-49) David Evans postulates a theory of oral-poetic formula for the blues model. John Solomon Otto and Augustus M. Burns have dealt with diction, imagery, and levels of skin color in 1920–1930 blues recordings as indexes of sociofolk culture in "The Use of Race and Hillbilly Recordings as Sources for Historical Research: The Problem of Color Hierarchy among Afro-Americans in the Early Twentieth Century" (JAF 85/338 [1972]: 344-55). Robert Ladner, Jr. considers the Black urban protest of the 1960s in "Folk Music, Pholk Music, and the Angry Children of Malcolm X" (*Southern Folklore Quarterly* 34 [June 1970]: 131-45).

The findings of Ramsey, Courlander, and John Lomax challenge those of Samuel B. Charters in *The Bluesmen: The Story and the Music of the Men Who Made the Blues* (see above), a study of early commercially recorded blues from Mississippi, Texas, and Alabama. Charters concludes that Alabama folk blues either never came to birth or mysteriously disappeared, largely because of the general poverty of the state and a scant work-song tradition, and that field studies have not uncovered significant blues performers. This opinion is also held by David Evans (as quoted by Jeff Todd Titon in JAF 90/357 [1977]: 316-30) who says that the recordings of Courlander and Ramsey are "undistinguished from either a folkloristic or commercial viewpoint."

The paucity of Alabama bluesmen on commercial discs does not prove their nonexistence. The first performer recorded by the present editors was a Pike County bluesman whose pick was a drink-bottle shard, and our investigations over the past thirty years show that there were, and are, hundreds like him, thriving unmolested by folklorists' tape recorders. In fact, the economy of Alabama from 1865 until 1940 did not prohibit the development of folk blues any more than it did the continuing evolution of the spiritual and play-party song which Mrs. Tartt and other WPA workers collected in such number and variety. To the contrary, poverty is one of the lodestones of folk blues. The evidence reviewed in

---

[18]Originally appeared as *Screening the Blues: Aspects of the Blues Tradition* (London: Cassell, 1968).

[19]See JAF 87/343 (1974).

[20]One of Ferris's informants was James Thomas, Mississippi sculptor and tale-teller, who figures in Ferris's folk-life profile "Vision in Afro-American Folk Art: The Sculpture of James Thomas," *Journal of American Folklore* 88/348 (1975): 115. Thomas appears also in the film *I Ain't Lying: Folk Tales from Mississippi* (Center for Southern Folklore, 1216 Peabody Avenue, P.O. Box 4081, Memphis TN 38104), a study notable for its integrated culture approach to folk personae. See also Ferris, "Black Prose Narrative in the Mississippi Delta: An Overview," specimen field texts with comments, in JAF 85/336 (1972): 140-52.

this volume shows a strong, extensive, diverse Alabama tradition continuous with other Afro-American folk blues of the South yet articulated, especially in the case of Sumter County, by individual performers from a restricted geographical area and folk community, as significant poetic, musical, and cultural expression.

The argument regarding origins was fiercely renewed in the 1970s with the publication of Richard M. Dorson's "Africa and the Folklorist" in *African Folklore,* ed. Richard Dorson (Bloomington: Indiana University Press, 1972).[21] Dorson's position was attacked first by William D. Piersen in "An African Background for American Negro Folktales?" (JAF 84/332 [1971]: 204-14) and then more strongly by William R. Bascom in "Folklore and the Africanist" (JAF 86/341 [1973]: 253-59). In "African and Afro-American Folklore: A Reply to Bascom and Other Misguided Critics" (JAF 88/348 [1975]: 151-64) Dorson maintained that the anthropologist and the folklorist differ significantly in function and intent; that his own *American Negro Folktales* (Greenwich CT: Fawcett Publishers, Inc., 1967) were annotated against other printed American sources, collections, and indexes of Negro storytelling and motifs; and that a multiple-origins theory was more tenable than either the black-manner, white-subject reconciliation or the theory of single-line African ancestry adapted and expanded in the new world. The end of the quarrel is not in sight.

Several bibliographies of Black folk song and culture are available, including the following. *Afro-American Folk Culture: An Annotated Bibliography of Materials from North, Central, and South America and the West Indies,* American Folklore Society Bibliographical and Special Series 31 and 32, 2 vols., ed. John F. Szwed, Roger D. Abrahams, et al. (Philadelphia: Institute for the Study of Human Issues, 1978) is useful, despite the 1973 cutoff date and some inaccuracies and omissions. Irene V. Jackson, *Afro-American Religious Music: A Bibliography and a Catalogue of Gospel Music* (Westport CT: Greenwood Press, 1979) indexes articles in Black culture, gospel, hymns, blues, and spirituals, and offers a catalog of sheet music archived at the Library of Congress.

The bibliography of the *Southern Folklore Quarterly* is now being reproduced at Indiana University, and the Bibliography Committee of the American Folklore Society has arranged for a separate Folklore Division in the annual bibliographical publications of the Modern Language Association.

Other older bibliographical aids are Tristram Coffin's *An Analytical Index to the Journal of American Folklore,* Bibliographical and Special Series 2 (Philadelphia: American Folklore Society, 1950; rev. 1963); Charles Haywood's *A Bibliography of North American Folklore and Folksong,* 2 vols. (New York: Greenberg, 1951; rev. ed. New York: Dover Publications, 1962); and D. K. Wilgus's *Anglo-American Folksong Scholarship Since 1898* (New Brunswick NJ: Rutgers University Press, 1959).

The scope of Afro-American studies is indicated in the *Southern Folklore Journal* special issue on "African and Afro-American Folklore" (39/2 [June 1975]). Judy Peiser and William Ferris have prepared a useful listing of folklore films in *American Folklore Films and Video Tapes* (Memphis: Center for Southern Folklore, 1976).

The great shift of the late twentieth century towards electronic media as powerful, instant, and complex bearers of folk tradition and as tools of research, recording, and analysis facilitated the multi- and interdisciplinary approach to subject matter once regarded as taboo, and intensified general debate over the definition of folklore as an area of academic study. But controversy in scholarship is inherent, and no matter how apparently trivial or topical, the dispute must go on, for silence or total agreement may put an end to free intellectual inquiry.

[21]See Dorson's earlier chapter on "The Negro" in which he traces the history of Negro story and song, in his *American Folklore* (Chicago: University of Chicago Press, 1959).

Entranced by the possibilities offered by technology, folklorists annually turn out hundreds of folk performances on discs, cassettes, film, and video tapes, a far cry from Lomax's cylinders and Mrs. Tartt's pen. From laboriously inscribed stone, clay, and parchment to metal type and the printing press, and now the laser wand and magic-crystal microchip—man stands on the threshold of a new oral, verbal, and imagistic language. Given the obsessional desire for knowledge and the hunger for remembrance, this technology, save for some holocaust, can only advance.

But the problems of truth telling attendant on electronic methodology are morally and ethically vexing. Bruce Jackson has dealt with both the pragmatic aspects of contemporary folklore studies and the ethics of electronic methodology in *Fieldwork* (Urbana: University of Illinois Press, 1987), but still to be settled are specific issues regarding documentation, permissions, profit sharing, and producer-performer roles in determining the contours of the finished creation.

The "instant" folklorist of the future must have a multiple vision with which to view, all at once, the lore and its personae, the electronic presenter and recorder, and the interaction of the folk with both the lore and the media. This enterprise will require a willingness to witness as the folk experience unfolds, fairness and courtesy in the reporting and analysis of findings as opposed to a penchant for manipulation towards a thesis, and, above all, a vigorously held respect for the folk as fellow human beings.

Ruby Pickens Tartt
A Bibliography

The donation of the Ruby Pickens Tartt papers by her daughter Fannie Pickens Inglis to Julia Tutwiler Library, Livingston University, Livingston, Alabama, was commemorated by a tribute from Carl Carmer, author of *Stars Fell on Alabama* (New York: The Literary Guild, 1934), who observed that Mrs. Tartt's life was a book "she never got around to writing."[1] We were allowed a glimpse of the Tartt papers in the summer of 1978. Subsequently, Ethel Scott, special collections librarian, who cataloged the bequest, provided us a check list. At the time of this writing the collection has not been opened for examination, but much about Ruby Pickens Tartt as a woman, a writer, and a folklorist may be gleaned from this check list.

Included on the list are sketches, poems, and photographs; taped interviews with Dr. Robert Gilbert, former chairman of the English Department at Livingston University; books from the childhood of her daughter; and a daybook kept by Miss Ruby's mother. Like many folklorists, Mrs. Tartt had a lifelong interest in local history, and among the papers held at Livingston are her histories of Gainseville, Epes, and Demopolis, and a rough draft of a history of Sumter County. An inveterate newspaper and magazine clipper, she hand-copied or typed numerous articles from nineteenth-century Sumter County newspapers about Reconstruction and slavery, many of which were deposited in the Library of Congress as part of the WPA Document Series. Other newspaper articles include several about the Lomaxes along with Mrs. Tartt's review of John and Alan Lomax's *Folksong U.S.A.*, biographical and critical assessments of her own work as a painter and folklorist, and several articles about the outlaw hero Steve Renfroe. Some check-list entries suggest it was her intent to collect all the folklore genres recommended by the WPA guidelines and memoranda: she made collections of remedies, superstitions, epitaphs, and sayings (especially those of Rich Amerson and Josh Horn), and there are two folk sermons (by A. A. Anderson and Birdnell Hall) on deposit.

The journals and autobiographical sketches in the Tartt collection are especially illuminating. Here she jots down recipes, clothes sizes, directions for mixing paints, picture-frame measurements, important dates in her life, memories of her youthful

---

[1]Carmer came to know Mrs. Tartt when he was teaching English at the University of Alabama. In his account of Alabama folklore she appears as "Mary Louise," his delightful hostess and mentor.

In his article "Ruby Pickens Tartt Inducted in the Alabama Women's Hall of Fame," *The Alabama Librarian* 32 (November-December 1980): 2-6, Livingston University Librarian Neil Snider includes Carmer's tribute, as well as those of Alan Lomax and Professor James A. Hand, and Livingston University President Asa Green's speech delivered on the occasion, along with a general assessment of the Tartt papers by William Stanley Hoole, dean emeritus of the University of Alabama Libraries.

New York experiences, price lists of antiques, directions to rural churches, addresses of singers, humorous and inspirational quotations which struck her fancy, rules for library usage (the Livingston city library was named for her and a special "Miss Ruby" day was held in her honor), notes for an organization of young readers styled the "Dancing Rabbit Club," and shopping lists.

The letters held at Livingston show that by 1944 she was widely known as an inexhaustible source of Alabama folklore. Benjamin A. Botkin writes for material to be included in another anthology, advises that her materials are "frozen" at the Library of Congress, and later, that her manuscripts would be loaned for two months. Fletcher Roberts of Texas asks for Alabama Christmas-cake recipes. Myrtle Miles, Alabama WPA director, thanks her for her WPA manuscripts. The *Georgia Review* wants articles on middle-class whites and mill workers. Sculptor Geneva Mercer (with whom Mrs. Tartt shared a great enthusiasm for the achievements of Julia Tutwiler) encourages her to write a book. Carl Sandburg thanks her for a letter. Elie Siegmeister sends a copy of *The Music Lover's Handbook* (see below) and his regret for Miss Ruby's recent accident. Glenn Sisk asks for her assistance with his dissertation. Harold Courlander thanks her for a newspaper story. Houghton Mifflin urges her to write a book about Negro folklore. And the Carl Carmers maintain a friendly correspondence throughout the 1940s.

Numerous letters from John Lomax reveal their mutual interests, personal affinities, and practical concerns. In one Lomax announces that *Adventures of a Ballad Hunter* is about to be published, and in another he informs her of her employment with the Library of Congress. He refers to his Christmas gift to Sumter County folk singer Dock Reed and encourages her to write a book about Dock, that he is keeping "all her beautiful letters," that he has sold her story "Blue Stockings" for fifty dollars,[2] and that her writings "will make you immortal." In still another letter Lomax requests more stories from Rich Amerson and a copy of John Horn's will. In the last of the Lomax letters, Ruby Lomax writes of her husband's illness and death and acknowledges Mrs. Tartt's letter of sympathy.

The bulk of the Livingston Tartt papers consists, first, of her WPA manuscripts in Slave Narratives, Life Histories, and folk songs, and second, of the manuscripts of her published writings. All these bear evidence that Mrs. Tartt made many revisions of her work and retained duplicate and/or multiple copies of manuscripts in various stages of their evolution. More important, the check list shows that she did indeed consider writing full-length volumes: there is a chapter outline for a book

[2]One of John Lomax's letters reassures Mrs. Tartt about copyright laws, and two undated letters from Alan Lomax, according to Mrs. Scott's check list, concern "royalties on recordings and future plans for recordings" and "contract for songs recorded in Sumter County." That Mrs. Tartt was conscious of certain legal and ethical considerations in the use of folklore materials is clear from a letter written by Oliver Bing granting permission to use his WPA interview in one of her stories. The WPA manuscripts and recordings are in public domain: project workers and editors were remunerated by federal allocations, but, so far as is now known, folklore informants were not paid.

We have found no evidence to show whether or not the Sumter County singers or Mrs. Tartt were paid royalties from any of the commercial recordings and/or books by any of the folklorists whom she aided. The problem of who owns the material in folklore collection and other similar undertakings is still unresolved. Numerous cases involving the use of both folklore and literary materials, especially posthumously, are currently being adjudicated in various courts. The executive board of the American Folklore Society addressed the ethical problems in methodology in 1987 with the position paper "Statement on Ethics: Principles of Professional Responsibility" (*The American Folklore Society Newsletter* 17/1 [1987]: 8). Some scattered attempts have been made to negotiate contracts between folklorists and informants: Henry Glassie, for example, divided royalties among the contributors of *All Silver and No Brass: An Irish Christmas Mumming* (Bloomington: Indiana University Press, 1975).

on Josh Horn, and in several entries she appears to be advancing various definitions of folklore field collections. The overriding question of why she did not write this or any other book may never be answered satisfactorily, but the check list holds a good clue: here was such a full life, however might she have done more?

Nevertheless, some fiction and WPA materials were published during her lifetime. Benjamin Botkin, the last director of the National WPA folklore program, who supervised the final disposition of thousands of manuscripts, set aside, among others, several Tartt manuscripts in the Archive of Folk Song for possible publication. More than a dozen of these manuscripts, some heavily cut, were included in Botkin's anthology of WPA Slave Narratives, *Lay My Burden Down: A Folk History of Slavery* (Chicago: University of Chicago Press, 1945). In addition, "Guinea Jim," a tale told by WPA informant Josh Horn, and the folk song "Po' Little Johnny" appeared in Botkin's *A Treasury of Southern Folklore: Stories, Ballads, Traditions of the People of the South* (New York: Crown Publishers, 1949).

The first of Mrs. Tartt's stories to be published—derived from her experience as a folklorist—were "Alabama Sketches" in *Southwest Review* 29 (Winter 1944): 234-44, and consisted of "Richard, the Tall-Hearted," "Bing Oliver Is a Pushing Man," and "A Pair of Blue Stockings." Martha Foley selected "Alabama Sketches" for her *Best American Short Stories* (New York: Houghton Mifflin, 1945) and for her and A. A. Rothberg's *U.S. Stories: Regional Stories from the Forty-Eight States* (New York: Farrar-Strauss, 1949). The Bing Oliver sketch was also included in the anthology *Son-of-a-gun Stew: A Sampling of the Southwest,* ed. Elizabeth M. Stover (Irving TX: University of Dallas Press, 1945). "Carrie Dykes—Midwife" (originally a WPA Life History) was chosen for the Texas Folklore Society publication #19 *From Hell to Breakfast* (Austin: Texas Folklore Society, 1944). "Earthy-Ann" (Hester Frye in a Tartt WPA Life History) was published in the *Southwest Review* 29 (Spring 1944): 397-405 (repr. in *Mid Country: Writings from the Heart of America,* ed. Lowry C. Wimberly [Lincoln: University of Nebraska Press, 1945]). And four Negro animal stories were offered by the *Southwest Review* 37 (Spring 1952): 137-40.

In addition to those manuscripts held by Livingston University, there are three depositories of Mrs. Tartt's folklore collections and other writings. The Alabama Department of Archives and History (Montgomery) holds her large collection of Afro-American secular and religious folk songs from Sumter County and her WPA Life Histories, Slave Narratives, and documents. Those Histories, Narratives, and folk songs that were received by the Washington office of the Work Projects Administration Federal Writers' Project, Folklore Division, are stored in the Library of Congress, Archive of Folk Songs.[3] Mrs. Tartt's correspondence with John Lo-

---

[3]The holdings of the Library of Congress in WPA Slave Narratives, together with other documents relating to slavery have been issued by George P. Rawick, ed., *The American Slave: A Composite Autobiography,* 19 vols. (Westport CT: Greenwood Press, 1972ff.): Alabama (along with Indiana) narratives appear in vol. 6. Later Rawick gathered supplementary manuscripts from various depositories and these were published in a supplement series of twelve volumes (Westport CT: Greenwood Press, 1977) with the Alabama materials in supplement vol. 1. (Narratives from Mrs. Tartt are included in both the original and the supplement series.)

The Alabama WPA Manuscripts in Life Histories and Slave Narratives present numerous difficulties. Multiple manuscripts, for example, led Rawick to believe that all his Alabama supplements were "new" when in fact almost half were earlier, later, or different manuscript versions of the same interview. We have prepared an index of the Alabama Archives holdings in Alabama Slave Narratives and Life Histories, annotated with number of manuscripts and their location in Rawick's collection, and emended by Archives librarian Sarah Ann Warren. This index is available for use in connection with the Tartt and other WPA materials. Short excerpts from Mrs. Tartt's WPA Slave Narratives, Life Histories, and one folktale are included in *Ghosts and Goosebumps: Ghost Tales, Tall Tales, and Superstitions from Alabama,* ed. Olivia Solomon and Jack Solomon (University AL: University of Alabama Press, 1981).

max is held by the University of Texas, Eugene C. Barber Texas History Center, Lomax Collection, Texas Collection Library. It is our understanding that, as in the case of the Tartt papers at Livingston, the Lomax Collection, formerly of limited access with permission by Alan Lomax, is now closed. Therefore we have had to rely principally on the evidence of manuscripts and of folksong recordings within the public domain, and then on scant published secondary materials.

Among published secondary materials, the most useful is *Toting the Lead Row: Ruby Pickens Tartt, Alabama Folklorist,* by Virginia Pounds Brown and Laurella Owens (University AL: University of Alabama Press, 1981). *Toting the Lead Row* brings together the Life Histories and Slave Narratives and presents important bibliographical data, thumbnail biographies (with some photos) of the Sumter County folk singers from whom Mrs. Tartt gathered her collections, and a biographical essay based largely on the Tartt-Lomax correspondence and John Lomax's "Alabama Field Notes" (Archive of Folk Song, Library of Congress).

John Lomax's field notes became part of his memoir *Adventures of a Ballad Hunter* (New York: Macmillan, 1947) in which his Alabama episodes figure prominently. Included are accounts of the Sumter County singers Vera Hall,[4] Dock Reed, Rich Amerson, and Enoch of the Long Bridge, and here Mrs. Tartt is presented as hospitable, warm, and energetic in her pursuit of performers, whom she always regarded with affection, loyalty, and respect.

Of the "Yankee" folklorists who visited Livingston, Elie Siegmeister recalls his three-day visit with Mrs. Tartt (whom, following Carmer—see below—he disguises as "Mary Louise") in his "Letter from Alabama" in *The Music Lover's Handbook,* ed. Elie Siegmeister (New York: William Morrow and Company, 1943).[5]

Kathryn Tucker Windham honors Mrs. Tartt as folklorist and painter in *Alabama: One Big Front Porch* (Huntsville AL: Strode Publishers, 1975). In their story of Alabama for young readers, *Alabama: From Mounds to Missiles,* 2nd ed. rev. (Huntsville AL: Strode Publishers, 1969), Helen Morgan Akens and Virgina Pounds Brown describe Mrs. Tartt's work with John Lomax and others in the gathering of Sumter County folk song and lore. All these sources can provide the basis for a much-needed full-scale biography and evaluation of Mrs. Tartt's contributions to American folklore collection.

The Tartt manuscripts are by far the most numerous and comprehensive of the general Alabama WPA collection of folk songs gathered concurrently throughout the state. Identification of Tartt folksong manuscripts which appear in this volume was made by inference from mandatory WPA data and by comparison of handwriting and typescript. The presentation order and arrangement of the manu-

---

[4]Alan Lomax based his fictional "Nora Reed" on Vera Hall Ward in *The Rainbow Sign: A Southern Documentary* (New York: Duell, Sloan, and Pearce, 1959). There is some evidence that Mrs. Tartt did not fully agree with the re-creation. Virginia Pounds Brown and Laurella Owens report that when Mrs. Tartt "chastised" Alan Lomax "for his portrayal of Vera Hall . . . he replied that she should have written about Hall herself" (*Toting the Lead Row,* 52). Brown-Owens cite a letter from Alan Lomax to Mrs. Tartt archived at Livingston University. (Vera is variously designated in the several sources as Vera Hall, Vera Ward, or Vera Hall Ward, even Vera Ward Hall. Her maiden name was Hall; she was married to three men—Riddle, Ward, and Adair. Evidently—on the basis of mention in published sources—she was Mrs. Ward for the longest period of her married life.)

[5]Rev. ed. as *The New Music Lover's Handbook* (Irvington-on-Hudson NY: Harvey House, 1973). Siegmeister tells of "Mary Louise" introducing him to several singers, including Vera Hall and her husband, Sally Ann Johnson, and a work-song-singing railroad section gang lining track. All the singers sang for Siegmeister. He was especially impressed by Vera Hall's rendition of "Black Woman." And he says he "got about thirty songs noted down and the most wonderful introduction to some fine people and exciting music in the Deep South" (25). Siegmeister's "Letter from Alabama"—in the "Fiddle Strings and Ballads" section of his well-known anthology—is on pp. 23-25 of the first edition (the 1943 wartime Victory Edition—small type, cheap paper) and on pp. 9-11 of the revised edition (1973).

scripts indicate that Mrs. Tartt intended a broad division of "secular" and "religious" songs. Her collection of secular songs, which she usually designated as "play party," is included in the present editors' *Sweet Bunch of Daisies: Folk Songs from Alabama*.[6]

With very few exceptions the manuscripts of the secular songs bear Mrs. Tartt's name or initials, typed or handwritten, and the name and address of the informant, and one, "When I Was a Young Girl," is dated "November 28, 1938."

The manuscripts of the religious songs fall into five distinct groups. Group 1, the largest, bears the handwritten title "Old Songs Collected by Ruby Pickens Tartt, Livingston, Ala., District #4, Sumter Co., Ala." Group 2, entitled "Twenty-Four Songs as Sung by Sumter Co. Negroes Collected by Ruby Pickens Tartt, Livingston, Alabama," contains thirty-four pages, all carbons, with no identifying WPA data. Group 3, "Unpublished Folk Songs," contains fifteen songs, all of which may be found also in group 1, and bears the notation "Washington Copy/11-8-37/L.H." Group 4 consists of six song texts on five carbon pages, the first page bearing Mrs. Tartt's name and address, the last "Wash. Copy/6-3-37/L.H." Group 5 bears the title "Songs submitted by Ruby Pickens Tartt, Livingston, Ala." and the notation "Washington Copy/ 9-20-37/L.H." Five of the group 5 songs also appear in group 1; the title page indicates that group 5 originally included two other songs. For one song only, "Clear the Line before You Call," no identification or association with any of the five groups can be discovered. Except for the convenient placing of a few variants and parallel texts, the presentation of religious folk songs in the present volume follows the order of the manuscripts deposited in the Alabama Archives.[7]

Our every examination of a Tartt manuscript shows her to have been a meticulous, sensitive, and accurate collector who recorded and re-created thousands of details which she preserved and arranged in an orderly, workmanlike manner remarkable for one whose life, both interior and exterior, was so intense and various. Her skills of organization, her faithful—it would seem daily— preser-

---

[6]Ed. Jack Solomon and Olivia Solomon, with musical notations by Sarah Scott and illustrations by Ophelia Walker (Bessemer AL: Colonial Press, 1991).

[7]The check list of the Tartt papers shows that approximately twenty-four "secular" song texts are held by Livingston University. Of these the following do not appear among the Tartt manuscripts at the Alabama Archives: "Bird Eye"; "Blue Bird, Blue Bird"; "Charlie over the Ocean"; "I Must See"; "I Wonder and I Wonder"; "Oh, Johnnie Brown"; "Old Lady Sally"; "Rosie"; "Stoopin' on the Window"; "That Old Mule Bray"; "Hello, Mary (subtitled "Wood-Chopping Song")"; "You Don't Miss Your Water till the Well Goes Dry"; "Pretty Betsy"; "Ha, Ole Hen Cackle"; "Me and My Wife Live Jes"; and "whose hat is that Where Mine ought to be? (*sic*).

Further, the Tartt check list suggests that approximately twenty "religious" song texts at Livingston University do not appear in the present collection or among her manuscripts at the Alabama Archives. These include "If You Ain't Got Religion, You Can't Cross"; "Jesus Knocking at Your Door"; "Certainly, Certainly, Certainly, Lord"; "Dear Lord, Take Er Me Through"; "So Soon, So Soon I'll Be at Home"; "Nothing But Joy, Joy, Joy Once There"; "Oh, Death"; "Oh, Didn't It Rain"; "Over in Zion"; "Sinner Man"; "I'm Troubled"; "Pray Hard fer to Enter de Gate"; "God Told the Angel, I'm Gwine Home Tomorrow"; "Over My Head I See Trouble in the Air"; and "Oh Lord I'm So Glad."

Without access to these texts it is impossible to determine precisely which songs among the Tartt papers do not appear in the manuscripts deposited at the Alabama Archives, since Mrs. Tartt often assigned alternate titles to the same text. (Variant titles—indeed variant texts—is characteristic of the materials with which Mrs. Tartt worked: previously unpublished folk songs preserved only by oral tradition and thus subject to the vagaries of the medium.) The Tartt papers check list indicates that Mrs. Tartt made periodic inventories of her collection: many titles mentioned in her "miscellaneous song lists" are not included in the Alabama Archives collection or, for that matter, in the Livingston Tartt papers—for example, Rich Amerson's very fine "Black Woman Blues" which was recorded by both Lomax and Courlander.

vation and interpretation of Sumter County folk culture, her bold concourse with that culture and with the larger world represented by Lomax, the conscientious discharge of her WPA position, her moral commitment to what was then and is now a stern task (that is, the presentation of a culture that was both alien and familiar to its interpreter), the unwavering pursuit of music and language she loved, and her deep fidelity to the folk who possessed those arts—all these have made our own efforts much lighter than they might have been.

The whereabouts of the Tartt song texts, both recorded and published, are well established. The jacket notes and oral comments on the Lomax and Courlander recordings; the bibliographical citations in this volume and that of the Brown-Owens book; the *Check-List of Recorded Songs* issued by the Archive of Folk Songs, the Library of Congress (1940; currently being revised); the Lomax Alabama folksong recordings for the Library of Congress together with the present editors' index in the Thomas Russell Library, Alexander City State Junior College, Alexander City, Alabama; and the bibliographical listings of published appearances of Tartt songs in the anthologies of the Lomaxes and others. When the Livingston University Tartt papers and the Tartt-Lomax correspondence become available, scholars may begin to explore in depth this Sumter County segment of Afro-American folk song.

The Folklore Division of the Federal Writers' Project had as its ultimate aim the publication of folklore collections such as Mrs. Tartt's, but unfortunately the entire federal arts structure was phased out before that aim was realized. In fact, hundreds of manuscripts, including perhaps many texts submitted by Mrs. Tartt, were never even mailed to the Washington office. In recent years there has been a revival of interest in WPA literature and folklore, and many holdings from various depositories are at last seeing the light of publication. In Alabama,[8] in addition to the Brown-Owens edition of Mrs. Tartt's WPA histories and narratives, James Seay Brown, Jr. has edited twenty-eight of the Alabama Life Histories in *Up before daylight* (University AL: University of Alabama Press, 1982) and Virginia van der Veer Hamilton has relied heavily on the Alabama Slave Narratives for her *Alabama: A Bicentennial History* (New York: W. W. Norton, 1977). It is to be hoped that more such publications, including the reissue of important early folklore collections now out of print, are forthcoming.

---

[8]For an assessment of the Alabama WPA folklore effort, see *Ghosts and Goosebumps* (see above, n. 3). For a history of New Deal art projects, see Jere Mangione, *The Dream and the Deal: The Federal Writers' Project, 1935–1943* (New York: Little, Brown, and Company, 1972; paperback by Avon, 1972) and William McDonald, *Federal Relief and the Arts* (Columbus: Ohio University Press, 1969). A preliminary bibliography of relevant WPA publications is available upon request from the Library of Congress, Archive of Folk Song.

A Discography of Alabama Afro-American Folk Songs

As was true of most WPA folklore collectors, Mrs. Tartt evidently had no access to "recording machines."[1] However, "the government recording fellow"—as one Alabama project worker styled John Avery Lomax—with Mrs. Tartt as his guide, recorded more than 600 separate songs in Sumter County during his Alabama field trips in 1937, 1939, and 1940.[2]

In 1977 the Thomas Russell Library of Alexander City State Junior College purchased duplications of those recordings from the Library of Congress Archive of Folk Song as well as those Lomax recorded in Alabama prisons and parts of the state other than Sumter County. The Sumter County segment occupies eighteen seven-inch reel-to-reel tapes, recorded at 7.5 ips. We have prepared an index of titles and singers, cross-indexed with the Library of Congress folksong acquisition number, for use with the Tartt Alabama Archives folk-song collection.

In addition, Sumter County folk songs may be heard on the six-volume commercial disc anthology *Negro Folk Music of Alabama* collected by Harold Courlander who recorded many of the Sumter County singers encountered by Lomax a decade earlier—again with the invaluable assistance of Mrs. Tartt. The Courlander anthology consists of eighty-four recordings (out of "several hundred" recorded in the field) compiled in 1950 under a grant from the Wenner-Gren Foundation for Anthropological Research and issued by Folkways Records 1950–1956 on records numbered FE 4417, 4418, 4471, 4472, 4473, and 4474.[3]

---

[1]An annotated bibliography of six tape recordings held by Livingston University indicates that Mrs. Tartt possessed at least one field recording of ten Sumter County songs, the tale of Rabbit and Buzzard, and an interview with Vera Hall Ward conducted by Alan Lomax. The remaining five tapes are comprised of lectures and interviews with Mrs. Tartt by Dr. Robert Gilbert and the dedication of the town library in her honor. (Ethel Scott, letter to the editors, 5 October 1978.)

[2]John Lomax recorded folk songs in Alabama prisons at Wetumpka, Montgomery, Speigner, and Atmore, as well as in Mobile and North Alabama. These, together with his Sumter Country recordings, place Alabama high in the Library of Congress, following disc collections, being outranked only by Texas, Virginia, and North Carolina.

A few of the Sumter County songs appear on Archive of Folk Song (AFS) recordings as follows. *The Ballad Hunter,* ed. John A. Lomax (Library of Congress AFS, 1941): songs from Sumter County appear on parts 1, 2, and 5-10. *Afro-American Spirituals, Work Songs, and Ballads,* ed. Alan Lomax and John Lomax (Library of Congress AFS): includes songs by Dock Reed, Henry Reed, and Vera Hall. *Afro-American Blues and Game Songs,* ed. Alan Lomax, John Lomax, et al. (Library of Congress AFS): several Sumter County songs, notably including Vera Hall's "Another Man Done Gone."

[3]A descriptive booklet (notes, texts, illustrations) is included with the records in addition to the jacket notes. *Negro Songs from Alabama,* collected by Harold Courlander with music transcribed by John Benson Brooks (New York: Oak Publications, 1960; rev. and enlarged 2nd ed., 1963), also sponsored by the Wenner-Gren Foundation,

A third series of recordings from Alabama, Louisiana, and Mississippi was recorded by Frederick Ramsey in 1954: *Music from the South,* 10 volumes (Folkways Records FA 2650–2659), field recordings with jacket notes, compiled under a grant from the Guggenheim Foundation. Ramsey's collection provides parallels and contrasts to the Sumter County folksong tradition documented by Lomax and Courlander.

Although Mrs. Tartt did not identify singers of spirituals on the manuscripts held by the Alabama Archives—in startling contrast to the manuscripts of her Afro-American "secular" folk songs where every song is attributed—there can be no doubt that previously and concurrently she took down texts from those who sang for both Lomax and Courlander, and that she gathered songs from other singers known to neither Lomax nor Courlander.[4] Because the Lomax, Courlander, and Ramsey recordings are significant for Afro-American folksong study in general and specifically the Tartt songs in the present collection, these series of recordings will be considered here in some detail.

The John Lomax WPA Recordings

The Sumter County Library of Congress recordings encompass every genre of religious and secular Afro-American folksong tradition and present a gallery of gifted Alabama folk singers, among whom were Vera Hall, Dock Reed, Rich Amerson, Blind Jesse Harris, Rich Brown, Hattie Godfrey, Florida Hampton, Celina Lewis, Joe and Mollie McDonald, Mary and Clabe Amerson, Liza Witt, the B. D. Hall family, Mary Jane Travis, Ed Cobb, Tom Bell, Enoch Brown, "Peeler Hatcher," Harriett McClintock, and the Mt. Pilot school children.

Summoning up the psychological and physical landscape of their music, the singers sometimes pay Lomax the ultimate compliment—performing as if he were not there. Their bard is Rich (Richard Manuel) Amerson, jokester, tale-teller, singer, preacher, and conjure man.[5]

An uproarious leg-puller, ad-libbing and embellishing with quick fluent strokes, Amerson's monologues, ruminations, and tales are animated by the trenchant self-mockery, incisive wit, sly parody, and clownishness of a born comic.[6] Save for

includes sixty-seven (of the eighty-four Courlander recorded during 1950) texts of the songs Courlander recorded in Alabama along with Brooks's music transcriptions. Folkways issued the additional Courlander recording *Ring Games* (Folkways Records FC 7004) in 1959, with song texts and game directions "assisted by Ruby Pickens Tartt and Emma Courlander." Courlander's *Spirituals with Dock Reed and Vera Hall* (Folkways Records FA 2038) appeared in 1965, and includes ten songs of the original sixteen sung by Dock and Vera on Courlander's 1950–1956 Folkways recordings.

[4]A comparison of the singers attributed to the secular songs collected by Mrs. Tartt with those recorded by Lomax for the Library of Congress is instructive. The only informants common to both Mrs. Tartt and Lomax are Celina Lewis, Florida Hampton, and Joe and Mollie McDonald. Curiously, Mrs. Tartt does not cite Vera Hall as an informant though Vera sang four of Mrs. Tartt's texts for Lomax. Among the singers identified on the Alabama Archives Tartt collection manuscripts who do not appear on the Lomax recordings are Clara Bell Witt, Laura Hines, Nannie Pratt, Mary Eason, Mat Vaughn, Carrie Dykes, Roberta Lewis, Helen Smith, Tom Tartt, May Pearl Jackson, Jennie Lee Russell, and Stella Russell.

[5]Amerson is the subject of Mrs. Tartt's WPA sketch "Graduated in Lies" (manuscript deposited in Alabama Archives and Library of Congress AFS). John Lomax's impressions of Rich Amerson appear both in his field notes and in his *Adventures of a Ballad Hunter* (New York: Macmillan Co., 1947). Also, Amerson was the subject of Harold Courlander's *Big Old World of Richard Creeks* (Radnor PA: Chilton Book Co., 1962) which includes stories by Mrs. Tartt about Amerson and several tales told by Amerson.

[6]Lomax recorded Amerson's narratives of his education, his experience in the U.S. Army, his steamboat exploits, conjuring acts, and a long folktale about a deacon and his new mule. In her brief biographical sketch of Amerson, Laurella Owens gives an extensive list of Amerson's songs and tales, as recorded in Courlander's book (see n. 5 above) and elsewhere. Virginia Pounds Brown and Laurella Owens, *Toting the Lead Row: Ruby Pickens Tartt, Alabama Folklorist* (University AL: University of Alabama Press, 1981) 155; the Amerson sketch begins on 154.

Blind Jesse Harris, Amerson is unrivalled among the Sumter County bluesmen: his "Black Woman" is the finest folk-love blues ever documented in Alabama,[7] his "Boll Weevil" a miniature comic-blues epic of the Depression in the Deep South, his "John Henry" a stunning tragic-blues saga of an Afro-American folk hero, and his tie-tamping, track-lining, and levee songs are a small textbook in Afro-American secular-religious folk song reciprocity.[8]

As a singer of spirituals, Amerson nowhere matches the artistry and emotional power of Dock Reed and Vera Hall, but his familiarity with all the performance traditions of Afro-American religious folk song and his bardic genius are apparent in supple restructuring of narrative, figurative, and melodic elements. His skills, talent, and position as high priest of lore grant him almost unlimited freedom of personal interpretation, yet this license is tempered and balanced by his role as perpetuator of a folk-music tradition. Thus, in many of his songs, notably "John the Revelator," "Jonah," "Didn't You Hear My Lord When He Called," "Zionee," "One Born Israelite," and "King David," may be discerned the quiet intensity of the teacher who expounds mysterious beauty and wisdom.

Amerson's improvised church service shows him to be bearer of Afro-American folk oratory, rhetoric, narrative, and litrugy. He warms up as a ring-tailed roarer, swearing he can't preach without a pot of greens and ten biscuits under his belt. His overture is the Job song: alternating sung verses with blues recitative and dialogue, he telescopes the Old Testament story of Job and the New Testament ministry of Christ and Day of Judgment. In his prayer of invocation to the Holy Ghost, the God of Daniel and the Hebrew children, the "Good Spirit," the "root of David," Amerson is the ancient prophet come down to "the little town of Livingston" to sing for Lomax who, like all men, must "stand in judgment," and a chorus of women moan "Amazing Grace" as he cries "Have mercy, Lord! Help us, Jesus!"

The ensuing sermon explores the motifs of the Job song: the first portion presents Job as the prototype of suffering, the second dramatizes the Crucifixion, and the third imagistically creates the Apocalypse, the transitions marked by great pulpit shouts— "Oh, John!" "Ah, Judas!" "Ah, Gabriell!" Both Job and Christ are contemporary: Job "sings the blues," his termagant wife "wasn't treating him right," Jesus walked so far that his feet "cracked open like corn pone," and the Crucifixion is poignantly humanized in a folk conversation between Christ and his mother.

Amerson's perfectly miniaturized service demonstrates the aesthetic wholeness of Afro-American Protestant folk worship—so great are his powers that the listener forgets the performance is staged for recording, and so deep is Amerson's own immersion that the con man becomes the authentic preacher.

Lomax recorded two worship services that actually occurred, both at Johnson Place Baptist Church.[9] The first, a prayer meeting, includes excellent samples of congregational hymn singing in the leader-respondent manner and several prayer

[7]Amerson's version is a paradigm of the Afro-American lyric blues ballad: clusters of folk images and vocal style, moan and falsetto, capture the emotions of a betrayed lover.

[8]The most-memorable of Amerson's songs are the work-and-woman blues "Evelina," the track-lining "Captain Can't Read, Captain Can't Write," the blues work-shout "I Ain't Gone Be Here Long," the complexly structured "Wake Up" levee song, and "Hurry Up, Sundown," the poignant blues holler of a levee worker separated from his wife and children. In all these, Amerson intersperses long melodic passages among moans, chants, shouts, and hollers. Lomax also recorded Amerson's harmonica music, freight-train blues, hunt songs, and barnyard mimicry.

[9]The Lomaxes and Mrs. Tartt were trying to reach Dock Reed's church for this recording session but violent rains forced them off the road and they stopped at Johnson Place where Dock was presiding over the prayer meeting. Lomax's field notes for this session are dated 1939. Song texts are given, but texts for prayers "were not taken down."

chants backed by a moaning chorus.[10] The second, a funeral service for Sallie Ann (?), among the most significant of the Lomax recordings in Alabama, offers a view of early twentieth-century Afro-American funeral rites which, though conforming generally to the liturgy of the Anglo-American Protestant office for the dead, are, in sermon, eulogy, and song, distinctly expressive of this folk continuum: mourners view the body while a chorus of women sing "Were You There When They Crucified My Lord?" Dock Reed and Vera Hall sing the moving "This May Be Your Last Time," women keen, suddenly Dock begins to shout, and there follows an indescribable merging of song, prophecy, chant, and pentecostal tongues. Doubtless, the service went on, but here the recording ends.[11]

All the singers Lomax recorded knew numerous religious folk songs, but unquestionably the Sumter County tradition is best displayed in Dock (Zebediah) Reed and Vera Hall. Those who would understand the spiritual can do no better than hear their songs on these Library of Congress recordings.[12] From the very first phrase, the listener knows he is hearing extraordinary musicians who sing the history of their people. Singly, they are impressive; together, they are attuned, a combination of voices unsurpassed in field recordings of Afro-American religious folk song.

Sometimes he leads, empowered by strong piety and unshakeable faith. Softly she leaves him, retreating to a shadow, her tongue kindles and she comes home, their reunion a marvel of music and worship. Or Vera will lead, her voice holding all needs and griefs and loves, and her every sound he strengthens, counterparts. Usually they begin with straightforward melody and simply rhythmic response, gradually assuming emotional, poetic, and musical complexities until, finally, meaning is distilled in a single phrase, a single note.

"Job, Job," the summit of the Sumter County spirituals, was recorded by Lomax again and again, and Dock and Vera's every performance of this traic folk hymn, which coherently fuses song, story, prayer, sermon, and chant, and mingles lyric, dramatic, and narrative modes, is flawless. Their duet repertoire includes the triumphant hymn of freedom "Free at Last," the superb funeral song "Please Jesus, Don't Leave Us Alone," the moaning sorrow song "Oh, Lord, Trouble So Hard," the jubilee "Oh, Lordy Give Me a Long, White Robe," an energetic, rigidly antiphonal "Plumb the Line," the Christmas carol "Good News," the hypnotic elegy "Low Down Death Right Easy," the great death songs "I Don't Know When Death Gone Call Me Home" and "Jesus Gonna Make Up My Dying Bed," the shouting "I've Done All I Can Do for the Lord," and the syncopated, hand-clapping "Handwriting on the Wall."

The splendor of their talents and spiritual vision shines over the grief-laden "Lord, I'm Rolling through This Dark, Dreary World," the elegiac farewell "I'm Going Away and Leave You," the Pentecostal "Waiting on You," the yearning "This Time Another Year I May Be Gone," the subdued chant "Praying at the Hills of Mount Zionee," the prayer song "In'a My Heart," and the joyous salvation songs "I'm So Glad I Got My Religion On Time" and "I Been Baptized."

---

[10]Dock Reed is the chanter. The hymns, led by Mary Tollman, include a Sacred Harp-style "I Want My Mother to Go with Me," a moaning "Well, I Guess I Will Make It to the Kingdom," and a chanted solo of Psalm 23.

[11]Two ministers preside. The first preaches a sermon on the text "Ye must be born again" (John 3:7), eulogizes the dead, and leads the congregation in antiphonal moan and chant. The second addresses the white visitors (whites, he says, taught us how to steal, lie, and cuss, but also "to know Jesus"), remembers Sallie Ann's last days on earth, and leads the congregation in "Have You Decided Which Way to Go?"

In his field notes Lomax comments that he will remember Dock's seizure "as long as I have conscious feeling. . . . Dock's soul must have had animations of immortality, not given to ordinary mortals."

[12]The field notes include eleven complete texts of Dock and Vera's songs, a sketch of Vera as a singer of "reels," and the texts of several of her secular songs. See Brown-Owens, *Toting the Lead Row,* appendix, for convenient biographical sketches of Vera (162-63) and Dock (167-68, with photo).

Dock and Vera's Revelator song "John Saw That Number" points up the importance of individual performance styles in Afro-American song tradition. First, Vera sings it solo, a vocal correlative, in chant, recitative, and melody, of the dreadful images of the Beast of the Apocalypse and the angel's flight to the bottomless pit. Dock's solo is a long cry across the fathomless gulf that separates the twentieth-century Black preacher and the exiled John, and in the silence of the singer's pause, one waits for the answer from Patmos. In their duet the apocalyptic symbolism of Revelation is brilliantly translated by his preaching shout and her richly elaborated melodic line.

Their last performance is a miniaturized re-creation of Sabbath worship service, a folk liturgical music-drama of salvation and faith. In the introductory moaning hymn, the soul, garbed in the symbolic shoes and crown of the redeemed Christian, approaches Heaven. Vera chants and moans "Have mercy on me, my Lord," Dock breaks in with a long-phrase counterpart, and after a time he takes the chant lead, her melodic response a flute aainst his impassioned prayer: "Hear my prayer, bless my white friend, come a long way from home; bless my white friend in her home today; I am your child, you are my father." And their benediction is a stirring "When I Can Read My Title Clear" beautifully modulated to "Amazing Grace."[13]

With one exception, Dock's solos are all religious songs.[14] In "For the Holy Ghost," a song of repentance and salvation, his style is evangelical preaching. The lament "Just Because I'm a Poor Child" vocally evokes the symbolic fugitive slave who begs for food and shelter. His "Death Come Creepin' in the Room" is a piteous prayer to Death, imaged as the slave merchant who seizes the mother from her family. And "God's Word Will Never Pass Away," a composed hymn which Dock says he learned recently, is sung with the sincerity of a personal religious testament.

Solo, Dock sometimes lacks the fiery exaltation he reaches with Vera, but like her, with unwavering control he explores a sound, builds a small scale around it, imparting subtle tints which can only be suggested by the term *quaver*. This vocal peculiarity is apparent in Dock's mystical communion hymn "Drinking Wine," in the psalm of exile "Down on Me," and the lovely petition "Bear Me Over till Another Year." And like Rich Amerson, Dock borrows freely: his "Good News" carol is expanded to evangelical sermon, and in "We All Have Something to Do in This World" he assembles several migratory stanzas for his didactic purpose. But Amerson's performances, however moving, are ordered out of intellectual mastery and intuitive theatricality while Dock is always the minister whose improvisations arise from some deeper, less-well-understood source.

Though Vera's vocal talents are always in evidence, without Dock's undergirding the listener may feel vaguely that something is missing. "Ananias, Ananias" exhibits, however, the forceful passion they always achieve in duet. "One Monday Morning," a salvation song which utilizes the days of the week as a unifying device, presents an interesting female preaching style. "Home in That Rock" shows her finest lyrical tones. And in "The Hearse Keep a'Rolling Somebody to the Graveyard" she conveys the desperate fear of imminent death. In "Down on Me" her voice trembles with despair and in "Motherless Child" she is the weeping orphan of the whole world. "I'll Sing with My Mother Some Day," in her highest operatic range, delicately counterpoises the sorrow of this world against hope for the next. Her most-exciting vocal display is the melodic chant "Death Is Awful," an invocation of the monstrous spectre Death, thief and cold-blooded murderer whose weapons are disease, beatings, and starvation.

[13]In their last session Dock and Vera sing "Let Your Will Be Done" and the song of the Crucifixion "See How They Done My Lord." Lomax then asks Dock to pray, and there follows a similar music-drama.

[14]Dock sang one secular song for Lomax, "Tell Me, Little Children," a didactic animal-dialogue song, but clearly he was uncomfortable with even this worldly innocence.

Vera also sings solo numerous play-party songs, and here her vocal style is notably articulate and disciplined. "Eeny-Meeny-Miny-Mo" and the hide-and-seek call "All Hid" imitate children at play. Her knee-bumping lullaby "Little Lap Dog" is sung faster and faster until it becomes a wordless chant, and she garlands the ring-game song "Miss Sallie Walker" with an ornamental melody, though in a similar children's game song "Hold the Gate" her presentation is direct and uncomplicated. In "Little Girl, Little Girl, Did You Go to College?" folk conversation is stylized as secular antiphonal dialogue. And her Christmas lullaby "Hang Up, Hang Up the Baby's Stocking" is a charming paean to motherhood.

There are other fine singers of religious folk songs on the Library of Congress Sumter County recordings. Mary Jane Travis and her children stringently observe a spirited leader-respondent antiphony in their ecstatic Pentecostal "Move de Member." Liza Witt and Betty Moore borrow a tune from Sacred Harp hymnody for their wailing "Time, Time Is a'Winding Up" and give a vivacious performance of the handclapping gospel "This Little Light of Mine."

Ed Jones recorded several hymns and spirituals, including "Jonah," "Am I a Soldier of the Cross," and "Drinking Wine," all of which exhibit contemporary gospel modifications of the leader-respondent dialogue.[15] Jim Carter, a strong, clear singer of bold, simple melodic phrase yet capable of harsh tones and complicated rhythmical patterns, transforms the Protestant hymn "I Heard the Voice of Jesus Say" into elegaic moan, intensifies "Come My Lovin' Brotherin' " to a rapid ecstatic chant, and in "Lookin' for Me" he takes the roles of both leader and respondent.

The Reverend B. D. Hall family group is distinguished by their vocal clarity and blend of Sacred Harp, gospel-quartet harmony, and antebellum worship music, yet their most-outstanding performance is the traditionally interpreted, rhythmically complex "Plumb the Line."[16]

The Sim Tartt-Clabe Amerson group from Boyd (then Boyd Station), Alabama, yielded numerous spirituals sung solo, duet, and in congregational manner. Though her voice is more strident and less given to nuance, Mattie Bell Tartt proves herself a near rival to Vera Hall Ward in "You Gone Reap Just What You Sow" and "Low Down, Chariot," and Mary Amerson's masculine tones provide supportive contrast in their duets "What More Can Jesus Do" and "Wonder What the Matter in Zionee."

Like his kinsman Rich Amerson, Clabe is a mature folk singer who varies vocal qualities according to mood and meaning. Of all the Sumter County singers who interpreted the great blues spiritual "Down on Me," Clabe best captures the despair of the bonded slave and the troubled Christian, and in "I Never Heard a Man Speak Like This Man" and "Job, Oh, Job" he is the peer of Dock Reed.

Though none of these singers challenges the high musical, poetic, and religious expression of Dock Reed and Vera Hall or the bardic role of Rich Amerson, they expand and deepen the Sumter County religious folk song tradition.

Rich (Richard) Brown, however, is his own tradition. An Ariel who lives in a whimsically self-created world with his own personal history, mathematics, philosophy, and religion, his vocal qualities are faintly Carribean, and his language is the gibberish of a sprite, at once male and female, crone and child, witch doctor and bard. His favorites are "Rock-ee My Soul," "When the Saints Go Marching In," and "I'm Gwine Jine, Jine, Jine That Heavenly Choir," all delivered in the sweet manner of a children's ring game. He obliges Lomax with a

---

[15]Liza Witt and Betty Moore were recorded on 27 October 1940 at Mrs. Tartt's home. Lomax's field notes also list several secular songs performed by Ed Jones.

[16]Lomax's field notes list eleven songs recorded by the Halls and includes a letter from Rev. Hall, 31 December 1940, in which he thanks Lomax for a Christmas card and requests copies of the recordings. In his prayer at the end of the recording session, Rev. Hall insists that the singer is, like the preacher, divinely inspired.

few hollers, but when prodded to "Holler some more," he answers "That's all the hollers I know." Asked to pray, he obediently chants the Lord's Prayer in the style of an auctioneer and concludes with "He That Believeth," an odd little song he apparently invented on the spot.[17]

Sumter County also has its Caliban, Enoch Brown, a kinsman of Rich, a strange, half-wild creature, "Enoch of the Long Bridge" who fascinated Lomax. Enoch, too, speaks a personal language, a holler with his own fantastical signature, a long cry of exile intermingled with snatches of secular and religious folk songs and random images and metaphors that seem to spring from his unconscious self.[18]

The Lomax recordings document the natural generational transmission of Sumter County folk song.[19] The musical and social interaction of families and friends is especially evident in their modifications of Anglo-European lyric and play-party tradition and may be most fully observed in Hettie and Annie Godfrey, Joe and Mollie McDonald, Celina Lewis, Harriett McClintock, Caroline and Jim Horne, and the children of Mt. Pilot School.[20]

Though the Mt. Pilot children hold their game songs in common with their elders, predictably the young introduce numerous blues and boogie variations. In the duets of Hettie Godfrey[21] and her daughter Annie, the contrast of high, clear childish tones with Hettie's mature contralto sharply reveals the antiphonal structure of their ring, dialogue, and chant specimens. The Hornes, husband and wife, perform spirituals in duet, but interestingly sing secular songs solo, Caroline a cotton-picking work song and the lovely lyric "Little Red Bird," and Jim an elaborate version of the blues holler "She Brought Me My Breakfast."[22]

The bonds of marriage, consanguinity, and community existing in the rural folk culture of the American South for two centuries are exhibited in Joe and Mollie (Mary) McDonald who grew up as house servants on adjoining plantations, married in early youth, and raised a large family.[23] Children and grandchildren sing along, all are perfectly at ease with each other, and the session provides revealing clues

---

[17]In one session, Rich Brown was more interested in making ice cream for Miss Ruby's guests than in singing for Lomax. The incident, along with Rich's sayings and fragments of song texts, is reported in Lomax's field sketch, "Uncle Rich Brown." Rich also appears in Lomax's *Adventures of a Ballad Hunter,* along with Dock, Vera, Rich Amerson, Blind Jesse Harris, and others, in the chapter entitled "Alabama Red Land" (189-208). For a brief sketch of Rich Brown, see Brown-Owens, *Toting the Lead Row,* 156.

[18]In world folk culture the holler exists as three broad types: the shout of greeting and identification over physical distance; calls to animals; and the work shout, derived from images, rhythms, and sounds of labor. The musical, vocal, and substantive aspects of the holler are determined by the individual performer. For Mrs. Tartt's comments on the holler, see *Toting the Lead Row,* 148; also see *Adventures of a Ballad Hunter,* 198-201, for Lomax's description of Enoch Brown. Another of Enoch's accomplishments was the delightful "billy goat talk," a created folk language, like "pig Latin," spoken also by Joe Fred Williams and his brother Booker who recorded samples of it during Lomax's 1937 visit.

[19]The B. D. Hall ensemble includes brothers and their father. Clabe Amerson is cousin to Rich and brother to Earthy Anne Coleman who sings duets with Rich on the Courlander series. Dock and Vera are cousins.

[20]Lomax's field notes for November 1940 list the songs recorded and include the texts of "Steal Miss Liza," "Susie," and "Go In and Out Your Windows"— attributed to Minnie Mae Coats and Vera E. Brown—none of which Lomax recorded, though all three texts appear in Mrs. Tartt's Alabama Archives collection.

[21]Hettie, Mrs. Tartt's housemaid, sang solo "Jaybird" and "Old Lady Goose," neither of which was recorded by any other Sumter County informant. The field notes include several song texts from Hettie which are not on the Library of Congress recordings. Owens sketches Hettie and includes a full-length photo in Brown-Owens, *Toting the Lead Row,* 160-61.

[22]The field notes include six texts from the Hornes. Owens sketches Caroline (and mentions husband Spencer) in *Toting the Lead Row,* 164.

[23]The McDonalds recorded the greatest number and variety of play-party, game, and dance songs for Lomax who held sessions with them during all his visits. The field notes describe the 1939 session and include texts for fifteen songs.

both to the question of the family as folksong repository and to the Afro-American origins controversy.

Though Joe and Mollie learned their numerous comic courtship songs from white employers,[24] vocal, musical, and structural elements are distinctly Afro-American, and they are adept at crossbreeds. Their "Old Gray Goose" duet is a doleful elegy closer to its English ancestor the "Cock Robin" ballad than to the more familiar comic nineteenth-century nursery song. Conversely, in Mollie's "Little Bitty Man," Anglo-American lullaby performance styles give way to the vibrant melody and rhythms of the ballad of "John Henry." Their exuberant clapping, stomping reel songs[25] reflect the passage of play-party and game songs into American folk dance where tunes and texts from who-knows-where are tossed higgedly-piggedly into the caller's bag of instruction. Mollie's frankly sexual "Titty, Mamma, Titty" might be shocking were it not for her artless performance. "Little Girl, Little Girl," though rooted in English lyric tradition, has, like Rich Brown's songs, a Carribean flavor, and a Mother Goose nonsense refrain is attached to the amusing drinking song "Ride the Blind." Mollie's "Cotton Needs Chopping" shows the work song as blues ancestor, and her "Let Him Go" the affinities of the rambling-gambling blues hero with the weary pilgrim of the spirituals. And their zany "mule songs" are interpolated with work hollers and animal cries.[26]

From the accumulated evidence of Lomax's memories and field notes and from the conversations on the Archive of Folk Song recordings, one may discern something of these Sumter County singers as individuals and of their attitudes towards their own folksong tradition. For example, the bardic assurance of Rich Amerson, the authoritative moral and musical stance of Dock Reed, Vera's anxiousness to please and her awareness of the recording situation as an official government act. Above all else stands their willingness to oblige Mrs. Tartt and John Lomax, their habitual courtesy, and their pride and sheer joy in the music. This last is especially obvious in the singers of play-party songs which celebrate the harmony between self and the universe.

Florida Hampton playfully chastised Mrs. Tartt for causing her to sin by singing reels, but clearly she relished her songs and animal tales.[27] The delightful Celina Lewis chatted happily about games and dances[28] and the spirit of childhood is incarnate in Harriett McClintock who was enchanted by the playback of her own voice.[29] Asked if she enjoyed the Rachel-Jacob blindfold kissing game she giggles, "Yes, sir! Else we wouldn't be playing it!" Ruby Lomax's photograph of Harriett, which appears in the Pounds-Owens edition of Mrs. Tartt's writings, shows a sturdy old woman, in work dress and brogans, with just the beginnings of a smile, her deep-set eyes staring hard at the camera, a solemnly posed great grandchild on either side, a third in her

---

[24]Among the songs from white tradition are "O, No, John," "Darling, Don't You Miss Me," "Shoo-Fly," "When I Was a Young Girl" (one of Mrs. Tartt's favorites which she herself often sang), "Sweet Love, My Home's in Boston," "Remember Me," and "When You Cook a Chicken, Save Me the Wing,"

[25]Among these are "Rena," "Sangaree," "Rosey," and "'Taint Gonna Rain No More."

[26]The "mule song" was widely current in Sumter County as reel, game, dance, and pantomime. Both Joe and Mollie claim to have authored "Humpback Mule": Joe swears he and his kin made it up to "play in the band" but Mollie says she and her siblings used it to dance by "in the yard." See *Toting the Lead Row,* 29, for Mrs. Tartt's comments on the mule song.

[27]The field notes date the first session with Florida as 23 July 1937, when she recorded the tales and "Go to Sleepy, Little Baby." The 29 May 1939 entry mentions Florida's concern over "sinful reels" and gives three song texts.

[28]In the field notes for 29 May 1939, Lomax wrote that Mrs. Tartt brought the "dainty" Celina to Livingston for the session during which she sang "Peep, Squirrel," "Shortenin' Bread," "Sangaree," and "Whoa, Mule."

[29]Field notes, 29 October 1940, "near Sumterville, Alabama": the account of the session is taken from a letter written by Ruby T. Lomax to her family. Since the road to her house is impassable, Harriett comes to the car and soon gathers an audience, including a preacher who discusses his theories regarding the origins of spirituals.

arms. Surely, this is not the Harriett of the recordings! Not the child who impatiently churns milk, chanting "Come, Butter, Come," and then flies through house and yard to play "Peep, Squirrel" and "Ching's Dress." Through song and remembrance, the old woman turns herself into "Po' Little Johnny," the man-child moaning woefully over his cotton picking, or a mother chanting a sleep song, and the infant sleeping under the charm of lullaby.

Harriett and Hettie, Joe and Mollie, Celina and the Hornes, the children of Mt. Pilot—their songs, too, are sweet honey seized from the rock of bondage.

In comparison to the large body of spirituals and play-party songs, Lomax's recordings of Sumter County folk blues is scant but far from negligible. Ranging over every genre (shouts, hollers, laments, boogie, moody blues, and ballads), varied in performance styles, reflecting the evolution from work and religious songs, and continuous with the Afro-American folk blues of other Southern states (especially Georgia and Mississippi where proximity facilitated the exchange of fellow bluesmen), the tradition is represented, in addition to Amerson, by Vera Hall, Blind Jesse Harris, Tom Bell, and the railroad men "Peeler Hatcher," Ed Cobb, Jeff Horton, and Ed Jones.

In her spirituals Vera incants thousands of subtle musical and poetic images but in the blues ballads of Stag-o-lee, John Henry, Lazarus, Railroad Bill, the boll weevil, and the black woman, she is only a shadow of her mentor Amerson, her vocal style marked by clarity of diction, a shy detachment from the emotional intensity of dramatic events and heroic characters, and by strict adherence—without so much as a handclap variation—to melodic and rhythmical patterns.

Vera's lyric blues, however, recall the purity and complexity of her spirituals. Her voice is once more magical on "Another Man Done Gone," the bleak elegy of a chain-gang fugitive which fascinated Carl Sandburg, and in the strangest and most touching of all Lomax's Alabama recordings, "Good-bye, Sammie," she sings a farewell lament for a runaway with the solemnity of a child who mourns more deeply than is in her power to express. In "Dink's Song," a love blues of singular beauty, she is the abandoned woman who bitterly wears the high apron of pregnancy,[30] and in "Kansas City Blues" she is the country-girl-gone-wrong, doomed to prostitution and cocaine. Had Vera wished, she might have become a famed lady of the blues.

Today there is a blues canon of regional style and idiom—Mississippi, Memphis, New Orleans, Chicago—and a calendar of folk celebrities—Ma Rainey, Bessie Smith, Leadbelly, John Lee Hooker, Muddy Waters, Jelly Roll Morton. But long before radio, the blues travelled, and a bluesman always knew another bluesman and often played under his tutelage. Many went North to work in factories by day and play bars and parties at night. Some came to town long enough to record several songs for a few dollars. But hundreds never went anywhere and died unknown except by friends and relatives. Of such relatively unknowns were the hamlet and crossroads bluesmen Mrs. Tartt presented to John Lomax.

Tom Bell, the resident Sumter County danceman who turns blues into "shimmy" and "two-step" dances, gave Lomax the best and longest version of "Stag-o-lee" and an excellent rendering of "I Can Eagle Rock," a tragic ballad about a man whose beloved wife dies young.[31] Jeff Horton recorded a moody blues version of the Appalachian ballad "Down in the Valley," "blacksnake" and "hard-woman" blues, and a version of the Lazarus ballad interesting for its John Henry tune adapted to tie-tamping rhythms.[32] Ed Cobb provided Lo-

[30]Lomax first heard "Dink's Song," according to both the field notes and *Adventures of a Ballad Hunter,* in the Brazos (River) Bottom, Texas, thirty years earlier.

[31]See Lomax's field notes "Tom Bell," 1940. Bell also sang "Corinna" and "Tell Me, Mama" both of which utilize migratory blues stanzas and poetic conventions, as well as a worried-man blues and "Rocks and Gravel," a chain-gang blues progenitor of rock.

[32]The field notes for 29 May 1939 record that Mrs. Tartt saw Horton as she and Lomax were leaving Johnson Place Baptist Church. Too drunk to sing, he came to her house the next day for recording. Horton also sang sev-

max with the one Casey Jones ballad among all the Sumter County recordings, a version he learned from a New Orleans minstrel troupe that once entertained in Livingston.

A large portion of the blues recordings reflect Lomax's long-standing interest in railroad songs. "Peeler Hatcher"[33] talked at length about his railroad work, performed numerous tie-tamping and track-lining shouts with percussive response and melodic blues intervals, and his "White Lightning" is a very fine drunkard-gambler blues.

The champion bluesman of Sumter County is Blind Jesse Harris, a local legend at the time of his recording for the Library of Congress. His voice, harsh and ragged, approaches from the distance and hovers above the heroes of blues balladry, as if he had known Stag-o-lee in the flesh and now re-created him before the listener's very eyes. Losers and outcasts gamble, drink, ramble, fight, run from the law, and make love in epic proportions, and Blind Jesse is their minstrel casting spells with his long-ago and faraway lore, brazenly altering narrative events, rearranging time and place, changing outcomes, unmasking social and political protest: "Railroad Bill" thumbs his nose at every deputy in the woods and flees to the West where he continues his Robin Hood exploits; a bluesman stubbornly keeps singing and playing his guitar in the face of his police captors; and in his masterpiece "Kansas City" the troubador becomes a satirist drawing on the springs of Afro-American mother wit.

Rarely is the accordion a blues instrument, but Blind Jesse makes it so, and more. As accompaniment, his accordion provides rhythmical counterpoint, responsive dialogue, variations and improvisations on a melodic theme, and countermelody, simulating strings, pipes, horns, and drums, sometimes sweet and nostalgic like the sidewalk organ grinder or the circus calliope, or elegant as 1890s ballroom dances, again boisterous as the town saloon.

Lomax first recorded Blind Jesse in 1937 but when he returned to Livingston in 1939 the bluesman was dead. Surely Blind Jesse understood, as the spiritual says, that this was his last time, and though he must have known many more songs, it cannot be said that he left his work unfinished.[34]

Significantly, John Lomax recorded only three white singers: Jewel Hyatt, a student at then Livingston State Teacher's College, Mrs. Tartt, and an unidentified female.[35] After four years, Lomax had fulfilled his intent to investigate every genre of Afro-American secular and religious folk song in Sumter County. A carefully edited and electronically enhanced series of these Alabama recordings is very much needed for both the scholar and the general public.

The Harold Courlander Recordings

When Harold Courlander came to Sumter County a decade after Lomax's last visit, the indomitable Mrs.

---

eral spirituals, the best a versified sermon "Now, Ain't That a Witness." With Robert Chapman and Ben Donner, Horton performed a boogie variant of the play-party "Speckled Lady" and, with Chapman, a track-lining blues holler with hummed response.

[33]See field notes, 1940. "Peeler Hatcher" is also Manuel Jones and "Pelahatchie" Jones. "Manuel" was probably his given name, and "Pelahatchie" a nickname derived from the town of Pelahatchie, Mississippi, with which he was associated either by birth or other circumstances. Two of his work blues are noteworthy for their imagery of the merciless "black woman."

[34]Field notes, 25-30 May 1939. Lomax hopes Blind Jesse is not given a harp in heaven, but a new "macordium." The recordings also include "Lose a Dollar" (one of Mrs. Tartt's three blues manuscripts), the puzzling, complex "Ballad of the Spanish American War," "Boll Weevil" with onomatopoetic freight-train rhythms, and "Willie Joe," a barroom-rambling-man song.

[35]Hyatt sang "Paper of Pins," "Frog Went a'Courtin'," "Old Shoes a'Draggin's," "I'm Travelling to the Grave," and "Press Onward and Upward." Mrs. Tartt recorded a riddle and "Jack, Jack Davis," a hide-and-seek chant. The unidentified singer performed "Come, Butter, Come," "When I Was a Young Girl," "Alone, Alone, by the Sea," and "Go to Sleepy, Little Baby." The session with Hyatt occurred, according to the field notes, on 29 October 1940, at Mrs. Tartt's home. Lomax included a copy of the riddle in his field notes, and Mrs. Tartt filed it with both the Alabama Archives and the Washington Office of the WPA.

Tartt again summoned the singers, and if now and then some of them seem constrained by the recording situation, the passing years had not diminished their powers nor corroded the song tradition.

Foremost among the new singers are the children of York School and Lily's Chapel[36] whose performances of ring and other games, play-party and dance songs illustrate the diverse functions of leader and responding group and specific orientation towards musicalization, oral recitation, dance, dramatic and narrative pantomime, or game actions. The choice between unison chant and leader-respondent is not one of personal preference, but rather is dependent on internal game structure and the relative importance of oral, musical, and physical elements. Hence, in "Charlie over the Ocean" the game song is only a warm-up and signal for the chase while "Loop de Loo" is fully musicalized as dance accompaniment and instruction. "Green Field, Rocky Row" features a strong leader who directs game action and determines forfeits, but the simpler ring dance "Miss Sallie Walker" is sung in unison. "Merry Mac" (a lengthy recitation of "Old Gray Hoss" and other migratory folk rhymes) is intended primarily as humorous oral entertainment, but in "Old Lady Sally" cumulative rhymes are chanted as instructions for pantomime, and in "Rosie" and "I Must See" the leader chants a series of rhymes that serve as reel calls. "Satisfy," replete with veiled sexual allusions and social comment on the 1930s migration of thousands "up North," though orally oriented, features complicated handclap. "See, See Rider," with the traditional "Satisfy" refrain attached, uses the fully musicalized blues song of adults for a children's pantomimic dance. And the play-party "My Gold Needle" becomes "May Go Round the Needle" to accommodate the ring-game structure.[37]

Among the adult performers of children's songs, Celina Lewis obstinately refused to record her "Little Bitty Man" lullaby, but vivaciously sang "Bull Frog," "Sangaree," "Rosie," and "Kush-ee-dye-o," playfully noting that she might be "turned out of church." Vera Hall sang only two of the "Devil's songs," her beautiful complaint "Give My Heart Ease" and the "Little Lap Dog" lullaby.

The Sumter County singers' designation of secular songs as "reels" is not without some basis, for the child's ring game and the adult's dance blues sometimes share comparable poetics, vocal qualities, and interior musical structure—in Courlander's recordings of Joe Brown the harmonica often sounds like a fiddle. Indeed, one of the attractions of the inexpensive "mouth harp" as a folk instrument is its capacity for re-creation of mechanical and natural sounds, but Brown's "Southern Pacific," like other American folk train blues, moves beyond the simple imitation of clattering wheels, engine roar, and long whistle to full symbolism of the yearning wanderer.

Nevertheless, the supreme expressive instrument of Afro-American folk song remains the human voice. Davie Lee's tongue quivers with the fear of the fugitive in "Meet Me in the Bottoms," and Archie Lee Hill spits out bitterness in his chain-gang work blues, while in contrast Red Willie Smith's "Kansas City" and "Salty Dog" take the slick, cynically comic turns of the juke-joint performer.

The performances of Annie Grace Horn[38] demonstrate individual vocal accommodations to folksong

---

[36]Since Lomax's recordings of children's game songs are technically flawed, Courlander's collection (in vol. 5) is especially welcome. See Courlander, *Negro Folk Music, U.S.A.*, for musical notations of "Old Lady Sally," "Green, Green Rocky Road," "Sally Walker," "Merry Mack" (275-79), "Satisfied" (150), "Rosie" (156), and "Amasee" (155).

[37]The needle game draws its refrain from the practice of "shooing" chickens. Among other specimens are "Stooping on the Window," in which the winding of a yarn ball suggests a reel or line game, and "Watch That Lady," a ring game of capturing "prisoners."

[38]Annie Grace was the daughter of Josh and Alice Horn, subject of one of Mrs. Tartt's WPA sketches, whose married name is given as both Dodson and Downson. In *Negro Folk Music, U.S.A.* (New York: Columbia Univer-

type. In the elegiac "Wonder Where My Brother Gone" she is leader-choragus, in "Go Preach My Gospel" the liturgical incanter, and her Rufus greeting calls, field hollers, and blues moans illustrate the formative processes by which a performer structures wordless syllables and interprets traditional oral-musical formulas.[39] Annie Grace is proof that the human voice may convey every level of meaning.

And so are Dock Reed and Vera Hall. In ten years they have forgotten nothing. Still, they sing together as friends, kinsmen, and fellow Christians, and though isolated from the sacred precincts where their music belongs, on display as it were to unnamed, invisible listeners, they seem to feel a deep obligation to set down their legacy forever. Mystically wrapped in glory, they achieve the emotional transport and aesthetic command of which every performing artist dreams.

In "Trampin'" Dock is the weary sojourner nearing Heaven and in "Somebody Talkin' about Jesus" the inspired preacher melodically intoning salvation. As the man of faith, he hears the approach of the death angel's chariot and begs "Low Down, Death" so he may wrap his bloody feet in immortal shoes. And in "Jesus Gonna Make Up My Dyin' Bed" he seems to moan his own elegy.[40]

Vera Hall's "Noah" solo has about it the wonder of an eyewitness to miracles, and in the rarely heard "What Month Was Jesus Born In" she patiently, gently teaches a child the months of the year.

Of their duets for Courlander, Dock and Vera's Job song again sets the standard for the performance of spirituals, and "Look How They Done My Lord" is a monument to Afro-American folk musical, vocal, and poetic art. Across the millennia, they enact the martyrdom at Golgotha, and so skilled are these singers, so delicately enmeshed their voices, so enraptured these believers, that metaphor, symbol, image, rhythm, and melody wear the living flesh of the Word.

Rich Amerson's recordings of spirituals on the Courlander anthology sometimes lack the vocal clarity, sincere piety, and graceful execution always present in Dock and Vera. But Amerson is accomplished in moan, chant, and shout, and here again, as bardic singer he has no peer in Sumter County, authoritatively adapting, complicating, and improvising.

Rich's "Late Over in the Evening" molds various Judgment Day and Revelator songs with the mood of elegy into a new liturgical moan. "Death Have Mercy" is vocally hoarse with apocalyptic fear, and in the chant "When You Feel Like Moaning" a Holy Spirit song of classical four-line balance, his voice is suffused with the intensity and bewilderment of mystical states. In the leader-respondent-dominated "Waiting on You" and the melodic heaven song "Come On Up to Bright Glory" his articulation is uncommonly clear. "Little David" and "Bear Me Over till Another Year" are thick with borrowings from the Bible, sermons, and other religious songs. And his Job song is a musical version of the Job sermon he preached for Lomax.[41] "Didn't

---

sity Press, 1963), 83-87 and 228, Courlander subjects her field calls to intense musical analysis. See *Toting the Lead Row,* 158, for a photo and biographical sketch.

[39]Courlander also recorded several of Enoch Brown's calls. The jacket notes call attention to Enoch's hollers as rites of magical summoning performed before he crosses the "long bridge."

[40]Other performances by Dock include the salvation hymns "Plumb the Line" and "The Blood Done Signed My Name" and an ecstatic prayer chant. Vera's "Death Is Awful," though shorn of some of the morbid images in the Lomax version, stands the listener's hair on end, and in "Travellin' Shoes" Vera is the balladeer-like narrator of a small Pilgrim's Progress. Dock and Vera's duet "Dead and Gone" is surely the finest of the many Afro-American folk elegies recorded by Lomax, Courlander, and Ramsey. See Courlander, *Negro Folk Music, U.S.A.*, for musical notations of "Noah" (246), "What Month Was Jesus Born In" (245), "The Sun Will Never Go Down" (238), "Let Me Ride" (250), "Prayer Song" (22), and "Everywhere I Go" (247).

[41]The harp refrain of "Little David" unifies stanzas on Satan, Mr. Hypocrite, and the tree of Paradise. Similarly, in "Job" the Rock Mt. Zion chorus is attached to stanzas on Pilate, Gabriel, the Apocalypse, the death angel, and Elijah's chariot. See Courlander, *Negro Folk Music, U.S.A.*, 223, 225, 227, 229, 234, 236, 238, 241, 248, for musical notations of songs recorded by Amerson and Coleman; also 266 for Amerson's "Black Woman."

You Hear My Lord Call?" supported by Earthy Ann Coleman, a skilled and talented respondent, shows liturgical antiphony to be fundamentally lyric, that is, clusters of metaphors, images, and symbols, as in the psalms and prophetic books of the Old Testament, convey transcendent meaning within the structured context of dramatic dialogue.

Amerson the tale-teller and preacher is given full display in the Courlander series. As in the earlier performances for Lomax, he announces his bardic role: "I'm sent to preach. . . . I'm built up in the frame of it. . . . I'm swallowed up in the words like Jonah swallowed the whale," he says in the brief Sunday School lesson "Animals in the Church." The Brer Rabbit tales[42] are handed down ritualistically in the manner of a conscious transmitter of traditional narrative, as if Trickster himself were recounting his own adventures. Amerson's Jonah narrative is a folktale of supernatural marvels set in Alabama, and "Texas Sandstorm," a fable of cosmic destruction and resurrection embedded with mythic symbols, is told as a deadpan, poker-faced tall tale. Though Amerson surely knew that the David-Goliath slave contest in "The Champion" was entertaining fiction, he swears to its factual truth,[43] as he also does in the tongue-in-cheek accounts of his encounter with the draft board and his visit to a Mississippi doctor who cures his "ugliness." How he ever concocted a fable set in ancient Rome is a bit puzzling—the tale of children who escape death when their would-be murderers mistake ordinary geese for angelic guardians probably owes something to the story of the infant Moses and to the New Testament Slaughter of the Innocents—but given Amerson's intelligence and talent, one would not be at all surprised if he narrated tales from Chaucer or Ovid.[44]

The Frederick Ramsey Recordings

What is missing in Courlander's *Negro Folk Songs of Alabama* may be found in Frederick Ramsey's *Music from the South.* While Courlander confines his field survey mostly to Sumter County and focuses intently on traditional spirituals,[45] hollers, blues, work songs, ring-game and play-party songs, Ramsey ranges through the Black Belt to Talladega and over into Mississippi, gathering, in addition to the types Courlander collected, brass and string bands, buck dance, blues boogie, gospel, and Afro-American modifications of nineteenth-century Protestant hymnody. Though the oral interview is prominent in Ramsey's collection, he gathered no folktales, a genre well represented in Courlander's recordings of Rich Amerson's monologues. Both collectors found memorable interpreters of Afro-American folk culture.

Ramsey's bard was Horace Sprott (of the town of Sprott in Perry County), grandson of a slave, bluesman, buck dancer, harmonica player, and singer of worship songs. In his oral narratives Sprott quietly ruminates over his experiences as a cotton picker, Mobile dock hand, and inmate of Kilby Prison. Citing banjo-player Will Harris and Blind Lemon Jefferson (whom he met in Eutaw, Alabama) as musical influences, Sprott holds, like Rich Amerson, the world and the devil in one hand and

---

[42]In addition to the famed tales of the Briar Patch and the Terrapin Race, Amerson recounts other stories of Brer Rabbit triumphs: on a courting jaunt he wears a hibernating blacksnake as a necktie; in one tale he chokes Brer Fox on a rail fence; in another he outwits Hawk and Buzzard by talking them into "waiting on salvation"; and in the most inventive and longest he gets revenge on Alligator at a cotillion in the sagebrush.

[43]Mrs. Tartt's WPA tale "How White Oak Tom Got His Name" is based on Amerson's oral version.

[44]Like Lomax, Courlander was interested in liturgy. The Courlander series includes a prayer meeting at Shiloh Primitive Baptist Church, Bogue Chitto, Mississippi, and Rev. E. D. Luckey's sermon on Abraham and Lot.

[45]Courlander recorded only samples of gospel. The trio of Joe Brown, Harrison Ross, and Willie Strong performed "When the Roll Is Called Up Yonder" (from white Protestant hymnody, written before 1892 by Methodist hymnwriter James Milton Black, 1856–1938) and "I Moaned and I Moaned" in radio quartet harmony. Rosie Winston, a delicate contralto, sang the gospel ballad "Standing in a Safety Zone." And Rosie Hibler, with family, recorded "Move, Members" in Sister Rosetta Thorpe style.

God in the other. Antiphonal liturgist, bluesman, and gospel-ensemble leader, he is vocally adept at every performance style, blues guttural and falsetto, Sacred Harp, moaning lament, strong chant, free holler, and radio gospel, in particular the solo "Jesus song."

As bluesman, Sprott "makes up" his songs in time-honored ways, yet his indebtedness to church music is evident throughout. The murder ballad of Luke Mullen begins like a chanted pulpit narrative of the Old Testament and its diction echoes liturgical psalmody. In his hammer-work songs, the travail of John Henry's spirit is rendered as an agonized prayer moan. And in "Shine On, Rising Sun" the glory shout of church worship becomes a defiant cry hurled by a grieved lover to the immortal sun. The elegiac "Smoked Like Lightning," introduced by a yodelling holler, is structured like the dramatic antiphony of spirituals:

> I follow my baby to the burying ground
> Call her! Call her!
> Lonesome dead, don't you hear me crying?
> Lord! Lord!

The liturgical lament is vocally and rhythmically perfect for Sprott's lyric blues. In "Early One Morning" blues is palpably present as falling rain and drives the rejected lover to the verge of insanity. A husband is crazed by his wife's unfaithfulness in "House Full of Nickels." In his composed ballad of a girl who would marry Jesse James the heroine flees the blues with compulsive paranoia. And in "Blacksnake," though veiled by folk nomenclature, the phallic serpent coils through the bluesman's tormented hallucinations.

The blues setting is often the juke joint, but all Afro-American folk song is an organic presence in daily life, at work, play, and in the home where family and friends often assemble for get-togethers. At Richard Jolla's house in Pond, Mississippi, Ramsey recorded the exhiliarating blues dance of Celeste Dunbar and her daughter Rose to Scott Dunbar's guitar-accompanied "Easy Rider."[46] And at a catfish supper held by Sprott's crowd at Dobine Creek, he recorded Sprott's "Rocks and Gravel," Philip Ramsey's "I Feel Good," and Mrs. Ramsey's honky-tonk dance song "Me and My Pork Chop" as well as the gospel "Talk about Jesus," children's game songs,[47] and buck dance from Sprott and Harry Rutledge.[48]

The bluesman is never far away in Sprott's religious folk songs, though clearly he conceives of himself as a singer of praise song. To "Jesus Gonna Make Up My Dying Ged" he imparts all the blues tonalities and phrasing latent in that famous spiritual. In "Oh Glad, Oh Free" the antiphonal leader declaims freedom like a blues chanter. "Steal Away" is styled as blues falsetto, and the melody of "Mean Old World" features honky-tonk embellishments. Early radio influences are evident in Sprott's harmonica train songs,[49] his sentimental ballad "One of These Days," and in the gospel quartet-Sacred Harp style of "When the Saints" and "Over in the Glory Land." By far, his most-interesting perfor-

---

[46]Another session, at Scott Dunbar's house, yielded his dance blues "Memphis Mail" and "Forty-Four," a bad-man blues dominated by phallic imagery of the outlaw's pistol.

[47]Ramsey's few specimens are valuable for their documentation of the evolution of contemporary ring dances and play parties toward sophisticated adult blues and dance. The lengthy composite "Merry Mac" includes "Rubber Dolly," a faintly lewd World War II pop-folk song. "Head, Shoulder Baby" is a boogie dance derived from the more-innocent "Loop-the-Loo" ring type. And the veiled fertility symbols of the traditional "Hobble-Li" (which Mrs. Tartt also collected) have acquired the transparent sexual implications of blues poetics.

[48]A folk invention comprised of a series of rhythmic movements learned traditionally but altered by improvisations of the talented performer. The minstrel imitation evolved into stage tap routines. The contemporary break-dance ensemble now choreographed for media entertainment originated as the solo of one virtuoso dancer from the ring.

[49]Sprott often accompanies himself and other singers with the harmonica, and his fox-hunt pieces are first-rate folk improvisations.

mance is the work song "My Hoe Leading My Row," with Nellie Hastings, a complicated antiphony, vocally light and fragile, which evokes the season of spring with its images of fresh earth and the call of lovers down the rows of tender plants.[50]

Afro-American instrumental ensembles have been largely neglected by folk song investigators;[51] hence is it gratifying to have Ramsey's recordings of the Mississippi String Band, the Lanville-Johnson Union Brass Band of Perry County, Alabama, and the Lapsey Band of Scott Station, Alabama. The rural string band, rarely recorded,[52] plays dance blues for parties, blues sessions, and weekend stints at local honky-tonks.

The distinctive musical quality of the Afro-American band tradition is designated by Alfred Frankenstein in the Ramsey jacket notes (vol. 9) as "heterophony." As in worship song, many voices of various timbres, pitches, tempos, and rhythms all proceed at once under the mysterious control of archetypal imprints. It is the wholeness of Afro-American folk culture, its receptivity to the principle of cosmic harmony, which makes possible the blending of secular and religious musical elements in Ramsey's bands.

In both the Lapsey and Lanville-Johnson bands the trombone is leading instrument, the bass drum is heavy and persistent, alto and bass horns provide response as echoing tag, simple repetition, or as complicated counterrhythm and chromatic inventions, and the snare drum may take on melodic function. Moreover, the march style is infused with jazz syncopation, blues atonalities, the common meter and partsong of Protestant hymnody, and the antiphonal dialogue of antebellum folk worship music.

The Lapsey Band excels in the jazz march ("Shine On," "Dixie," and "John Brown's Body") and their "Just Over in the Glory Land" is indebted to the American folk hymn "Unclouded Day" while "When I Lay My Burden Down" is similarly derivative of "Amazing Grace." The Lanville-Johnson ensemble favors ragtime and urban street blues ("Farewell, Daddy," "Rocks and Gravel," and "Sun Gone Shine") and adapts hymns and spirituals to brass jazz. "Precious Lord" and "Let Thy Will Be Done" are markedly syncopated, the jubilee spiritual "I'm Goin' On" is styled as street march, and in "Preaching Tonight" percussion replaces the congregational response *uh-huh.* Fascinating in their exotic mingling of styles and moods, these Alabama brass bands remind us that Saturday's children also belong to the Sabbath.[53]

[50]The Brown-Owens volume *Toting the Lead Row* is titled after the field-worker "row leader" (chopping cotton, corn, peas, but especially cotton)—the fastest "chopper" who leads all and helps slower workers. The "chop" is the sharp, quick stroke of thinning the young plants; the "hoe" a gentler scrabbling to loosen the soil around young plants. This duet suggests the latter.

[51]The brass or community band, now largely replaced by the financially well-endowed high school band, was once an important part of small-town American life. Volunteer musicians, with little or no formal training, their uniforms borrowed or subscribed by merchants and citizen supporters, played at political rallies, municipal ceremonies, and socioreligious festivals—Christmas, Independence Day, Mardi Gras. American folk types include circus, theatrical, medicine show, urban "beggar," evangelical or Salvation Army, and community bands. Long association with the military has determined their general character—resplendent dress, the primacy of percussion and brass instruments, and the march tempo.

[52]In the jacket notes (vol. 5), Ramsey points out that only two early recordings of such folk-string bands exist, one arranged by Edmond Souchon for a New Orleans group and the other of the "Mobile Strugglers" by William Russell. The Mississippi group recorded for Ramsey "See, See Mama" and "It's Right Like That" in Jelly Roll Morton style and "Hootchie Kootchie," a 1920s roadhouse shuffle.

[53]The law of decorum in Afro-American folk musical performance is observed both literally and in the subtle realm of intent and attitude. Beyond the church walls religious song serves the same purpose as it does in the sacred setting, that is, the expression of feeling, conceptual knowledge, and spiritual impulse through melody, rhythm, and language. Solo or ensemble, arising spontaneously at work or leisure, or "staged" for the collec-

Emmett Brand and Wilson Boling of Talladega typify Ramsey's "elder songsters" of deep religious faith. Brand is a straightforward melodist steeped in both the spiritual and American folk hymnody. "Rough, Rocky Road" and "Old Time Religion" recall Dock Reed's fervent preaching-singing style. In "Some of These Days" incremental repetition perfectly realizes its function as intensification of mood and theme, in this instance the surging hope for the freedom of Jordan. And "Preaching on the Old Camp Ground" is filled with the great affection most Southerners hold for the church as a religious and folk center.[54]

Wilson Boling, ninety-three at the time of his recording, his voice quivering with the frailness of the very old, strongly reflects the performance styles of Sacred Harp in "I'm So Glad That I Am Free," "We Have Mothers Over Yonder," and "Come to Jesus," all of which are delivered in bold, regular, percussive rhythms and strident vocal tones.[55]

George Herod's position as brass-band leader in Perry County is evident throughout his vocal performances. "I Shall Not Be Moved" begins as pulpit declamation in leader-respondent style but gradually acquires a syncopated intensity. "Lord, When I Was a Sinner," initially delivered in the rhymed stanzas and syncopation of boogie gospel, develops into ecstatic prayer chant. "Travellin' Shoes," with the young voices of Fanny and Peggy Lou Herod, is performed in partsong overlaid with the cumulative chant of children's games. "Sister Mary," sung to a Barbara Allan tune, is flavored with brass-band blues. And "Oh the Sun Don't Never Go Down" utilizes the balanced stanza of antebellum worship song but borrows its flower and sun metaphors from the nineteenth-century Protestant sentimental hymn.[56]

The trio of Jake Field, Eastman Brand, and Arthur Holifield of Talladega sing a congregational-style "Waitin' On You," the slow wailing of their melodist-liner well suited to this stirring prayer for deliverance.[57]

Richard Jolla, a Mississippi church deacon recorded first-rate performances of the famous Afro-American communion hymn "Lord, Have Mercy" and the spiritual "De Road Is Rough and Rocky," both sung to the Sacred Harp tune "The Old Ship of Zion" (by Thomas W. Carter, 1850) and both marked by clear melodic line, Sacred Harp vocal style, and the incremental repetition and caesural pause of leader-respondent antiphony.[58]

---

tor, re-creating, if unconsciously, liturgical structure and mood, it is a sincere act of worship.

Ramsey's survey of religious song (vols. 6-9) documents that sincerity in every syllable of every singer. Moreover, in his numerous performers from various geo-folk backgrounds, may be seen the evolutionary scope of Afro-American folk liturgy from 1850 to 1950: antebellum spirituals, metrical psalmody, liturgical chants, eighteenth-and nineteenth-century Protestant hymnody, ecstatic moans, melismatic song, Sacred Harp, invocatory and petitionary prayer, holy dance, charismatic and Pentecostal instrumental and vocal music, piano-accompanied rites, oral-religious species, and folk gospel.

[54]Emmett Brand also performs "My Old Mother" as a work song, a Revelator song, "Boats Up the River" as a field holler, a hammer song, a lullaby, and "Ridin' My Buggy," a composite of wagoner's lad and gambler motifs from white traidtion.

[55]"Come to Jesus," as Ramsey notes, is set to the Clementine tune, but both melody and text are influenced by the chorus of John Hart Stockton's (1813–1877) hymn "Only Trust Him" ("Come every soul by sin oppressed," 1873 or before). "Over Yonder" is a "camp meeting" song of the nineteenth-century Great Awakening.

[56]The Protestant hymn "I Shall Not Be Moved" is current in both Sacred Harp and boogie gospel. "Travellin' Shoes," of antebellum origins, is still a favorite on "choir day" and other all-day song fests.

[57]They also chant the Charles Wesley hymn "Father, I Stretch My Hands to Thee" (ca. 1741). Ramsey notes the spread of Methodist song tradition in the Black Belt and Talladega areas through missionaries Lorenzo Dow and Matthew P. Sturdivant. Dow also travelled to the Wire Grass region of South Alabama where folktales about him still circulate. Sturdivant's mission field included Montgomery and what is now parts of Elmore, Tallapossa, Macon, and Lee counties, an area which preserves to this day a strong Watts-Wesley hymn tradition.

[58]Jolla also recorded specimens of expository and

Afro-American usages of both the Watts-Wesley hymn and of Anglo-American Protestant worship types, including psalmody, chant, responsive dialogue, and prescribed prayer, are represented in Ramsey's anthology[59] by John and Lovie Griffin of Perry County, Sudie Griffiths of Talladega, Dora Bliggen of New Orleans, a worship service at Morning Star Baptist Church in New Orleans, and by Elder Effie Hall, minister of the First Independent Holy Church of God Unity near Marion, Alabama.

Like the Sprotts and Dock and Vera, the Griffins distill the leader-choir-congregation musical and psychological interaction. Significantly, they sing from a hymnal.[60] John "deacons" or "lines out" a stanza, Lovie responds with echo choral refrain, and melodic or chanted variation. Their one performance from memory is "Dark Was the Night and Cold the Ground," a nineteenth-century hymn by Thomas Haweis (1734–1820) which appealed deeply to the newly Christian Afro-American immigrant slave.[61]

The Griffins' vocal style exemplifies a duality common in Afro-American religious folk song performance, two distinct yet related approaches to oral and musical worship. The first and older leans towards the intoning and reciting qualities of cadenced chant, and is derived both from African antecedents and the antiphonal dialogue of Christian liturgy in general and Anglo-American Protestantism in particular. The second leans toward melody and is associated with the historical rise of Protestant hymnody. In both the reciting and melodic approaches the presiding or initial tone may be broken, equally and unequally, into a small surrounding scale, usually of three to five tones of chromatic progression which may or may not be resolved, and rhythmical properties may be similarly broken and elaborated. John and Lovie are masters of both the recitative and melodic modes. In their performance of "When I Can Read My Title Clear," the Watts hymn of American brush-arbor fame, syncopation, syllabic elongation, chromatic expansion of melodic line, counterpart, and vocal contrasts create the illusion of congregational song.[62]

The assumption of ministerial office by the female, until recently relatively unknown in white Protestant churches, occurs historically throughout Afro-American folk Christianity. In the role of priestess, women may serve as foremost choir singer, lead chanter, usher, testifier, deaconess, and even

---

narrative oral discourse of a type well known in folk Protestantism, the "Sunday School talk" of pedagogical intent and conversational delivery.

[59]For purposes of comparison, we examined the following hymnals. *The Hymnal of the Protestant Episcopal Church in the United States of America* (New York, 1940); *The Broadman Hymnal* (Nashville: Broadman Press, 1940); *Baptist Hymnal* (Nashville: Convention Press, 1956, 1975); *The Methodist Hymnal* (Nashville: Methodist Publishing House, 1939); and *The B. F. White Sacred Harp as Revised and Improved by W. M. Cooper and Others* (Troy AL: Sacred Harp Book Co., Inc., 1949).

[60]The jacket notes imply an 1820 American edition of *The Psalms and Hymns of Dr. Watts*.

[61]Ramsey singles it out as an example of composed song which "pulled away" from hymnody and was transformed into a "passionate personal expression of sorrow and suffering." Jacket notes to vols. 6, 7.

[62]The anonymous early American "Amazing Grace" tune setting is their choice for several texts, including Charles Wesley's "A Charge to Keep (I Have)," usually sung to the tune "Boylston" by Lowell Mason (1792–1872), and Isaac Watts's "Am I a Soldier of the Cross" which, in Baptist and Methodist hymnals, is set to "Arlington," a melody by Thomas A. Arne (1710–1778). John and Lovie also use Arne's Arlington melody as underlay for psalmodic chant.

The composer of the text (excepting the "When we've been there" verse) of "Amazing Grace" (writen before 1779) was the prolific hymn-text writer John Newton (1725–1807). Before his conversion Newton was for ten years crewman and then captain of a slave-trading ship; was influenced by John Wesley and George Whitefield; became a minister of the Church of England (1760); befriended the poet William Cowper (1731–1800) with whom he issue the *Olney Hymns* (1779); and as a strong abolitionist influenced William Wilberforce (1759–1833), a leader of the "Clapham Sect" and of the abolition movement in England. That "Amazing Grace" would be taken to heart by the slave South, both black and white, and become the best-loved hymn of all Protestantism is one of the striking ironies of American history.

founder of a sect. Raised to eminence by reason of personality, knowledge of the Scriptures, and religious inclination, they function in the same manner as the male, though their sex imparts observable but hard-to-define differences in the celebration of worship rites. Dora Bliggen, "the blackberry woman," is such a priestess. Unselfconsciously aware of her powers, she prays a blessing for Ramsey, "the man who desires my voice" and utters the Watts hymn "Come, We That Love the Lord"[63] as invocatory rite. As priestly mediator, she recites a divine ode of praise and petition in exalted pulpit mode. And as leader-preacher she moans and chants "Somebody Touched Me," the famous gospel song which describes a mystical encounter.

That the "call to preach," of doctrinal import in Protestant folk religion, does not discriminate sexually is apparent in Sudie Gifffith's antiphonal chant of the Watts hymn "Go Preach My Gospel," and her performance of "I Heard the Voice of Jesus Say"[64] illustrates Afro-American usage of hymnody within the sermon where, under the influence of strong emotion, a familiar melodic phrase may be given complex musical and rhetorical development.[65]

The female as preacher and priestess is brilliantly portrayed in Elder Effie Hall who leads a Pentecostal sect in Marion, Alabama. Her discourse offers a model of the folk ministerial prayer: the invocation of blessing and offering of praise and thanks; the petition of divine inspiration for the priest; the litany of sorrow and sins; the kyrie and the promise of immortality. A choral introit serves as prelude, and moans, handclaps, counterchants, shouts, humming, and individual prayers break out like brushfire under her urging. The "weak, humble servant" enters the "holy presence" to pray that "peace continue existing in my time"; that sinners be cleansed; that the "Lord God of Heaven" send blessings on "the boys in Korea," her grandson "on the battlefield somewhere," her children and neighbor's children, the sheriff, police, doctors, lawyers, undertakers, and all the city of Marion; that the Lord grant mercy and carry the soul "high in the Kingdom."

Afro-American in vocal, musical, and poetic expression and Anglo-European Christian in its liturgical substantive and sequence, Elder Hall's prayer shows the workings of both the moaning chant, in which strophic cadence and sonorous vocal tones invoke the divine presence, and of the charismatic chant, where acceleration of tempo and percussive effects may lead to the sacramental "speaking in tongues."[66]

---

[63]Dora's tune is derived from "House of the Rising Sun," a ballad of a New Orleans prostitute, and the chorus is interpolated from "I Am So Glad Salvation Is Free." In white hymnody the common tune for "Come, We That Love the Lord" (Watts's original "Heavenly Joy on Earth," before 1707) is "Marching to Zion" (1867) by Robert Lowry (1826–1899).

[64]The text is that of Horatius Bonar (1808–1889). Few Protestant hymns have been given so many lovely settings. The American Episcopal *Hymnal* (1940) offers "Vox dilecti" (1868) by John Bacchus Dykes (1823–1876)—also the tune in *The New Baptist Hymnal* (Nashville: Boardman Press, 1926)—and another (dated 1567) attributed to Thomas Tallis (1505–1585), the "father of English cathedral music." The *Methodist Hymnal* (1939) includes the Dykes setting and a tune by Joseph Holbrook (1812–1888). The (Baptist) *Braodman Hymnal* (1940) uses a Baylus Benjamin McKinney (1886–1952) arrangement of the tune associated with Ben Johnson's "Drink to Me Only with Thine Eyes." In the 1956 *Baptist Hymnal* (it is not in the 1975 edition) the tune setting is by Louis Spohr (1784–1859). Sudie Griffith's own tune is a severely limited scale chromatically elongated to moan.

[65]The departure, sudden or gradual, also occurs in musical performance. In the Ramsey series, the lead singer of the Mississippi Wandering Travellers, after an introductory stanza, breaks into a rapid chant in which short phrases are interrupted by a caesural sharp intake of breath.

[66]Both species may occur at any time during a worship service. At the New Orleans Morning Star Baptist Church anniversary service Brother H. Stevenson chants the Watts hymn "I Know the Lord's Laid His Hands on Me" as opening invocation, his "lining out" answered by a long, syncopated congregational wail, and Brother F. Lewis chants the twenty-third Psalm, with responsive moan, during the main sermon.

Appropriately, the musical tradition of the Marion sect is also female and Pentecostal. "Precious Lord, Take My Hand" and "Don't Let His Name Go Down," with drum, tambourine, and guitar accompaniment, are performed in the charismatic style associated with Sister Rosetta Thorpe whose radio shows and recordings have exerted enormous influence upon Afro-American gospel from 1940 until the present.

As Ramsey observes (vol. 8 jacket notes), the gospel ensemble encapsulates the congregation-choir-leader structure into a "more or less self-conscious art form" which, it may be added, is often rigid and predictable in formal musical requirements, simplistic in content, and conventional and sentimental in language and figurative devices. Yet even within these limitations, its vocal styles often tap authentic folk precedents and express genuine religious feeling.

The Starlight Gospel Singers of Perry County, Alabama, were superficially influenced by early radio gospel—apparent in the occasional showcasing of a virtuoso bass singer, in metrically and vocally monotonous short-phrase response, in concluding stanzas of stereotyped harmonic and rhythmic resolution, and a restrained, polished antiphonal warm-up. But, for the most part, they draw straight from the well of antebellum worship song, particularly in the range and variety of congregational response and the prominence of the Everyman persona.

Often two talented Starlight leaders rival and complement each other in preaching and singing. In "The Lord Is My Shepherd" a lyric solo gives way to operatic duet. In "Say a Word for Me" the two singers alternate a preaching solo over insistent congregational partsong repetition. In "The Tree of Life" their ecstatic chants compete over percussion accompaniment and moaning, harmonized response.

The communion hymn "Lord Have Mercy" is metamorphosed into a sermon chant delivered in rapid-fire syncopation, the gospel ensemble responding as sinners who hypnotically repeat the cry for forgiveness, while in "I Done Just What He Said" congregational response gradually quickens and strengthens until it matches the leader's melodic shout.

Another communion hymn, "Come Over Here, the Table Is Spread,"[67] illustrates the role of the folk minister as singer in his own right and as musical leader of choir and congregation. Without the least hesitancy he moves from the formulas of preaching rhetoric to those of sacramental song, and worshippers follow with celebratory moan. Clearly, the boogie, blues, and radio-harmony selections of the Starlight group are nourished by antebellum apocalyptic and salvation spirituals, and they are highly skilled in all the vocal styles associated with historic Afro-American folk liturgical music.[68]

The accomplishments of the song leader, who is the musical exponent of Christian theology, myth, and rite, were readily transferred to the solo gospel ballad which, though the species has obvious resemblances to the secular pop love song, also employs the vocal techniques of worship chanters and melodists. Dorothy Melton, Plantersville, Alabama, has learned her mellifluous phrasing in "I Want Jesus to Walk with Me"[69] from radio, but under-

---

[67]The implications of this song are not only for Communion but also the "love feast." In both white and black folk Protestantism, the love feast is a communal banquet of food, hymns, Scripture readings, prayer, and testimony, which emphasizes through ritualistic gestures— kissing, embracing, handshaking, exchanging flowers, and, sometimes, footwashing—the brotherhood of Christian believers. Often occurring during "revivals," it may evoke charismatic and ecstatic behavior. The more decorous—and probably today more common—expression for "love feast" is "fellowship supper."

[68]Ramsey's fears that groups like Starlight would vanish have not been realized, at least not in Alabama. Our recordings of a choir day at Sylacauga, Alabama, during April 1984 indicate that the quartet flourishes, and to it has been added the larger ensemble, the travelling church choir, which performs in rural and small-town churches over a large area at the annual choir day, an all-day event which draws large crowds.

[69]The chorus derives from "Close to Thee" (or "Thou My Everlasting Portion") by Fannie Crosby (1820–1915) set to a tune by Silas J. Vail (1818–1884). Dorothy also

neath lies the lyric field moan. And Ella Cash, loosely structures "All My Trouble Soon Be Over" as personal religious testimony.[70]

Adaptations of gospel to leader-respondent choral modes also occur in the Morning Star Baptist Church service. The largely female choir performs "When the River Cease to Flow" as surge song, but the accompaniment is tavern piano. Their "Sweeter as the Days Go By" spontaneously acquires traditional handclaps, fugal passages, and antiphonal complications. A boogie-blues-ballad piano solo by Sister Annie Pauageau accompanies a ritualistic processional of worshippers.[71] Coexisting with these gospel elements are ministerial "talks," prayers, and portions of sermons as well as congregational surge hymns led by Sister L. Brown.[72]

The final volume (10) of the Ramsey anthology, appropriately entitled *Been Here and Gone,* is a pleasant, well-conceived mosaic that effectively juxtaposes secular and religious genres and demonstrates the range of individual Afro-American folk song performance styles. Over in Louisiana, Louis Bonner blows his hunting horn, and from Alabama Horace Sprott answers with a harmonica hunt piece and a blues holler. Gandy dancers of Frisco Line, Alabama, call and sing track lining. The Lanville-Johnson Band plays a trombone dirge. Elder Effie Hall incants "When the Saints Go Marching In." The Dunbars of Mississippi repeat their best number, "Vicksburg Blues." Sprott and his friends have a "Skiffle." And New Orleans ends it all with Dora Bliggen's pulpit chant "O Lord, Have Mercy" and the Eureka Brass Band's performance of the street jazz "Panama" and the hymn "Just a Closer Walk with Thee."[73]

In his essay of general introduction Ramsey urgently calls for more field studies,[74] though he believes that Afro-American folk song is "fading irrevocably as changes come to the South." In 1990, however, it still flourishes—beautiful, strong, and a tribute to those who continue to sing it.

---

chants "The Day Is Past and Gone" (1835), a hymn for vespers by John Leland (1754–1841; in Sacred Harp hymnals set to the tune "Evening Shade" from *Baptist Harmony* [1834]). The vespers hymn, with origins dating to the fifth century, now declines in most American Protestant churches; its symbolic associations of evening, sunset, and approaching darkenss held special appeal for the slave who re-created its melancholy mood in field cries.

[70]Ramsey says Ella Cash's voice was "breathtaking in its impact." She also provides supportive harmony to her brother's lead in "Yes, He Cares."

[71]The performance of Elder David Ross of "He Gave Me a Heart to Love" is more suited to the honky-tonk than the church, but acceptable perhaps because the service is an anniversary occasion.

[72]Our recordings of the centennial anniversary at Mt. Zion Baptist Church, Tallassee, Elmore County, Alabama, during October 1984, are similar to Ramsey's Morning Star celebration recordings: surge song, moan, chant, and leader-respondent spirituals and hymns have, by no means, been replaced by "gospel."

[73]The jacket essay for vol. 10 concerns this religious and secular dualism. Throughout, Ramsey's notes are cogent and useful. Though he cites Courlander's studies in the folklore of Haiti and the recordings made by Courlander and Lomax in Sumter County, Ramsey assays no comment on these investigations.

[74]Bibliographies of recorded Afro-American folk songs are available on request from the Library of Congress, Archive of Folk Song, Washington DC 20540. Commercial folk song field recordings are produced by Folkways Records and Service Corporation (117 West 46th St., New York 10036) which offers title catalogs and mailing service. See also the recordings essays in quarterly issues of *Journal of American Folklore* and Ray M. Lawless, *Folksingers and Folksongs in America,* 2nd rev. ed. (New York: Duell, Sloan, and Pearce, 1965; [1]1960).

An Index to the Song Texts